Bernadette Strachan has a peculiar CV encompassing managing a wool shop, silverware buying for John Lewis and representing various household names for voiceover work. The author of six novels, she lives in Kingston, Surrey with her husband Matthew, daughter Niamh and Mavis, the most stupid spaniel she has ever met.

Bernadette also writes musicals with her husband. See her website bernadettestrachan.com to find out more. If you want to. And you can also follow her on Twitter. Again, only if you want to.

Praise for Bernadette Strachan

'It's official: the drought of fre
sparkling language and hilarious
from the first page'

heat

'No-nonsense sharp, dry wit with larger than life characters . . . a mosaic of sparkling fun'

Woman

'Fresh, funny and full of romance'

Company

'Delightful and refreshingly different'

The Bookseller

'Affectionately humorous at times, tongue-in-cheek and then poignantly astute . . . highly recommended'

Lovereading.co.uk

Also by Bernadette Strachan

The Reluctant Landlady
Handbags and Halos
Diamonds and Daisies
Little White Lies
How to Lose a Husband and Gain a Life

Why DO we have to live with Men?

Bernadette
Strachan

sphere

SPHERE

First published in Great Britain in 2010 by Sphere

A CIP catalogue record for this book
is available from the British Library.

ISBN 978-0-7515-4229-5

Typeset in Garamond by M Rules
Printed and bound in Great Britain by
Clays Ltd, St Ives plc

Papers used by Sphere are natural, renewable and recyclable products sourced from well-managed forests and certified in accordance with the rules of the Forest Stewardship Council.

Sphere
An imprint of
Little, Brown Book Group
100 Victoria Embankment
London EC4Y 0DY

An Hachette UK Company
www.hachette.co.uk

www.littlebrown.co.uk

This book is for Robert Berry,
for lots of reasons, with love

Acknowledgements

I borrowed some names for this novel, so thank you to the following for letting me use their monikers – Riona (or Cat) O'Connor, my cousins the Collets, and of course the peerless Jozette Lee.

A big 'Thank You' and the macaroon of your choice to the following:

Annette Green, my agent and dear chum: Jo Dickinson, my preternaturally serene and wise editor at Sphere; Caroline Hogg, a Sphere gem who makes me laugh while doing the work of ten men; Penny Killick, Kate Haldane, Sara Jade Virtue and Janet Partridge for cheerleading throughout my career; Louise Candlish and Dorothy Koomson for authorly support and giggles; Sanae Matsunaga for giving me this book's title over supper a very long time ago; Matthew and Niamh for being the point of it all; Mavis . . . well, for not very much, but she gets annoyed if she's left out.

1

Cat O'Connor whispered a fervent prayer before opening the fridge.

If there was no milk left she would have to kill her lodger and she really couldn't spare the time. Cat needed to see a drop, a smidgeon, a *smear* of milk in the fridge.

Moments later Cat was banging on Mary's bedroom door in the style of the Flying Squad. 'Come out! Now! I need to assault you!' she yelled peremptorily.

'Eh?' On the far side of the door Mary sounded weak and early-morningish.

'I don't ask much from life,' shouted Cat untruthfully. 'But I do like a nice cup of tea before I go to work. I am denied that small pleasure because, once again, you've used the last of the milk.'

The door opened a chink, revealing a slice of dishevelled expatriate Dubliner. 'But you couldn't have had a cup of tea,' she pointed out reasonably. 'I used the last tea bag.'

Cat made a black coffee and Mary agreed to stand on the sofa in her pyjamas for exactly one minute while Cat threw cushions at her.

'Right,' said Cat gravely when the minute was up. 'Let that be a lesson to you.'

'Oh, consider me reformed,' said Mary piously.

One of Cat's talents was the ability to switch effortlessly from cushion-throwing big kid to shoulder-padded she-wolf. The transformation claimed her every morning in the revolving doors of Percival Cant Jablowski; soft-centred Cat was spat into the marble and glass lobby made over as a fearless careerist. This duality was one of the reasons Hugh had fallen for her, and he told her so in the lift after their breakfast meeting with new clients.

'You impressed the hell out of them. You were assertive, knowledgeable, commanding, and I was the only one in the room who knew you were wearing Mr Men knickers.'

When the lift doors slid open Cat had stalked back to her office to bash out an email.

FYI I threw out my cartoon-related lingerie last week, the same day I told you to go to the devil.

Snorting, Cat pressed 'send' and jabbed the intercom on her desk. 'Marian!' she barked.

On the other side of the glass wall, a white perm jerked and an elderly lady scrabbled for her intercom. 'I wasn't asleep,' she said loudly.

'Could you round up the team, Marian? I need to brief them on the new clients. No excuses. They're all in the meeting room in ten minutes or I detach them from their rude bits.'

'Oh dear.' The perm nodded knowingly. 'I think a certain little lady got out of bed on the wrong side. Somebody could do with one of my special ginger and nettle infusions.'

'I'm sure somebody could, but *I'd* like a black coffee with some heroin in it.' Cat released the button, neatly silencing Marian's tut.

The daily transformation in the revolving doors turned Cat into a superb employee, but addled her manners. She should have been gentler with her PA, Cat knew that. Marian's loyalty was as invaluable as her encyclopaedic knowledge of company lore: Marian knew the whereabouts of the MD's biscuit stash and wasn't afraid to embezzle a Bahlsen in an emergency. Cat overlooked the napping, tolerated the nosiness and positively revelled in the affront to the advertising world's cult of youth that Marian represented shuffling to the kitchenette in wider fit slippers. Head to toe in tea-coloured BHS separates, Marian was a comfortable blot on the pristine, minimalist landscape of the advertising agency.

The super-modern open plan office was carefully designed to scream 'Money!', 'Creativity!' and, in Cat's opinion, 'Wank!' Polar white cubbyholes housed men with hair gelled to a point, and women head to toe in black, like a herd of very thin Latina widows.

Percival Cant Jablowski took itself seriously. It was a cathedral to the god of advertising: getting in late was a sin, and going home on time was heresy. Everybody was only as good as their last idea.

It was impossible to resist the paranoia. As the newest accounts manager, Cat felt the eyes of the board upon her as she steered her creative team through the genesis of thirty-second epics exhorting Mr and Mrs Average to buy this washing powder or that ready meal. Struggling to keep each commercial on budget, Cat constantly looked over her shoulder for the next hotshot lusting after her job. No wonder her muscles were tense.

And the headaches . . . these days Cat only noticed when her head *didn't* throb. Tense as a sentry, Cat kept up the pace that Percival Cant Jablowski demanded. This meant that the majority of her evenings were spent supine on the sofa, sucking up Wotsits and shouting the wrong answers at *Who Wants To Be A Millionaire?*

As for her keen-as-mustard colleagues, Cat suspected they spent their evenings throwing together macrobiotic salads, Debussy tinkling in the background. Not for them the lowbrow consolation of a cheese flavoured puff and Chris Tarrant. She was, she suspected, fundamentally different to these effortlessly trendy people who chewed up the demands of their working day like so many corporate goats.

Checking her reflection in the glass wall (account managers were honoured with their own, albeit transparent, offices; higher-ups merited real, honest to goodness walls) Cat hoped she looked the part. To the casual eye she fitted right in, but Cat fretted she was half a stone too heavy, an inch too short, and a trend or two behind. Her black trousers were only Next's take on Armani, and the towering heels which had broken the bank threatened to do the same to her ankles. She'd invested in one of those 'perfect crisp white shirts' fashion editors bang on about, but after umpteen washes it was neither perfect nor crisp.

Black hair, shiny as a rook's wing, fell in a neat, expensive-to-keep bob around the pale oval of Cat's face. Her eyes were blue and inquisitive, flecked with darker blots to reward those who took a second, closer look.

Cat's pearly skin never tanned and her nose was straight and short enough to compensate for the unruly nature of her bottom. Average height, average weight, Cat's average looks belied her hunger to succeed. Despite this ambition, Cat had promised herself never to step on people, never to bitch. She avoided the lure of office politics by keeping herself aloof from her colleagues.

Such aloofness didn't come naturally, and it was easy for Cat to feel lonely under the soaring white ceiling of Percival Cant Jablowski.

Strictly speaking, it was Marian's job to prepare the meeting room for the team briefing. 'Oh no you don't,' said Cat firmly, hijacking the pile of folders and pressing her assistant gently back into her seat. 'I'll do it this time.' Marian's bad legs were famed throughout adland; they were veined, they were weak, they were tingly; one memorable morning leprosy had been suspected. Cat's conscience wouldn't allow her to sit while Marian winced her way across reception.

Feather footed, Hugh appeared from nowhere to open the meeting room door for her. 'Cat,' he began, in that honeyed, well bred voice that had once fluttered her underwear. 'Might I sit in on your meeting? I like to keep up to speed.'

'Sure.' Cat preceded him into the room, her bared teeth just about qualifying as a smile.

Working her way around the table, plonking down a folder in front of each chair, Cat resolutely did not look at Hugh. He lounged – Hugh was *born* to lounge – against a filing cabinet, arms lazily crossed in his bespoke suit. He was a naturally elegant man. On meeting him Cat had theorised that he would probably even puke elegantly, a theory borne out after a bad oyster at Claridge's. He'd puked much as Bill Nighy might, or Louis XIV.

'Darling,' he said.

And then Cat had to look at him: that word was flammable in these surroundings.

Ignoring the hen's bum of disapproval that was Cat's mouth, Hugh pushed recklessly on. 'Can't we stop this cold war? I can't bear it. Seeing you every day, close enough to touch.'

Cat flung down a folder with unnecessary force, then stalled the next one in mid-air, breathing hard. In theory, Hugh was easy to resist: the briefest inventory of his shortcomings would include vain, shallow, dangerous, *old*. She could just imagine her twenty-something team's communal 'Yew!' of disgust at the idea of getting naked with a man in his fifties. But Hugh, Cat had to admit, wasn't old, and possibly never would be. The twinkly golden boyishness that ensured his blond hair flopped just so had no sell-by date.

And at this distance, the man was hard to resist. Hugh smelled unbelievably good, like a lemon grove. In Harrods. She recalled how it felt to be pressed against that irreproachably cut suit, his arms greedily tight around her . . . Cat resumed the folder-plonking.

Five days of cold turkey couldn't be abandoned just like that. Tonight was her fortnightly girls' night out, a rare Wotsit-free evening, and Cat couldn't wait to tell her friends that she'd finally taken their advice. 'I'm not listening,' she said tartly.

'You're cruel,' Hugh whispered as the first of Cat's creative team wandered in.

The new copywriter had too many teeth. Cat wondered why she'd never noticed before. His smile was like a sale in Ikea's crockery section.

Cat was seeing a lot of those teeth that morning. Eager to impress, the new guy fired one idea after another at her, each lamer than the last.

'Come on, people!' Cat stalked the room, aware of Hugh's silent scrutiny from the corner. 'We're getting nowhere.'

A junior writer, equipped with the requisite spiky hair but lacking the requisite talent, muttered 'It's a shit product with a shit name. What do you expect?'

Cat expected him to earn his impressive salary instead of toying with the man-bling on his lilywhite fingers, but she said diplomatically, 'There's not much we can do about the product. It's useful, practical, and we all have something like it in our homes.'

'It's a fucking toilet fucking gel,' sneered the young writer. 'And the name sucks. It's a blatant rip-off.'

'Perhaps the name is a little, er, unfortunate.' Cat picked up the bulky orange bottle of toilet cleaner and tried her best to gaze upon it fondly. 'But Toilet Pigeon is our new baby and we're being paid – well paid – to give it our best shot.'

An art director wearing a sequinned beret that would get her sectioned in any other workplace piped up. 'A celebrity endorsement? Kind of drag Toilet Pigeon upmarket?'

'Need a bloody strong rope.' The junior writer's chin was on his chest.

Instinct told Cat that the clients were after something fresh, strong. Her instinct regularly let her down when it came to men, shoes, and whether or not she'd look good in leggings, but it was rarely wrong about work. She was about to open her mouth when Hugh spoke from the back of the room.

'Guys,' he said languidly. 'This is painful. In case you've forgotten, we're running ideas past Mr Toilet Pigeon next week.'

'I hadn't forgotten,' snapped Cat, rising to the bait. She longed to send him a blistering look but that would be too dicey. Time to take control. 'No celebs,' she said firmly. 'I know you all want to meet Joanna Lumley but we need to be brave, to grasp the nettle. It's a terrible product name, so let's go with it. Make a so-bad-it's-good ad. Do you get me?'

Blank faces suggested they didn't.

Sensing Hugh's interest quicken, Cat grabbed a marker and turned to the whiteboard. 'Irony. We need a lorry load of irony. Make a funny, colourful, crazy, OTT film about how fan-fucking-tastic this silly little toilet cleaner is. With a song. And dancers. And fireworks. And an excruciatingly cheesy endline. Like ...' Cat uncapped the marker and paused. She hadn't thought this far ahead. 'Oh, something like . . .' She began to scribble. '*Your toilet will love you for it.*' She heard Hugh cough, or it might have been a laugh. 'Not exactly that, obviously.'

Raising his chin for a moment, the junior writer said, 'It sucks.'

'No.' Cat was adamant. 'It doesn't suck. It's the answer. Ironic. Over the top. Done carefully, this little ad could be career defining.' They all perked up, as she'd known they would. 'I'm talking awards.' She was fairly certain that gave the junior writer an erection. 'Now sod off and come back in a couple of days with something sketched out.'

The team trailed out, baffled and mutinous, as Cat tidied the room. 'Still here?' she asked wryly over her shoulder.

'You're *good*,' whistled Hugh.

'Thank you.' Cat was stiff. She went a little pink at his praise. Hugh knew how much she needed it. She risked a peek behind her.

Hugh was smiling. He could smile to Olympic standards. It transformed his lean, wry face.

It would take a heart of stone not to return such a smile. And Cat didn't have a heart of stone.

'That's better. It's no fun being public enemy number one.' He took a step towards her. 'Can't we put an end to this silliness?'

'No,' said Cat impatiently, her smile dying. 'And it's not silly.' Resentment lit a flame under her words. 'It's something I should have done years ago.' She glanced, paranoid, out at the open plan office: and lowered her voice. 'I can't do it any more. All the secrecy. And the shame.'

'You,' said Hugh vehemently, and with a roughness that made the moment suddenly intimate, 'need never feel ashamed.'

'Go away, please,' asked Cat sadly.

Dejected, Hugh left the room. Passing a wall of glass bricks, his outline rippled and swam, the way it did every night in Cat's dreams. *You bastard*, she thought.

That wasn't fair. Cat knew Hugh inside out: he wasn't a bastard. He was just a weak man.

The real problem, of course, was that he was somebody else's weak man.

2

Cat distrusted tapas. Too many little plates. Too much opportunity for Mary to snaffle the lion's share and leave Cat with a lone tentacle. 'Why do we come here?' she grumbled.

'It's good value,' said Germaine, who had approximately eighteen times as much money as the next richest person in the restaurant. 'And it's convenient.' Tall and handsome, Germaine was draped in her customary boho, vaguely ethnic layers. Mary likened her to a jumble sale in Eritrea, but Germaine's slubby layers were cashmere and silk. 'And I like tapas.' That was the clincher: Germaine generally got her way. Generations of strong minded women, who'd owned horsewhips and weren't afraid to use them, had spawned this modern day suffragette.

'Plus the staff are fit.' Mary was unkempt after a hard day's temping. Officially an actress, she took office jobs to pay the bills.

'We have no fucking imagination!' laughed Jozette, whose language had deteriorated since arriving in London from the States a decade ago. Her awesome Afro bobbed to the rhythm of her laughter: an ex-model, Jozette was gorgeous enough to hate on sight, but God had given her, along with mile-long legs and tilted eyes, a seam of pure sweetness that was impossible to resist. These days she was a freelance stylist, and it showed in her effortless funky glamour.

The gang was all there. I'm too old, thought Cat, to have a *gang:* it's unseemly. Gangs are for sixth form: no thirty-six-year-old should be in a gang. But a gang the women indisputably were. For some reason these four individuals, all very different, needed each other. Differing perspectives, Cat had learned, can be illuminating.

Sitting back to savour a chunk of chorizo, Cat watched the others gabbling and interjecting and giggling. She and Mary were the bedrock of this unlikely gang, the first to meet – Cat counted on greasy fingers – an astonishing seventeen years ago.

Perhaps it was inauspicious to meet your future BF in a nightclub toilet. Mary had been fleeing a small man who'd bought her a drink and now expected an Access All Areas pass to her erogenous zones. Bursting into the ladies' loo, boob tube awry, she'd asked Cat urgently, 'Is there a way out through here?'

'No. Maybe. Dunno.' Cat, the far side of eleventy-four margaritas, was peering in the mirror, wondering which of the four eyes she could see needed more kohl.

Mary slowed down, peering over Cat's shoulder. 'Hey, go easy,' she advised. 'No more eyeliner. You look like Cleopatra's slutty mate.'

Vacillating between laughing and swearing, Cat decided on the former, and somehow found herself committed to smuggling Mary out to the taxi rank. On the cab journey home they discovered how much they had in common: favourite Angel Delight – Butterscotch; favourite type of knicker – big; favourite Osmond – none.

The buzz of Cat's phone woke her the next morning, suggesting they meet for a milkshake and the rest was history. Messy, rather loud history.

Ten Christmases ago, Germaine had come along. Back in the days before she'd amassed her inherited fortune, Germaine worked for next to nothing in a women's refuge and was scraping by in Chelsea (where 'scraping by' constitutes a higher standard of living than most of the UK enjoys). No doubt, like Cat and Mary, she'd been attracted by the promise of a 'bespoke uniform' in the advert for Christmas department store staff.

'I assumed bespoke would mean smart,' Cat had wailed, looking down at herself.

'You *are* smart,' insisted Mary, swishing about in front of the broken mirror in the staff changing room. 'You're quite the smartest elf I ever saw.'

Not ideal casting for Santa's Little Helper, Germaine had thrown all six foot of herself into the role with gusto. Rouged of cheek, green of tight, she'd swooped on weeping children with a loud 'Come along now. You're just looking for attention. Nobody likes a whinger.' It was how her nanny had raised her and it worked. 'Hop on to Santa's knee, poppet. NOW!'

For days, Cat and Mary avoided the tall, posh anti-Poppins at tea breaks, admitting that she scared them witless.

'She's so . . . *certain* about everything,' grimaced Cat in the canteen, over a very hard bun.

'And so feckin' loud,' said Mary.

'Anybody sitting here? No? Splendid.' Germaine had appeared on the far side of the scuffed table. 'You two interest me,' she'd said. 'Talk.'

The three of them had been talking ever since. It had taken a while to cultivate a skin thick enough to withstand their new friend's brand of honesty, but Cat came to enjoy being hosed down with Germaine's stream of consciousness. It was kindly meant. When Mary complained covertly that Germy was meddlesome, or know-all, Cat would remind her that Germaine's motives were pure.

The extreme political correctness could be hard to take, but Cat had learned to tune out while Germaine ranted about her latest feminist/sexist/homophobic bugbear. This zeal sprang from the same root that made Germaine go the extra yard for her little gang, and she wouldn't be Germy without it. A vain woman, Germaine expected thanks – *copious* thanks – for her loyalty but Cat and Mary were accustomed to her quirks and either supplied it uncomplainingly or told her to sod off, as the mood took them.

It would have amazed Germaine to know how protective Cat was of her, how she worried about her. Germaine's strong personality wasn't to everybody's taste and Cat kept an eye on her. Discreetly.

The fourth musketeer, currently turning her elegantly sculpted nose up at a prawn ('They feed around sewer pipes, people!'), had been gifted to them by Cat's older brother. Cat rarely got to meet Trev's conquests: the hapless girls had short shelf lives. When he'd admitted to racking up a whole month with a woman, that he was *living* with her, Cat had engineered a rendezvous. 'Please, please,' she'd told him later on the phone, 'hang on to this one.'

Four years later it was Jozette who was hanging on: Trev could be slippery. Cat and Mary had ushered her into their fold, despite their assumption that Jozette and Germaine would have nothing in common. They were wrong. Jozette, a liberal to the core, thoroughly endorsed Germaine's right-on approach and Germaine was susceptible to Jozette's happy, lit-from-within beauty.

A graduate of the fashion world, Jozette's address book bulged, but she had the knack of making people feel that they mattered to her. She was a shot in the arm when Cat, Mary or Germaine were feeling downcast or dowdy, and yet there was a hinterland to their fourth gang member that they knew little about. Confiding, warm, but light of touch, Jozette seemed to like it that way.

And so the four women had fallen into the habit of meeting up every other Thursday, building up a formidable closeness and an encyclopaedic knowledge of each other's foibles as they swigged house wine, devoured the specials of the day and gossiped about their lives.

'About *men*,' Hugh used to tease. 'Admit it. You get together with your coven to complain about us heartless brutes.'

'Don't,' Cat had advised, 'flatter yourself.'

The women discussed politics, television, shaving versus creams, work, weight, ambitions, disappointments, cellulite, immigration, shoes. Fears were shared and downsized, bubbles pricked. They didn't moan about men.

Not until the house wine kicked in. Cat looked at her watch. So far the evening had unfolded strictly to schedule. Germaine had arrived first, fussing and looking at her watch. Jozette had arrived last with improbable tales of drama on the Northern Line. There had been the usual squabble about what to order, the foursome splitting tidily down the middle into pro-calamari/anti-calamari factions, followed by the usual plea from Germaine for the purchase of some decent wine this time. This had triggered Jozette's well worn phrase 'We're not all made of money, Germy,' before a familiar finger-marked carafe had been plonked on the table.

Moaning about men wasn't pencilled in to start for another half hour or so. Cat took advantage of a waiter bending down to tie his shoelace right beside Mary to snaffle the last spoonful of paella: she didn't like paella, but sharing with Mary brought out her inner hyena.

'Bloody Trev,' said Jozette, elbows on table and Miami drawl rendering the dullest of British names exotic.

'What's he done now?' asked Germaine, with a long-suffering sigh.

Cat frowned. The schedule was awry. They were still, to all intents and purposes, sober. It was too early to moan about men.

'It's what he hasn't done,' spluttered Jozette, head wobbling with backdated outrage. 'Fill me in, guys: I'm guessing foreplay has reached Britain, yeah?' After a doubtful 'Kind of', from Mary, Jozette carried on, 'Then where was Trev when they handed out the leaflets? That guy hasn't been further south than my neck for months.'

Cat gulped at her wine. Moaning about sex was timetabled for even later: they were usually plastered before anybody said 'foreplay'.

'Sorry, hon. Too graphic for ya?' Jozette swung herself against Cat, giggling. Jozette was physical, her long arms and legs in constant motion. She was a hugger. And a prodder. And a nudger. Meals with Jozette meant a lot of ketchup on your bodice.

'Well . . .' Cat didn't care to picture the apple-cheeked boy she'd beaten at Buckaroo getting jiggy with it.

'I know, I know. Lord, if he was a female version of you, everything would be fine. How did your mama raise two such different kids?'

Germaine had an answer. 'Trev has a penis. Therefore he is untrustworthy, feckless and flawed. Cat,' she added sagely, 'does not own a penis.' Germaine nodded, in a 'case closed' kind of way.

'Give over with the man-hating thing,' scoffed Mary. 'It's so last season. You need a good seeing to, Germaine, that's your problem.' Her fork hovered over the empty paella bowl and she shot Cat a filthy look.

'I don't hate men,' said Germaine calmly, waggling the empty carafe in the direction of the bar. A distinctive woman with a noble profile, she tended to get good service. 'I'm a realist. I see them for what they are. I don't cook for them, I don't pander to them, I don't bat my eyelashes at them, and I don't expect them to validate my existence. And I can assure you that I don't need a good seeing to.' She shuddered, as if somebody had just walked over her grave. 'I have been penis-free for many years and I intend to keep it that way.'

'How many years?' Mary's tone was light, but this information was gold dust; she and Cat had often speculated on the subject but been too sensitive/cowardly to ask.

'If,' said Germaine imperiously, 'that was any of your business, I'd tell you.' A seasoned busybody about other people, she could be tight lipped about herself. 'Suffice to say, I prefer a simple life without the emotional upheaval sexual relationships inevitably cause.'

'What about *love*?' asked Cat urgently, tucking her black bob behind her ears. 'Germaine, you must miss love.'

'I love my life. I love me,' said Germaine. She could be cheesy without wincing: if Cat had been forced to say *I love me* she'd have climbed the curtains with self-consciousness like an electrocuted cat. 'I am complete. I don't need petrol station roses and a Terry's Chocolate Orange with half the segments missing to bolster my self-esteem.'

'Once, *once*, Alun did that,' protested Mary, her Dublin tones fishwife shrill. She tugged at her cleavage. Mary was built on extravagant lines, a series of fleshy rollercoaster curves. Tonight's woollen dress wasn't quite up to the job of containing her milky-skinned bosom.

'Anyway, never mind Trev's prowess or Alun's taste in presents, I have news!' Germaine's eyes glowed under the untamed hedge of her fringe. She regarded beauty products as the devil's work; her hair and skin had to get along as best they could without pentapeptides. Luckily nature had granted her soaring cheekbones and the self-belief of a Sherman tank. 'I have *big* news.'

'So has Cat,' Mary interrupted. 'Go on. Tell them.'

'You're not . . .' Jozette glanced down at Cat's tum, confusion written all over her face.

'No, God, no.' Cat paused, and flattened her hands over her belly. 'Why? Does it look—'

'Not the whole *am I fat* conversation, please,' groaned Germaine. 'What's your news, Cat?' She was tapping her foot impatiently under the table, keen to race on to her own bulletin.

'I finally did it,' said Cat sheepishly. The moment wasn't like she'd rehearsed: she'd imagined herself standing on the table and crowing. Where was the joy, she wondered, the relief? 'I dumped Hugh.'

'Yeay!' Jozette high fived Cat so hard her palm stung. 'Girlfriend, that is worth celebrating. About time! Germy, tell those waiters to swing their asses into action and get some champagne on this table.'

'Should we . . .? It's so expensive,' said the woman who'd paid cash for her house.

Mary, who struggled to pay cash for her Travelcard, shouted Germaine down. 'Two bottles!' she barked. 'This is historic. Hugh is kaput. Deadingtons.'

'Tone it down,' hissed Cat. 'I've dumped him, not assassinated him.'

'Unfortunately.' Mary was not and had never been a fan of Hugh. 'At least that way he'd *stay* dumped,' she said darkly. Being Irish, she was good at saying things darkly: in Celtic households toddlers can ask for a Cornetto darkly.

'Our Cat is a sensible girl,' said Germaine, aiming for supportive but landing on patronising. 'She won't go back to him.'

'Not this time,' said Jozette, beaming a megawatt smile that sold everything from orange juice to insurance back in the day. 'She's got us. She doesn't need that a-hole.'

'But no doubt,' said Germaine wearily, 'there'll be another bum-hole along in a minute.' She was genetically programmed to resist Americanisms.

'Oh, they're all bumholes,' claimed Mary sweepingly. 'But Hugh was dangerous. A father figure. Classic scenario,' she said, sagely.

'No. He. Wasn't.' Cat gave each word equal weight. She was tired of Mary's pet theory. 'Hugh was a boyfriend figure.'

'You went looking for your daddy and found a sugar daddy instead.' Mary was smug, satisfied with her hypothesis.

'Cat's gonna find out who she is, get in touch with herself.' Jozette seemed very sure of this.

Cat was less sure. She had never opened a self-help book and was allergic to notions of finding the real her, suspecting that the real Cat was a small hairless thing that really should be locked in the wardrobe.

'You're going to heal,' said Jozette, evidently liking the word and lingering over it. 'This is the first step of a beautiful journey.'

A bottle of Romania's finest champagne was plonked down by a bored waiter.

'The first step on my beautiful journey,' simpered Cat, 'is to get smashed.'

The big hand was on the twelve. The little hand was on eleven. An awful lot of bad champagne had flowed under their bridge.

Cat's news had been efficiently filleted, Germaine's news shushed, and a general man-rant had broken out. Alun came off particularly badly and it was his lady love who, bang on schedule, supplied the set-up for their girls' nights' habitual conclusion.

'Why do we have to live with men?' wailed Mary, her Guinness moustache in no way hampering her Dublin rhetoric. 'All the buggers do is trample our hearts and leave wet towels on the bed.'

Cat clambered on the drunken bandwagon. 'Yeah, they don't deserve us,' she claimed, ignoring an odd sensation that the room was tilting.

The glittery green eyeshadow, hailed as trendily retro when Jozette arrived, had slid about her face. 'Trev has no idea – *no idea* – how his dinner arrives in front of his fat face every night.' Her Afro had diminished. 'And the face he pulls if I ask him to empty the bin!' she spluttered.

They'd reached the moment they'd been crawling towards: the cheese platter to their metaphorical meal. 'You know what, ladies,' said Jozette, hands on her hips. 'We should all—'

'LIVE TOGETHER!' chorused Cat and Mary rowdily, clinking glasses as if it was the official Best Idea Ever.

Sphinx-like, Germaine folded her arms and regarded the others with pursed lips. 'If you'd let me tell you my news, it would—'

'Look at us,' exhorted Cat, with the faintest of slurs. 'Smart. Funny. Good looking. Ish. How the hell have we got into our thirties, *well* into our thirties, without a decent man between us?' Sober, Cat renounced self-pity and loathed females who banged on about men. But Cat was not sober. 'If we're not sorted by the time we're forty, listen, *listen*, you know what, we should club together, buy a big house and all live in it.' Over fresh cheers for this old chestnut, she shouted inspiringly, 'Imagine it! We could enjoy *Sex and the City* without being judged! We could arrange cushions on the bed in the certain knowledge that they'd stay that way!' This nirvana felt so real to Cat she could almost touch it. Mary and Jozette whooped, burped and banged the table as she rose to her feet for the crescendo. 'We grow old and not care about under-eye bags and have cats and keep the bathroom clean and be really really really nice to each other!'

Germaine buried her head in her hands.

'Exactingly!' yelled Jozette, who had fallen asleep and woken up during Cat's call to arms. 'I mean it, though. You'd better fucking mean it, too, girls. Let's do it.' She prodded Mary, who was attempting, cross eyed, to light a toothpick. 'Stoppit, girlfriend,' she chided. 'You gave up, remember?'

Gazing wistfully at the toothpick she would never get to smoke, Mary grunted emotionally 'Alun doesn't care enough to knock cigarettes out of my hand. Let's really do it! Let's live together! I love you lot, I really do.'

'And we love you. *Sho* much,' gushed Cat, unsure who had spoken but confident that she loved the out-of-focus blob across the table. 'Let's do it. Let's promise.'

'Huh.' Germaine's sour exclamation freeze-framed the groggy love fest. She pulled her shawl tighter about her broad, valkyrie shoulders. 'Tomorrow you'll forget all about this. I've heard it a thousand times before.' Her sozzled expression mingled lofty disdain with the desire to vomit. 'You complain and you whine but you never actually *do* anything about the power these men hold over you. You're happy to talk about living in an all-woman paradise, yet never lift a finger to achieve it. As you know, *I* put my money where my, erm, you know, thingy is.' Alcohol always landed a direct hit on Germaine's vocabulary. 'I've been trying to tell you all night, but you're too busy obsessing about your worthless menfolk to listen.' Germaine took a moment, lifting her nose before announcing, 'You all know how many years I've longed to set up a social experiment to prove that women have no need for men beyond sperm donation. You pretend to be bored when I bring it up, but I know that, deep down, you share my dream. Cat's speech proved it.' She paused, her face pink not only with booze, but with excitement. 'I have rented us the mythical big house in the country. We can live together, without men, with cats, just as soon as you please.' She nodded, pleased with herself, swaying only slightly. 'Now, ladies, after all these years of talking about it, who'll be the first to sign up?'

Mary slid off her chair, but Cat didn't notice. She was intent on concocting a polite way of telling Germaine she was bonkers. 'Germaine,' she finally came up with, 'you are bonkers.'

3

The revolving doors were a maw, primed to swallow her whole. Cat gulped, a reckless move that set off an entire troupe of bongo-playing mice in her hungover head, and squared her shoulders. 'Get a grip, Flowerpot,' she told herself, employing the private mantra that nobody, not Mary, not Hugh, knew about. As ever, it did the trick.

It was a bad day at the office. Cat seemed to be working through some dire karma from a former life, perhaps one spent serial killing, or estate agenting. Not only were her team in open revolt about her Toilet Pigeon strategy, muttering rebelliously in their cubicles, (or 'thinking pods' as the MD insisted on calling them) but Cat had been summoned to the accounts department to examine the budget for her previous project. The owner of a feminine products company was beefing about the cost of his TV campaign: Cat supposed it served her right for referring to him as Tommy Tampon behind his back.

Weathering the day's banal storms, Cat couldn't miss the figure constantly in her peripheral vision. Even with a hangover she sensed Hugh's sinuous outline stalking her. He was a puma: Cat a gnu with a gammy leg.

On her way to the Ladies, Cat passed Simon Cant, the *capo di tutti capi*, who offered her a slight nod, its inclination and length in perfect correlation with her position in the Percival Cant Jablowski hierarchy. Cat tried to nod back, but it was more of a twitch. Since embarking on her affair with Hugh she'd been jittery around the MD, like a teenager with a shoplifted Curly Wurly passing a policeman. Simon's attitude towards office romances was simple: he prohibited them. Discovery of her relationship with Hugh would have meant instant dismissal for Cat. Hugh would fare better: he was on the board, a big name in the industry and a close friend of Simon's, but the fallout wouldn't be pretty. A natural risk taker, Hugh had always laughed at Cat's fears. If she'd been blessed with Hugh's wealth, power and position, perhaps she could have laughed too.

A quick inspection of herself in the mirror in the ladies' loos made Cat recoil. That hangover was good at its job, afflicting Cat with grey skin, lank fringe, and eyes that looked as if they'd never slept. And was that a spot? It was. *I'm too old for spots*, groaned Cat, who was secretly rather vain about her white skin. Hugh had christened her 'Geisha' the first time she'd stood naked in front of him.

Hugh Schmoo, thought Cat briskly and not particularly convincingly as she applied concealer.

The seldom-used tannoy crackled into wakefulness. 'Would Cat O'Connor return to her desk for a *personal* visitor.' The temp receptionist had GCSEs in Nail Art and Sadism. 'That's a *personal* visitor for Cat.'

Hastily rubbing in the concealer, Cat flew back to her office to see her personal visitor sitting in the chair opposite her desk.

'Trev.' Cat's voice was wry. 'Long time no see.'

'Don't start,' warned Trev, with the shatterproof good humour of a man whose dimples have charmed women since he was in his pram. 'You look tired, sis.'

'And so the compliments begin,' sighed Cat, perching on the edge of her desk. This was of course glass: Percival Cant Jablowski was like the Snow Queen's palace. 'What are you doing here?'

'Nice to see you too.'

This arch toing and froing was how the elder O'Connor siblings communicated. Cat couldn't tell if it bothered Trev as much as it bothered her: seeing him with his long legs spread out comfortably in front of him, she wondered if it bothered him at all.

'Mum's fine.' Cat couldn't keep the soupçon of lemon out of her tone. 'Jon's responding really well to the new physiotherapist. But you'd know that if you rang them more often.'

'I refer you to my previous *don't start.*' Trev shrugged. 'I ring, OK, Cat? I ring. I'm here if they need me.'

There was no point pursuing this. The relentless smile pasted on Trev's handsome face, a broader masculine version of Cat's own features, precluded any real questions. Like how he could neglect their divorced mother who cared singlehandedly for their younger brother, Jon. Twenty-five years ago the new baby's cerebral palsy had changed the whole family's roles: Cat and Trev had morphed overnight from giddy pre-teens to mini-adults; their mother had given up her job to stay at home; their father had left the house for twenty Benson and Hedges and never come back.

Sending half her salary home kept Cat poor, but it was the least she could do, along with the one weekend a month she spent in the suburbs, giving her mum a break. Friends chorused, 'You do your best,' but her mother's wan face and Jon's vulnerability demanded more than her best. Cat would never admit, even if thumbscrews were employed, how much she dreaded those weekends.

Only Mary and Hugh knew Cat well enough to pinpoint her family situation as the blue touchpaper for her ambition. One day she would be responsible for Jon. That would take resources as well as love, hence the carefully planned career. Cat hoped she'd inherited more than shiny hair and a fondness for Quality Street from her mother: when the time came she'd need her grit, too.

One thing was certain. Trev would be little or no use. He'd inherited their father's swagger, and his reluctance to 'do' emotions.

'Mum's always fine,' he was saying glibly. 'You worry too much.

I'd be there in a flash if they were in trouble. Anyway, how's work?'

'Fine. You know.' Cat made an attempt to lighten up. 'And you?'

'Not so bad. Plenty of naughty motorists to tick off.' Trev was possibly the sexiest traffic warden in London, but Cat had never done the research to back this up. 'Actually I dropped in to pick your brains. About Jozette.' He paused. 'Did she seem all right to you last night? Did she say anything, you know, about me?'

'We don't *just* talk about blokes, you know.' Cat made a good show of indignation. 'She didn't even mention you,' she fibbed.

'Come off it.' Trev inhabited a Trev-shaped universe that ended abruptly at the tip of his nose. 'I was hoping you could shed some light on why she's being so odd.'

'Odd how?' Cat peeked out at Marian, covertly knitting a bed-jacket under her desk.

'Cross-examining me. Checking up on me, kind of. That's not like Jozette.' Trev laced his fingers in his lap. As if confessing some sin he blurted, 'Caught her going through my pockets the other night'.

'Did she find anything?'

'Course not!' Trev looked affronted, before adding slyly, 'I always dump any incriminating evidence on the way home.'

Marvelling that Trev expected her to find this amusing, Cat said wearily, 'You shouldn't mess with Jozette. She's a good woman.'

'What she doesn't know can't hurt her.'

'It disrespects her.' Cat hoped that was a real word. 'And maybe she does know.' Her brother's smug shake of the head angered Cat. 'You're undermining her self-esteem.'

'Oh, do behave. Self-esteem didn't even exist until Oprah Winfrey invented it. Jozette doesn't know, all right?'

'Doesn't know about what?' Cat had never dared to speak so plainly before.

'About . . .' Those dimples again. 'My little lapses.' He held up his hands as if to ward off a punch. 'Good clean fun. Nothing that would scare the horses.'

Taking a deep breath, Cat swallowed the speech she'd been honing for years. Trev would simply tune her out. 'Have you asked Jozette what's up?'

Trev's eyebrows shot up into his hairline.

'Perhaps you should,' suggested Cat. 'I've got a degree from the Institute of the Bleedin' Obvious and I know from my studies that the person to talk to is your girlfriend, not your sister.'

'How come you got all the brains?'

'Christ, if I'm the brains of the outfit this family is in real trouble.' That was a little too close to the truth: the O'Connors *were* in trouble. They'd never fully recovered from the fallout of their father's defection. 'Listen,' she said, as she stood up to see him out. 'Don't just turn up when you've got a problem. Come and see me, you know, any time.'

'*Starting.*' Trev waggled a finger as he crossed the floor.

'I'm not, I just . . . oh forget it.' Cat pushed him out of the door. She'd had a taste of what Jozette put up with and she didn't like it one bit.

'No, no, no,' scowled Germaine. 'This won't do. I want to sit in the window.'

The tiny café was packed, but miraculously a man laying waste to a tuna baguette got up from a window seat just as Germaine spoke.

'Ah!' She turned to make her way to the table, her cape swirling and knocking an elderly spring onion off a side salad. 'Perfect.'

Nobody else of Cat's acquaintance wore capes. Nobody else behaved like visiting royalty when buying a cheap lunch at Luigi's.

'What's good here?' asked Germaine, putting on her glasses to peer at the laminated menu.

'Nothing,' whispered Cat, aware that Luigi's temper was as foul as his panini.

Their dejected platters arrived mid spiel: Germaine was in proselytising mood. 'You *have* to be involved, Cat, it'll be the greatest social experiment of our times.'

Such hyperbole brought Cat out in hives. 'Gosh, really?' she asked, knowing the irony would be wasted on Germaine.

'Really. I've leased the most idyllic farmhouse for six months, slap bang in a plot of gorgeous Dorset countryside. Lyme Regis is a few miles away, but there are no aeroplanes roaring overhead, no music blaring, no traffic honking, just peace, blessed peace. No internet connection. No news. No mobile phone coverage. For six whole wonderful months.'

'I have a job, Germaine.'

Ignoring her, Germaine frowned at the espresso in Cat's hand. 'How many is that today?'

'Three. But who's counting?' Cat nodded, catching her friend's drift. 'OK, OK, *you* are. Won't this *experiment* cost you a fortune, Germy?' She knew how attached Germaine was to her money: each penny was like a favourite child she couldn't bear to see leave home.

'An absolute fortune,' agreed Germaine. 'I've dipped into the inheritances.'

'Blimey.' Germaine's wealthy great-aunts had been polite enough to die in sequence over the space of a decade and bequeath her their estates.

'Each commune member will contribute according to her means. Life skills will be accepted in lieu of payment. This is about sisterhood,' said Germaine fiercely. 'I'm doing this for women everywhere. It's my dream.'

'But,' said Cat gently, 'not *my* dream.'

'It is when you're drunk,' said Germaine caustically, nailing Cat with a glare. '*In vino veritas.* Deep down you long to shrug off the tyranny of the male/female relationship. Every time you get tipsy you fantasise about a big house where you could live with your friends.'

'That's the drink talking,' said Cat. The coffee was bitter on her tongue. She looked out at the thronged street, mentally photoshopping a West Country meadow in its place.

Sensing an advantage, Germaine pounced. 'It would get you away from Hugh,' she whispered.

Blinking away the pastoral, Hugh-free scene, Cat said, 'It's a daydream, Germaine, and more fool you for not realising it. Women everywhere fantasise about how great it would be to live without their other halves, but they don't act on it. Besides, I don't have any money to contribute, and last time I looked I didn't have any life skills either.'

'You must have,' scoffed Germaine, extracting a long, dark, Italian hair from her lunch.

'I make TV ads. All-female communes don't have much call for TV ads, I imagine. You need somebody who can bake bread.'

'Oh, any fool can bake bread,' said Germaine dismissively.

Cat recalled her domestic science classes and disagreed. 'This is all beside the point, anyway. Even if – *if* – I wanted to join you – *and I don't* – I have no option but to keep working. You know my situation. Jon and Mum rely on me.'

'Not half as much as you think,' said Germaine. 'Oh go on, bluster away, but it's true. They'd be *fine* for six months. You're a saver, I bet you have enough squirrelled away to keep them going, don't you?' She reached over the table to prod her victim. 'Don't you?'

'Ow.' Cat rubbed her arm. Germaine was bossy enough in normal circumstances: running a commune she would give Pol Pot a run for his money.

'You could take a six-month break from your career, surely?' Germaine had all the conviction of a woman who had never had a proper job in her life. 'All you'd need to do is make a small contribution upfront, to cover your share of the food, then I wouldn't ask for anything more. The aim is to grow our own, anyway. The only money you'd need is spending money, and we'll be out in the wilderness so you won't require much of that. Think of it as a holiday from all your responsibilities. Imagine that! Come on, woman, a little career hiatus won't kill you.'

It was useless trying to explain the cut-throat nature of advertising to a woman born with a silver spoon in her opinionated mouth. 'Enn oh, Germy.'

'Where's your spirit of adventure?' goaded Germaine, knocking over an encrusted ketchup dispenser in her zeal. 'It's an opportunity for us women to show that we don't need men, that women can look after themselves and each other. Think of it! No conflict. Rational discussion. The lack of sexual tension will foster honesty, openness, simplicity.'

'I'm quite a fan of sexual tension myself,' teased Cat. 'Have you actually signed anybody up yet?'

'Yes.' Germaine leaned back, smugger than a WAG at her own *Hello!* wedding. 'Three so far.' She suddenly leaned forward, her hawkish profile hanging over Cat. 'But I want Mary. And Jozette. And you.' She frowned. 'No. I *need* you, Cat,' she said in a softer voice. 'Please.'

The change of tack unsettled Cat. Need was not something Germaine ever admitted to. 'You don't need me,' she said briskly, regretting it when Germaine's face flooded with hurt. 'I can't. I'm sorry, but I can't.'

'Imagine it, though,' said Germaine, refusing to give up. 'The marvellous isolation. All that time for contemplation.'

'That,' said Cat, 'clinches it.' There was a long shopping list of needs and wants in Cat's mind: contemplation had never been on it. 'No!'

4

When Mary's call was put through that afternoon, Cat was ready to deliver a blow by blow account of Germaine's lunacy, but the sound of Mary's voice stopped her. 'What's up?'

'Everything!' Mary was squeaky with tears. Mary never cried. She hadn't cried when Alun gave her a McDonald's voucher for their fourth anniversary: this was serious.

'Tell me.' Cat gripped the phone harder.

'The landlord just rang. We've got a fortnight to get out of the flat.'

'Hang on. He can't do that.' Cat was in full shoulder-pad mode. This was twenty-first-century England, there were rules and regulations: you couldn't bait bears, you couldn't shoot people who smelled of BO on the tube, you couldn't evict tenants who had signed a contract. 'We never signed that contract, did we?' she sighed, the shoulder pads melting.

'Nope.'

A long-running dispute about the skirting boards – the bloody skirting boards! – meant that the women had refused to sign the latest lease.

'Don't cry,' Cat advised. 'We'll sort it out.'

'How?' wailed Mary, enjoying the novelty of sobbing. 'This flat is the last bargain in Fulham. We'll have to live . . .' Horror coloured her tone. '*Somewhere else.*'

Somewhere else with boarded up shopfronts, syringes underfoot and a personal hoodie for all your street crime needs: Cat was realistic about how far their money would go in London. She lived on half her salary, and Mary's earnings were fitful, barely keeping her in Bacardi Breezers. 'We'll sort it out,' she repeated, sounding much like the captain of the *Titanic* as he told the third-class passengers to keep singing.

A quick word with Marian produced a stack of property magazines. 'There's always my spare room if you're stuck,' said Marian, shambling off.

'Thanks, M.' Cat imagined herself and Mary swaddled in a bri-nylon sheet on a single bed, ogled by a conga line of the pottery cats that Marian collected. Because there was no doubt that wherever Cat went, Mary would follow.

A frustrating half hour of circling studio flats in the arse end of nowhere followed. If Cat really stretched herself financially, if she gave up, say, food, she could afford a lock-up garage behind a handbag factory.

'Isn't London fun?' she thought.

The agency kitchenette was, natch, white, but tucked away, so it didn't have to conform to the rigid rules of Percival Cant Jablowski interior design. Multicoloured mugs, some from courier firms, some proclaiming their owners to be the world's best aunt/dad/girlfriend, littered the surfaces. They were never quite clean, and Cat was peering at them, searching for the least offensive one as she scanned a property paper.

'Fancy meeting you here,' said Hugh, appearing around the corner like a well-dressed genie.

Ignoring him, Cat rinsed a mug. Mollycoddled board members never made tea: she marvelled that Hugh had found the kettle without a sherpa.

Leaning against the fridge, Hugh said in a posh undertone, 'You look so bloody pretty.'

'Shut up,' hissed Cat, her eyes flicking towards the open plan office where Marian was watering an aspidistra she'd nursed to trif-fid proportions.

'Ah yes, Marian, the arch-spy,' deadpanned Hugh, his clever eyes lit up with amusement. They both watched as one of Marian's American Tan stockings slid down her leg. 'She's on to us.'

'There is no us,' Cat pointed out. The atmosphere was too chummy for her liking.

'There'll always be an us.' Hugh threw Cat a smile drenched in such sadness that she almost returned it.

'Since you're here,' she said, 'I have a favour to ask.'

'Anything, beautiful.'

With a repressive glare, Cat carried on in a businesslike tone. 'Could you have a word with Simon for me? Kind of soften him up? I'm going to ask him for a meeting.'

'Why? Is it money?' Hugh's gaze flitted to the pages open on the worktop. 'Moving house, are we?' Too late Cat attempted to snatch away the magazine, and Hugh nabbed it. 'Fifth floor studio?' He raised a derisive eyebrow. 'Attic flat above off licence?' Hugh tossed the paper down as if it had scorched his fingers. 'In *that* neighbourhood? You'd need an armed guard to get home at night.'

'It's all I can afford. We have a fortnight to get out of the flat.' Cat wanted to fold Hugh up and file him under S for Snob. 'This is how normal people live, Hugh. We're not all ex-public school.'

'That's hardly my fault,' smiled Hugh, unperturbed. 'I can't help it if my pa wanted me beaten up by a better class of sociopath.' He leaned towards Cat over the spattered microwave.

Cat leaned back, as if a panther had slapped a velvety paw on her knee.

'I can't let you live in one of these dumps. I have a solution.'

Cat was arch. 'Really?'

'There.' Hugh's long fingers flicked to another page. 'That's more you.'

'Hardly,' guffawed Cat. 'Lux 1bed,' she read incredulously. 'Balcony/use of communal gardens/Chelsea square.' With a growl she told him, 'This isn't helping, Hugh.' Muted golds and creams winked up from the photographs. The carpets were soft, and the windows framed treetops like works of art. 'You know my situation. I can't afford that.'

Hugh's voice was so low it could have crept under the carpet tiles. 'I can.' He was regarding her with a focused energy quite unlike his customary nonchalance.

Cat held his gaze, their eyes locked. 'What are you saying?' she whispered.

'I take a lease on that flat. Or one like it. And you live in it.' He bit his lip: more un-Hughish behaviour.

'And?' Cat joined the dots to draw a picture she didn't much like. 'You *visit*?' she asked coldly.

'Hopefully, maybe, we can pick up where we left off,' was Hugh's preferred way of describing it.

'What, with me still alone at Christmas and birthdays?' spat Cat, as loudly as she dared. 'While you witter on about how it's never the *right time*?' Mimicking him cruelly, she jabbered, 'I can't leave her now, she's depressed, she's having an operation, her mother's sick, there's a vowel in the bloody month.' Cat shuddered. 'I've had enough, Hugh. It's not right, what we've been doing. I want to face myself in the mirror each morning.' She crossed her arms as tightly as a straitjacket. 'What on earth makes you think I'd agree to something so sordid?'

Hugh flinched. 'No. Not that. Nothing we do together could ever be sordid.' Intense now, the way he could be during client presentations, or sex, he said, 'It's awful without you, Cat. Nothing makes any sense.'

'Oh, you and your words,' groaned Cat, longing to yell at him, maybe hurl the Canderel dispenser. 'It's my stupid half-life that didn't make any sense. The waiting and the fantasising about something that's never going to –' This was veering close to self-pity. 'Your life makes perfect sense, you buffoon. You have a wife, a career, a beautiful home, a—'

Hugh butted in desperately. 'But no Cat'.

At the same moment they both realised how that sounded. 'Surely, with all your money, you could afford a little tabby?' chuckled Cat. She gave a gentle moan, glad that the temperature had lowered. 'Don't you see how insulting this is? Setting up your bit on the side in a love nest so you can pop in for a touch of how's your father every now and then?'

'You've got the wrong end of the stick. Of so many sticks. To be frank,' said Hugh, 'I never knew how many sticks I had before you started getting hold of the wrong end of them all.' Cat's reluctant giggle gave him confidence. 'Think about it. That's all I ask. It would give you a breather, help you save up a nest egg for your future. For you and Jon, when the day comes.' Hugh rarely mentioned Jon by name: Cat gave a tiny start at her brother's condition being referred to so fearlessly by a man who shied away from the entire spectrum of physical frailty, from period pains to the Black Death. 'And I'd only turn up if I was invited.' He lowered his head and pinioned her with a stare. 'But I hope you'd invite me often, because I'm crazy about you, Cat.'

'Get out,' said Cat sadly, screwing up the page and aiming it at the bin.

Hands in pockets, deflated but still *soigné*, Hugh backed away. 'Don't worry about Simon. I'll make sure he's receptive.'

'Thanks,' said Cat, awkwardly.

From the bin the apartment's warm colours sang out at her, even after she'd draped a discarded Pop-Tart over it. From this angle it didn't look sordid. It looked safe.

Alun stood, phantom white, in antique underpants, the milk carton halfway to his lips. 'All right, Cat?' he chirruped.

'Alun, I hate to be picky, but why are you almost naked?' Throwing her keys and handbag on the kitchen table, Cat averted her eyes, but there was an awful lot of Alun to ignore, most of it hairy.

'Mary's doing my laundry.' Alun nodded complacently at the drier. 'That's why I'm here.'

'She's too good to you,' said Cat lightly, meaning every syllable.

'Fancy the pub tonight?' Alun drained the milk carton and wiped some stray dairy off his stubble. 'I've got a big match. You could cheer me on.'

'Why not? Sounds great.' The White Hart was no Claridge's, and darts wasn't Cat's favourite sport, but she had sorrows that needed drowning. Pubbing with Alun tended to be costly: an actor like his girlfriend, he didn't share Mary's practical approach to temping, preferring to keep himself in eternal readiness for his break. Perhaps, Cat sometimes suggested, actors who slept for twenty-three hours out of every twenty-four didn't get many breaks. Mary glossed over Alun's laziness with talk of how he needed his rest, what a talent he was, and how he would repay her for all the dinners/nights out/copies of *Nuts* when he 'made it'. 'But put some trousers on, eh?'

'Sure thing. Mustn't drive the ladies wild with desire.' Alun wandered off, scratching his left testicle with loving attention to detail.

Something peeked out of Cat's handbag at her. Puzzled she tugged at it and saw the corner of a page ripped from a magazine, an image of an immaculate living room with a marble fireplace and parquet floors. Hugh's arty handwriting disfigured the sofa: *'say yes!'*

Emerging from her room in a low-cut jumper that made the most of her wenchish curves, Mary didn't bother with a hello. 'What the feck are we going to do?' she yelped.

'Personally, I'm planning to panic. Then maybe a spot of despair.' Coat still belted, Cat dropped to the sofa. 'We'll have to move further out of London. Way out.'

'I've been on the internet all day at work.' Mary wasn't the most conscientious of temps. 'Anything we can afford is horrible. The world's gone mad. Soon the only people left in London will be billionaires. But, listen, right,' she began, plopping down beside Cat, 'we're sticking together, aren't we? You and me?'

'Yes.' Cat meant it. She couldn't bear to split up her double act with loud, interfering, irreplaceable Mary. And yet . . . she hugged her handbag close to her chest, as if the photo of the elegant flat might leap out and lapdance.

Betraying her witchy tendencies, Mary studied Cat's face and asked abruptly, 'Has Hugh been oiling about? Wangling his way back into your good books?'

'He doesn't oil. And I've never witnessed any wangling. Is there any hot water?'

Laughing at such whimsy, Mary persevered with the Hugh-bashing, leaning forward to study Cat's face. 'Not weakening, are you? Bet he's trying his usual mind fuck on you.'

'What mind fuck is that?' scowled Cat.

'The one where he bamboozles you into abandoning your perfectly valid reasons for dumping him. He's done it four or five times now.' Mary was warming to her subject. 'One waggle of his demi-centenarian bum and you're back in his bed. Well, a hotel bed, obviously, seeing as his wife's in *his* bed.'

'Enough.' Cat held up a gloved hand. 'Hugh is history. We have other stuff to worry about.' Cat stood up and made for her room. 'And just so you know, his wife's not in his bed. Hasn't been for years.'

'Could you possibly pull the other one?' asked Mary politely. 'It's got the loveliest little bells on.'

'Hugh doesn't lie. Well . . .' Cat reconsidered: this was a man who'd slept with her behind his wife's back for four years. 'Not to me.'

'Jaysus, I'm a trained actress and even I couldn't pretend to believe such guff.'

Cat wondered what Mary would make of Hugh's offer. Buying a flat for your younger mistress was classic sugar daddy behaviour: Cat disliked the Pavlov's dog way she salivated at these gestures. If she'd grown up with an actual daddy, one who took proper care of her, perhaps she wouldn't be so needy. Or, she sighed inwardly, perhaps she would. Who knew? Cat was too punch drunk to analyse herself.

'But you're right, we need to concentrate on finding a flat.' Mary leapt up, bosoms bouncing. 'We'll go to the pub, pretend to cheer Alun on, have forty-eight gin and tonics and set our world to rights.'

'Great idea.' Cat paused and turned. 'It's your pay day today, isn't it? Any chance of that tenner I lent you?'

'Sure thing.' Mary knelt on the sofa and reached behind it (this no man's land was the flat's main storage space) to retrieve her battered Gucci rip-off holdall. "Oh,' she said blankly on opening her purse, 'I was sure I put fifty—' She pursed her lips.

'Get a wiggle on, ladies.' Alun appeared, fully clothed and smelling of own-brand fabric conditioner. 'First drinks are on me.'

Mary kept her head down.

Cat looked at Alun for a long moment. He had last bought a round when Michael Barrymore was heterosexual. 'Actually, changed my mind.'

'Shame!' groaned Alun, before shoving Mary out of her reverie with a bear-like prod. 'What about you, bugalugs? You're coming, aren't you?'

'Yes,' said Mary, snapping her purse shut. 'I am.'

5

Negotiating her way into sleep that night, Cat was *almost* there, her consciousness melting into a spangly, drifting dream, when her mobile had an aneurism on the bedside table.

Give it a rest, Hugh, she grumbled, reaching out for the phone. *Oh*. The message was from Germaine.

Jst heard yr homeless. Y not live rent free 4 6 mnths? U no it makes senz.

Snarling, Cat tossed the phone under the bed. Only somebody as batty as Germaine could advise leaving your job the moment you lost your home.

It made no senz at all.

Thanks to an ill-timed swerve to avoid the post boy, there was more coffee on Cat's perfect crisp white shirt than there was in her Starbucks cup.

'Bollocks,' she said quietly but vehemently as she sat down at her desk.

'I heard that,' said Marian, limping in to hand her a kilo of kitchen roll. 'Dab, don't wipe,' she ordered as she left.

Dabbing obediently, Cat grimaced at the Post-It note on her strategy outline for Toilet Pigeon, recognising Simon's self-consciously unusual handwriting. 'Sure about this? Seems risky?'

Cat *was* sure, but it wasn't a good omen for their meeting. She'd rehearsed her speech, honing and polishing, trying to render it less of a terrified barf. Simon didn't respond well to sob stories, and Cat was too proud to offer one, but even so it was hard not to just run in, leap over his desk and shriek 'YOU HAVE TO GIVE ME A RAISE OR I'LL END UP ON THE STREETS!'

'Got anything to show me on the Toilet Pigeon account?' asked Hugh over-emphatically, like the lead in an amateur play. He ventured further into Cat's office. 'I adore you, you little trollop,' he said in a far more intimate tone.

'Up shut,' said Cat briskly, eyes on her laptop.

'I've softened Simon up for you. He'll see you at three.'

'Right. Brilliant. Thanks.' Panicking slightly, Cat wondered how she'd hide the coffee stain. She wished she'd worn her other trouser suit. And her other brain.

'Which is your favourite?'

'Sorry?' Cat looked up, puzzled.

'The mansion block? Or the one with the roof terrace? I circled four or five that seemed very "you".'

'Stop talking, Hugh, please.' Cat pressed Esc when she meant to press Pg Up.

'Never. I never want to stop talking to you,' whispered Hugh.

'Don't. Don't be Satan,' pleaded Cat, tired of withstanding him. She studied his full, pink lower lip. She wanted to touch it with one finger, the way she used to. 'Don't tempt me with things that are bad for me.'

'Since when were marble bathrooms and porter service bad for you?'

'What about my independence?' hissed Cat. 'My self-respect?'

'This isn't some sugar daddy you're talking to.' Hugh wasn't designed to frown, it looked odd. 'I want to make your life better, easier.'

'You're manipulating me.'

'Thanks a bunch. Anything else you'd care to accuse me of?' Hugh's face was turning an interesting puce colour. 'Why must my motives be so base? You're a fool, Cat, to turn down a no-strings offer like this.'

'It's all fucking strings!' snarled Cat, squirming as Hugh pressed at the chinks in her armour. 'We aren't together any more, remember? Tell me this: how would you feel if I entertained a new boyfriend in this de luxe little pad of yours, mine, ours?'

Nostrils flaring, Hugh said that he wouldn't mind at all. 'Although,' he added, 'I'd have to kill him.'

Cat shook her head in wonder. 'How do you do that? Make me laugh at the precise moment I want to staple your head to the filing cabinet?'

'I'm not at all sure but I'm awfully glad I do.' Hugh put his head to one side and regarded her wistfully, much as Cat regarded size ten skinny jeans in Topshop. 'We don't really want to lose what we have together, do we, darling?'

The temp receptionist popped her head round the door just as Hugh unleashed that last incendiary word. 'Sorry. Am I interrupting?' she asked hopefully.

'No, no,' said Hugh blithely. 'We're just discussing a client we're wooing. Darling deodorant. Fabulous product.' Hugh lifted an arm. 'Care to sniff?'

'No, ta.' The girl backed away. 'Hugh, your wife's here to see you.'

Cat managed to turn the strange noise she made into a credible cough, as the receptionist carried on. 'I've put her in your office.' She turned to Cat. 'And there's a giant crate of bog cleaner in reception for you.'

'Thank you so much,' said Cat, falsetto.

*

There was no point trying to concentrate. Cat threw down her pen as if it was all its fault and crossed her arms, uncrossed them, and crossed them again. From outside Cat's lair, Marian regarded her over the rims of her bifocals. 'Tea?' she mouthed.

Nodding ferociously, Cat picked up her phone. Then she put it down again. She had learned the hard way that there is no point phoning a friend, even your best one, for sympathy in married-man-related anguish.

Knowing this agony was her just deserts made it no easier to bear. Cat's hitherto reliable moral compass had snapped the day Hugh first kissed her, and now it was spinning crazily. If she kept her head down at her desk perhaps she could avoid seeing the woman who played such a bizarre dual role in her life. Hugh's wife was both Cat's duped victim and the woman who stood in the way of Cat's happiness. An innocent in the tangle of her husband's affair, the faceless spouse nonetheless stirred a bewildering array of emotions in Cat. Over the past few years she'd worked her way through guilt, resentment, the desire to confess, rampant jealousy and an occasional late night drunken urge to ring her up and shout 'I'm in love with your husband!' Most of these feelings reflected badly on Cat and now they bobbed to the surface and circled her like smug sharks who were finally getting their elevenses.

As Marian bumbled over the threshold with a china cup and saucer, a door crashed open in the outer office with such force that Marian dropped them both. 'What was . . .' Marian clutched her pearls.

It was Hugh's door that had opened so dramatically. And across the floor, cashmere coat askew, flew the tall, discreetly beautiful and very pregnant Mrs Hugh.

Cat stood, shakily. Here it came: the official worst moment of her life. She deserved every name the woman would throw at her. *Get a grip, Flowerpot.* Cat straightened her shoulders and took a deep breath as Hugh's wife approached her door at speed.

Legs caving, Cat sank down again and watched, rapt, with the rest of the Percival Cant Jablowski workforce, as the furious woman with a huge belly passed her office and kicked open Simon's door. Cat remembered Marian, and jumped up. 'Marian, no, let me,' she insisted, stopping her assistant on her long slow descent to pick up the shards of china.

Marian put her lips to Marian's ear. 'Better prepare yourself, Cat.'

Cat straightened. 'For what?' she twittered.

'The game's up, dear. Be strong.' Marian patted her arm. 'This won't be nice.'

For a second Cat considered the *I don't know what you mean* route, but Marian's expression was so kind and so knowing that she said instead, 'I've been stupid, haven't I?'

'Only as stupid as a million other women before you.' Marian took the shattered pieces from her.

Outside there was a buzz of delighted speculation as all pretence of work was abandoned and the staff stood about like meerkats.

The buzz stopped abruptly when Hugh emerged from his corner office. Still perfectly groomed, not a hair out of place, he was subtly changed, as if his batteries were failing. With obvious effort he threw back his shoulders and walked with roughly ten per cent of his usual swagger towards Simon's office. He looked neither left nor right.

Marian put an arm around Cat and they stood in silence as Hugh closed Simon's door behind him and the speculation revved up again.

It didn't take long for Simon's line on the reception desk to buzz. All eyes upon her, the receptionist answered with the gravitas demanded by the wonderful situation she found herself in. 'Yes, Simon. OK, Simon.' A long fingernail with diamantés glued to it pressed a button on the switchboard to cut off his call. Toying with her audience the receptionist looked down at her desk for a long moment before craning her neck and shouting 'Cat! Simon wants you in his office! Pronto!'

'Eh?', 'What?', 'Cat?!', 'Nooooo!' A whirlwind of mutters trailed Cat on her long walk across the open plan Serengeti. She opened the door of Simon's office to discover a tableau that would feature in her nightmares for some time to come.

Silhouetted by the floor to ceiling window was the willowy figure of Hugh's wife. Willowy, that is, except for the glorious bump filling out her silk dress. She had long, expensively highlighted hair, and the kind of fine face that stares out of inherited portraits. Soho's drab rooftops didn't merit the fierce concentration she was bestowing on them through the glass.

On a chrome and leather chair sat Hugh, legs apart and his head in his hands.

Simon, slight and sharp in a silk suit, was glaring. Cat thought she saw hellfire dancing in his eyes but that could have been nerves on her part.

'You wanted to see me,' she said.

'You're fired,' said Simon.

'Oh.' Cat wobbled on her patent heels. 'Er, thanks,' she muttered, uncertain of the etiquette.

'Clear your desk and get out. I'll give you . . .' Simon glanced at his watch. 'Ten minutes.'

'I'm sorry,' Cat told the room at large. 'I really am.'

The lady at the window snorted. Cat heard tears in the noise.

'Bit late for that.' Simon was cold. 'I don't think my cousin wants to hear your cynical apology in her condition, do you?'

With a tiny gasp, Cat had to look directly at Hugh, if only for a moment. So his wife was the boss's cousin. That detail had never made it to their pillow talk. She frowned. 'I didn't know,' she faltered. About the baby. About the family connection. About just how secretive her 'boyfriend' could be.

'You know now,' spat Hugh's wife, grappling a tissue out of her pocket, her eyes still fixed on the view. 'Simon,' she begged in a strangled voice. 'Get her out of here.'

'You heard,' said Simon. 'And don't think about a reference. In fact,' a thought struck him, 'don't even think about finding a job in advertising. Not in London. I have many friends in this business.'

'You can't . . .' began Cat, but she stopped herself. He could. 'The Toilet Pigeon folder is on my desk.'

'And what a pig's ear you made of that,' said Simon caustically. 'I'm sure we'll cope without you.'

Still Hugh hadn't lifted his head.

Cat carefully shut the door behind her. Ignoring her newfound fans' questions on the long walk back to her desk, Cat dropped her pen, phone and diary into her bag, hugged Marian hard and went out through the magical revolving doors which this time transformed her into a jobless woman with scalding tears of shame on her cheeks.

6

Cat didn't pass Go; she didn't collect two hundred pounds; she went straight to her mum's.

To an armchair psychologist, that might sound regressive, but in fact it was novel: Cat had never before fled to her mum. Jon's arrival and diagnosis just after Cat's eleventh birthday had put paid to such fluffy notions; Cat's mum had enough on her plate. Her father's defection reinforced Cat's determination to protect her mother. Homework had been tackled alone, the early stirrings of romance angsted over without maternal input. Cat had soldiered through a Kajagoogoo obsession without once crying in her mother's arms over the realisation that Limahl was spoken for.

The egg mayonnaise sandwiches (her favourite) on the kitchen table touched Cat's heart, as did the familiar toast-crumb smell of the room. Her mum travelled on tram lines from cupboard to fridge to table assembling a consolatory feast of sandwiches, crisps, tea and an all-important Penguin for afters. Small and frail looking, the woman was a bison in sparrow's clothing. Her fashion sense had stalled in the eighties, and she wore a kaftan that, perversely, was once more on trend. Nobody would take them for mother and daughter – one so pale skinned and dark haired, the other blonde and tan – unless they looked at their eyes. They shared blue eyes, empathetic and moody, that shifted shade with their state of mind.

'So,' said her mum, sitting on a pine chair that pre-dated Cat, 'you've been in the wars, love?'

'Mmm.' It was hard to unload when accustomed to holding back.

'Why on earth did they sack you?' Umbrage had evidently been taken: her mum sounded aggrieved. 'You work all hours.'

'I made a few mistakes,' lied Cat, picking at the crust of her sandwich.

'You? Never. Not my cautious Cat.' Her mother assumed a knowing look, her chin lifted. 'I know what happened. I know you.'

'Eh?' Cat took a crisp from a bowl. All savoury snacks were decanted into bowls at the bungalow: it was 'nicer'. 'Do you?' Cat had never told her mother about Hugh. Perhaps maternal intuition had read her mind. Cat's pulse quickened slightly: it would be wonderful to be noticed like that by her mum.

'Yes, young lady.' Cat's mum looked stern. 'You've taken the blame for somebody else, haven't you?'

'Yes,' said Cat, crunching the crisp. The medicinal tang of salt and vinegar stung her lips. 'That's it.'

'Knew it.' Cat's mum looked triumphant. 'You're such a decent girl. Well, love, *I'm* proud of you,' she said, reaching over to pat her daughter's hand. 'You'll find another job no problem. With all your qualifications and know-how.'

'Yeah,' said Cat brightly, the crisp dying soggily on her tongue. 'How's your week been?'

There had never been pressure for Cat to settle down. No hopeful maternal murmurs about big days or happy events. Mrs O'Connor distrusted men, and her daughter learned at her knee. Her plan to nurture independent offspring had worked: both Cat and Trev were autonomous, determined individuals who'd left home early and always held down a job, paid their bills, kept their noses clean. Relationships, however, were another matter: the O'Connors just didn't have the knack.

A snuffling noise from the room on the far side of the sitting room interrupted Cat's mum's extended riff on what she'd turned round and said to the woman next door and what the woman next door had turned round and said to her. 'He's waking up.' She leapt to her feet. She did everything quickly, with the same neat economy of movement as Cat.

'I'll pop in and say hello.' Wiping mayonnaise off her chin, Cat followed her mum past the red velour three-piece suite and the family studio portrait that hung over the coal effect fire despite Cat and Trev's pleas over the years for her to take it down and burn it (nobody likes to be reminded of their 1985 dress sense).

'Jonny!' sang her mother, preceding Cat into the extension that had sprung up a decade ago. 'Look who's here, sweetheart.'

'Hello, trouble.' Cat rounded the high, wide, white bed, the centrepiece of the cheerful room. It had cost almost as much as the extension, a virtuoso piece of medical equipment that could be notched up or down, or around. Jon's sleepy face beamed at her, and he pointed with a crooked finger at the control buttons.

'He wants to sit up,' translated his mother smoothly. 'Go on, love, the bottom button.'

Cat knew what John meant, and which button to use, but allowed her mum to instruct her. The bed buzzed, raising Jon in to a sitting position. 'All right handsome?' grinned Cat.

Jon nodded, an untidy move that tossed his dark fringe over his eyes. He was so like Trev, as if a sarcastic God had made one robust version and one flawed one. His dark, liquid eyes slid about the room, alighting nowhere, ringed by dark opulent lashes. His mouth lacked his brother's sardonic pout, but it was wide and full lipped just the same. Jon moved constantly, his right arm in perpetual revolt. He stuck his left hand out to Cat and she took it, feeling the long strong fingers in her own smaller ones.

'I've missed you,' said Cat. 'I've had nobody to do *this* to.' She blew a loud raspberry on his palm as her mum tutted comfortably. Jon thrashed in delighted horror, his gaze slithering, landing occasionally on Cat.

Her heart tightened. Cat was accustomed to Jon's condition, it was a fact of their family life, like her mum's passion for macaroons or Trev's hay fever, but she had never quite accepted it. It still felt unfair.

Trev's insistence that talk of fairness was neither here nor there was right, Cat knew that, but she had another Jon in her head. Not a perfect Jon, because the man in the bed was a perfect Jon, but an independent Jon, who could make his own decisions and mistakes, feed himself, maybe even fall in love. She would have liked to have an argument with Jon, to hear his opinion on the prime minister, borrow money from him, tell him off.

Jon pressed his fingers fleetingly to his lips, prompting a 'Thirsty?' from his mum. She bent to a fridge that stood against the wall and extracted a plastic goblet half full of orange juice. A straw protruded from the lid, which screwed on tight: like so much of the stuff in Jon's room, it had an antiseptic hospital look, designed for practicality not pleasure.

'Look at this,' said Cat's mum proudly, carefully wrapping the fingers of Jon's left hand around the vessel. 'He can almost—'

The goblet fell on to the sheet.

'He's managed it before,' she said, undeterred. 'He drank his milk on his own yesterday.'

'Clever old sausage,' said Cat fondly, stroking Jon's hair away from his forehead. Eyelashes crowded round his brown eyes like fur. It was overwhelming to be around Jon, to witness his little battles and triumphs, to know that one day she would be responsible for his well-being. She had a feral love for him that nothing else inspired: pure feeling, powerful and plain. Cat felt more alive beside Jon than anywhere else on earth.

*

'The main problem,' Cat said carefully as she sat down to a dinner of fishcakes and chips, a meal her mother believed to be her favourite, 'is money.'

'I can help you out if you're in trouble,' said Cat's mum hastily as she placed, with the asbestos fingers patented to mothers, the last few chips on Cat's plate.

'No, no,' said Cat. 'I mean, if I can't get another job straight away, you know, I might not be able to, you know . . .' Cat, bullish at work, was mealy mouthed at the bungalow.

Her mum was not. 'We'll get by,' she said. 'You give us too much anyway. A quarter of your salary is over the top, love.'

And only half the truth: Cat gave her mother half of her earnings.

'You'll never guess,' started Cat, changing the subject, 'what Germaine's up to.'

The expected hoot of derision didn't come. Wryly, Cat's mum said, 'Wish I'd had somewhere like that to escape to.'

Cat recognised the oblique reference to the O'Connors' D-Day, when Cat's father had left with only a cheery 'Back in a minute!' as a farewell. The portrait over the fireplace was post D-Day, and no photos of Mr O'Connor existed any more. At least, Cat had never found any in the furtive searches she'd carried out as a teenager when her mother was out. Cat didn't take the opportunity to try and talk about her father: she knew better than that. 'But it's a crazy idea. I mean, *all women*. They'll drive each other mad.'

'There's more than one way to go mad,' said Cat's mum with the gnomic, ask-me-no-questions style she'd perfected over the years. 'At least nobody would get their heart broken.' She speared a chip.

'Well, anyway,' said Cat, pushing the supermarket fishcake ineffectually around her plate, 'obviously I'm not joining her silly commune.'

'She wouldn't have to ask me twice,' said Cat's mum, adding hastily, 'If I could bring Jon of course.' She jumped at a sudden noise. 'You're beeping, love,' she said, motioning towards Cat's handbag slumped on the kitchen floor.

'I know who it is,' said Cat. 'It can wait.'

It waited until Cat was on the last train home.

> Please call back. I'm going mad. Please Cat let me know you're all right.

There was another.

> I'm so so so sorry. How can I make things right? Tell me and I'll do it. Anything.

And another.

> Don't shut me out. Perhaps this is for the best.
> Call me, Cat!

And another.

> My offer still stands.

And another.

> Just say the word and the flat is yours. I owe it to you. You deserve it. No strings, promise. Call me and we'll work something out. I love you. I love you. I love you.

Not enough to stand up for me in front of Simon, thought Cat. She deleted ten more messages without reading them.

Am I really, wondered Cat, watching the light show the passing headlights provided on her bedroom wall, *this weak?*

The answer was an incontrovertible yes. Despite the day's revelations she longed to talk to Hugh. He would make it all right, just as he promised. It would be all right in a shallow, surface, cosmetic way: it would be better than nothing.

Reaching out from under the duvet, she grabbed her mobile and stabbed out a number she knew she shouldn't be calling. 'I give in,' she barked, when a sleepy voice answered. 'I'll do it. I'll join your stupid social experiment. Goodnight!'

7

'So,' said Cat.

'So,' echoed Mary.

'So this is it.'

'This is bloody it.'

'This bloody is,' agreed Cat, 'bloody it.'

A few feet away a minibus idled in the narrow car-lined street outside their flat, its engine ticking over asthmatically. Inside it, along with Germaine, were Cat's companions for the next six months. Through the unwashed windows they looked like any other gaggle of random women, but they were strangers and Cat felt her folly keenly. She had never been in such need of warmth and familiarity, yet here she was, heading off down the yellow brick road with what could well be a selection box of psychos.

'You can still get out of it,' wheedled Mary, a seasoned getter-out-of-things. 'I'll say you're not well.'

It was tempting. But too late. The practicalities had been hammered out. Cat had transferred six months' worth of contributions to her mum, leaving a startled and blinking handful of cash in her account. Germaine had snaffled the lion's share of that for Cat's portion of the food bills, leaving an unimpressive figure for spending money. 'I'm committed now.'

'You fecking should be.' Mary sighed and looked around her. 'I thought Jozette was coming to see you off.'

'Last minute styling emergency, apparently.' Cat pulled a face. 'Maybe somebody caught their loafer in their snood, or something.' She scanned the street, wishing that Jozette would materialise, all coltish legs and jangling accessories: six months without her suddenly seemed like an age. 'Funny thing is, I had this feeling she was kind of keen to join the experiment.'

'Never,' said Mary robustly, ringlety hair falling in her eyes. 'Who travels all the way from the States to end up in a field in Dorset? Jozette told me she thought you were mad. Very mad,' she added, for emphasis.

'The truth is she can't leave Trev on his own. He'd be like Hugh Hefner, only in a traffic warden's uniform.'

'There is that,' conceded Mary. 'But you're still mad.'

'You know why I'm doing this. There's nothing for me in London.' Cat was tired of this circular argument. Tentative calls to the HR departments of the bigger ad agencies had confirmed the reach of Simon's tentacles. 'Hugh is still bugging me. I need to break the cycle. Clear my head.' The daily flowers, texts and emails offering love, devotion and a rent-free sanctuary made Cat either scream or sob, depending on her mood. 'Change your mind, Mary. Come with us!' Cat kept the pleading this side of dignified. Just.

'You're kidding.' Mary threw a scornful look at the minibus. An inept hand had attempted to paint over the slogan *South Staffordshire Pig Disease Unit* on its side. 'I'm committed too. To my new flatshare.' Mary had found a berth in a three-bedroomed attic with four other actors that made Anne Frank's accommodation look spacious. 'Anyway, Alun's right. You and I see too much of each other. A break'll do us good.'

Cat pulled her chin in. She hadn't realised Alun thought that way. 'See you, then,' she said in a coiled voice.

'Yeah,' laughed Mary tightly. 'See y'around.'

Turning to clamber on to the minibus, Cat paused. 'My pink duffel bag,' she exclaimed. 'I left it on my bed.'

'I'll go.' Mary dashed back through the peeling front door. This was out of character: she never physically put herself out for a fellow human.

Bracing herself, Cat stepped up on to the minibus. Her erstwhile creative team wouldn't have recognised the diffident woman with her meek 'Hi, I'm Cat.'

'Ah, Miss Broken Heart,' sang Germaine from the seat beside the driver. 'Remember, ladies? The one whose married boyfriend *was* still sleeping with his wife – in fact, she's expecting! – and who lost her job? Well, this is her. Our poor little Cat.'

The sympathetic greetings were laced with enough pity to make a Care Bear gag. 'It's not as bad as it sounds,' lied Cat with a toothy smile as she manhandled her suitcase on board.

'Oh, and she's homeless too,' added Germaine.

At school, Cat had been a consummate back-seater, a flinger of empty juice cartons and a fund of ribald songs. She didn't feel up to a chorus of 'Oh! Sir Jasper!' sitting there alone, staring at the backs of unfamiliar heads. There was a pale, ashy blonde head, a shiny brunette head and a head mostly covered by a khaki cap in the driver's seat. There was an absence of excited chitchat, or any sort of chitchat at all. The others were evidently as tense as she was.

Cat stuffed her case, with its judiciously edited selection of her possessions, under her seat. Everything else was cluttering up her mother's spare room, alongside the exercise bike and a broken lawnmower.

'Good for you!' her mum had said as she waved her off. 'You show 'em!'

Unsure who they were, or what to show 'em, Cat had extracted a solemn promise from her mum to get in touch the moment there was a problem, any problem.

'Are you listening, Cat?' snapped Germaine. 'I *said*, this is Antonia.'

A pallid woman bent sideways out of her seat, peeking back at Cat through a curtain of hair that shade of timorous blonde which is next door to green. 'Hi,' she offered in a wintry voice, her shoulders up around her neck.

'She's devastated by life's cruelties,' was Germaine's summing up.

Antonia pulled her crochet cardigan tighter over her narrow frame.

'Aren't we all?' laughed Cat, attempting to dilute Germaine's callous shorthand. Antonia looked down at her child-sized feet. Cat guessed that she and Antonia were about the same vintage, but Antonia was ushering in middle age with her floral dress and her shapeless cardi, whereas Cat was, in theory, keeping it at bay with her black leggings and biker jacket.

Fidgety now, unimpressed with Antonia, Cat peered out of the scuzzy window. Where was Mary with her bag? Alun had probably ambushed her. He'd been lurking all morning, surveying the girls' emotional leave-taking with Neanderthal incomprehension.

'And that's Lucy.' Germaine waved a hand in the direction of the woman sitting in the seat just behind the driver. 'Journalist. Single. Very single.'

'Right. I see,' nodded Cat.

'Really very very single.'

A hand waved above a seat, but Lucy didn't turn around. All Cat knew about her was that her brown hair was unfeasibly shiny and she was really very single.

Germaine twisted in her seat to place a hand on the shoulder of the figure at the wheel. 'And this incredibly useful little human is Sarge.'

A small, wiry woman, head to toe in army surplus, gave Cat a cheerful thumbs up from the front seat. Sarge was built like a muscly child. Shrewd eyes gazed frankly out from a bony, boyish face, and raggedy fair hair curled beneath a forage cap. Sarge's asexual face offered no clue to her age: she could have been seven, or one hundred and three.

'Nice to meet you, Sarge,' said Cat.

Sarge saluted.

Cat saluted back, and felt like a moron. 'What's your real name?' she asked with a smile.

'No names, no pack drill,' spat Sarge. She leaned towards Germaine and muttered, 'We've got to get a move on. The schedule is already kaput thanks to a certain somebody.' She glowered at Antonia.

'Oh goodness, yes that was me, I'm sorry I—'

'Never explain, never apologise,' advised Sarge sharply. She fizzed with energy, as if it took immense effort not to bounce up and down on her seat. 'Let's get on the road.'

With a nervous, rather small, 'But my duffel bag . . .' Cat looked fearfully out of the window to see Mary tearing out of the house.

'Here.' Pink and perspiring, Mary leapt aboard, shoving the pink bag at Cat. 'Budge up.' She dumped two more bags on the seat.

'No, hang on, these aren't mine,' gabbled Cat.

'They're mine.' Mary's smile split her face.

'Another convert!' Germaine clapped her hands and Sarge crunched the van into gear.

'What?' Cat was incredulous. 'Alun . . .?'

'I need some perspective on Alun.' Mary battled with a threadbare seat belt. 'That whole purse episode made me think.'

'What about your agent? She won't be impressed by a move to the wilds.'

Mary stopped battling with the seat belt and looked down at her lap. 'Let's be honest, she never calls me wherever I am.' She shrugged. 'She'll find me if the National Theatre suddenly want me to play Phedra.' She frowned, her lush dark brows knotting over her gold-flecked brown eyes. 'Don't you want me to come?'

'Of course I do!' laughed Cat, punching her. 'It's just that it's a big step.'

'Bollocks,' said Mary robustly. 'It's an adventure!'

'Tally ho!' cried Germaine as the minibus reversed neatly over Alun's moped.

Four hours on the road with only a James Last cassette for entertainment took its toll on Germaine's reserves of enthusiasm. 'Ta-daah!' she croaked unconvincingly as the minibus bumped through a pair of high, crooked, wrought-iron gates. The women had been lost for the last hour, crawling up and down narrow lanes that snaked along the coast. 'This is it!'

Through the wet windows of the bus, the women peered at their new home.

'Lovely,' said Antonia bravely in the defeated voice which seemed to be the only one she'd packed. With her hair tucked behind her ears, Antonia's eyes were visible for the first time. They were a pretty grey-blue colour, like clouds full of rain approaching a picnic.

'Oh sweet Jesus God Christ, it's a dump,' cursed Mary with Catholic fluency. 'Listen to that wind. And look at that rain.'

Nature had laid on quite a welcome for the social experimenters. SFX-style torrential rain bounced off the cobblestones of the courtyard and the low roof of the farmhouse on its far side. The sulky moon was overwhelmed by mist: the darkness prompted a sudden grumpy nostalgia for Fulham's street lamps in Cat's townie heart.

'Jump to it, ladies! Hup hup!' Sarge darted out of the van and raced through the monsoon back to the gates, heaving them shut with a doom-laden clang. The smack of her hobnail boots in the puddles prompted Cat to peer down at her own wedge-heel ankle bootees; they wouldn't last long out there.

Unfolding from their seats, their bottoms vivid testament to the shortcomings of the vehicle's suspension, the women disembarked one by one and dashed for the house.

Cat's handbag-size umbrella, so handy for darting from kerb to cab, couldn't cope with the downpour and blew inside out. She dodged under the superior umbrella that Lucy had unfurled. Cat noted with a stab of envy that Lucy's cashmere and denim were immaculate after four hours in a minibus that smelled of vomit: Cat looked as if she'd been mugged by a lint monster.

Mary passed them, shouting, 'I should have packed a sou'wester!' into the wind, adding 'What the feck *is* a sou'wester, anyways?' as she skidded across the slick cobblestones on suede ballet pumps even less suitable than Cat's footwear.

'Oh dear,' said Lucy, in a deep arch voice as they looked up at the house, the first words she'd said since they'd left London. She had delicate level brows over dark eyes with a slight oriental tilt to them.

'Oh dear indeed,' sighed Cat.

Twin rows of squat unlit windows glowered at them from a long, low farmhouse with none of the grandeur Cat had recklessly imagined. A turret erupted from the upper floor, a crumbling hexagon topped by a witch's hat of cracked slate. From either end of the house a row of outbuildings shambled out to meet the pillars attached to the gates, enclosing the damp, mossy courtyard. Unmolested by modernity, the house looked as if nobody had lit a lamp, built a fire or laughed there for a long time.

The peeling front door was broad and black, studded with nails and pocked with age, distinctly lacking what a lifestyle journalist might term 'kerb appeal'.

'My fellow pioneers,' shouted Germaine portentously above the keening wind. She brandished an enormous rusty key. 'One small step for woman, one giant leap for—'

'Girls!' The door swung inward. A golden-haired young man, off the scale handsome, with dimples that could undo a bra at ten paces, grinned at them.

'Ooh,' said Mary in an urgent quiet way.

Cat pulled her tummy in and tried to look interesting, sexually knowing, intelligent and thin.

Perhaps because he'd spoiled her big moment, Germaine looked furious. 'Who the hell are you?' she snapped.

'Jamie,' replied the god mildly. 'You know. My dad leased you this place.'

'Hello Jamie,' muttered Mary, injecting mucky promise into the innocuous greeting.

'What are you doing here?' Germaine was recoiling.

'I thought it would be nice for you to arrive to a hot meal.' Jamie stood back and allowed the women a glimpse of another, glowing, open door at the far end of a narrow gloomy passage, A tantalising tang of something oniony drifted out to mingle with the cold clean smell of the rain.

'That's really ever so really nice of you,' said Cat.

'Yeah,' said Mary breathlessly, edging closer to Jamie with a greedy look Cat recognised from their special kebab 'n' Magnum nights.

Not so easily seduced by the interplay of biceps and tight shirt, Germaine asked sternly, 'Didn't your father make you aware of our no men rule?'

'Well, yes . . .' Jamie seemed ready to laugh. 'You mean you were serious?'

'Sort of,' said Mary hastily.

'Absolutely,' said Sarge.

Snorting puffs of frosty air like an affronted racehorse, Germaine stood back to let him pass. 'So. If you don't mind . . .'

Nobody else moved. Antonia had pressed her own pause button and Mary was treating Jamie to the kind of frank and filthy once-over patented by Sid James.

'There's just one little problem.' Jamie hadn't budged. 'My car's kaput. I'm afraid I'll have to ask for a lift.'

'Me!' barked Mary, who couldn't drive.

'I'll do it,' said Antonia, just as Cat put her hand up.

'Don't look at me,' said Sarge, although nobody was.

'We'll call you a cab,' said Germaine.

'A cab?' The cuckoo in their nest smiled. Betraying a local twang he told them, 'This isn't London, you know. There's only a couple of decent cabs and in this rain they'll be busy and besides, there's no mobile coverage up here.' Cat twitched at this, but recovered to hear him say, 'The landline acts up and it's not working, I just tried. I really do need a lift. Sorry.'

'We appear to have no choice,' said Germaine grimly. 'I'll drive you home.'

Lucy chose to speak up, tucking a silky hank of poker-straight brown hair behind one ear. '*After* dinner, surely,' she said, sounding exasperated.

'Yes.' Cat bulldozed the idea through. 'After dinner, Germy.' She felt like a smoker on the verge of giving up a hundred a day habit. What harm could there be in one last puff?

8

The house didn't improve on closer inspection. Ceilings were low and stained. Floors were uneven: the flagstones would have looked *mahvellous, dahling* in a London refurb but here in Dorset they were treacherous underfoot. Dim, bare bulbs failed to illuminate murky corners, and the tightly turning narrow stairs were so crooked and dark that the women postponed exploring the upper floor until they had some food inside them.

'It's all very rustic,' suggested Antonia.

'That's one way of describing it,' agreed Mary, thin of lip.

The kitchen was a relief, big and square and toasty warm, thanks to a wide old Aga. The women clustered around it.

'The electrics don't work in here.' Jamie turned up a paraffin lamp and placed it on the table, where it threw out an unsteady yellow circle.

Warming her outstretched hands, Cat took in the very basic amenities. Defiantly unfitted, the kitchen was sanctuary to various wooden cupboards and shelves of differing vintage. Painted in drab utility greys and browns, they were lorded over by a magnificent dresser, crowded with cracked crockery. Under the black rectangle of the un-curtained window was a Belfast sink, a massive tap drip drip dripping into it.

Centre stage stood a huge square table, knocked and chipped and past its best. *Know how it feels*, thought Cat, running a hand over its rough surface.

'Hope you all like hotpot.' Jamie opened one of the small doors on the elderly range cooker.

'I love hotpot,' said Mary, who had never tasted it.

Ladling out the oozing stew and fussing over portion size, Jamie was presumably unaware of how efficiently he was capsizing Germaine's pet theories about the male's inability to be domesticated. He gave them the rundown on their new home in his gentle local accent.

'The house has full central heating.' This was surprising, and the women nodded approvingly at each other. 'But it doesn't really work. The boiler's a bit iffy but you should be able to coax a full bath out of it every other day.'

'*A* full bath?' A frown knotted Antonia's pretty, pale, very English face. 'Just one?'

'Yeah. Sorry.' Jamie shrugged. 'So you'll just have to get dirty!'

Cat smiled indulgently at Jamie's weak joke, just before he lost her for ever.

'Or *share*,' he said lewdly, and began to giggle at such speed and at such a high pitch that his audience all sat back abruptly.

Discussing Jamie's laugh later, Cat and Mary couldn't agree: was it poodle in blender? Or more eunuch on helium? Either way, it neatly negated his charms.

The women heard that laugh rather a lot over the next hour. Jamie found most things funny. He laughed when the oven handle came off, he laughed when Antonia's earring fell in her dinner, he almost coughed up a lung when Sarge got the hiccups. If there was nothing for him to laugh at, he tapped into his fund of anecdotes, struggling to finish them while wiping his eyes and guffawing. 'Hang on, hang on, let me tell you about the time me nan knocked over the Ferrero Rochers in the Co-op!'

'Wine, I think,' said Lucy, producing two bottles from a carrier bag.

'Yes, I think so too,' said Cat, hurrying to find glasses on the dresser shelves. The complicit look of amusement and pain she shared with Lucy as they poured gave her hope for some sort of relationship in the commune.

'Not for me,' said Antonia piously, refusing a glass. 'I don't drink alcohol.'

'I'll have hers as well,' said Mary, nabbing the dusty tumbler. 'Do you have a problem?' she asked Lucy, who had raised a finely drawn eyebrow.

'No,' said Lucy languidly, the edges of her mouth a-twitch. 'Do you?'

Cat silently applauded Lucy. Mary was a steamroller and it was best to draw distinct boundaries early on. Lucy, so laid back she already sounded bored by everybody, was no pushover.

At least the hotpot was good. Slumped over her glass, Cat stared at Jamie, willing him to please, please stop laughing, relegating him to at least one hundredth position in her personal league of fanciable men.

'You ladies won't be alone here,' said Jamie, in what he patently hoped was a leading way. When nobody pressed for further information, he pressed himself. 'And why's that? you ask. Because you have a ghost.'

That got their attention.

'Get off,' snorted Mary, delighted.

'Ooooh yes.' Jamie leaned back in his chair, thumbs hooked self-importantly in his belt. The chair wobbled and he righted himself hurriedly. 'In the turret room.' He raised his eyes to the ceiling, a move mirrored by the others.

Except Lucy, who said, wearily, 'No such thing as ghosts, Jamie. Rational people discarded them some time ago, along with other myths such as the Earth is flat and men are superior.'

Ignoring, or possibly not noticing, the slur, Jamie grew animated. 'Moans, it does,' he said. 'I've heard it. Groans. Weeps. Whines.'

Mary shuddered happily. '*I* believe in ghosts,' she declared.

'True,' said Cat. 'But you also believe that Victoria Beckham's boobs just grew that way so I'm not sure we should listen to you.'

Antonia shivered in her crochet cardigan. 'I don't think we should joke about the afterlife,' she said, her face even gaunter in the lamplight.

'I only believe in things I can touch,' claimed Sarge. Her lean face was clenched and tense, her whole body taut with readiness at all times. *How exhausting,* thought Cat, draining her glass, *to be Sarge.*

'It's a right cheeky ghost, our one,' offered Jamie. 'Likes to mess about. There's no harm in it.' He paused, as if reconsidering that statement. 'Although of course we never did discover how old Fluff got disembowelled.'

Hastily, Germaine moved the conversation on to other topics, so Cat never managed to ascertain whether old Fluff was a farm cat, or an affectionate nickname for Jamie's grandmother. Chatting about the undead wasn't the best way to spend one's first night in an old, dark house: luckily Jamie was a mine of stories on all sorts of subjects. He seemed keen to tell them everything that had ever happened to him. In detail.

A century had passed by the time Germaine stood up and said, in a tone that invited no argument, 'Time to go, Jamie.' She waggled her car keys and he trotted behind her obediently.

'Bye, girls!' he trilled. 'Have fun playing at communes!'

The upper floor was in darkness. The lights didn't work. The women barged into each other's heels as they opened doors, searching for a habitable room.

In the candlelight the short flight of steps to the turret room wobbled.

'Let's,' said Mary, her cheeks red from the wine.

'No, let's not.' Antonia drew back, her frame ethereal in the gloom.

'It's just a room,' said Lucy impatiently, climbing the steps and opening the door.

Accustomed to being the bravest, the boldest, Cat took the steps two at a time: Lucy was threatening her turf.

'Don't leave me!' Antonia chased the others as they looked over Lucy's shoulder into the haunted chamber.

The far side of the room, lined with a row of small mullioned windows, curved out from the house. One of the windows was open, shuddering in the storm.

'It smells rank.' Lucy's ski-jump nose twitched.

'That's the stench of death,' whispered Mary, as Celts are contractually obliged to at such a juncture.

'Or pigeons,' said Sarge knowledgeably. 'I could survive on the carcass of a dead pigeon for a week if I had to.'

After everybody had stared at Sarge for a long moment, Cat said, 'I hate to admit it, but there's a distinctly creepy vibe in here. It feels . . .' she groped for an appropriate word. 'Unhappy,' she concluded. Unhappily.

The open window crashed back on its hinges and the candle blew out. Even Lucy was down the steps sharpish, although she managed not to shriek along with the others as they stampeded along the dark landing.

'I saw something!' breathed Antonia.

'Enough of that,' said Cat, a little of her old backbone returning. 'The candle went out, that's all.'

'I did,' insisted Antonia.

'So did I,' said Lucy sombrely. 'I saw five women old enough to know better.' She grasped a door handle, muttering, 'there must be a bed somewhere in this godforsaken house.'

And there was. In that very room were six beds, facing each other in two neat rows, all of them dressed with old-fashioned quilts and coverlets, all with pillows that looked full of rubble.

'Ah now here,' said Mary, in broad Dublinese, 'Germaine has lost the plot if she thinks we're all going to sleep together.'

'Well,' said Lucy reasonably, 'it *is* a commune. We signed up for it.'

'I bloody didn't,' said Mary. 'I'm not sharing with the likes of youse,' she said heartily, adding a pallid 'no offence'.

Laying the re-lit candle on a wonky chest of drawers, Cat resigned herself to her fate, gazing up at the beams that ran across the ceiling. What ran across the beams, she didn't care to imagine. 'Let's make the best of it for tonight. I'm too tired to start dragging beds around, anyway. We'll bring it up at breakfast tomorrow,' she said.

'Or during Group,' said Antonia, drifting to a bed under the window.

'Group?' repeated Cat, flopping down on to the nearest quilt. The mattress was hard, and unyielding. Much like Simon had been. She banished the analogy. 'What do you mean?'

'Group therapy. It's part of the experiment.' Antonia looked to the others for corroboration, uncomfortable at being the centre of attention. 'We all discuss what's brought us here. And how we can help each other to heal.'

'Feck that,' said Mary with gusto. She'd peeled off her jumper and looked furious in her D-cup balconette. 'I'm not sharing my innermost workings with bloody strangers.' She threw a long, loose Mickey Mouse T-shirt over her head. 'No offence,' she said in a muffled voice.

Wishing Mary would stop not offending people, Cat struggled into her silk pyjamas. They were a gift from Hugh, a relic of a distant time and place, when dinosaurs roamed the Earth and Cat had sex in peachily lit hotel rooms. She chided herself for not asking more questions about daily life in the commune: talking about her feelings didn't appeal. She'd never discussed her father with her mother. They didn't even ponder Jon's impact on their family life, focusing instead on practicalities.

The wind howled like a lost dog, rattling the windows and whipping the trees outside into a frenzy. A soft sniffling crept from under the covers Antonia had pulled over her head. Wondering if they should go to her, Cat caught Mary's eye and inclined her head towards Antonia's bed.

No, mouthed Mary. *Let her be.*

*

At midnight, or later, a noise woke Cat. She sat bolt upright, sheet to her chin, like a Victorian miss.

A voice hissed from Mary's bed, 'Did you hear that?'

'What was it? A kind of clatter?'

'I heard a groan.'

'Don't say groan,' begged Cat.

'It was probably just Germaine getting in.' Mary didn't sound convinced.

'Yeah,' agreed Cat, thinking *it was the ghost, it was the ghost, it was the ghost.*

9

A cock crowed. A Cat stirred. Wrenched from a warm dream of having her feet kissed in Claridge's it took a moment for her to realise where she was.

In the olden days, by the look of things. Dawn, surprisingly vehement, scoffed at the thin curtains on the leaded windows and nosed all over the room.

Cat pulled the heavy quilt over her nose. She'd had a restless night, her sleep punctured by coughs, sneezes and groans that may have been the ghost but were probably Germaine. She would never have guessed that Mary snored like a tuba falling down a spiral staircase: Cat had always credited Alun with the otherworldly noises from the flat's other bedroom.

Two beds were empty. Germaine and Sarge were, predictably, already up. Possibly shooting men like pheasants out in the fields. Across the room, Lucy slept on, her hair spread over her pillow as carefully as if an art director had overseen it. Just as Cat was dwelling enviously on Lucy's complexion – no pillow marks, no inexplicable red blotches – the woman's eyes opened.

'Oh. Good morning,' said Cat self-consciously, caught out.

Lucy closed her eyes and turned over.

*

Breakfast was interesting. As interesting as rye bread can be. Germaine had thought to shop, but she hadn't thought to plan meals. There was bread but no butter. Soya milk. A lone herring. Some seeds. There was the biggest tub of tofu Cat had ever seen outside her nightmares, and a box of Lidl Turkish Delight.

'We need a supermarket,' said Cat, surveying the desolate larder, picking rye shrapnel from between her teeth.

'And waste precious petrol?' scolded Sarge. 'We'll forage.'

No, we fucking won't, thought Cat, ashamed of her scorn. Sarge baffled her: she couldn't imagine any common ground between them. Sarge's khaki ensemble owed nothing to fashion, and everything to surviving a nuclear attack on Lyme Regis. The woman was springy and tough, like a Jack Russell; Cat preferred spaniels.

Sunlight cruelly exposed the kitchen's nooks and crannies, reminding Cat of that moment when the lights go up on the school disco to expose the pimples crowding your slow-dance partner's chin. She pulled her stool nearer to the Aga: March was misbehaving beyond the leaded windows, and this was the only warm room in the house.

A cursory tour of their new home in daylight had revealed their 'idyllic' farmhouse to be more Addams Family than Waltons. The other bedrooms, though numerous, were derelict. Beams were rotten, skirting boards had been nibbled away by generations of mice, and the scarred floors were crazily uneven. An unhappy smell of neglect curled through the rooms, blossoming into a different and rather more robust smell in the one bathroom.

Mary had backed away, a hand to her throat. 'I'm weeing in the bushes,' she'd announced. 'That bathroom is a museum.'

A loo with a chain, taps ruddy with rust, and a bath with feet and a furry ring of other people's grot, the bathroom had provoked an 'Urrgh' from even Lucy, who prided herself on inscrutability.

By tacit agreement, the turret room would be left to its own devices: the living occupants were quite enough for now. Cat could almost taste her regret as she stretched a hand out to the range. By now, she could be ensconced in a chichi flat with a smart postcode. Of course there would be strings attached: silken strings, though.

'Get a grip, Flowerpot,' Cat chided herself, unfurling from the stool and sadistically reminding herself of Hugh's wife's gloriously pregnant tum.

'Everyone happy?' Germaine breezed into the kitchen, curls bouncing, confidence scraping the ceiling.

'No.' Lucy stood, spare and lean in her well cut jeans and pristine white tee.

'Oh.' Germaine braked. 'What's the matter?'

'The sleeping arrangements,' said Lucy calmly. 'I refuse to share a room with the entire commune. It's juvenile. We're not at boarding school, after all.'

'What about the rest of you?' Germaine looked around, gauging the mood. 'Do you feel the same way?'

'Well, not really, well, kind of, no.' Antonia's body was twisted into a reef knot. 'But yes.'

'I want a room of me feckin' own,' said Mary impatiently. 'We all do.'

'I'm . . .' Cat, generally so decisive, was unsure where she stood. 'Actually, I'm just glad to have a roof over my head,' she said eventually.

'Nice to know *somebody* appreciates the work it takes to set up a venture of this size.' Like a sitcom housewife, Germaine's lips were pursing and her arms folding. 'This property is old and neglected. The other bedrooms are falling apart. I understand the need for privacy but unfortunately it's not possible. Besides,' she asked pithily, 'isn't this meant to be a *commune*? Aren't we supposed to pull together?'

'I'd sleep in the dirt for the good of the commune,' said Sarge superciliously, as if sleeping in the dirt was a talent.

'That would be up to you, but for me it's a deal breaker,' said Lucy, without rancour. 'I haven't unpacked yet. I'll get back to London today. No hard feelings.'

Antonia squeaked. Mary muttered, 'Jaysus, she's hardcore.'

'But . . .' Germaine's demeanour altered. 'You've only just got here. Don't be rash, Lucy.' She sounded on the verge of tears.

Serene and uncreased, Lucy's face reflected none of the high emotion in the room. 'It's simple. I need a room of my own and if I can't have that, I have to leave. I'm not having a hissy fit, merely stating my needs.'

From where Cat stood, Lucy's fit seemed pretty hissy. 'Why don't we take a fresh look at the other rooms?' she suggested diplomatically in the voice she'd used to steer her creative team away from many a storm. 'See if we can fix them up?'

The upper floor didn't improve on a second viewing. 'I don't say this often,' muttered Mary, 'but I see Germy's point.'

'It's derelict,' offered Antonia.

'D'you see?' Germaine towered above her flock on the shadowy, narrow landing. 'Imagine how much it would cost to make them habitable.' She turned to Lucy. 'It would be absurd when we're only staying for six months. Despite what some of you think,' she threw a look Cat's way, 'I'm not actually, literally, made of money.'

Before Lucy could open her mouth, Mary spoke. 'Anyway you can't go,' she said pertly. 'You just feckin' can't. You're one of us now, Lucy.'

'Yeah.' Cat backed her up, risking a hand on Lucy's shoulder. Lucy regarded it as she would a long-dead fish. 'You owe the commune a shot.' Cat and Mary, rugged individualists both, usually gagged at the notion of 'joining', but for some reason the thought of Lucy deserting the ramshackle house panicked Cat. She'd leapt nimbly from denigrating it to defending it. 'Or,' she asked, knowing it to be a low blow, 'are you a quitter?'

'Purlease!' Lucy shook Cat's hand away. 'I'm not falling for tricks gleaned from your Ladybird Book of Armchair Psychology.' She started down the stairs, saying blithely, 'I appreciate your argument, Germaine,' over her shoulder. 'It would be fiscally inappropriate to refurbish the other rooms. I'll stay.'

The other women did a silent, frantic, rather cramped dance of victory and then, by tacit agreement, didn't mention it again.

Bright as a born-again, the outdoors was a shock. Cat screwed up her eyes against the twin onslaughts of the sunlight and the smell. A dozen different scents assailed her as she stepped out into the windy courtyard, a place transformed by daylight. Cat sniffed and recognised the green smell of grass and the glassy tang of the sea, but there were yeasty notes and earthy undertones and a clean sharpness with the whip of a cold shower. She shivered pleasurably, and longed for wellies.

Gingerly making her way over the damp cobbles, Cat examined the outhouses that reached out from either end of her new home. Stables, she supposed, or pigsties, they were run-down boxes, with slates missing from their low roofs. Tiptoeing to the gates, she looked out through the bars and caught her breath. The green went on and on, undulating into the distance, clean and fresh and moist.

And empty. Cat sighed. She wasn't built for the countryside. Its charms were invisible to her. She liked noise and dirt and crowds and buses and sirens. Out here she felt insignificant and forgettable, just another dot of colour on a massive canvas.

What if there's an emergency? she said to herself in a wittering voice she barely recognised. One of the women could fall over. On to a sharp implement. And what about snacks? At home, Cat's slippers had worn a furrow in the pavement to the corner shop, a godforsaken repository of depressed assistants and very old bread. She'd relied on the good offices of a chippie, a Chinese takeaway, a Tex Mex restaurant and a café that understood the magical properties of a Full English. Here there wasn't even a Starbucks. Cat fingered the useless lump of metal that used to be her mobile in the pocket of her jacket.

Wrinkling her nose, Cat forced herself to see the positive side of the lack of mobile phone coverage. The constant messages from

Hugh had been irritating, insulting, unwanted. And strangely comforting.

It felt, thought Cat, seating herself on a kitchen chair that wasn't really up to the job, rather momentous: their first house meeting.

'Gather round the table, ladies,' said Germaine, patting her hair and preparing herself. 'Sarge, would you take notes?'

Sarge clicked her heels, setting off a barrage of sniggers from Mary, who, after a glare from the terrier, put a finger to her lips and assumed a sanctimonious expression.

Germaine, a heroic figure in the ruined landscape of the decrepit kitchen, drew her storm-coloured mantle about her. 'Rules!' she began imperiously. 'You know the main one already, of course.' She mimed cocking an ear.

'No men,' muttered the women, except for Lucy, who looked bored.

'Correct,' said Germaine, gratified. 'Break that rule and, I'm sorry sisters, but you're out.'

'Charming,' said Mary, shifting lazily in her chair.

'Surely,' said Cat, uneasily, 'we'd have to discuss it? You can't sling one of us out into the cold without consulting the others.' She licked her lips, meeting Germaine's gaze. 'I mean, Germy, this is a commune after all: the clue's in the title.'

Wavering, Germaine's fingertips went to the tabletop to balance herself. 'Of course we'll discuss it. At length.' She paused, and then lifted her chin. 'And then you're out.'

'OK, we get it,' sighed Cat who had prophesied that power would go to Germaine's head. 'Really, absolutely, definitely no men. Not even a teeny tiny little man at weekends. What else?'

'We are all equal. We have all contributed financially according to our purses.' Germaine faltered. 'Oh, except for you, Mary. We'll talk about that privately later. We'll all share the everyday chores. There is no hierarchy.' If Germaine noticed the array of disbelieving expressions she didn't show it. 'Nobody will make work for the others, i.e.

none of us will behave like men. Let there be no bewilderment about where the toilet rolls are kept.'

Antonia raised a finger. 'And we won't leave dirty mugs by the sink.'

'And we won't mess up the entire kitchen if we make cheese on toast,' said Mary, her face suggesting a bad memory.

'And we won't leave wet towels on the floor,' said Lucy.

'Or the bed,' said Mary, with passion.

'Yeah, no wet towels on the bed,' echoed Cat, remembering past boyfriends who had draped her entire bedroom with damp towels after a bath. 'If this place had a coat of arms it would be a wet towel on the bed with a red line through it.'

Germaine had one more rule: 'The rota must be obeyed.'

'What rota?' Mary folded her arms and looked sideways at Germaine. 'I never met a rota I liked.'

'A rota of duties,' said Germaine. 'We must all pull our weight.'

Sarge was on her feet in a shot, unfurling a large sheet of wipe-clean laminated paper, covered with a grid featuring the women's names. 'These,' Sarge pointed out, 'are the household chores. Those are the garden chores, the maintenance chores and lastly the miscellaneous chores.'

The others leaned forward to take a look.

'It's like the Dead Sea Scrolls,' murmured Lucy.

'But with fewer jokes.' Cat spotted her name beside Mary's under 'BATHROOM (CLEANING OF)'.

'Oh dear,' said Antonia, which amounted to swearing for her. 'I don't know if I can dig the garden like it says there.'

'Of course you can,' said Sarge dismissively. 'You've got two hands, haven't you?'

'Ye–es,' agreed Antonia, looking nervous about where this confession might lead.

'Then you can dig. No room for slackers here.' Sarge pinned the rota on the distempered wall, just over a large stain that looked like Melvyn Bragg if approached from the right direction. 'Well?' she glared, hands behind her back and legs apart. 'Get cracking.'

10

The bathroom repaid Cat and Mary's efforts by looking more like a bathroom and less like an abattoir. It was still old fashioned and badly designed and arctic cold, but now it was clean.

'There!' said Cat, with proprietorial pride, giving the ungainly old boiler a last rub with her sponge. 'That's better.'

'Hmm,' said Mary, peeling off her Marigolds with a squelch. 'Bagsy I have a bath tonight.'

'Your bagsies are no good here,' Cat told her, scrutinising as much as she could see of her red, sweaty face in the sliver of broken mirror leaning on a copper pipe above the sink. 'It's written in stone in the rota. I think you're due one a week tomorrow.'

'No way,' snorted Mary. 'That'll put my exfoliation schedule right up the cock.'

'If nobody's going to see you naked, is there any point exfoliating?' mused Cat.

'I don't keep myself nice for *men*,' said Mary, sounding affronted. 'I do it for myself.'

'You shave your pubic hair into an A for yourself?'

'Oh shut up,' said Mary, throwing a rubber glove in her direction.

The house was buzzing with industry. Dustballs, years in the making, fled from Sarge's broom; strange brown stains melted under Lucy's cloth.

The only person absent, Cat noted, was their leader. Germaine had shot off in the van to shop for food. 'Shall we give Antonia a hand with the sitting room?' she asked Mary, as they came down the stairs. 'I think she's a bit overwhelmed.'

'But I'm knackered,' claimed Mary. 'I'm an actress, not a charlady.'

'Then act a charlady for the next half hour,' suggested Cat, knowing that Mary's warm heart would outvote her lazy limbs. 'Right,' she said heartily, bursting in on Antonia. 'Let's transform this museum into a comfy haven.'

'Oh. Well.' Antonia did a good line in disconnected exclamations. 'Yes. Hmm.'

'Get the dust covers off,' ordered Mary, sweeping up a squall of antique dust.

'I wasn't sure if I should,' said Antonia, tweaking a corner of one.

'We'll do it together.' Cat tugged at a grimy dust cover and the shapeless blob beneath it turned out to be a handsome old settle, ornately carved in blackest wood. It was uninviting, designed for puritanical bottoms of a bygone age.

'*That* is vile,' said Mary, harassing a skirting board.

'So's this.' Cat excavated a flowery sofa, sunken in the middle like a failed soufflé. 'And this.' An ebony dining table, its stout legs sculpted into gnarled bunches of warty grapes stood stiffly like a loitering vicar in a corner of the low, gloomy room. 'This room is more of a parlour, isn't it? Sitting room is too modern a word for . . . this.' She waved a hand at the chintz curtains at the diamond-paned windows, fastidiously keeping out the sunlight.

Antonia had to be watched and chivvied, or her engine puttered and she slowed to a stop: Cat could have washed the windows in half the time it took Antonia. She guessed that the woman wasn't unwilling, just timid to a disabling degree. She pitied her, but couldn't quell the irritation Antonia's passivity inspired. Over-compensating for these dark thoughts, Cat praised her as she would a child: 'Well done, that's lovely, you're doing a great job.'

'Oh. My. God.' Mary straightened up suddenly, pausing in her punishment of a small cushion. 'Where's the TV?' She looked wildly around, as if a television set might be hiding, waiting to pounce.

'Let's just calm down.' Cat approached Mary warily, under no illusions about the scale of the crisis. 'There must be one here, somewhere.'

'Germaine couldn't be that cruel.' Mary banged the carved doors on a tall dresser and checked pointlessly behind the curtains. 'There must be one! We're missing Jeremy Kyle!' She collapsed on to an unforgiving chair. 'What'll I do? No *EastEnders*. No *Casualty*. No *Emmerdale*.' She turned stricken eyes to Cat. 'No *The One Show!*' she mewled.

'We'll get through this somehow.' Expert in Mary psychology, Cat didn't bother with the *there's never anything on anyway* approach. Television was Mary's religion, the Rovers Return her cathedral. 'Perhaps,' she cooed, taking a careful step backwards, 'it'll be good for us. You know, we could do something more constructive with our time.'

'Like what?' raged Mary. 'Read? Listen to music?' Her lip curled, Elvis-like, as she forced out, '*Talk*? Oh yeah. That's so us. We're so read-y music-y talk-y.'

Now wasn't the moment to suggest that reading, listening to music and chatting might be preferable to wallowing in reality shows. 'Be brave,' Cat counselled. 'Suffragettes threw themselves under the hooves of horses for us. Perhaps you can live without Judge Judy for six months.'

Antonia paused in her methodical rubbing of a bumpy window pane, screwing up her misty blue eyes. 'Oh dear. There's a pig at the front door.'

A pig?' queried Mary.

'A pig,' confirmed Antonia.

'There is,' repeated Cat for the sake of clarity, 'a pig at the front door?'

'At the gate, to be precise.'

Straightening herself, Cat wiped her hands and called out 'Lucy!' dismissing the others, in Germaine's absence, as being of any practical use.

Cat and Lucy sauntered across the courtyard. There was indeed a pig at the gate. A youngish man stood beside it, wearing overalls so dirty they could have stood on their own. 'All right?' he asked brightly. 'Here's your pig.'

'Ours?' Cat studied the pig. The colour of nudity, and upholstered with bristles, it was shitting spectacularly in the lane.

Lucy shook her head. 'I wasn't told about a pig.'

'Nor me,' grimaced Cat.

The pig belched contentedly.

'I don't know nothing about nothing, 'cept I was told to deliver a pig.' The young man turned to his battered pickup. 'I've left you some hay as well. I'd offer to help but the lady on the phone was adamant about me staying outside the gates.' He patted the animal's broad back. 'Think of it as a pile of sausages, eh?'

'You can't just leave him!' squawked Cat. 'What do we do? What does he eat? What's his name?'

'That's a good one.' The pig man's raucous laugh drowned out the diesel engine as he drove off down the lane.

On the other side of the gate the pig stared in at them.

'Looks like a Dave to me,' said Cat.

If, in some absurd maths exam, Cat had tackled the question 'How long would it take woman A (36 years old, 10 stone) and woman B (34, 9 stone) to manoeuvre a pig (age unknown, about 14 stone) across a yard measuring 30 feet by 30 feet?' she would never have risked 'two fucking hours' as her answer. And yet it would be correct.

'Dave! No!' she yelled, then 'Good, Dave, good!' then 'Dave! Are you mad?'

Using branches culled from a tree bending lazily over one corner of the courtyard, Cat and Lucy tickled and prodded and pestered

Dave, who ambled thither, and occasionally yon, sniffing and licking, breaking into a trot when he felt like it.

Dave had zero interest in the outbuilding designated as his new home. The most solid in the row, it had a proper door and had been strewn with hay in his honour. Tempting him with tofu was successful, but there were insufficient supplies to lure him all the way to his new front door. When it ran out, Dave turned and sprinted on surprisingly elegant ankles back to the gates.

'I've had boyfriends like him,' Cat confided to Lucy as they took a breather on an empty stone trough. 'Volatile. Didn't listen to a word I said.'

'I hope they smelled better.'

'A little.' Lucy, Cat had decided, was cool. Supercool, even. Lucy had yet to squawk or yelp, and managed to look Audrey Hepburn-ish even when chasing the less pretty end of a pig. She didn't waste words, it was all pithy. 'Why are you here?' Cat risked a personal question.

'Why are you here?' Lucy batted it back.

'Not because I hate men.' Cat was proud of her deflection: she could be mysterious too. Kind of.

'Same here.' Lucy got to her feet. 'Let's show Dave who's boss.'

It transpired that Dave knew perfectly well who was boss: Dave. Only when Germaine returned, pink cheeked from her foray to the outside world, and the others were recruited into a yipping phalanx behind and around Dave was the pig cajoled into his new quarters.

'Aw, he's lovely,' cooed Mary, surprising Cat, who saw only a porcine bundle of raw-looking flesh and spiky hairs; maybe he triggered memories of Alun.

'He's a lovely *food source,*' said Germaine. 'He'll supply us with a freezer full of organic meat eventually.'

'He?' snorted Sarge, goggling up at them from her magisterial four foot eleven. '*He?*'

'Yes,' snapped Mary. 'Dave's a boy's name, isn't it?'

Fists on hips, Sarge signalled a witty comment with a wobble of her head. 'I've never met a Dave with twelve nipples.'

Neither had Cat. 'Oh. You mean . . .'

'This,' said Sarge confidently, 'is a female.'

And so Dave joined the commune, settling down to a dinner of cheese sandwiches with the crusts cut off, followed by a pleasant evening's squitting.

11

There was some competition for the chore of emptying the shopping bags Germaine had brought home. Cat won, but as disappointing food item after disappointing food item hit the table she rather wished she hadn't. Germaine had bought the cheapest versions of everything: the biscuits all seemed to be made of sawdust, the marked-down bread was teetering on its sell-by date and the fruit was bruised.

'Is there chocolate?' asked Mary fearfully.

'Any camomile tea?' Antonia stood behind her.

'Dare I hope for an artichoke?' asked Lucy.

'Personally I could live on a squirrel,' said Sarge.

There was no chocolate ('bad for you,' said Germaine), only own-brand economy tea ('damn good value,' said Germaine) and Spar didn't sell artichokes ('Don't be bloody ridiculous, Lucy,' said Germaine).

Dinner was omelette, approximately: Sarge had sweated and cursed over some eggs for a while and then something yellow that tasted of feet landed on Cat's plate. She'd refused dessert, a personal first.

The women drifted into the parlour, and deposited themselves on the various uncomfortable chairs within the reach of the two-bar electric fire. Outside the wind made its feelings known and inside Cat drummed her fingers on the arm of the settle. About this time, most evenings, she rang her mum and was debriefed about Jon's day. Her mother had been adamant: 'Take a break from us. We'll call if we need you.' Cat knew that a new massage therapist was due to start: Jon could take an age to get used to new personnel. She shifted on the chair, a sour look on her face. Apron strings were stronger, with a longer reach, than she'd imagined.

'Come along, come along!' Germaine was all activity, pashmina askew, as she whisked into the room, and began to haul chairs about. 'Help me form a circle, please. It's our first Group tonight.'

With heavy feet the women moved to the circle Germaine created, except for Sarge who practically skipped in her Doc Martens. They settled themselves gingerly down, coughing and brushing imaginary lint off their laps. Lucy fussed with her hair, which was always perfect and never needed fussing; Antonia bit her thumbnail to the quick. Mary waved her hand in the air like a primary school pupil desperate for Miss's attention.

'What now, Mary?'

'Telly,' said Mary. 'I need a telly. We all,' she motioned to the others, 'need a telly, Germy.'

'Need?' Germaine queried the word.

'Yeah, need.' Mary was adamant. 'I'm sure there's a bye-law about it. Maybe something from the Human Court of European Rights,' she nodded confidently. 'Isn't it classified as torture to deprive a woman in her thirties of television? I'll be at a social disadvantage when we get back to civilisation. Main characters could have left *EastEnders* and I'd be none the wiser.'

Looking disappointed, Germaine said, 'You have this marvellous, once in a lifetime opportunity to expand your mind without the twitter of the media and you're worried about missing . . .' Germaine groped for a pop culture reference and pulled out a plum. 'Simon Cowell.'

'I don't particularly want a television,' said Lucy.

'I only watch documentaries and the news, anyway,' said Antonia.

Mary glared at her. She held a special reservoir of distaste for individuals who claimed to watch only documentaries and the news.

'It's all brain-rotting rubbish,' declared Sarge. 'Mind-bloating pap. Head-mangling—'

'Thank you, Sarge dear, we get the gist.' Germaine had sniffed victory and said 'Let's vote. Hands up who thinks the commune needs a TV.'

Up shot Mary's lonely hand. She grunted at Cat.

Shaking her head apologetically, Cat kept her hand by her side, happy to escape the dictatorship of television for a while. 'I wouldn't make any difference,' she whispered consolingly: 'you're heavily outvoted.'

'Democracy,' said Germaine piously, 'is a wonderful thing.'

'When it goes your way,' muttered Mary.

'Healing,' said Germaine suddenly, and with a self-conscious gravity that made Cat long to laugh. Standing straight and tall in the centre of the circle, she continued in a sonorous voice, 'Hearing. Sharing. Growing.'

'*Bullshitting*,' murmured Mary.

Sarge glowered at her, nose twitching.

Germaine said, as if leading a prayer, 'Let's remind ourselves of our reasons for being here.'

Hugh, thought Cat.

'We are here to escape the constraints of the archetypal male/female union.' Germaine looked at each face in turn. She'd obviously rehearsed at length. 'We are here to slough off the dull strata of urban life. We are here to explore ourselves.'

'Now now,' said Mary, who had the capacity to misjudge a moment spectacularly. 'None of your smut, Germy.'

Sarge bounced on her seat, furious.

'Mary, *dear*,' said Germaine, with a brave attempt at sounding saddened, but quite unable to cloak her desire to lamp Mary one. 'To create confidence within the Goddess circle, we must resist cheap cracks.'

'As the actress said to the . . .' Mary tailed off. 'Eh? *Goddess*? What are you on about?'

'We are all goddesses,' claimed Germaine. 'We have the power to remake ourselves. Stronger. Flexible like a reed. More serene.'

Despite her aversion to such talk, Cat found herself hungry to believe that this was possible.

'Above all, we are here to reconsider our lives as modern women. You!' She pointed sharply at Mary. 'What benefits did your relationship with Alun bring you?'

'Me? Oh. Well.' Mary pulled a face. 'He was somebody to go to the pictures with.'

'And on many occasions,' Germaine reminded her, 'you told us of the drawbacks. Of his inability to cook a Cup-a-Soup without explicit written instructions. Of expecting an arch of swords for said Cup-a-Soup. Of his belief that women can't tell jokes. Of his, and I'm quoting here, "toenails of Satan".'

'Well, yes, but I was usually drunk when I said—'

Cutting Mary off, Germaine rumbled on like a juggernaut. 'Some of us,' she said, 'have never experienced a male/female relationship.'

Sarge, thought Cat immediately.

'But we have all suffered beneath the jackboot of male patronage.'

Cat imagined Hugh in jackboots. He looked rather sexy. Which wasn't helpful.

'You, Cat, have recently experienced the horrible inequality of the traditional male/female romantic pattern, dovetailing neatly with the traditional male/female business pattern, have you not?'

'Mmm,' said Cat, mealy mouthed with fear. She didn't want to share, not yet. Not ever.

'But we won't hear from you today.' Germaine lifted the sword of Damocles as adroitly as she'd dangled it. 'Today we are going to share the story of a remarkable and brave woman. An individual who has lost everything. I met this incredible spirit when we both reached for the last organic kohlrabi in our local greengrocer's. To me she seemed a typical Chiswick housewife. I saw her as a kept woman, a modern-day geisha. We came to an agreement about the kohlrabi: she let me keep it.'

'*Surprise surprise!*' mouthed Cat to Mary.

'*What the feck's a kohlrabi?* mouthed Mary to Cat.

'As a thank-you I treated her to a soya latte and we chatted.' Germaine regarded Antonia with a complicated look of sympathy and puzzlement. 'There was a lot more to this woman than I had realised. More afternoons, more soya lattes, and I learned how she has suffered under the cosh of male oppression.' Germaine waved a melodramatic hand in Antonia's direction. 'Come, Antonia. Share. Enlighten.'

The slender, childlike woman stood hesitantly and changed places with Germaine, barely responding to the theatrical hug. The others were silent, watching her with interest, pity, and profound relief that it wasn't them.

'I am Antonia,' began Antonia redundantly. She looked around, garnering an encouraging smile from Mary, an intent gaze from Lucy and empathy from Cat, who was sure that her own voice would sound every bit as hamsteresque when her turn came. 'And this is my story?' she ventured with a questioning glance at Germaine, who threw her a queenly nod to reassure her that she was doing it right.

Hands writhing like mating eels, Antonia shared. She shared, as Mary would later comment, like billy-o.

'I was not,' began Mary contemplatively as she trained an inexpert hose on Dave's living quarters, 'expecting *that*.'

'Me neither.' Cat was still recovering from Group. She'd expected tedium but had found high drama, culminating in a swooning Antonia being led to a chair, like a Jane Austen heroine who's glimpsed a bare male ankle. 'That Paul character, the husband, sounds like a monster.'

'Yeah,' agreed Mary grimly, concentrating the hose on a blob of something she didn't care to analyse. 'She got the fairy-tale wedding, the big house, the limitless spending money but at a cost. As soon as she didn't toe the line Antonia was out.'

'That's not quite how she put it.' Cat remembered Antonia's stricken face, her pale eyes. 'What was it she said? *I'm not terribly good at things.* She has no confidence. The poor woman's self-esteem is in the basement.'

'Mind you,' said Mary, switching off the water. 'She's not much good at anything, is she?' Ruefully, regretfully, she admitted, 'it's her mousy ways that get on my nerves.'

'Hmm.' Cat felt the same way. 'But if you're constantly policing the mouse, criticising the mouse and telling it it's stupid, like this Paul character, the mouse will get even, well, mousier.' The country air might have been good for Cat's complexion, but it wasn't helping her skill with metaphor.

'What a bastard, asking her if she was mad. Just because she forgot the odd thing here and there.'

'Like picking her son up from Cubs.' Cat pulled in her chin. 'Actually, that's quite a big thing to forget.'

'But that doesn't excuse what he did,' said Mary, winding up the hosepipe all wrong.

Snatching it impatiently, and winding it up even wronger, Cat concurred. 'No. Keeping her children away from her, telling everybody she was an unfit mother.' She shook her head sadly. 'Poor woman.' The recessive, red-eyed Antonia had filled out into a real person during her Group confession. 'A virgin when she married him, always in his shadow, always trying to please.' She could vividly imagine the bowing and scraping that went on in the Chiswick 5 bd. des. res. 'Only to be chucked out with the rubbish.'

'And his accusation that she drank is so transparent.' Mary was rather enjoying Cat's tussle with the hose. 'Like Lucy said, a foolproof way to gain custody of the children. Antonia barely touches the wine when we open it. She's the type to get squiffy on one sniff of a barmaid's apron.'

'She's so vague when she talks about her marriage. Like it's a dream she's remembering.' Cat tutted at the hose and shook it. 'It was sad, wasn't it, when she was talking about how she worries about her sons, how she's the only one who knows what yoghurts they like and which bits of the Harry Potter films scare them.'

'Ah, yeah,' said Mary, her face melting in sympathy. 'The tears were tumbling down her face by then. She reckoned even her own mother said *no smoke without fire* about the drink. Old bitch.'

'Lucy seemed pretty certain about what has to be done.'

'Fight him!' Mary did a creditable impersonation of Lucy. 'Easier said than done,' she added.

'Antonia's got us now,' said Cat, enjoying a warm gush of comradeship.

'S'pose.' Mary turned and began to walk across the courtyard. 'Life,' she said sagely, 'is too short to spend this much of it watching you wind a fecking hosepipe.'

12

'Nothing,' said Mary, laying the table, 'happens here.' She banged down a fork missing a tine with uncalled for force.

'Not true,' Cat corrected her. 'Things do happen, but they're the same things over and over again.'

It had taken a week for the commune to settle into a routine. An early start, followed by a breakfast involving eggs and bread and strands of hair. A brief row about the rota as Sarge did fifty sit-ups on the kitchen floor, then the chores began. It could be clearing out an outhouse, or doing the laundry, or digging the new vegetable patch or one of a hundred tedious tasks. Lunch was greyish soup and bread, followed by what Germaine dubbed 'Personal Reflection Time': Cat called it 'Terrifying Void Needing To Be Filled Without Dwelling On Recent History Time'. There had been no further group therapy, but Germaine had led a couple of post-dinner workshops. (Cat considered 'workshop' a misleading term for a couple of hours spent listening to Germaine free-associate on a topic she had researched in the *Reader's Digest Encyclopaedia.*) Then it was yet more Personal Reflection (Cat usually lay on the bed and fantasised about saddling Dave and galloping home) before bed.

'Something happened this morning!' Cat was toothily glad to prove her friend wrong. 'We got a postcard from Jozette.'

'Ah. Yes.' Mary picked it up from a shelf where it stood propped against a jug, and reread it aloud: '*Hey you guys, how could you? I'm all alone in London Town. Mary, you're a traitor! Hope you're all happy in the country. Miss you! Love you! Mwah! Mwah!*' She put it back, and looked wistfully at the Beefeater on the front as if he was a close personal friend before resuming laying the table. 'She's being decent about it, but we deserted her.'

'I suppose.' Cat put herself in Jozette's shoes and, although far trendier than her own, they felt lonely. Six months without your support team was a long time. Especially when your significant other was as tricksy as Trev. 'What's on the menu tonight?' asked Cat fearfully, shadowing Mary and laying down table mats.

'It's brown and that's as far as I can go,' shuddered Mary.

'It's a warming stew,' said Sarge, appearing like a resentful sprite at Mary's shoulder. 'All organic.'

'And afters?' prompted Mary, who had grown up in Dublin where a meal without afters can be offered as provocation in a murder case.

'Fresh fruit,' said Sarge.

'That's not afters,' Mary explained patiently, as if explaining our ways to a Martian. 'That's fruit. What's for afters?'

Sweeping into the kitchen in a small selection from her shawl collection, Germaine said tartly, 'Don't pester Sarge, Mary. If you don't like the food why not volunteer to cook?'

'Because I can't cook,' admitted Mary with no visible shame. 'I can reheat. And if you put a gun to my head I might arrange things on a platter. But I can't cook.'

'Then perhaps you should learn,' said Germaine, pushing a dejected curl out of her eyes. She was looking tired today, worn, like a library book that's been thumbed a little too much.

Cat empathised: demotion from career wonderwoman in push-up bra to commune drone was hitting her hard. She was a decision maker, a leader, but here Cat was a mere cog in Germaine's ill-designed machine. Her natural bossiness found no outlet here: Cat's 'life skills' had been perfect for her old life but were redundant in her new one.

Eventually, after much hand to hand combat with saucepans, Sarge yelled 'rations!' It was dark outside, and, thanks to the capricious nature of the commune's electricity supply, it was dark inside too.

Itchy and unwashed (it wasn't her day for a bath), Cat took her usual place at the big square table. Each woman gravitated to their regular chair at mealtimes, their faces sympathetically lit by the oil lamp that sat in the centre of the check tablecloth and cast a soft halo that just took in their faces.

The phrase Cat recalled from holidays with her granny was right: hunger really is the best sauce. There is no other explanation for the way the women fell on the food, even though experience told them it would taste of socks.

Ostentatiously ladling her portion into a metal tuck dish, Sarge attacked it with a curious instrument, part cutlery, part weapon. Noticing Cat stare at it, she waggled the little implement. 'This could save your life in a combat situation.'

'Really?' Cat feigned polite interest. 'Lovely.'

'I'll get you one for Christmas, Cat,' promised Mary, breaking herself a piece of bread. 'Hey, this would be useful in a combat situation, too, Sarge,' she said innocently, bashing Cat neatly on the head with a stony wholemeal nugget.

'I'm not hungry.' Antonia pushed her plate away.

'You should eat,' said Lucy firmly.

Applauding her in her head, Cat backed her up. 'Yes. You're wasting away.'

This was true. They were all dropping weight – the Atkins diet had nothing on Sarge's cooking – but Antonia was becoming skeletal.

'Is it because you're missing the kids, wondering if they're languishing without a mother's love and possibly suffering long-term psychological damage?' asked Germaine with sledgehammer compassion, groping for Antonia's hand on the tablecloth.

Nodding mutely, Antonia stood up and rushed from the room.

'Should I—' Cat half stood, looking after her.

'No, no, leave her,' said Germaine wearily. 'Where does she go? Half the time I have no idea where she is.' She hesitated before adding, 'Sometimes she's not in her bed at night. I've woken up in the small hours, and Antonia's off somewhere, alone, crying no doubt.'

'Tomorrow,' Cat pointed out, 'is her day to see the children.'

Sympathetic noises were made over the puddles of stew. Mary's sympathetic noise segued into a delighted 'Ooh!' She leaned over to Germaine. 'So you'll be dropping her to the station? Can I come? Can we all come? It'll be fun.'

'It won't be fun, it'll be a chore like all the others on the rota,' said Germaine primly. 'We're not here to have fun. I'll drop Antonia off and then go to the bank and pay some bills. Unless, Mary, you'd like to do that for me?' She raised a sardonic eyebrow.

Mary wouldn't and she said so.

Scraping her chair back from the table, Cat stood up and excused herself. 'I've got a date with a pig.'

Rhett and Scarlett. Antony and Cleopatra. Dave and Cat.

The pig's welfare had somehow devolved on Cat. It gave her days a sense of purpose, trotting back and forth to the sty with buckets of slop marginally more appetising than the women's dinner. With no experience in pig husbandry, no way of googling the subject and a history of pet rabbits who starved to death in sordid hutches, Cat had discovered how to look after the newcomer by trial and error. She let Dave trit-trot about in the courtyard for exercise, scrubbed her pink frame every few days, mucked out her plentiful emissions from the courtyard, forked fresh hay into the sty and supplemented the commune leftovers with noxious-smelling pellets that Germaine had sourced in Lyme Regis.

The other women's initial interest in Dave had waned; there were fewer crustless sandwiches, fewer mawkish exclamations ('Aw, look at it I mean him I mean her!') and fewer visits.

'*I* still love you, Dave,' Cat cooed, leaning over the half-door to scratch the pig's back with a stick. 'Oooh,' she laughed at the intense pleasure on the animal's face as it wiggled against the pressure. 'Fancy a stroll?'

Interpreting Dave's guttural grunt as 'Yes', Cat unlocked the door. Stepping daintily over scattered cabbage leaves, Dave joined Cat in the courtyard. Cat wondered if it would work this time. She kept expecting it to be a fluke, but no, Dave was following her again, keeping close to her heel like the politest of Knightsbridge chihuahuas.

It tickled Cat every time. 'Good pig,' she encouraged her companion. 'Clever pig.' She looked down into Dave's unchanging face, the dark pinkish eyes and the chomping jaws. 'Pretty pig.'

Stopping by the gates, Dave butting gently at her calves, Cat gazed out at the view. She hadn't explored beyond the courtyard. The view was just that – a view. Dark now, during the day it was green and damp and full of possibilities. Cat turned away, ashamed of the panic it lit in her breast.

Footsteps drummed on the cobblestones, and Mary was at her side, almost obliterated by woolly scarves and a bobble hat. 'Christ it's cold,' she complained. 'It's late March. This is supposed to be spring. We should live in Jamaica or Italy or somewhere.' Her breath snaked visibly from her lips before dying on the night air.

'Look at the stars,' said Cat.

'I'm over the stars,' said Mary crossly.

Stargazing was their new hobby, since they'd discovered how much brighter and nearer the blazing little points of light were out here in the wilderness.

'I'm not,' said Cat placidly, turning to lead Dave back to her boudoir.

'Never mind the stars,' said Mary, keeping close. 'Are you over *him*?'

'Him who?' asked Cat, aiming to annoy. She was annoyed herself: did Mary really expect her to step away from four years of loving a man just like that?

Apparently Mary did. 'Him Hugh, of course,' she said rattily. 'Mr Posh Pants, your father substitute.'

'Hugh is many things,' conceded Cat, opening the sty door for Dave to trot obediently through, 'but he is not a father substitute. I have a perfectly good father, thank you very much.' She dropped the latch and reconsidered. 'Well, not good, not good at all, crap in fact, but I do have one.' She sighed and found Mary's dark-lashed eyes in the moonlight. 'I don't want to talk about Hugh or my father, thanks very much. Can we drop it?'

'Can *you* drop it?' Mary persisted. 'Do you miss Hugh?'

'Of course I bloody do!' Cat exclaimed. 'I saw him every day for years. I'm only human. I loved him, you know.' She closed her eyes against whatever it was that Mary had opened her gob wide to say. 'And please don't go all cod-Freudian on me and tell me it was a father complex. Whatever it was, I liked it and it's gone and I miss it. OK?' She opened her eyes again. 'Am I allowed to miss him without being a traitor to the cause?'

'Of course,' said Mary, softening. 'Let's go back indoors. There's a red hot game of Snap about to kick off.'

'Join us!,' trilled Germaine from the ugly carved table where she sat with Sarge and Antonia, her hair pinioned in a shaky bun. 'High stakes tonight.' She winked. 'Sarge has just bet two matches.'

Cat shook her head and passed Lucy, sitting in her usual spot in an old armchair with a notebook. Lucy had a proper silver pen with a Tiffany 'T' on it: Cat assumed it could only produce elegant intelligent prose. Lucy had proper kit for all activities. Cat rather envied her her shagreen address book and her tortoiseshell manicure set.

'*EastEnders* would be starting now.' Mary drifted across the room and looked mournfully yet bravely past the scene around her. She tapped out the famous drum roll – 'dum dum dum dum dum da da da da' – funereally slow on the window. '*Rickaaay*,' she whispered, a catch in her voice.

Dropping to the depressed sofa with a paperback, Cat brayed 'Oh for God's sake, Mary. We can't take this. Not every night. Do something else with your time. Remember doing something else?'

'Later,' said Mary in the scary half-whisper she used for this kind of thing, 'it would be *Watchdog*.' She threw back her head and groaned, eyes tight shut. 'All those rogue double glazing firms, and me none the wiser.'

'You *hate Watchdog*,' Cat reminded her through gritted teeth.

Leaping to her feet, Germaine asked hungrily, 'Do you ladies need some conflict resolution?'

'No,' said Mary. 'I need a telly.'

A grandfather clock, the only male for miles, ticked and tocked the evening away. At some point, Antonia slipped noiselessly down beside Cat on the lumpy sofa.

'All right?' asked Cat in an undertone.

'Fine. Fine. Just, you know . . .' Antonia tapered off.

Cat didn't know but nodded anyway.

Curled up in an uncomfortable chair, her russet hair gleaming in the amber light of the standard lamp, Mary murmured, '*Location Location Location*'s starting now.'

Ignoring this gauntlet, Cat turned a page of her novel. The cover promised psychological suspense, but didn't mention a plot so complex that Cat was cross-eyed trying to keep up. She closed the book, finally admitting that she didn't give a monkey's about whodunnit. She yawned. The black rectangle of the window above the card game seemed to look out on to nothing, as if there was no life beyond the outline of this house.

In a way, that was true. Cat had no idea what was going on with her wonky little family. Accustomed to being the linchpin, she missed them. Far more acutely, it would seem, than they missed her, despite all the neurotic attention she'd shown them down the years.

And somewhere out in the dark, over the hills and far away, was

Hugh. Did he miss her? she wondered, the question turning in on itself like a snake eating its own head. There was no way of knowing. Certainly he hadn't left his job, deserted his wife and mounted a white steed to track her down. He hadn't even written. Not having her address was no excuse: Hugh was resourceful enough to approach her mum. He was letting go.

An image flared in her mind: Hugh was letting go and Cat was spiralling off, spinning into the pull of those bright stars over the house. The picture was vivid and made Cat catch her breath. She was adrift. Cat clasped the solid arm of the sofa, and looked about her at the other women, their various shapes and colours and attitudes. They were ballast. She fell to earth again.

What would the commune think of her if they knew the truth? Cat felt acutely ashamed of her desire for another woman's man, a pregnant woman's man. Hugh was about to be a father and here she was wondering if he still thought of her. Her feminist credentials lost even more lustre with this sorry admission.

The truth was that Cat had zero idea what was going on in Hugh's head. One human could never truly know another: she wouldn't have guessed at Antonia's hinterland of pain if she hadn't heard her history in Group. *Whatever Hugh is doing or not doing,* Cat reminded herself, in the manner of a stern nanny, *is none of my business any more.* She repositioned herself and tucked her feet under her bottom.

The torpor in the room must have got to Sarge, too. Springing to her feet, she asked brightly, 'Why don't I tap-dance for you all again?'

A ripple of fear swept the room. It was Lucy who spoke. 'Another time,' she said languidly. 'You've spoiled us enough for one week.'

13

Out in the scrubby yard, Sarge was performing exhibitionist one-armed push-ups in the dirt. Beyond the rickety fence that defined the edge of the commune's empire were shadowy hills of green and grey and mauve, but within the yard all was dust and pebbles.

'Thirty-eight,' puffed Sarge. 'Thirty-nine.' She paused, poised on one impossibly strong little arm to shout at Cat, watching from the door, 'Aren't you supposed to be beating the rugs?'

'Yes,' said Cat unworriedly, sipping her tea. The rota's power waned when Germaine was absent: this morning she was dropping Antonia at Axminster station for her day in town. 'Oh shit,' said Cat hurriedly, banging down the mug and hurrying guiltily out when she heard the minibus wheeze into the forecourt. She'd just reached the blood-coloured old Persian rug hanging over the washing line and picked up the curly rug beater when Germaine emerged into the yard.

'Look!' Germaine was shouting, a look of bliss on her face familiar from Renaissance depictions of saints. 'I bring you life! Precious life!'

The rug beater was put down again. Cat squared her shoulders: she was required to be an audience once more. Seeing Germaine weekly back in London had been, she now realised, just about right: living with her, the histrionic passion was wearing.

'Behold!' Germaine held up a nugget of something which was next door to being no colour at all. 'The universe is in there!'

'Translate, please, Germy.' Mary had joined them, bad tempered and bovine.

'It's a broad bean seed,' beamed Germaine, far too happy for such mundane information. 'Our first seed. Our first connection with good Mother Earth.'

'Don't like broad beans,' said Mary sullenly.

'You,' said Germaine, a hint of threat among the bliss, 'will like *our* broad beans.'

'Yessir!' Mary clicked her heels together and Sarge stopped mid-push-up, wondering if she was being sent up.

'We'll be genuinely self-sufficient thanks to the vegetable patch,' said Germaine, rolling up her kaftan's voluminous sleeves.

'What?' scoffed Mary. 'You're growing Pot Noodles in it?'

Ignoring her, Germaine disturbed the ground with a spotless trowel. She dropped the seed daintily into it and patted the crumbly brown earth over it with one finger. 'There!' she said, delightedly.

Cat, feeling it was expected, applauded.

Sarge resumed her regime, saying in a strained voice as she completed push-up number sixty-three, 'Germaine, there aren't many women like you'.

That was certainly true, thought Cat, getting back to her rug as Germaine carefully planted some more seeds, Mary alongside her, helping.

On her knees, a smudge of mud on her nose, Mary looked wanton. Wanton came easily to her: sophisticated was harder. Whereas, if Cat gave it half a day and concentrated, she could do sophisticated, but wanton was beyond her. She envied Mary her jezebel touches. The way her breasts jiggled, the slalom curve of her hips. Cat's own hips felt podgy, not voluptuous, and she knew that she could never work the whole 'mud on the end of her nose' thing without looking like a tinker.

When Germaine went inside to meditate, Cat strolled across to the vegetable patch. 'Was that a letter from Alun I saw this morning?' she asked, careful to bleach the envy out of her voice: Hugh hadn't put his expensive pen to paper yet. 'Is he in shock?' Cat still found it hard to believe that Mary had just walked out on him.

'I told him at the time it wasn't the end,' said Mary defensively. 'He knows we're still a couple.' She bullied a small cabbage cutting into a hole. 'As much as we ever were.' She sat back on her heels and regarded the wilting little plant as if it could advise her. 'Maybe I was a meal ticket. Somebody to warm his bed and wash his smalls.' She sighed, and made another indentation with the end of the trowel. 'That's the problem – *one* of the problems – with this place. It gives you space to think.'

'That's a good thing, surely?' suggested Cat when it didn't look as if the cabbage had an opinion. 'Maybe we don't think enough about our choices.' Cat wasn't sure she'd thought at all. 'Do you miss him?'

'Alun?'

'No, Noel Edmonds. Of course bloody Alun.'

'God yeah.' The fervour of the reply surprised Cat. 'It's so peculiar not talking to him. I rang him the other day, from that big old-fashioned phone on the kitchen dresser, and he wasn't in. And he's always in!' Mary looked peeved by Alun's sudden predilection for being out. 'I don't know what to do with myself. There's nobody to nag,' laughed Mary. 'I can't, you know, *let rip* at anybody. I have to be polite twenty-four seven. And that,' she said thoughtfully, 'is not easy for me.'

'Really? You astonish me.'

'Obviously I'm not polite to *you.* With you I can act natural, accuse you of fancying your father and whatnot, but it's not enough of an outlet for my nagging needs. Alun was so naggable. All those clothes on the floor. The stubble in the sink. The amazing noises that came out of his nose.' She sighed nostalgically. 'And nobody here leaves the toilet seat up and widdles on the floor.'

'I can try if you like.'

'Do they look all right to you?' Mary frowned down at the shaky row of green things. 'I'm no good at this. I couldn't pick out a cabbage plant in a line-up.'

Passing them, a yoga mat tucked under her arm, Lucy said 'They're fine. Water them now, to settle them in.' She laid her mat down on the far side of the yard.

'Ta,' shouted Mary, before saying under her breath to Cat, 'Jaysus, she's such a know-all. Look at her, doing *yoga*.' Mary pronounced the word with disdain.

'What's wrong with yoga?' Cat loved her yoga gear: footless tights, soft grey tee, bright pink mat. She'd signed up for a term of lessons at the gym near the office, and she had a selection of DVDs. She'd never done any yoga in her life. 'It's good for your body and soul.'

'Feck off,' said Mary heartily. 'Little Miss Superior only does it to show off.'

'She *is* good, though,' said Cat admiringly, watching Lucy stretch and bend her thin, supple limbs. 'Wish I could do that.'

Returning her attention to the vegetables, Mary shook her head. 'Nah, she's too snooty for me. And so secretive about what she's writing. As if we want to know.'

'Well, we do want to know,' Cat pointed out mildly. Every evening they attempted to look over Lucy's shoulder, and every evening she caught them.

The lack of mobile phones and internet at the commune meant that mail enjoyed the importance it enjoys in prisons, or Eton. Cat was accustomed to being left out when Sarge doled out the letters, but the next morning she heard the magic words 'Letter for you' and a pink envelope landed in her lap at the breakfast table. Tucking it into her jeans pocket for later, Cat pushed her burnt Quorn sausage around her plate and asked if anybody had heard the noises last night.

'Yeah!' said Mary immediately. 'Me, I did.'

'I did too,' said Germaine reluctantly. 'I think it's the pipes.'

'Since when,' asked Cat, 'do pipes howl?'

'Oh come now,' said Germaine, 'they were hardly howls.'

Sarge, setting down a smoking sausage on Lucy's plate, said, 'I hate to disagree with you, boss, but they were howls. Definite howls.' She turned back to the Aga. 'Human, I'd say.'

'*In*human.' Mary relished the word, and tipped her sausage covertly into Germaine's handbag, open on the floor.

Cat turned to Antonia, whose woebegone face was closed and distant, looking at but past her plate. 'Did you hear them?'

'What?' Antonia dragged herself from the dreamscape she inhabited. 'Sorry. What?'

'The noises.' Cat fought to engage her. This morning she was pale, even for her, and looked chewed up. 'In the night.' She hesitated. 'The ghost.'

This sparked off a spirited debate. Cat slipped away just as Lucy was declaring in her certain way that 'when you're dead you're dead' and Mary was retelling for the umpty-fifth time the story of how her great-grandma pulled a pint in a Dublin pub an hour after she was buried.

Out in the sty, all was peaceful. Dave was chomping her placid way through some smuggled sausages to a muted soundtrack of birdsong. The hay was warm and soft beneath Cat's bottom, the bitter snap of the late March weather safely beyond the door.

Retrieving the letter, she read Dave the highlights. It was a long letter, newsy and full of asides. 'Ooh, Dave,' said Cat, flattening the page to follow her mother's meandering hand along a crease, 'Jon's had a haircut. The fringe is a bit too short, apparently. And the woman next door put up a new conservatory. Aw, Dave, Jozette's been down to visit!' She put out a hand and rubbed the pig's bristly rump. 'And Mum's gone off Eamonn Holmes, and she's treated herself to a new rain jacket but the zip's stuck so she's taking it back.' Cat didn't read out the PS: *'Meant to post this tonight, but my eyes are closing! Must get off to bed. God bless.'*

Just like her daughter, Cat's mum rarely admitted to tiredness. Perhaps, thought Cat, it was the distance between them, or the time delay of the written word, that made her mother feel able to say she was weary.

Cat folded the letter carefully back into its original creases, as if it was a precious ancient artefact. 'No mention of Trev,' she said ruefully to Dave, who snorted in disgust. Or perhaps a morsel of Quorn went down the wrong way.

14

Dinner was just a traumatic memory: they'd survived worse. In the parlour the electric fire did its best but cardigans had to be fetched before Group could begin.

'Settle down!' Germaine was impatient to begin, a towering divinity centre stage in her flesh and blood Stonehenge. 'Tonight, sisters—' was as far as she got before she was interrupted.

Parting the fringe that was growing into her eyes, Cat said, 'May we vote? On buying a washing machine?'

The slumped audience perked up.

'It's bad for our morale,' said Cat cunningly, 'to look so scruffy.' She plucked at her once-smart lambswool jumper.

'Hand-washing in cold water just doesn't cut the mustard.' Mary stretched out her sweatshirt, offering a visual menu of all their dreadful dinners.

'Have you any idea how much such an item costs?' spluttered Germaine, as if Cat had asked for the Koh-i-noor diamond.

'Two hundred pounds?' ventured Cat, whose knowledge of white goods was shaky.

'Four thousand?' suggested Mary, whose knowledge was shakier.

'This is too dull,' declared Lucy with a refined groan. 'Of course we need a washing machine, Germaine. Nobody agreed to step back into the Dark Ages. I'll pay for it.'

'Oh.' Ready for a fight, Germaine was taken aback and had to reluctantly lay down her weapons. 'Fine.' She remembered her manners. 'And thank you.' Under the heartfelt avalanche of 'thank-yous, Germaine murmured, 'Why didn't anybody bring this up earlier if it means so much to you? Am I really so unapproachable?'

'Hell yeah!' nodded Mary.

'Oh.' Germaine touched her temples with her forefingers. 'Oh dear.'

'Come on, start the cabaret,' said Mary impatiently. 'I'm a busy woman. There's Scrabble to play and my navel to gaze at.'

The withering look sent her way skated right over Mary's untidy head and hit the wall above the pockmarked marble fireplace. Germaine launched herself at her preamble, swinging from hyperbolic statement to hyperbolic statement like a gibbon. 'Tonight we're privileged to hear the tale of a woman whose true grit has been forged in the white heat of male dominance, only for her to emerge from the furnace an oestrogen-powered phoenix.'

Nobody in the room lived up to that description, but then, thought Cat, nobody in the world lived up to that description.

'Sarge!' roared Germaine, throwing her curls back.

'I am Sarge!' announced Sarge leaping up, feet apart, chest out. 'And this is my story!'

'Is she,' whispered Mary to Cat, 'going to put exclamation marks after everything?'

She was.

Sarge's story, thought Cat as she absent-mindedly made cocoa for six much later that evening, had ticked all the boxes she'd expected it to. And one unexpected one.

A father desperate for a son: tick. (After five daughters, Sarge's daddy had wanted a boy; Mummy had wanted a swimming pool.)

A vow to be better than the son her father never had: tick.

A decision to work in a man's world: tick. (Sarge had chosen a career 'few women would dare to': she'd become a milkman. Milkwoman? Cat was still unclear on the nomenclature.)

An army connection: tick. Sarge had joined the TA where, apparently, the other soldiers were terrified of her 'awesome female power'.

Meeting Germaine: tick. Sarge's consciousness had been raised by 'this incredible individual'.

There had been much waxing lyrical about the commune, about its lack of distraction, its scorn for 'puny fabricated notions of romance'. 'You live,' Sarge had declared, 'and you die. Simple.' The finale had been Sarge raising a fist and bellowing 'I am unapologetic. I am what I am. I am power. I am WOMAN!'

'She am nutty,' Mary had muttered under her breath.

So, no surprises there. Sarge was exactly what Cat had surmised her to be: a neglected child who'd grown up to be a marginalised adult, growing spikes along the way to repudiate the world before it got a chance to do the same to her. The surprise was how protective Sarge's history made Cat feel towards the commune's very own feminist hedgehog. She popped an extra Economy Fig Roll on to the tray beside Sarge's chipped mug and carried her watery offerings through to the other women.

15

March was done. It had howled and hailed and been generally pre-menstrual but now April had arrived, and she was proving to be a more mellow character.

In London, the weather stayed politely out of doors: in Dorset it had no such manners. Sunshine improved the house no end, dressing up its dingy corners, but clouds lowered the atmosphere, slowing the women's tread and deadening their chatter.

It had been a clean, sharp arrow of a day, filling Cat with enough energy to paint an outhouse, fix some guttering and withstand dinner. Now, up in the dormitory, rubbing hand cream into her sorry paws, Cat stared out into the navy blue night-time hills, oblivious to the muted babble around her.

The women wandered about stroking lotions onto their cheeks, folding clothes, turning back the heavy bedclothes: a typically calm end to a commune day. Without men there were no bear-like yawns, unthinkable explosions in the bathroom, or enthusiastic scratching of regions better tended to in privacy.

Outside, in the dark, the emptiness reigned. Cat shuddered and tugged at the inadequate curtain. She was still struggling with the scale of her new life, starring in 'Honey, We Shrunk the Londoner'.

A small mobile unit back in the city, she'd jumped from pavement to cab to tube to lift to office to (twice a week) hotel room, all snug and centrally heated and sure of herself. In the wilderness of the west, Cat was a wisp, fragile and prey to the whims of nature.

At least, if she was feeling melodramatic, that was how it seemed. And Cat felt melodramatic quite often these days. She still hadn't ventured beyond the gates, despite her maternal desire to see that Dave got enough exercise. It was just too bloody *big* out there.

Her immediate surroundings had changed. After weeks of care the house was clean, if shabby, and even the desolate backyard was improved by Sarge's pet project, the hen house. The chickens were yet to arrive but their handmade home was waiting for them. The women had marvelled at the scale of Sarge's ambition: the hen house was turreted and Gothic, with a drawbridge and several balconies and, for all Cat knew, underground parking spaces. Antonia had sewn tiny gingham curtains for it and Germaine had pronounced it a symbol of the commune, provoking Mary to a 'Yeah, it's bleedin' ridiculous' which managed to prod a laugh from Lucy. Dave was thriving, despite being referred to as 'Breakfast' by Sarge.

The boiler's caprices were familiar to them now, the washing machine had arrived (greeted like a victorious Caesar), and the rows about the rota, although still a reliable staple of daily life, involved fewer threats of violence.

The turret room was still out of bounds. Even the most sceptical commune member (step forward Lucy!) couldn't explain the eerie noises that floated about the house some nights. Cat felt almost fond of their very own ghost. Almost: it was hard to be fond when she sat bolt upright at 3 a.m., woken by the sound of somebody long dead expressing themselves.

Making the slightest of humps in the bed nearest the door, Antonia was already asleep. Germaine peered at her, and shook her head, semaphoring something along the lines of 'oh dear oh dear oh dear' to the others.

Cat reached out and tucked in the end of Antonia's quilt, while

Mary pushed the woman's hair from her puckered eyes. Antonia had got back from London an hour or so ago, looking as if she'd been through the spin cycle of the new washing machine. Cryptic half-sentences about Paul 'making things difficult' and 'sabotaging' the visit were all they'd got out of her.

The light went out. Cat found her bed in the moonlight and inserted herself between cool, much-mended linen sheets, ignoring Mary's inventive cursing following the sound of a toe being comprehensively stubbed.

'Let's hope,' said Germaine piously, 'that our ghost behaves itself tonight. Poor Antonia needs her sleep.'

Cat apologised to Dave for yawning openly as she filled her trough with horrid-looking items. 'Sorry, Dave, it's not that you're boring, it's just that I had a disturbed night.' The ghost had not co-operated. Its keening had driven off Antonia, who, as she so often did, fled the dormitory and spent a sad and solitary night elsewhere, presumably on the lumpy sofa.

Difficult to insult, Dave chewed stolidly on, savouring the potato peelings and apple cores and congealed rice and lumpy gravy. Cat watched over the feast: occasionally a lazy or inaccurate hand threw something inedible into the swill bin.

'Whoops! Hang on, Dave.' Cat gingerly dipped into Dave's breakfast to fish out a piece of paper. 'This'll give you indigestion.'

A careless once-over of the scrap stilled Cat. It was the corner of an envelope, with just the first name of the addressee still legible. 'Cat O' it read, in an unmistakable *fin de siècle* hand.

At times, Mount Olympus has faultless timing. Some chuckling god sent Mary through the door. 'Jaysus, it's bedlam in the house. We've run out of toilet paper and Germaine is suggesting we improvise, whatever that means, and Antonia is going around looking like leftovers, and Lucy is critiquing the scrambled eggs and . . .' She puttered out. 'What's the matter with you?' She frowned. 'You look ready to kill somebody.'

'I am. I'm ready to kill whoever threw this letter from Hugh into Dave's bucket.'

'Ah,' said Mary blankly. She sucked her lips and looked all around the sty. At some point her eye had to meet Cat's again and when it did she said, 'Sorry'.

'Is this the only one?'

'Could you shout at me?' asked Mary. 'It'd be easier to deal with than this horror film calm.'

'Is it?'

Mary sighed. 'No. It's the second.' She spoke to be heard over Cat's growl. 'That's better. Let it out. But you know I did it for your own good.'

'Did you read them?'

'Of course not!' Mary looked aggrieved: evidently she had standards.

'How could you?' At last the volume went up. 'Mary, you know I've been in agony!' Cat brushed the slop off the scrap of paper, and her name blurred. 'I thought he'd forgotten me . . .'

Taking a brave step forward, Mary said in a wheedling, placatory voice she rarely used, 'You're doing cold turkey, remember? What could he say that would change anything? He can't make his wife unpregnant. Letting Hugh into your head would set you back weeks.'

It was, Cat knew, pointless being angry. Mary meant well: poking her freckled nose in came naturally to her. Cat tussled with the desire to strangle her friend, and won. 'You had no right,' she said eventually.

That didn't get through, Cat could tell. Mary considered herself to have a statutory right of entry to all aspects of Cat's life. 'I'm trying to help.'

'Well, don't,' said Cat waspishly. She didn't want to tear into Mary, but didn't feel able to let her off the hook either. 'Leave me alone for a while, would you?'

'Can't.' Mary pulled a comically regretful face. 'We're on Dave shampooing duty together.'

*

'That,' said Mary standing back, hands on her hips, 'is the cleanest pig in the world.'

'And the happiest.' Dave enjoyed her shampoos, and had shimmied with pleasure through the whole process. She smelled of ylang ylang and avocado, an improvement on her customary smell of plop.

Peace had broken out between the friends. Life was either too short or too long (Cat wasn't sure which) to argue with the one person standing between her and insanity in this outpost.

'I'm *trying*,' bellowed Mary from the top of the stairs, 'to feckin' meditate! Me ying and me yang are all over the kip! What's going on down there?'

Cat, too, drawn by the sounds of a scuffle in the hall, was beetling through the house from the garden.

Spreadeagled against the front door, Sarge was withstanding a tattoo from Antonia's tiny fists.

'Let me out!' Antonia was crying, tearful and, despite her passion, ineffectual. 'I can go home if I want to!'

'Control yourself, woman!' barked Sarge, barely flinching.

'Antonia, dear!' Germaine was gingerly trying to get a grip on Antonia's wriggling torso. A suitcase lay on its side by the stairs. 'She's leaving,' said Germaine, her eyes helpless, as Cat approached.

'She can't.' Cat's breath quickened. 'You can't,' she stammered, trying to grab Antonia's wrists and stop the onslaught on Sarge.

'I can! I'm a grown-up! I can do what I want!' Antonia's sudden assertiveness was dismaying, accompanied as it was by My Little Pony-style violence. 'I HATE IT HERE!' The sudden change in volume seemed to wear her out and she slumped back on to the lowest stair, sobbing.

'You don't,' soothed Cat, hunkering down beside her.

'Maybe she does.' Lucy had appeared on the top step, behind Mary.

'I do-o-o!' keened Antonia, beginning to rock.

With some fancy footwork and lots of cooing, the women

shepherded Antonia into an armchair in the chilly parlour. They clustered around her, apart from Lucy who struck an elegant shape against the mantelpiece. After much nose-blowing, Antonia was able to explain.

'I can't bear being so far from the children,' she faltered, pulling apart the sopping tissue in her hands. 'And I can't take any more of the . . .'

'The cooking?' Cat was sympathetic.

'The company?' Lucy was sardonic.

'The existential pain of communing with your true self?' Germy was baffling.

'Yes, all those things.' Antonia hiccuped. 'I'm lonely . . . and crowded . . . all at the same time. Does that,' she queried, meek once more, 'make any sense?'

From the grave faces about her, Cat could tell that it made perfect sense. 'We all feel displaced,' she said gently, taking off before knowing where she would land, hoping inspiration would strike. 'It's not easy.'

'It's not meant to be,' interjected Germaine.

'But it's *important*,' said Sarge with customary certainty. 'We're facing a challenge. It will change us,' she said, 'for ever'.

She's right, thought Cat, surprised to be agreeing with Sarge. 'And if you think about it,' said Cat gently, praying she didn't sound patronising, 'we're all here because there's some aspect, some facet, of our lives or us that we want to change.'

'And isn't it better to do that amongst friends?' asked Mary, perching on the arm of the chair. 'Cos we are your friends by now, you silly little moo.'

Antonia giggled, and the others exchanged 'we're getting there' looks above her bedraggled head.

'We're building something solid together.' Germaine leaned down and put her hands on Antonia's shoulders. 'You're part of it.'

'Exactly!' Cat nodded vehemently. 'If we took you out of the picture, it wouldn't be the same. If you took any one of us out . . .'

She gestured around the room. 'We're all vital.' She looked over their heads and murmured, 'And isn't that a nice feeling?'

'Now,' whispered Cat in the chilly dark of the narrow hall. 'Let's do it now.'

'I think she's going out, though.' Mary squinted through the sliver of light showing around the partly opened kitchen door. 'She said something about having to talk to the farmer, some problem with the lease.'

'At this hour? It's gone nine. Farmers go to bed by, ooh, eight,' said Cat authoritatively. 'Come on!' She prodded Mary. 'Now!'

Together they burst through the kitchen door, startling Germaine who was peering critically at herself in a compact mirror. Stuffing it into her bag she tutted, 'What are you two up to creeping about like that?'

'We're on a secret mission,' giggled Cat, advancing on Germaine.

'We're kidnapping you.' Mary completed a pincer movement on the other side. They grabbed an arm each, and manhandled her towards the hall.

'No, stop, no, I have to go and visit the landlord, I really must' Germaine was tall and it wasn't easy manoeuvring her towards the hall door when she was defiantly in reverse. 'Let me go, it's urgent, I have to go out!'

'It can wait,' said Cat, tightening her grip.

'NO!' bellowed Germaine.

'Shush!' ordered Cat sternly. 'Or Sarge will hear you and rescue you using her milkwoman jujitsu skills and I don't need the bruises, thanks.'

'Milk*person*,' said Germaine, before exhaling and wilting like a reed in a storm. 'All right.' She rolled her eyes. 'I give in. Where are we going, you silly, silly girls?'

The silly silly girls, who recognised that tone of voice and knew that Germaine was enjoying herself, led their captive to Dave's door.

'Absolutely not,' said Germaine, digging her unfashionable heels in.

'It's warm. And clean. Don't worry,' said Cat, shoving her in, 'Dave doesn't poo where she sleeps. She's far too sophisticated for that.'

The squawks petered out once they'd ceremonially seated Germaine on a rug on top of a hay bale. The flickering lantern light and the background music of dozing pig apparently brought the venue up to her exacting standards. 'What,' she asked, trying to sound stern and not doing a terribly good job, 'is all this about?'

'We miss you,' said Cat, handing her a mug of wine.

'Or rather,' corrected Mary, settling down on a lower bale. 'We miss the old Germy, the one we knew in London who wasn't always going on about the feckin' rota.'

'Somebody has to—' began Germaine. Perhaps she caught sight of herself in Cat's blue eyes. She stopped and her shoulders sagged. 'I miss her too,' she said, a wry look on her face.

'*This*,' Cat gestured at the moodily lit sty, 'is the nearest we could get to recreating our fortnightly girls' nights back in London.'

'This isn't your way of telling me you're leaving, is it?' Germaine's face creased.

'Of course not, you eejit,' Mary reassured her.

Cat put an arm around Germaine. 'Self-doubt doesn't suit you,' she advised. 'We're not going anywhere. We're behind you.'

'You mad old bitch,' added Mary, lest things got too mawkish.

'Maybe I don't deserve your support.' Germaine twisted her lips together, as if gagging herself.

'Of course you do!' Cat was having none of that. 'You're a miracle worker. You've made Mary live without telly. You've surgically separated me from my mobile.'

'So you never think about walking out? About giving up?' The answer was evidently terribly important.

'Every day.' Mary went further. 'On the hour every hour.' She nudged Germaine heartily. 'But I'd never do it.'

'I don't *seriously* consider it,' said Cat, hoping that that was true, and feeling that Germaine needed to hear it. The letter she'd written to her mum earlier that evening had gone through three drafts before the stench of regret was rinsed out. *I miss you* it had ended, shamefaced.

'It's not like I imagined,' said Germaine slowly, watching their reaction. 'We're not all quite as . . . *nice* to each other as I'd envisaged.'

'We're right cows at times,' agreed Mary philosophically.

'We're only human.' Cat defended herself and her fellow pioneers.

The thought bucked their leader up. 'I never expected anybody to actually join up, you know. Why *did* you agree to come?'

'Absolute truth?' On a nod from Germaine, Cat said with a wince, 'Nowhere else to go. Sorry,' she added.

'Now ask us why we stay,' said Mary.

Dutifully, Germaine did just that.

'Oh. Er.' Cat scrabbled. 'Because I have nowhere else to go, and because I'm committed.' She paused. 'Mainly because I'm committed. I want to see this through.' Until she'd said so, Cat had been unaware that she felt that way.

'It would be, I dunno, wrong to leave,' said Mary, curling her lip with concentration. 'It's like I've been glued into a mosaic.'

'Or sewn into a patchwork.'

'Nothing loftier than that?' Germaine sounded mildly disappointed.

'Sorry no,' shrugged Cat.

'Remember who you're dealing with,' advised Mary. 'I can't do lofty.'

'But,' said Germaine warmly, 'you can certainly do sincere.'

'Aw shuddup,' said Mary, true to form.

Germaine looked around the sty as if just realising something. 'Jozette should be here.'

'The fourth musketeer,' said Cat dreamily. 'I miss her accent.'

'I miss her stories,' grinned Mary.

'I miss her, well, her niceness,' laughed Germaine.

'To Jozette!' Cat held up her mug.

'Jozette!' harmonised the other two.

'She's probably watching *Come Dine With Me* right this minute, lucky so-and-so,' said Mary, with an elegiac air.

'I'm sorry,' said Germaine suddenly. 'About the television. I know how you love it.'

With a look of deep suffering, Mary clasped Germaine's hand and squeezed hard. 'Bless you for that,' she whispered. 'I'm coping.'

Exchanging a look over Mary's head, both Cat and Germaine knew that she wasn't joshing.

16

'Is this . . . poultry?' queried Cat, trying to sound interested in and not at all judgmental about the mound of whatever it was that squatted in congealed sauce on her plate. She knew that Sarge had spent much of the day in the kitchen.

'It's fish!' Sarge was indignant. 'It's good for you,' she added, menacingly.

'And so delicious,' declared Germaine, in the tone newsreaders employ to announce royal deaths.

'I'm sorry,' said Lucy, pushing her plate away with a certain, swift movement. 'I simply can't eat it. I know you did your best, Sarge, and I appreciate it.'

Why can't I be like that? Cat was envious. She'd been prepared to eat the fish and risk spending the rest of her life on the toilet rather than offend Sarge. Lucy had been perfectly polite while neatly sidestepping gastroenteritis. 'Shall we knock up a Welsh rarebit?' she suggested.

'No bread,' said Sarge flatly. 'Unless you count rye bread.'

Cat didn't.

'And no cheese,' sighed Mary.

'Who wrote the shopping list?' demanded Cat.

'Let's not point the finger,' said Germaine soothingly, pointing it neatly at herself. She glanced at her watch. 'The chickens should have been delivered by now. The phone's on the blink, so I can't chase them up.' She made an impatient noise in her throat. 'I'll pop over to the farm in a bit.'

'I'll go,' said Sarge immediately, springing to attention.

'No, no, Sarge, you do too much. I'll take care of it,' said Germaine.

'Do too much?' Sarge seemed puzzled by the concept. 'I'll go. It's the next farm, isn't it? Straight over the brow of that hill. I hike that far every other day. I could do with a run.'

Cat goggled at Sarge with the amazement a life form so different to herself merited. 'It's pitch black out there,' she reminded the spring-loaded little creature.

'Perfect opportunity to use my night vision goggles.'

Deadpan, Mary lamented, 'Damn, I left mine at home.'

Even people with no sense of humour know when their mickey is being taken. Sarge's uncomfortable expression wasn't lost on Cat.

Germaine was adamant. '*I'm* going, Sarge.'

'Then I'll come with you.'

The doorbell intervened before Germaine could speak again.

'That'll be the chickens!' said Sarge.

'I'll get it.' Cat was glad to get away from the ley lines of tension criss-crossing the table. She raced along the passage – for some reason she suspected that the long, one-person-wide hall with no working light was the most likely place to meet their ghost – and dragged open the stiff front door.

Outside in the drizzle stood a comfortably built woman who Cat judged to be in her seventies. A buoyant white cowlick peeped out from under a scarlet headscarf.

'Hi,' said Cat brightly. 'Are you the chickens?'

The visitor looked confused. 'Sorry, am I . . .?'

'The chickens,' repeated Cat patiently. 'Are you the chickens?'

Mary appeared behind Cat. 'Is she the chickens?'

'I'm sorry, but how could I be the . . .' The woman looked down at her sky blue raincoat helplessly. 'What do you mean, my dears? Am I,' she echoed their question, 'the chickens?'

'She's not,' said Mary disappointed, 'the chickens.'

Beulah sat at the table, the others having moved round to make space. A mug of tea sat in front of her, the steam curling in kinks around her lined, heavy face. It was, thought Cat, a handsome, ruined kind of countenance, a relief map of experience. *Great casting,* Cat mused, *for a beloved grandmother.* She shook herself. Nobody looked to her for casting suggestions out here in the wild west.

Cat tuned back in to hear Germaine fibbing fluently. 'There is a stringent procedure to being accepted here,' she was saying, with haughty self-importance. 'One can't just knock on the door.'

'Tell me about this stringent procedure,' said Mary, leaning her chin on her hands, a dangerous expression in her eyes. 'Cos I don't recall it in my case.'

'Every commune member must demonstrate why she wishes to retire from the world of men,' said Germaine. 'Then her case is put to the committee for consideration.' She bestowed a lady of the manor smile on their interloper.

Wondering where this committee was hiding, Cat said, in a strenuously friendly way, 'How did you hear about us?'

'In Lyme. I was just passing through,' said Beulah, her eyes hard to read in the wavering lamplight. 'A shopkeeper was chatting to a young man. James, or somebody.'

'Oh, Jamie,' said Mary, and did a quick but accurate impression of his laugh.

The others giggled, except for Germaine, who snapped. 'We're trying to have a serious conversation, Mary.'

'Sorry,' said Mary, without a hint of contrition.

After a sip of the scalding tea, Beulah carried on. 'I heard how you're living together without men, and I thought, gosh, that's interesting. A group of women supporting each other, working together.' She cast a glance at Germaine. 'Accepting each other.'

'What makes you eligible to join us?' asked Germaine.

Eyes cast down, Beulah seemed to be picking her way through a maze of thoughts. 'If you need a tale of male cruelty, I'm afraid I can't supply one. I came here because I have nobody,' she said simply.

'Oh dear.' Softening, Germaine put a hand on the old lady's shoulder. 'How very—'

Lucy cut in. 'Can you cook?' she asked.

'I have cooked three meals almost every day of my life.'

'You're in,' said Lucy.

Both Beulah and the chickens were settling in.

According to the pitiless rota, Cat should have been out of doors alongside Lucy, feeding the feathery newcomers and cleaning up their droppings. She hesitated on the back step. The plump little letter from home had been cooing to her all day from her pocket. She surrendered to its charms and hungrily tore it open at the kitchen table.

It was as packed with detail and incident as the last letter. Cat tittered at the vivid description of Jon's refusal to countenance a change of breakfast cereal and groaned at the report of Trev's brief, disruptive visit, during which he'd broken a cup and played with the lever that raised and lowered Jon's bed.

As Cat read, Beulah moved about the kitchen, placing a pot here, stirring a sauce there. 'A letter from my mum,' said Cat by way of explanation, although Beulah hadn't asked. She refolded the piece of paper.

'Ah,' smiled Beulah. 'Biscuit?'

This habit of Beulah's of ending at least a third of her sentences with a questioning 'biscuit?' endeared her greatly to Cat. 'She's got a lot on her plate. Mum, I mean.'

Beulah made an indistinct but sympathetic noise in her throat as she assembled the alchemic ingredients for dinner.

'My younger brother has cerebral palsy.' Cat nibbled at the lemony edge of her home-made cookie. 'Do you know what that is?'

Beulah shook her head no, and began to weigh flour on the rusty old scales.

Cat explained. She told Beulah how Jon's brain had been damaged in the womb. She told her that cerebral palsy was non-degenerative, that not all cases were as crippling as Jon's. She spoke of the various therapies that made such a difference to him. It took two biscuits to adequately describe her family's set-up. She stopped munching and talking to consider that she'd never sat down and told the story of the O'Connors like that before: with Mary and Hugh it had emerged episodically. 'Do you have brothers or sisters?' she asked conversationally, aware that she'd bombarded Beulah with facts without a word from the woman.

'Me?' Beulah looked up from the scales. 'Goodness no.' She spoke as if such a thing were impossible. 'It was just me. And him. For years,' she said, almost to herself.

The pause that Cat left remained unfilled, except for the slow ancient noise of flour drifting into a bowl.

'There's no cock,' said Lucy, when Cat finally joined her in the garden. She was scattering bran all around the vivid lavender-coloured hen house.

'Surely that's the whole point of the commune,' sniggered Cat, stopping abruptly on receipt of a withering look. 'Sorry. No, there's no cockerel.' She straightened up, her ladle dripping water. 'How will they make eggs?'

'They don't need a cockerel to make eggs,' said Lucy. 'Only to make eggs that grow into chickens.'

'Oh.' How did people know stuff like that? Where had Lucy learned it? She probably, thought Cat, knew about removing red wine stains from carpet. And how to split the atom. 'They're rather sweet, aren't they?'

As was so often the case, Lucy didn't answer.

Cat bent down on her haunches and peered inside the hen house, past the curtains. 'Oi, girls! Dinner!' she called. 'Look at that one.' Cat pointed to a plump bird, its russet feathers gleaming, strolling pompously across the drawbridge. 'It reminds me of Germaine.'

Lucy dipped her chin and regarded the chicken, as it neatly bumped a smaller version, with less opulent plumage, out of its way. 'I see what you mean.'

Smug to have earned Lucy's interest, Cat scanned the other birds. 'Obviously the one she's just knocked into the water dish is . . .'

'Antonia? You're cruel,' said Lucy approvingly. 'And who do we think the sinewy one making all that noise is? The one charging around self-importantly?'

'That'll be our lovely Sarge.' Cat put a hand out to stroke the feisty little hen, who pecked her and seemed to enjoy it. 'Yup. Sarge.' She shared a giggle with Lucy, aware that it was unhealthy to court approval in this way. Lucy was just another commune member, not Miss Jean Brodie. 'Ah,' Cat pointed to a scruffy bird banging its head off the drawbridge. 'That'll be me.'

Over dinner of ambrosia from on high (Beulah's shepherd's pie), Sarge found fault with Lucy and Cat. Finding fault was a hobby of Sarge's. 'You put chicken food on the *ground*?' she said incredulously. 'You *scattered* it?'

'Err, yeah.' Cat watched neurotically as Mary snaffled another portion: she wanted seconds too. 'What's so wrong with that?'

'We spent thirty of our communal pounds on a sophisticated feeder for those individuals,' said Sarge, her head lowered angrily. 'Food on the ground means rats.'

'And rats,' said Germaine comfortably, 'means dead chickens.'

'Oh no.' Cat's bottom left her chair immediately.

'If you've locked them in properly they should be all right,' said Sarge begrudgingly.

'We did.' Cat turned to Lucy. 'Didn't we?'

'We did,' said Lucy calmly. 'Sarge, perhaps we need a seminar on chickens.'

Growing a full two inches on her uncomfortable chair, Sarge tried to suppress a smile. 'Perhaps you do,' she said. 'I'll show you how to dispatch them with a chair leg.'

17

The kitchen was transformed. Beulah's gentle sense of purpose had changed it from a dungeon where ingredients came to die to the irresistible centre of the commune.

Food responded to Beulah's touch. Potatoes fluffed up beneath her fork, bread and butter pudding swelled with the joy of being understood, and porridge became voluptuous. That was how it seemed to the women's starved senses. Beulah had brought sensuousness to their mealtimes.

It was a quality missing in the lady herself. Stout, solid, filling her worn selection of outdated clothes, Beulah moved slowly, if deftly. She was quiet, easy to overlook, yet when Cat took the trouble to study her, she saw a striking woman, with the kind of head that begs to be sculpted. Beulah's dark blue eyes, a sort of stormy navy, were hard to catch. She was busy all day, taming the Aga until it was so amenable that it baked bread to perfection. The women fell on the warm chunks like lionesses bringing down a wildebeest.

'That is . . .' Lucy couldn't find an adjective up to the job.

'Beulah, I love you,' Mary said, tearing at a slice with her teeth.

Startled, Beulah smiled, tucked up a stray snowy hair which had escaped from a clip and demurred. 'It's only bread, dear.'

Less effusive, Sarge hoovered up her fair share all the same. 'Nice,' she conceded.

'Like the Taj Mahal is nice,' suggested Cat. Lingering in the kitchen after the last crumbs had been chased and eaten, Cat endeavoured to make herself useful. The contrast with the rest of the house was brutal: warmth and the smell of bread versus dark corners and the smell of her own confusion. 'Where do you live? Normally, I mean,' she asked Beulah, standing beside the bulky older lady and hacking at a garlic clove.

Taking the knife gently from Cat's hands, Beulah sliced and crushed the clove with precision. 'Oh, nowhere really,' she said, vaguely. 'Here, I suppose,' she added with a shrug.

Cat never admitted she *lived* in the commune: it was a holiday. A longish holiday with no sun loungers and peculiar locals. 'Germaine will be very disappointed if you don't conjure up a tale of male dastardliness for Group,' she smiled. 'We're all card-carrying bloke haters here.'

'So I was led to understand.' Beulah dropped the garlic into sizzling oil. 'I didn't like to say so in front of Germaine, but the shop lady wasn't very complimentary.'

'What did she call us? Bunch of nutters?' asked Cat ruefully.

'More along the lines of *probably can't get a man for love nor money.*' Beulah shook her head in happy disbelief. 'People are funny, aren't they?'

Antonia drifted in to join them. 'May I wash up?' she asked humbly, as if it was a great favour.

'Thank you.' Beulah smiled a broad, appreciative smile.

'You missed Antonia's story,' said Cat.

'Story?' Beulah held the word in mid-air, and found it wanting.

Shamefaced, Cat reconsidered. 'That was crass. Sorry.'

'I don't mind,' said Antonia, filling the big old sink with tepid water. She never minded.

Punishing some dough on a marble slab Cat hadn't noticed before, Beulah studied Cat's face. 'You're sickening for something,

Cat,' she decreed, in a tone balanced between kindness and bossiness. 'Biccie?'

Biccies were always welcome. Cat nibbled and said, 'I need to get out of here. Just for a while. It's all right for Germaine, popping out in the minibus all the time.'

'Go for a walk,' said Beulah.

'Hmm.' Cat nibbled on.

'Cat,' said Beulah, pausing in her pummelling. 'Go for a walk, dear.' She allowed those elusive eyes, bright and dark at the same time, to alight on Cat's. '*Now*,' she said. 'Dear'.

The gate complained. Cat stuck her head out into the narrow lane and took in the landscape. It was big out there. And intolerably verdant. Borrowed wellies chafed her toes.

Cat felt a nudge at her thighs.

'You sure?' she double-checked. 'You really want to come?'

Dave was sure. In fact, she led the way, trotting confidently across the field over the way that rose up to meet the sky like a mossy welcome mat.

'Hang on!' Cat was afraid. Of what, she wasn't sure. 'Get a grip, Flowerpot,' she counselled. Puffing, she caught up with Dave. It was weeks since she'd been to the gym, and even at her most ardent she'd never troubled the 'incline' button on the treadmill. That pretty field was steeper than it looked.

Beneath her feet the grass squeaked happily. A breeze toyed with her dirty hair as Cat reached the crest of the slope. Dave was getting her second wind, scrambling down the other side, her wide behind swinging like Marilyn Monroe's. Cat paused to contemplate the view. Greyish stone walls criss-crossed the landscape, sealing in geometric shapes of green, yellow and a ruddy red. There was a sense of beginning, of waiting. It felt, Cat thought, pregnant.

Stumbling after Dave, Cat found a stream and they followed it. A light rain fizzed and she pulled up the hood on her jacket (also borrowed – a perk of the commune was the amount of borrowable kit). Up in the sky, clouds dissolved and regrouped, irresolute. Before long Cat pulled her hood down again and unzipped the jacket – suddenly she was too warm: April was not only the cruellest month, it was the most indecisive.

'I was right about this.' Dave turned to listen as she ambled just in front of Cat. 'I thought it would make me feel insignificant and it does. But I kind of like it.' The heavy breathing had tapered off: Cat hit her stride. 'I hope you know the way back, Dave, cos I don't have a clue.'

A rabbit zigzagged in front of her, as if evading a sniper. Cat felt a thrill. A real live wild animal! She'd seen a fox once in Fulham, strolling past some bins, like a toff down on his luck, and of course she'd seen plenty of urban squirrels and pigeons, all of them scruffy, paranoid and disabled by Coke can rings, but a proper animal, going about its business in the honest to goodness countryside, was a revelation. 'A rabbit, Dave!' she yipped. The pig seemed unimpressed.

The power of her little incantation had made this walk possible. 'Get a grip, Flowerpot' was Cat's equivalent of a shove in the small of her back. It rarely failed her. In her head, she heard it in her father's low, rolling, singsong accent.

He'd been Mancunian. Still was, presumably, as it's not something a person can change, but Cat was accustomed to thinking of Harry O'Connor in the past tense. He was forever thirty-three years old, freeze framed in flares.

Flowerpot was Harry's nickname for his middle child, his only daughter. The day he'd coined it had been immortalised in a photo, a curling snap, three inches by three, bordered in white. Something had gone awry in the developing process, and the photograph was flooded with an amber wash, rendering Harry's black hair rusty, and his blue eyes a strange colour that no eyes could ever be.

There was no mistaking their expression as he held his girl out in front of him, proving that her tubby little body could fit into the large clay flowerpot. Harry was happy, grinning widely, his moustache stretched and his small even teeth all showing. That was when he'd re-christened Cat, her fat face cracked with toddler merriment. Just an untidy 1970s patio, a flowerpot and a hiccuping two-year-old, but Harry looked thrilled with it all.

All grown up and then some, Cat had Harry's colouring but no Harry. She hoped they didn't share too many personality traits: Cat didn't want to be the sort of person who could walk out on people who depended on her.

It always came to this when Harry sauntered across Cat's consciousness: she ended up damning his name. That infamous trip to the shops which had yet to end towered over all his other actions. It was his defining moment, rendering him impossible to love.

His exhortation 'Get a grip, Flowerpot' had stuck with her. Cleansed somehow of negative connotations, it came in useful whenever Cat was floundering, or cowardly. Harry had said 'Get a grip, Flowerpot,' when she had cried at the sight of next door's Corgi, when she'd crashed her new red scooter and refused to get back on. It had worked then, and it worked now.

The stream disappeared. The next field was barren and pebbly, furrowed in neat seams, like a corduroy picnic cloth. Dave faltered on the uneven ground, those skinny ankles buckling.

This terrain was more challenging than the velvety banks of the stream. Cat placed her feet with care. She looked behind her, expecting to see the roof of the commune, but it had been swallowed up. All she could see was land, quiet and contemplative.

The roomy house had grown claustrophobic. The benefits, much brayed about by Germaine, of living amongst women were indisputable: the cleaning was done without too much carping, the place smelled nice, there was always somebody to talk to. Sometimes, though, Cat didn't feel like talking, and Sarge's narratives of the cut and thrust of life on a milk float were growing thin. The big verdigris playground outside the gates was a relief.

Ahead of her, Dave picked up speed. Her flabby snout close to the ruts in the earth, she beetled across the field with great purpose, heading for a tree whose branches splayed out like a parasol at the far side.

'Wait!' called Cat, breaking into an ungainly run. Dave had reached the tree, and judging by the obscene snuffling, had found something there to her taste. 'What have you got?' laughed Cat, drawing near to see the pig's face buried in the dirt. Dave was laying waste to a paper bag, the first scrap of rubbish Cat had seen.

'Dirty girl!' she admonished her porky companion. 'Don't eat any old crap you find on the ground!'

'I made those sandwiches myself.' A man swivelled round to face her from where he sat with his back to the tree trunk. 'It's not any old crap. It's Brie and sweetcorn.'

'That's an unusual combination,' Cat found herself saying, after she'd jumped a foot in the air. 'Sorry. She's kind of greedy.'

'Well,' said the man compassionately. 'She *is* a pig.' He smiled an inward smile, as if somebody just out of Cat's earshot had made a joke. 'After all.' The stranger was regarding Cat with interest, keen interest. It wasn't lecherous, not even sexual; it was interest, as if he'd spotted a rare bird he'd only ever read about.

Cat took a step back. This, she reminded herself, was A Man: the gender was newly worthy of capitalisation. He was Forbidden (she was free and easy with her capitals this morning). 'May I recompense you?' she suggested stiffly, her vocabulary ossifying into priggishness: a pointless offer from a woman without a purse. She was relieved when he shook his head.

'They weren't great, to be honest. An experiment that went wrong.' The stranger reached out and patted Dave's broad head. 'Do you mind me asking,' he asked, turning large, sad-looking blue eyes on her, their innocent colour belied by the heavy, knowing lids, 'what you're doing out here with a pig? I mean,' that half-smile again, and a raising of dark brows, 'it almost looks as if you're taking her for a walk.'

'I am,' pouted Cat. 'Is that funny?'

'No,' said the man. The smile disappeared from his face

immediately, but he couldn't quite banish it from his eyes. 'Not in the least.' He kept Cat's gaze squarely, there was nothing of the fidget about him. He was taking her in the way people take in a view. A scenic view.

'Good.' It was novel to meet a man without sizing him up: it was against the rules to fancy this stranger, so Cat noted with detachment his wide shoulders and his dark brown curling hair while finding his face, manly but indelicate, no match for Hugh's aristocratic features. This was a bumpkin after all, albeit a sexy-eyed one. 'She's very good company.'

'I can imagine.' The man waited a beat. 'Although I bet you get thrown out of restaurants a lot.' He settled himself more comfortably, so he could sustain his slightly twisted position and still 'see her.' I mean, she's got the looks but her table manners need work.'

Dave belched and a gobbet of sodden paper bag flew out of her mouth and hit the man's Barbour.

'Oh God, sorry.' Cat winced. She clocked the battered jeans and the Barbour and the pedigree wellies soiled with good country mud. She wondered fleetingly how he'd look in a suit.

'You're supposed to walk the perimeter, you know.'

'How do you mean?' Cat frowned. 'What perimeter?'

'Of the field.' The man gestured with a nod at the hill behind her. His hair flopped over his face. Dark brown, it was messy and a stranger to the barber, but, Cat conceded, rather better groomed than her own. She put a self-conscious hand to where her hairstyle used to be. 'That's a ploughed field sown with maize you've just tramped over. You and . . . I'm guessing the pig has a name?'

There was an implication there, about women and their silly ways, that irritated Cat. 'The pig,' she said neutrally, 'is called Dave.'

'Dave.'

'Yes,' she said, a glimmer of impatience, a glimmer of the old Percival Cant Jablowski Cat, intruding. 'She's Dave the pig. May we move on?'

'Of course. Dave has a right to be called Dave. But like I say, when you cross a field, try to keep to the edges. Farmers prefer it.'

It hadn't even occurred to Cat that she might be trampling over a farmer's land. Open space, she'd naively assumed, was communal. She felt her ignorance keenly. 'I'll remember,' she said, disliking this stranger a little for telling her off. Even if the telling-off had been soft edged and somehow fond.

'Are you from the old farm?' he asked, 'Are you one of those . . .' he hesitated. 'Those women?' His eyes flickered, as if he regretted the phrase.

'Yes, I'm one of the man haters.' Cat rolled her eyes. 'I'm a mad, quasi-lesbian, bra-burning fanatic.' She stuffed her hands in her pockets and wished Dave would stop with the revolting noises for a moment: the pig was French kissing the Brie to death. 'Is that what they're saying?'

'Kind of,' admitted the man, some elusive joke affecting his generous mouth and wistful eyes again. 'Nobody mentioned the pig-walking.'

'Well, now you can tell them.' Cat turned. 'Dave!' she called, in the fluting voice she'd cultivated for pig-training purposes, which was mildly embarrassing in this situation. 'Dave! Heel.'

Dave turned and obediently cantered after Cat, the two of them keeping punctiliously to the rim of the field.

'Goodbye,' called the stranger.

Utilising a move she'd always longed to, Cat copied Liza's Minelli's wave at the end of *Cabaret*: a nonchalant yet elegant wave of the hand, the vital component of the whole manoeuvre was not looking back over the shoulder.

Cat was no Liza. Her cool dissolved and she did glance over her shoulder, to see the man still there, his broad back against the tree, one long leg bent, the other stretched out. What must it feel like, she wondered, to take up that much space? He had the same density as the ancient tree he leaned on.

The man moved his head, and his eyes, with their distant blue gaze, caught hers. Cat turned into the wind and hunched her shoulders, speeding up.

'Dave!' she nagged. 'Come on!'

18

Greeted by Sarge with a gruff 'The rota says you should be hoeing,' Cat longed to trill 'Guess what? I spoke to a man! So there!', perhaps blowing a raspberry for good measure, but she simply grabbed a hoe from the back porch.

Over by Hen Central, Cat saw two figures on their haunches. Mary and Lucy were peering in at the occupants, rocking with laughter. Cat detoured towards them and caught a snatch of their conversation on the breeze.

'Look!' Mary was sniggering. 'Hentonia's legging it! She's terrified of Gerhen!'

Leaning on Mary's shoulder with a casualness at odds with her ironed chinos, almost pulling the two of them over, Lucy said, her low-pitched voice unrecognisable in its giggly shakiness, 'Trust Chickensarge to rush over and sort everything out!'

Their shared laughter slowed Cat's wellies. (Or Antonia's wellies, to be pedantic.) The parallels between life in the hen house and life in the main house was a joke she'd shared separately with Mary, and with Lucy. And here they were, veering off piste without her. She shook herself, frowning at such childish pique. It was this place, she told herself. Cat blamed the commune for all her failings these days.

But all the same, they needn't laugh so damn hard.

Coming up behind them, Cat said jovially, 'Crikey, look at Hencat! She's trying to throw herself out of a window!'

Mary jumped up as if surprised. 'Didn't see you there,' she smiled.

Lucy stood up too, her habitual reserve reclaiming her. She bundled her shiny dark ponytail into a smooth bun and turned for the house. 'I've got some work to write up.'

'Was it something I said?' laughed Cat, edgily.

'Lucy's just busy,' said Mary mildly, with a slight *what's the matter with you* frown. 'I still don't know what she's writing. Probably very weighty, very literary.'

'Yeah,' agreed Cat, leaning on her hoe. 'Something philosophical, deep. She spends a lot of time on her laptop.'

'And I've seen big thick packages arrive for her. Probably manuscripts to, whatsit, copy-edit, or whatever.'

There was a moment of silence, either to mourn their own dead careers or envy Lucy's flourishing one, Cat wasn't sure. 'Hey,' she said, with a breathiness that denoted news, 'guess what?'

'What?' asked Mary obediently.

'I just spoke to an emm ey enn.'

'An emm . . .' Mary tailed off, puzzled.

'Man!' shot Cat impatiently. 'Man. A man. An man with a penis and everything.'

'NO!' Mary was a wonderful audience.

'Yes.' Cat filled her in.

'Was he a looker?' Mary cut to the chase.

'If you like that sort of thing. Not really.'

'You mean he was under fifty and didn't dress like a prime minister?'

'Hugh doesn't dress like—' Cat bit her lip. She would not be drawn into a spat about Hugh.

'Did he remind you of your dad?' asked Mary slyly.

'Hugh doesn't remind—' Cat bit her lip again. 'He was kind of beefy, very dark, quite . . .' She jettisoned her first choice of 'handsome' and opted for 'rustic'.

'Did you go all funny?' queried Mary.

'I'm a grown woman,' Cat reminded her, preferring to forget that she *had* gone slightly funny.

'So am I, and it's five weeks since I saw a grown man. Or heard a male voice. The only man in my life is the grandfather clock.' She sighed. 'And that bastard's spurning all my advances.'

A bark from the doorway of 'Is this what you call hoeing?' sent Cat scuttling off to the vegetable patch, bowed like a serf.

'Go on. Put your back into it,' advised Sarge, arms folded, expression grim.

'How long do carrots take?' Cat's tone was sulky. 'This is so boring, all this weeding and stuff, with nothing to show for it.'

'Carrots take their own time,' said Sarge. 'Sorry if that doesn't suit your MTV attention span.'

Stung, Cat asked, 'Are you going to tell Germaine on me?' She affected a comically military style delivery. 'Sir! Discontent in the vegetable patch, sir!'

'It's my job to be Germaine's eyes and ears. If you'd been in the TA for ten years you'd know how vital intelligence is.'

'But I would never be in the TA. Even for an afternoon.' Cat leaned down to pull out yet more spiky little green weeds. The things never got the message, like thick-skinned gatecrashers they came in the windows if you locked the doors.

'No,' said Sarge, enjoying a private joke. 'I don't suppose you would. Look,' she said, in a kinder voice. 'This yard isn't blessed with quality earth. It'll take effort to get results.'

'Germaine reckons the plot is a metaphor for the commune,' Cat reminded her. 'Green shoots of rebirth and all that.'

'Hmm.' Sarge, faced with nay-saying their magnificent leaderene, was conflicted. 'We'll have to be patient. The carrots will show green leaf tops in about a month. The potatoes are growing underground. The tomato plants are starting to thrive. Just like Dave will take time to be ready for slaughter, so the veg will take time to be ready for picking.'

'Don't,' said Cat, 'use the words *slaughter* and *Dave* in the same sentence, please.'

'You'll learn.' Sarge seemed to like the idea of Cat learning.

The chairs for the Goddess circle had already been arranged by the tireless Sarge. Cat caught the end of a bout of laughter as she wandered in. Mary and Lucy, on adjacent uncomfortable chairs, were leaning towards each other, mirrored like bookends, sighing the end of a shared joke.

'Ladies.' Germaine surveyed the faces around her. 'Here we are again in our magic circle, where we can cavort emotionally naked.' She left a space for an evil hoot from Mary but none came. 'Tonight's brave speaker has been a friend of mine since we met some years ago in a festive-themed sales project.'

Cat's buttocks clanged shut. Opposite her Mary looked serene, obviously unaware that she was also in the frame.

'This woman is talented. Fearless. A warrior.'

Squirming, Cat was torn between hoping she was worthy of such epithets and praying that it was Mary's turn.

'Shackled to a boyfriend I wouldn't wish on my worst enemy, I am talking about Mary Cavanagh.'

Ms Cavanagh, who hadn't recognised herself, went rigid.

'Yay!' cried Cat, flooded with *Schadenfreude*. 'Go, Mary!'

Taking Germaine's place, Mary burbled, 'Right. Well. Yes. Oh hang on.' She remembered the form. 'My name is Mary. And this is my, you know, story.' She pulled a face and looked up at the ceiling. 'I'm here because my life is not . . .' She paused, and fixed Cat with a look as she continued slowly. 'My life is not how I want it to be.'

Cat held Mary's gaze. It was the look of a person learning to swim by holding somebody else's hand. Mary leached energy from Cat as she groped along: the gravity of Mary's demeanour surprised her friend. Mary hadn't taken anything seriously since 1998.

'I'm not the woman my teenage self planned on becoming.'

A sigh of empathy escaped Antonia.

'I don't know how I came to be living in a smelly flat. Unable to get the work I trained for. Sleeping with a man who . . .' Mary faltered. Perhaps she clocked Cat's almost imperceptible nod. 'Steals from my purse.'

A collective intake of breath buoyed Mary up. 'Yeah, he actually *stole* from me, and bought me drinks with it!' she said, with relish. 'I didn't even challenge him.'

'Why not?' asked Lucy quietly.

Wheeling around to face her, Mary almost shouted, 'Because I was scared of losing him!'

'Scared,' said Germaine in a sage voice that Cat found irksome, 'of losing a man who steals from you.'

'But that's not all there is to say about Alun,' insisted Mary. 'He's kind. He's got a great sense of humour. He . . .' At this point she caught Cat's eye.

Perhaps Cat's thoughts could be read on her face. She was trying to remember the last time Alun had been kind, or had demonstrated this alleged sense of humour. Perhaps sellotaping a Polaroid of Mary's naked bottom to the fridge with the word *diet* felt-tipped across the buttocks counted as both.

'He cares about me,' Mary said with defensive emphasis, as if Cat had spoken. 'Alun understands how hard it is to get established as an actor. I'm supposed to be famous by now, ladies. Or at least a spear carrier at the RSC. I'm an actress. I *act.* I'm not a fucking temp,' she spat. 'I don't like putting people through to other people, or handing out mail, or making ChocOrange low cal drinks for women with bad hair I'll never see again.' She reached out her hands in appeal. 'Why can't I make a living at doing what I love? I'm not a bad actress, am I, Cat?'

'No,' said Cat immediately. She'd loyally watched each production her friend had been cast in, sitting in draughty fringe venues that smelled of old beer, and community halls where the aerobics class next door could be heard through the walls. Mary had always beguiled Cat, transforming herself, inhabiting the characters she played. But there had been no roles for a couple of years now. 'You're a good actress.'

'Of course you are,' said Sarge unexpectedly, raising a fist, presumably to denote Actress Power.

'I am. Honest, Lucy.' Mary laughed in Lucy's direction. 'But if a tree falls in a forest and nobody hears, has it made a noise? If an actress never acts, is she an actress at all?' wailed Mary. 'Am I actually a temp?'

'No,' said Lucy. 'You're an artist.'

'And Alun?' prompted Germaine, her eye as ever on the ball. Or balls.

Lucy sat back to ask, in a neutral voice, 'Are you scared of outshining Alun?'

Framing a 'no' with her lips, Mary hesitated over the word. 'Oh my God,' she said wonderingly. 'Maybe I am. I don't want to, you know, leave him behind.'

'Women,' said Germaine knowingly, 'can be their own worst enemies. Doing things behind their own backs. Scuppering their happiness in order to follow the script their men have written for them.'

'Maybe I was doing exactly that.' Mary was having an epiphany in the middle of the tatty circle. 'Like you and Hugh,' she said suddenly to Cat, pointing at her dramatically.

'Eh? This is about you, not me.' Cat shrank back in her chair, as if Mary's finger was loaded.

Leaning over to her, Sarge asked sotto voce, 'Is it, though?'

'Yes,' said Cat, leaning away from her, 'it is.'

'Is it, though?' repeated Sarge.

'Stop saying is it though,' snapped Cat.

'I need to chuck him,' said Mary miserably. 'He's holding me back.'

'This is excellent stuff,' said Germaine.

'Hold on, hold on.' Cat applied brakes to the runaway shopping trolley of Mary's new philosophy. 'He's not all bad.' Defending Alun didn't come naturally to Cat: not only had she witnessed the way he ate Kentucky Fried Chicken, but she'd had to endure the Polaroid of his own bum he'd also stuck to the fridge. But Cat knew how Mary relied on his dense, ursine presence. He was, Mary had often said, handy to lean on while watching *Corrie.* Now, Cat would never argue that this was reason enough to persevere, but she knew how impetuous Mary could be. 'Shouldn't you talk to Alun before you make these kinds of decisions?'

Antonia's voice was loud. She sounded like a different person, possessed by a long-dead militant feminist. 'And hear his lies and excuses?' she growled. 'Dump him!' she snarled. 'He'll only bring you down.'

There was a moment of respectful, possibly fearful, silence for Antonia's new personality, then everybody in the room let rip with their opinions. Cat's voice was the only one counselling caution. Even Lucy was saying, 'I think you know you want to leave him.'

'SHUT UP!' yelled Mary, her hands on her ears. 'This is *my* moment, you mad cows.' She melodramatically lifted her head to savour the silence. 'Thank you. This has been amazingly useful.' She smiled at Germaine. 'Germy, I thought this whole group therapy was a crock of pseudo-psychological poo, but it's helped. I'm a fecking actress, I'm going to go out there and hustle work for myself. And as for Alun,' she caught Cat's anxious eye, and shrugged her shoulders. 'He's on parole.'

Perturbed, Cat sought out Dave. 'You should have seen her,' she marvelled to her pink and hairy confidante. 'She was hugging everybody, with tears in her eyes. Tears!' she repeated, in case Dave was too engrossed in the snotty tissue she was savouring to appreciate the significance of the word. 'Mary doesn't cry. She's been turned. It's like that horror film, *The Bodysnatchers.* She's buying into all this, despite being at least eighteen times as cynical as me.' She sighed. 'It's that

Lucy,' she whispered. A thought which had been floating about for a day or two tightened into a compact ball. 'They've been getting all pally. Lucy is brainwashing her.'

Dave coughed.

'It is,' insisted Cat. 'It's that Lucy.'

19

'I feel as if I've had a shower,' said Mary the next morning.

'It's not your turn,' said Cat, preceding her out into the sunny courtyard.

'I mean that Group yesterday. It was like having my brain spring-cleaned.'

'Will you stop with the born-again shit?' Cat stalked to Dave's outhouse.

'Why won't you admit that there's real power in that circle?'

'Mary Kathleen Philomena Regina Cavanagh.' Cat put her hands on Mary's shoulders. 'I rely on you to be ironic. Sceptical. Wry. Not to prattle about the bleeding power of the bleeding circle. OK?'

'So you prefer me unhappy?' countered Mary, removing Cat's hands. 'You want me to stay with Alun?'

'Of course not,' spluttered Cat. 'I want you to be happy.' She really did. 'I just want you to be careful, that's all.' There was no map for this: Cat and Mary never really argued.

'Just because you didn't have the courage to chuck Hugh until you had to,' said Mary, her red cheeks betraying she knew exactly how far she was going. 'Just because you're scared of change.' She seemed shocked by herself. 'Actually,' she ended limply. It seemed that Mary was as cack handed as Cat at arguing with her best friend.

'Change?' repeated Cat. 'I eat change for breakfast.' It was a dumb thing to say but it was preferable to the *don't you know what I've given up for you?* teetering on her lips: in a straight choice between Mary and a rent-free nest she'd opted for the former, and now the former was coming over all New Age and getting cosy with Lucy. 'Oh forget it,' said Cat crossly, and turned away, her wellies flicking mud across the cobbles.

'Cat!' called Mary.

'What?' Cat was sour as she looked over her shoulder.

'Do you have any idea what we're arguing about?'

Considering this for a moment, Cat laughed. 'No. Not really.'

It was late. The kitchen was empty. The low oil lamp sketched shaky shadows on the walls. Burglar-like, Cat crept to the phone and dialled a London number.

The Bakelite receiver heavy in her hand, Cat felt like a little girl playing a game. It was a foolish game, Cat knew. Hugh wouldn't recognise the number, so he would let the call go to message. Just as she desired.

The stew of needs and fears that culminated in a grown woman craving the sound of her ex-lover's dislocated voice on his outgoing message had simmered nicely all day. Cat's breathing was shallow as somewhere out in the night numbers clicked and clacked, connections were made and a ringing tone sounded both in Cat's ear and in a Chelsea townhouse.

'Hello?' said Hugh immediately.

With a gargle of alarm, Cat threw down the receiver. And missed. She banged it on to the cradle. Heart jumping like a pneumatic drill, Cat backed away from the dresser. Clenching and unclenching her fists, she fought to reclaim her equilibrium. 'You fool. You bloody fool,' she scolded breathlessly. 'How old are you, for heaven's sake?'

'Seventy-four, since you ask.'

Jumping like her namesake on a hot tin roof, Cat pirouetted to see Beulah at the table with a cup of something hot in her large, capable hands. 'I didn't see you there,' gabbled Cat redundantly.

'I should have spoken,' said Beulah apologetically. Her face wobbled in the shifting dark: one moment it was the face of a tired old lady at the end of a long day, the next it was bleached into a shadowy caricature of how Beulah might have looked fifty years ago.

'A man, of course.' Cat gestured to the phone, with a flip smile that didn't match her feelings. 'Making a twit of myself. Again.' She shrugged clownishly, aware that the need to cry was impacting on her comic timing. 'You know how love is!'

'No, dear,' said Beulah, blowing on her drink. 'I don't.'

Two steps forward, thought Cat drearily, three steps back. Hugh would guess the identity of his late-night caller. Once again she cursed Mary's presumption in throwing away his letters. Better to curse Mary than curse herself.

The house was sunk in the deep empty silence that only the countryside delivers. No hum of traffic, no drunken row on the pavement, no sirens, no televisions, no nothing, except the gentle scratch of Cat's pen on paper.

She told her distant mum about the hens, about Beulah ('you'd love her!'), about Mary's volte-face, about her lack of headaches. She put her pen down and tousled her hair, yawning. Five pages in, midnight a memory and she was stuck.

Cat had something more to say, but couldn't work out how to say it. It was a question, an angry one, long postponed. Alone in the silence, she felt brave. And calm. She would ask her mother about the photographs.

It's not fair. Those words had swum moodily around Cat's head through her teenage years, and even beyond, whenever she contemplated the loss of every single photograph of her father.

Her mum, a mild woman, had been as ruthless as Stalin dealing with an enemy of the people: Harry had been uninvented, erased. There had been no crude lopping off of his head: every snap he featured in was simply destroyed.

The gaps in their photograph albums, cheery tartan-covered volumes, meant that Cat and Trev had given up leafing through them. Their mum hadn't warned them about the purge, and had never mentioned it. Quick learners, they'd buttoned their lips, although Cat had once caught Trev stroking the blank space in an album where there should have been a snap of him and Harry on a sled.

'Get a grip, Flowerpot,' whispered Cat, and scribbled a PS. The photograph of her in a geranium pot, laughing almost as hard as her mustachioed daddy, existed only in Cat's memory.

PS. Mum, this is an odd question, but why did you throw out all the photos of Dad? I mean, I think I can guess – you must have been devastated and probably didn't want to see his face – but didn't you feel you ought to keep a few for us? Me and Trev and Jon?

Cat couldn't leave it at that. Criticising her mum was blasphemous.

Sorry if this sounds harsh, Mum. Don't answer if you don't want to.

Before she could change her mind, Cat licked down the envelope and turned off the lamp.

Going slowly up the stairs, savouring her alone-ness in a crowded house, Cat's feet sped up at the first groan from the innards of the house. The howling followed her as she burst into the dormitory and leapt for her bed. The springs bounced and creaked, but were no match for the hellish chorus coming from the turret.

'Lucy!' hissed Cat. 'Antonia!' The occupants of the beds either side of the door, misty humps in the moonlight, didn't stir. In the bed beside her, Mary snuffled, but didn't wake.

Cat pulled the covers up to her chin. It was just her and the ghost.

'*Voilà!*' proclaimed Germaine, then, 'Ta-daa!' Illuminated by the sunshine flooding in the back door, she held aloft a carrot of minuscule proportions. 'Our first produce. Beulah! It's carrot for dinner tonight!'

Beulah took the carrot with due reverence, and refrained from wondering aloud how she would feed six women on two inches of root vegetable.

'That's impossible.' Sarge's frown was scored deep into her features. She strutted across the kitchen in her army issue boots and peered at the carrot. 'It hasn't had time to mature.' She added, lower, 'not in *that* soil'.

'Well it did,' said Germaine testily. 'We are sending out green shoots, ladies! We are overthrowing the penis!'

Beulah gagged on her tea, and Mary turned the pages of the local paper with a bored 'whatever'.

A clang of the bell at the outer gate sent Sarge racing from the room. Coming back what seemed like a moment later she roared 'POST!' and began to hand out the modest bundle of letters. One of them flew in Cat's direction, catching her neatly below the eye.

'Ow,' she said mildly, surprised at how speedily her mum had replied. Retreating to Dave's boudoir, Cat plonked herself on a bale of clean hay. She ignored Dave's questing snout and regarded the envelope. It was flimsy, a supermodel to the previous letters' chubsters: Cat sucked her lips anxiously, hoping she hadn't pushed her mum too far with her question about Harry.

Apparently not.

I'm glad you asked about the photographs

was the first line.

Relaxing, Cat dropped one hand to toy with Dave's ears.

I feel bad about them. It was wrong of me to tear them all up. After all, he was your dad.

Wincing at that 'was', Cat was reminded why the O'Connors never discussed this subject: it hurt.

You and the boys deserve better from me. At the time I was upset and I didn't stop to think.

The discreet understatement prompted a fond 'Aw, Mum!' 'Upset' hardly covered the feelings of a woman abandoned with three children, one of whom was brand new and facing a catalogue of challenges. Cat would have been 'devastated', 'distraught', possibly 'murderous': her mum was 'upset'.

I couldn't bear to look at his face. He had such a handsome face, your dad, but now I hated it.

It struck Cat that her mum's taut, cramped handwriting wasn't quite itself.

Listen, love, for me this is history. My life is so different now, so full and I'm so, so proud of all my kids that your dad seems like a character in a film I once saw.

Smiling at her mother's ability to see all her geese as swans, Cat read between the narrow lines. The lady protesteth too much. Remorse claimed Cat. She'd been cruel to turf the family skeleton out of the closet.

An aggrieved grunt from below signalled Dave's displeasure at a break in the ear-toying.

Why don't I ask Nana if she has any pictures? And Aunty Pam should have a few holiday snaps with him in them.

'Please, no, Mum, don't,' groaned Cat aloud, ashamed to have pushed her mum into such a panic. She should have thought harder before asking about the photographs. After all, the answer was obvious. Only a broken heart made people act that way.

Bloody Harry, thought Cat. Bloody bloody Harry. Still causing trouble decades after his Houdini moment.

20

Hot on the heels of the first carrot, the first potato from the yard had been chipped, affording everybody one each. Mary regarded hers emotionally, holding it this way and that, marvelling at how the light played on it.

The women were subdued, as they often were the day after ghostly high jinks. Only Beulah seemed her usual self. But then, Beulah was her 'usual self' at all times. This struck Cat as odd. In a house of temperamental women, Beulah was always faultlessly Beulah. Serene. Comfortable. Exuding the old-fashioned wholesomeness of gold top milk. As Cat studied the older lady, Beulah looked up and smiled. It was a non-denominational, blameless smile that signified, Cat couldn't help feeling, not much at all. She watched as Beulah handed Antonia a small white tablet and a cold glass of water with a discretion that verged on sleight of hand. She must have noticed something that Cat hadn't: Antonia looked the same as usual to her.

The silence was broken by Sarge. 'Dave,' she said, 'has a cough.'

'I don't think so,' bridled Cat, who did think so. She was possessive about Dave.

'She does. Some illnesses spoil the bacon,' said Sarge.

'Do not refer to Dave as bacon,' said Cat. 'Please.'

Looking sheepish, an unusual look for her, Sarge said, 'I've tried to find a female vet in the area and there isn't one.'

'Nonsense.' Germaine's robust sense of her standing in the universe meant that a female vet would appear if she wanted one. 'Are you telling me that Dorset women kowtow to the scrotal sac?'

Beulah's eyelids fluttered, as Mary said, 'Not everything is about feminism, Germy. We'll have to call a male vet.'

'Oh. *All right*,' conceded Germaine irritably, snatching the chip out of Sarge's grasp. 'Will you *stop* frowning at my potato?' she snapped.

'It's too soon. It's a miracle,' said Sarge.

'They do happen,' said Beulah, mildly.

Amongst the trivia of her next letter home, Cat buried a tiny bomb, what a news report would term a 'device'. Now that the O'Connors' ancient wounds were livid again, Cat asked another question she'd always yearned to, before the subject was once again out of bounds.

Why did you and Dad split up? Really?

Sealing the envelope, leaving it on the hall table, Cat touched it with her fingers. If the answer to her question included the word 'Jon' she would . . . well, something would die within her, something that had been holding its breath for a long time.

'The vet's here!' yelled Sarge up the corkscrew stairs.

Leaping down two at a time, Cat puffed, 'I'll deal with him.' She didn't want Sarge muscling in and taking over: Dave was Cat's business.

'Good. Cos I'm a purist,' said Sarge as Cat dashed past her out of the front door. She raised her voice. 'YOU WON'T SEE ME CONSORTING WITH THE ENEMY!'

A man in the inevitable Barbour stood outside the gates, leaning on the equally inevitable four-by-four. These country types had no imagination. Jogging closer, Cat called out, 'Hi, hi! Thanks for coming.'

'No problem.' The vet was tall, very tall, about six four. He pulled off a tweedy cap, and his thick, wavy, dark hair flopped about ebulliently.

'Oh.' Cat slowed. 'You.'

'You,' he echoed.

'I keep faithfully to perimeters now, honest to God.'

'Excellent.' They stood in silence for a moment, then the vet gestured to the bars between them. 'Are you going to let me in?'

'Oh. Yeah.' Cat tugged at the gates' oversized iron handles.

'Your friend,' said the vet, proceeding with caution as if there might be snipers in the outhouses, 'was cagey. I got the feeling she didn't like me.'

'Sarge? Oh, it's not personal,' said Cat breezily. 'She dislikes all men.' She glanced over to where Sarge glared at them from the front step, a cut-price Rambo with an axe dangling from one hand.

'What was that about the enemy?' The vet was inching forward, one eye on Sarge.

'You must have misheard,' said Cat. 'Do you want to see your patient?'

'Is it Dave?'

Impressed that he remembered, Cat smiled. Funny how jumpy she felt talking to a real live man. She glanced back at the house and saw a face at every window. Cat hustled the vet into Dave's presence, away from the starved expressions. She was, she realised, possessive about the vet as well as the pig.

'There she is.' Dave was rooting about in the half-light of the darkened sty. Cat wondered if it was her imagination that dulled Dave's eyes and wilted her punky fringe.

'I'm Will, by the way.'

'Oh. Right.' Cat dusted off her manners. 'And I'm Cat.'

'Cat. That's a nice name.'

Something in Cat that had been snoozing stirred. Cat looked at the vet. Properly. 'Thank you,' she said slowly.

'Let's take a look at this lady.' Will took off his coat and hung it on a rusty hook.

Cat gave Will a critical once-over as he felt what Cat assumed were Dave's fetlocks. Men, she knew, didn't go around complimenting women on their names for no reason at all.

Will was tall, and most of it was good value. Broad shouldered in his shirt sleeves, he was long of leg and arm, healthily and robustly built. But the hands roaming over Dave, Cat noticed, ended in tapering elegant fingers.

The face, half of it pressed against Dave's prickly torso as Will felt tenderly around her stomach, was heavily made, with a large well-shaped nose and wistfully expressive eyes. It was a face that promised something, a face with room for improvement – next door to handsome, rather than drop dead gorgeous. It was, in Cat's opinion, the face of a rather sad and loyal dog. Which was appropriate, she supposed, for a vet.

'Yes. I see. I see,' Will muttered gravely, running his hands over Dave as if she was a Braille copy of a worrying bank statement.

'Is it serious?' Cat chewed her lip, cursing Will for the slow, considered way he spoke. Come *on*, she thought irritably. Bullet point me.

Will stood up, and patted Dave familiarly on the back, as if they were old mates. 'The obvious diagnosis is influenza.' He paused.

'And?' Cat jabbed him onwards. 'Is that serious?'

'Extremely.'

Another pause. Cat, a sprinter by nature, was impatient with Will's plod.

'Implications for humans, too,' said Will cheerfully. 'But it's not influenza.'

Cat let out a loud breath and shut her eyes.

'It's a cough.'

'Well, with respect, we knew that.'

'But it's *only* a cough. And that's excellent news. Because we can clear a cough up very easily. I'll prescribe you something to mix with her feed.' He opened up the shabby, capacious briefcase at his feet and took out a pad. 'Keep going for walks. She needs her exercise. As do you.' He stopped writing and looked up, his blue eyes alarmed. 'Not that you, I mean, I didn't—'

'I know you didn't,' laughed Cat. She checked herself. 'At least I hope you bloody didn't.'

'No, no, you're . . . fine,' ended Will feebly, evidently regretting ever starting the sentence. 'I'll stick to pigs, I think. It's better that way.' He bent down and pulled at Dave's snout with confident playfulness.

'Ooh, she likes that,' smiled Cat, as the pig squeezed her eyes shut and leaned ecstatically against Will's leg.

'Like I say. Better with pigs,' muttered Will, giving his patient one last brusque caress.

Walking him to the gates, Cat said, 'I'd make you a coffee but you're not allowed indoors.'

'No. I suppose I've got the wrong, you know, equipment.' Will's broad cheeks ruddied: evidently another sentence he regretted. 'I mean—'

'I know what you mean.' Cat tried not to laugh. 'Again.'

'I should just, you know, bugger off, really.' Will clambered easily up into his Land Rover. 'Should I address the invoice to you?'

'No. To Germaine Hoskins, our head nutter.'

'Fine.' Will pulled the tweedy cap back on, where it sat with the assurance of a cap that has sat there contentedly for years.

Nothing about this man was fashionable or cool: the scavengers of Percival Cant Jablowski would eat him alive. 'Thank you for putting my mind at rest about Dave.' It was fun being the dynamic one, the town mouse handling the country mouse. 'We have chickens too. Do you do chickens?'

'I do all animals.' Will had rugged dimples when he smiled that broadly. 'Possibly not *do*. Treat.' He hesitated before putting the car into gear. 'Right. Rightyho.'

'Goodbye, Will the vet.' Cat waved the prescription as the vehicle bumped off down the pockmarked lane. Dawdling back to the house, Cat nibbled a corner of the prescription and smiled a slow, introverted smile. Unless she was losing her nose for such things, the vet was *interested* in her. She lacked the vanity to describe it as fancying: interested would suffice. The bumbling leave-taking. The comment about her name. Those dimples that exploded like fireworks on his cheeks.

Catching her reflection in the parlour window, Cat came down to earth with a bump. Will couldn't fancy – or even be interested in – that pudding-shaped bundle of other people's cast-offs, clattering about in ill-fitting wellies. Her hair was satanic topiary, and while supermodels may get away with showing their faces *au naturel* Cat needed the support of mascara and lipstick.

Maybe Will had a thing for hobbits.

'Is this what one conversation with a man does to you after a few weeks' cold turkey?' Mary examined Cat's face as the women played cards that evening. 'Blimey.'

'It's not that.' Cat laid down a jack. 'I'm thinking.'

'Good,' enthused Germaine, playing a ten of hearts. 'We're here to reflect. Consider.'

'True,' said Mary, earning a raised eyebrow from Cat: Mary was not a natural thinker, preferring to drink, sleep or argue.

'There is such a thing,' murmured Cat, 'as too much thinking.' Her Personal Reflection Time was not confined to the half hour after supper, it had leaked all over her schedule. Twin ghosts, her father and Hugh danced through her mind all day. She was accustomed to suppressing thoughts of Harry but since he'd become entwined with Hugh the pair of them arrived unannounced at all hours.

'The vet was bit of a dish.' Antonia's chin sank to her chest at her own daring.

'Down, girl!' Mary was amused. 'Wee bit heavy for my tastes.'

Coming from a woman who regularly played Hide the Rude

Thing with Alun this was rich. 'He was handsome enough. In his own way.' Cat forced out some weak praise for Will. 'Dave liked him. But even if he was Johnny Depp who cares? We're here to avoid men, after all.'

The hand that Cat laid down won her four matchsticks. While Mary collected the cards, Cat asked Antonia, 'How did your visit go with your kids?'

'It was lovely.' Antonia's smile was unruly and atypical. 'Toby sat on my lap the whole time and refused to get off. George showed me his new trike.'

Mary dealt a fresh hand. 'Sounds like a riot.'

'Do you feel better for seeing them?' asked Cat gently.

'Tons,' grinned Antonia. 'They're my reason for living, really.'

'Dangerous,' said Lucy. 'Shouldn't you find that within yourself?'

Cat gave Lucy a quick look, ready to leap to Antonia's defence, but Antonia didn't need a champion.

'When you've had children, you'll understand,' she said mildly, picking up her cards and fanning them out.

'I don't intend to have any,' said Lucy. 'And I have the imagination to empathise with you. I can read *War and Peace* without being Russian.'

'What's your reason for living, then, Lucy?' Cat cut in, surprising herself with the sharpness of the question.

'Did I say I had one?' Lucy answered lightly. 'Not the search for true love, that's for sure.'

'Aw, shame!' cried Mary. 'Don't you believe in it? I do.'

Germaine peered at her over her glasses. 'Even after Alun?'

'Oi. Don't talk about him as if he's Hitler.' Mary looked wounded. 'And what do you mean *after* Alun? It's not over yet. I am considering my options,' she said grandly.

Cat ignored the digression. 'Lucy, you didn't answer me,' she said quietly.

'Sorry. I didn't realise it was a serious question.' Lucy fanned out her cards on the table, face up. 'Twenty-one,' she announced.

21

The weather grew warm enough to penetrate the thick walls of the farmhouse. Beulah had shed a layer of her dated, unremarkable clothes and her bare arms wobbled as she beat eggs energetically in a bowl.

'In that light, with your back to me,' said Mary, who'd come in with Cat on a biscuit filching mission, 'you made me think of my grandma. Are you a grandmother, Beulah?'

Without pausing her abuse of the eggs, Beulah said quietly, 'I don't know.'

Mary looked startled, and Cat dived in to divert her from probing further with a 'Mary, your turn to sponge down the hen house.'

People, reflected Cat, her forearm down the U-bend, are fond of using the phrase 'just a piece of paper': marriage is often described as such. The rota was, undeniably, just a piece of paper, but nothing else had the authority to make Cat clean a loo.

There was the sudden thump of feet on the stairs. They sounded like furious feet, and Cat straightened up.

The furious feet belonged to Mary. 'That is *it*,' she growled, dangling a dejected sponge between two rubber-gloved fingers. 'I have officially had enough.' She tore the gloves off and stamped on them. 'I am stealing me a diseased pig unit vehicle and taking it to town.'

'She'll kill us.' Cat's voice bubbled like a cold fountain.

'Do I look like I care?' Mary was intent on the track ahead. Their progress down the pitted lane was slow.

Cat's knees were under her chin in the seat beside her. 'This is just what the doctor would order if he was here.'

'Germaine planned to go into town herself today.' Mary gave her partner in crime a sly sideways look.

Cat groaned, then recovered: her conscience was wonderfully elastic now that she and Mary had parachuted into the screenplay of *Thelma and Louise.* 'Germy's *always* in town,' she pointed out. 'She does all the shopping and she knows we're stir crazy but she never takes us.'

'Yeah!' said Mary.

'Yeah!' said Cat.

The minibus turned on to a B road and the fugitives picked up speed. Signposts appeared, all of them helpfully mentioning Lyme Regis.

'Wish Dave could come,' said Cat wistfully.

'Thought you were serious for a moment there,' giggled Mary.

Cat said nothing.

'Whoo!' yowled Mary, waving her fist in the air.

'Yessir!' yodelled Cat.

'Yippee!'

'Yowsa yowsa yowsa!'

A duck turned to watch the van speeding past its pond. Possibly Lyme Regis's genteel outskirts didn't usually provoke such ebullience in visitors.

'Fish and chip shops!' shrieked Cat, as the van hurtled down the hilly main street.

'Pubs!' roared Mary.

'People,' breathed Cat, grateful for the ordinary-looking folk trundling in and out of the shops in windcheaters and bad haircuts.

'*Men.*' Mary swung the minibus into a car park.

The fish and chips were good, and the view improved them. It was a turbulent day out on the Channel and choppy waves surged towards the Cobb, a bent finger of stone that beckoned out to sea.

'Isn't this where Meryl Streep stood, looking all premenstrual, in *The French Lieutenant's Woman*?' Mary affected an appropriately dramatic stance.

'But she was wearing a rather fetching black cape,' remembered Cat, popping a nuclear-hot chip into her mouth. 'Not a Primark poncho.' Cat wished she'd had notice of their awayday: she was dressed to bleach a toilet, not take Lyme Regis by storm. Her oldest cardigan over her oldest polo neck were matched with worn cords the colour of bile that belonged to Germaine: it was true that living with women meant that there were always clothes to borrow, but they weren't necessarily clothes you *wanted* to borrow.

'Ice cream next.' Mary bundled up the chip paper and flung it into a bin. 'We'll suck this town dry of fun!'

Guffawing, faces smeared with tutti frutti, the friends bowled into a bric-a-brac shop. Lyme Regis was, it transpired, the world capital of small useless second-hand things. They browsed several small boxes, countless small figurines and could have filled the minibus with small pictures of Edwardian strangers in brass frames.

There were shops converted into art galleries, stuffed with paintings of the sea. There were tea rooms, and a handful of shops selling shells and fossils. There was no Topshop, no Monsoon and no Reiss: Lyme Regis flummoxed Cat's consumerist lust and she loved it. She loved the way the main road clambered upwards to a pleasure garden that tumbled in its turn back down to the beach. She loved the open air table tennis tables so much that she chivvied a game out of a complaining Mary. She loved the benches sited to admire the grand curve of Lyme Bay. The only thing wrong with Lyme Regis was the fact that it took less than an hour to 'do'.

'Right.' Mary stood outside the largest shell shop, hands on hips. 'What now?'

'Er, we've done the Cobb. The front. The shops. The museum. The beach.' They couldn't afford the amusement arcade, a detail that was not at all amusing. 'All that's left is the pub.'

'Oh no,' groaned Mary with forged horror. 'Not the pub. Anything but that.' She was already halfway to the door of the Fisherman's Rest. 'Let's take a look at the fishermen. Resting.'

The interior, a vista of dappled glass and brown wood, appeared untouched since the heyday of the grotty pub some decades ago. The only pubs Cat ever ventured into were decorated in Farrow and Ball colours, but this was painted varying shades of *Vieux Homme*. The clientele, all four of them, turned to take in the newcomers. Unimpressed, they returned to their pints.

The barmaid, abundant in ill-advised stretch velour, raised her voice to say confidently, 'You'll be wanting Nelson's, girls.'

Cat and Mary bowed out, back into the twenty-first century. 'There,' Cat pointed across the road. 'She thinks that's more us.'

'She's right.' Mary led the way to the wine bar, where distressed pine floorboards and shabby chic kitchen chairs promised a more up-to-date experience. 'Must be some talent in there, surely.'

Settled in a corner table, with the cheapest bottle of house something or other on order and Mary in the loo, Cat picked unthinkingly at the candlewax stalagmite on the table. There was zero talent in Nelson's: they were the only customers. 'Talent' was a favourite word of Mary's to describe picturesque members of the opposite sex, and it made Cat cringe. Should women who had long ago waved farewell to thirty use language like that? No mortgage, no children, Cat had come through her twenties unscathed. Or, to put it another way, untried. None of her close friends were married, or mothers. The uncomfortable thought that maybe she had avoided proper grown-ups couldn't be ignored. She sighed. She'd felt grown up at Percival Cant Jablowski: only an adult could cope with the pressure there. Without her job Cat was a condemned building whose scaffolding had collapsed.

Pulling, snogging, fancying – these words were still in the friends' lexicon of love. After four years Cat was – she gulped – back on the market. Out there. She shivered: it was dark out there.

Cat was confused. Not about Hugh: she knew exactly what to do about Hugh, even if she couldn't quite trust herself to do it. No, the confusion was about what she wanted, now that her future was a blank page. She had to be careful not to doodle on it, ruin it like she had before.

There was no need to look for a relationship. None at all. Cat hadn't been raised to expect a fairy tale. She'd been appalled when her schoolfriends had fallen in love every five minutes, enduring grand operas of hope and betrayal before they were out of their teens. Cat had been different. *I'll know,* she'd told herself, *when it happens.* She had a career to build first. A mark to make.

Well, thought Cat dejectedly, rolling a ball of wax, the mark I made was a grubby one. When love finally came along – in her thirties, long after those schoolfriends were on their second marriages – it had been oddly shaped, difficult to describe and clearly stamped with a skull and crossbones.

A practical woman, Cat hated to admit how very bad she was at love. How come other women were so surefooted? How did they leap from romantic crag to crag? After years of her timeshare in Hugh, Cat couldn't imagine herself with another man. It would look skewwhiff, like one of those 'What's Wrong With This Picture?' puzzles of a dog hoovering.

When she'd first met Germaine, the older woman had said approvingly that Cat was 'a natural feminist'. Cat had never examined that statement before but now she wondered about it.

A bottle arrived, with two glasses, delivered by a girl whose complexion sang of cream and butter and fresh air. Cat envied her for a moment, resented the decade and a half that must surely separate them. Not, she chided herself, the reaction of a natural feminist.

Mary returned: quiet philosophising was postponed indefinitely. She wanted to talk about men. Her man, in particular. 'I still miss him,' she sighed. 'And you have my permission to hit me on the head with anything heavy that comes to hand.'

'What do you miss?' Cat was intrigued. Alun was not endearing. He was not interesting. He was barely bearable. 'The snoring? The farting? The . . .' she hesitated.

With best friend radar, Mary picked up what Cat couldn't say. 'Yes,' she deadpanned. 'I miss the stealing most of all.' She smiled. 'I don't really know. It's just an amorphous blob of missing. Nothing in particular. Just that sensation of having somebody. An other half.'

'You've got me.' Cat raised her glass in salute.

'Yeah, I know, but you're you,' said Mary. 'You're female. It's different. I love you but I need to be in love.'

'Ah.' Cat tapped her forefinger on the dented table. 'But why do you need to be in love?'

'I don't have an answer, but I refer my learned friend to the fifty billion other women before me who have needed to be in love. It's how girls are.'

'We're not girls,' said Cat carefully. 'We're women.' This was a delicate issue. Their enduring girlhood was scheduled to end some time in their eighties. 'And as women, we should examine our needs before we act on them, surely?'

'Are you a Germaine in Cat's clothing?' scowled Mary. 'I miss Alun. That's all. Doesn't mean I'm running back to him. But I thought that a separation would make my mind up, show me that I don't need him.' She took a thirsty gulp. 'Despite my euphoria after Group, it's not working out that way.'

'Go easy on the giggle water,' warned Cat. 'We can only afford that bottle. And besides, one of us has to drive.'

'I hate being poor,' grumbled Mary. 'And I don't like being dirty.

Look at my nails.' She waggled her fingers in Cat's face. 'I miss being blow-dried, waxed, self-tanned.'

'You're lovely the way you are,' insisted Cat, ignoring the quotation marks of hair between her friend's eyebrows. 'We're women, Mary. We don't need to be oiled and shaved.'

'Have you looked at your legs lately? You're verging on simian.' Mary looked over Cat's head. 'Isn't that the vet over there?'

A spanner the size of a Labrador was thrown into Cat's works. 'Where? God. No. Shit,' she said all in one breath.

'It is. It's the vet.' Mary rubbed her chin contemplatively. 'Not bad. Not bad at all.'

Will was standing at the door with a woman old enough to disqualify her as a girlfriend. This thought occurred to Cat, fully fledged, in a second. The lady was in her sixties, and her nose was so like Will's she just had to be a relative. It looked better on Will: a nose of such dimensions is hard to carry off.

'Don't stare. *Don't*,' ordered Cat, pulling Mary's ringlets to wrest her gaze back. 'Let's not, you know, say hello.'

'You like him!' Mary's mouth hung open as the truth hit.

'No I don't. Is he looking? I do not. Like him, I mean. Shut up, Mary. God.'

'You don't sound like no woman, bitch.' Mary was enjoying this a little too much for Cat's liking. 'You sound like a *girl*. Is this overreaction because you're dressed like a tramp?'

Cat had been nursing the forlorn hope that she looked a little like Keira Knightley might look in unkempt layers, i.e. adorably tomboyish. 'No, it's not that. It's just . . .' She sighed. Mary was her closest ally, she could talk to her. 'I kind of thought that something passed between us the other day but now I don't know and I don't really want to test it in case I'm disappointed. I just want him to . . .'

'Die?' suggested Mary.

'Well, no,' laughed Cat. 'I just don't want to sense him thinking *not that skanky bird again*. To tell the truth, I don't need the distraction while I get on with the serious business of getting over Hugh.'

'This is progress!' beamed Mary. 'Lucy and I reckoned you were still eating your heart out over Hugh.'

'Did you?' Cat didn't much like that *Lucy and I.* 'It's not really any of her business.'

'She's dead nice. You're so funny with her.'

'Funny?' Cat looked outraged. 'Me? I've been friendly. Easy going.'

'No. Funny.' Mary seemed certain.

'We should go,' said Cat, draining her glass. 'Germaine will be impatient to kill us both.' Laying down a crisp and precious ten pound note, Cat shrugged. 'It's been worth it.' She frowned. 'Hasn't it?'

'Yes!' roared Mary. 'It bloody has!'

At the noise, Will looked up from the window table where he'd settled down with his mother/aunt/miscellaneous female relative.

'Hi!' said Cat, raising a hand.

'Hi,' said Will.

'Hi,' said Mary.

'Hi,' said Will, frowning and obviously wondering who she was.

'Bye,' said Cat.

'Bye,' said Will.

'Oh for fuck's sake, let's get out of here,' said Mary.

The excellence of the whole let's-steal-the-van-and-paint-Lyme-Regis-red thing had completely worn off.

'She'll throttle us,' said Mary, pulling out of the car park.

The van put-putted up the hill. 'And leave our bodies out for the hens,' agreed Cat. They drove in silence, leaving the street lights behind.

'Careful!' exclaimed Cat suddenly as their headlights picked out a figure in the dark. 'Christ. You nearly hit her.'

'I did not,' protested Mary, braking. 'Let her catch us up then I'll advise her, in no uncertain terms, that hitchhiking in the dusk is bloody . . . Jozette!'

There she was in the rear-view mirror. Jozette's Afro was tranquillised beneath a bobble hat, and her model-y frame was disguised in denim and rainproof nylon, but the gait was unmistakably the catwalk lope of their London friend.

'Jozette!' yelled Cat, leaping down from the van. 'What? I mean, how?'

'Oh my God, you guys!' shrieked Jozette, her body language cranking up a few gears from dejected to berserk. 'I . . . I was going to . . . I . . .' and she sank into a chic heap on the grass verge and began to sob.

22

'This isn't a home for waifs and strays,' hissed Sarge in a stage whisper that Jozette, wrapped in a blanket by the Aga, could surely hear.

'Keep it down,' warned Cat. That was her kind of, almost, sister-in-law Sarge was talking about. 'She is not a waif, she's a woman in trouble. And she goes way back with Germaine.' She hesitated, then showed her blade: 'Before *you*.'

An arm around Jozette's shoulders, Germaine stood silhouetted in the lamp's marmalade glow. 'Ladies, let's not argue,' she said in her best Mother Superior tones. 'Jozette is welcome, Sarge. She is a victim of male misbehaviour. She needs us.'

'If you say so, Germaine, then that's fine.' Sarge glared at Cat, before moving pugnaciously across the room. 'Just didn't want car thieves making the decisions around here.'

Germaine waited for the door to slam behind Sarge. 'She can be a little extreme,' she said quietly.

There had been no anger from Germaine on their return: perhaps Jozette had defused it. Or perhaps Germaine was biding her time. Germy was a noted bider. Cat reached out and ruffled Jozette's Afro, which had sprung back to life after hours suffocated beneath her hat. She liked ruffling Jozette's Afro. 'How you doing?'

'Better,' smiled Jozette, baring her large white teeth in a wide smile. 'I thought I was going to die out there. Like a dog.'

Germaine pulled up one of the scuffed old chairs. 'What were you thinking of? Walking through the dark like that?'

'Oh hell, I don't know.' Jozette waved her hands in the air, the smile abruptly switched off. 'There were no cabs, the buses were finished . . .'

'You're here now,' said Cat, consolingly. Jozette could rarely explain herself. The woman lived in a mutable universe where nothing was definite: things just happened.

'You were *meant* to find me.' Jozette was confident. 'You guys were sent out in that minibus for a reason.' She clasped her long fingers together in a gesture of prayer. 'The universe doesn't make mistakes.'

Jozette had evidently never seen Alun in Speedo's.

'Hotpot dear?' Beulah placed a tray on Jozette's lap.

'Hawt pawt?' Jozette had managed to spend the best part of a decade in the UK and still retain her touristy surprise at dishes such as hotpot or mushy peas. 'That looks good!' She relished the last word, awarding it a few extra vowels, like a Miami girl should. 'You're a lifesaver, Beulah.'

Beulah had already left the room. Cat was accustomed to her quiet tread and knew that the older lady was being discreet. Because it was time to ask Jozette why the hell she was here.

Germaine got there first. 'What blew you to our door?' she asked, with more poetry than Cat would have employed.

'A phone number.' Jozette tried a spoonful of hotpot.

'Ouch.' Cat sighed. 'In Trev's pocket?'

Mid-chew, Jozette clarified. 'On his arse.'

'Oh.' Germaine pulled in her chin.

'In biro.'

'Did he, could he, explain it?' asked Cat hopefully.

'It was,' repeated Jozette with queenly emphasis, 'on his arse'. Some English words she'd taken to. Arse was amongst them, along with cuppa, bonkers and wanker. '*Nicky 0790* something or other. He said it was a mate's number. Nicholas. Another traffic warden.'

'O . . . kay . . .' Cat tried that explanation out for size. 'Blimey. It gets pretty lively in those traffic warden changing rooms.'

'Quite,' drawled Jozette. 'So I called the number.'

Both Cat and Germaine cocked their heads to one side.

'And she ain't no Nicholas.' Jozette's mobile face twisted with scorn. 'That bitch is a Nicola.'

'What did Trev have to say for himself?' Cat didn't really want to know.

'He went kind of crazy,' said Jozette contemplatively, as if recalling a dream. 'I expected him to turn it all around on me as usual, but he started telling me he loved me, that we should have a baby, that he didn't deserve me. But he wouldn't answer me about this Nicola girl. I kept asking him and he kept saying he loved me.' She put down her spoon and looked Cat in the eye. 'Girl, your brother *never* says he loves me. It's like there's a law against it.' She stirred the meaty goo around her bowl. 'I had to get out. He was suddenly saying everything I longed to hear, but it was just a smokescreen. He'd been caught and he knew it, and he used all the precious sacred stuff just to change the subject. To distract me, like a toddler. Does he think I'm that dumb?' she asked Cat passionately.

The answer was an inescapable *oooh yes,* but Cat didn't say so. 'He's the dumb one,' she said sadly, imagining the wild funk that Trev would be in right now. 'What's the plan?' she asked, keeping the question light.

'I'm gonna stay here. Sort my head out.' Jozette twisted around in her blanket to check out Germaine's expression. 'If that's OK with the boss lady?'

'Of course it is.' Germaine had a sizeable soft spot for Jozette. Anybody who appreciated beauty would. 'I'll get Sarge and Lucy to move another bed into the dormitory.'

When Germaine left the room, Jozette gave Cat what her grandmother would have called an old-fashioned look. 'Dormitory?' she repeated. 'Is this some kind of Mallory Towers shit? It's true, you Brits do all want to go back to freaking school.'

'It's not as bad as it . . .' Cat checked herself. 'It's actually worse than it sounds, Jozette,' she laughed. 'We sleep together. We do chores on a rota system. We're trying to be self-sufficient. There's hardly any hot water. The electricity keeps going off. And there's a ghost.'

'Girlfriend, after chasing your brother's ass around town, that sounds like a picnic.'

To Cat's townie surprise, eggs from the commune chickens tasted just like 'proper' eggs. She dunked Beulah's home-made soldiers enthusiastically, taking in the familiar faces around the sun-striped breakfast table. Jozette's arrival underlined how tight knit the group had become.

There was no point pretending they all adored each other's company. Cat was still a little scared of Sarge, bored by Antonia, conflicted about Lucy. But somehow the ramshackle machinery worked. Floors were swept. Meals were made. Washing up was done. Adding another person to this delicate mix could be ruinous.

Particularly if that person was Jozette. An orchid of a woman, she didn't blend in. She stood out. And Cat felt responsible for her. She hoped nobody had noticed that Jozette was still in bed.

'The Yank's having a lie-in.' Sarge shrugged. 'All right for some.'

'She had a terrible time finding us,' said Germaine. 'Sarge, darling, do show some compassion.'

'What bloody good is a model to us? We need women who can work. Not princesses who lie in bed all day.'

Feeling that 7.45 hardly qualified as 'all day', Cat corrected Sarge. 'Jozette used to be a model. Now she's a stylist.' She saw the incomprehension on the woman's face. 'She sorts out the props and settings for fashion shoots, and er, things.' Cat shut up and returned to her egg: she didn't really know what a stylist was either.

*

Cough-free and full of the joys of the spring that was undeniably in full swing all around them, Dave shot across the lane ahead of Cat, barely giving her time to close the gate.

May had dotted the trees with blossom, and conjured up wild flowers from nowhere. But the warm, softly scented breeze was not to be trusted: gangs of surly clouds lurked, threatening to plunge everybody back into the bad old days of winter at any moment.

A jumper around her waist as insurance against a downturn in the weather, Cat enjoyed the sensation of fresh air on bare arms. Her fringe was history, and she'd scraped her unwashed black hair into a ponytail which tickled the nape of her neck as she chased Dave up the hill opposite the house.

'Dave! *Perimeter!*' glowered Cat, as they skirted the corduroy field, now green and fluffy. The details of their walk changed every day, new growth here, a disappearance there. Cat marvelled that she'd ever thought the scenery boring.

There was Will's tree. Cat's feet stopped dead. *Will's tree.* That, she realised, was how she thought of it. It was just a tree, and Will was just a vet, a common or garden vet. This need to elevate the first post-Hugh man she met was irritating, girlish. Her feet, which had started up, stopped again. Post-Hugh. She shuddered. It reminded her of 'post-apocalyptic'.

Settling herself comfortably against the tree trunk, one eye on the foraging Dave, Cat unfolded the latest letter from her mum.

Jon's asleep, it began. *Poor thing, he's exhausted. Physio today, then his health visitor, who asked me a hundred questions I've already answered. Jon was very cheesed off, I can tell you.*

After a few more lines, the meandering tapered off and the letter got down to business.

Goodness, Catrina, you're very inquisitive all of a sudden. Why did me and your dad break up? It's funny, but at the time I asked myself that question over and over, and couldn't work it out. I haven't asked it for years, and now that you've brought it up again, it seems so obvious. That's hindsight for you!

It's simple. We were a mismatch. We married too quickly, when we were still madly in love, too young to realise that it couldn't last. I didn't really know Harry when we walked up the aisle, he was like a hero to me. And he thought I was gorgeous (don't laugh). But as for living together. I wound him up, cleaning our little flat all the time. He used to say I loved the hoover more than him. He didn't talk to me enough. I would ask about his day and get a grunt.

It was a long, sad falling apart. No one thing broke us up.

Cat wheezed with relief. Jon wasn't even mentioned. Harry hadn't walked out because of his new son's disability.

All that dreaded Personal Reflection Time had brought Harry into sharp focus. Growing up, Cat had been afraid to think about Harry too much because she was confused about *what* to think. At least now she knew he wasn't the kind of beast who'd walk out on a baby because it demanded too much of him.

Looking back, I neglected him after we had you kids. You were everything to me. Your dad became less important. All those months we talked about separating he kept saying we should spend more time together. As if! With all I had on my plate!

Cat's palms tingled. *All those months . . .*

'Dave, come here,' said Cat urgently, needing her pink bulk. 'He didn't just leave on the spur of the moment,' she told the pig, who took the news nonchalantly. 'They discussed splitting up for months.' Cat gulped. The Bayeux Tapestry of her childhood was unravelling. How much of the bungalow's folklore was true? Had Harry really gone out for cigarettes and kept on walking?

The truth is, your dad was a weak man. He couldn't cope with family life, and he took the easy way out. If that sounds harsh, love, remember you asked me and I want to tell you the truth.

I'm worried about you, Cat. Where has this interest in the past come from? We didn't need him then, and we don't need him now.

'But Mum,' said Cat quietly, 'I did need him then.'

Her feet flew a touch too fast as she thumped back down the hill. Other girls got to have daddies: when her friends' fathers attained past-tense status, they had the decency to be dead. Cat had never grieved: her mouth had been stitched up.

Backdated loss chased Cat as she raced back to the house. Anchorless, directionless, Cat needed her daddy. There was nobody to tell. Nobody would understand.

'Oh Hu-u-ugh,' she howled, stopping suddenly, mid-hill, pressing her knuckles into her eyes. 'Where are you?'

23

There was what used to be known as a 'to-do' at the house. Busy buzzing around the four trunks that had arrived for Jozette, nobody noticed Cat's red eyes.

'Four?' Sarge shook her head at the luggage blocking the hall. 'I could live out of a backpack.'

'Four!' cooed Antonia, greatly admiring.

Cat turned Antonia neatly by her shoulders. 'Come on. The rota says it's you and me out in the vegetable patch.'

The clouds had drifted off to pick on the next valley. 'Mild, isn't it?' said Cat conversationally, picking what she hoped were weeds out of the dusty earth.

'Hmm.' Antonia was vague.

Determined to reach her, Cat persevered. 'Sarge reckons this plot is barren.'

'Like me.'

'Eh?' Cat frowned. 'You've had two kids, Antonia.'

'But they've been taken away.' The familiar snuffles were threatening. 'I have nothing. My arms are empty.'

Cat didn't feel qualified to speak. She didn't dare to say she knew how Antonia felt. That wasn't true. 'This will pass,' she said eventually, in a quiet voice. 'Nothing lasts for ever.' She paused. 'Not even the good stuff.'

Antonia looked penetratingly at her, the fug lifting for a moment. She dragged the back of one hand across her eyes. 'How come Germaine always manages to dig something up when she tends the vegetable patch?'

Swerving gratefully to the new subject, Cat suggested that perhaps the carrots and potatoes were as intimidated by their leaderene as everybody else.

'Glad you could join us,' said Sarge pointedly when Jozette took her place in the circle.

'Thanks,' grinned Jozette, buttoning a cashmere cardigan the colour of dead red roses. 'What's this about?' she asked, looking around delightedly as if the drab old parlour was front row at the Follies.

'It's our Goddess circle,' said Lucy. 'We talk about what's troubling us. We open up to the group. It's a form of therapy.' It was impossible to tell whether she felt it was a useful pastime, or utter piffle.

'Cool,' cooed Jozette approvingly.

Don't say 'cool' to Lucy, thought Cat, her tummy churning. Any minute now and Jozette would start quoting *The Celestine Prophecy*.

'Attention, ladies.' Germaine wrested attention back to her. 'It's that time again, when we shed our spiritual garments and stand skyclad in the eyes of our peers.'

Cat groaned, but Jozette was leaning forward, her eyes glistening. 'Wow,' she breathed.

'Wow is right,' muttered Cat, clamping her arms around herself. She fought the impulse to stick her fingers in her ears in case she recognised herself in Germaine's preamble.

'Today's speaker is a stalwart of this commune. She toils at the very heart of our house, feeding us, nourishing us.'

Cat looked sideways at Beulah, sizing up her reaction: there didn't seem to be one.

Waving a hand towards Beulah, Germaine said, 'There's not much I can tell you. We all met Beulah at the same time. There was a reason she found her way here and perhaps tonight we'll discover it. This house was a beacon shining in the night and Beulah trekked towards it.'

'Germy, that is so beautiful,' said Jozette, with a slow handclap. 'Please stand up and share, Beulah Snow.'

There was the usual polite applause, bolstered by a whoop from Jozette, but Beulah didn't stand up. She was immobile in washed-out nylon, her wonderful lion's head bent, staring at the floor. When the clapping petered out, she raised her head and said, 'No. Sorry. But no.'

'You can't refuse,' said Germaine from the centre of the circle. 'It's what we do here, Beulah,' she said querulously. 'We share.'

'Not I. Not today.'

Get a grip, Flowerpot. Cat raised her hand. 'I really need to share tonight, Germaine,' she gabbled.

At her side, Mary, who'd been having an intense whispered conversation with Lucy, broke off to gasp, 'You?'

'Yup, me.' Cat strode to the centre of the circle, hugged Germaine to quieten the splutterings and trotted out the traditional 'My name is Cat and this is my story', leaving Germaine no option but to retire to a chair.

'I'm here because I . . .' Cat wondered why the hell she was there. 'Because I fell in love,' she decided.

'Aww!' Jozette's heart was always on her designer sleeve.

'Typical,' said Sarge, as if falling in love was further proof of Cat's feeble-mindedness.

'With the wrong person, in the wrong place,' continued Cat, gathering speed. 'He held all the power because he was older, and, possibly,' she winked at Germaine, 'because he was male. When the affair was discovered, I lost my job.'

'You're leaving out the best bits!' Germaine bobbed on her seat. 'He's still in his job, sisters, plus he's gone back to his abused wife, *who is with child!*'

'Personally,' said Cat, 'I think they're the worst bits. I couldn't afford to find somewhere to live. And so I'm here.'

'There are worse places to be,' laughed Jozette comfortably.

'What about your family?' asked Lucy, legs crossed and one foot jiggling a slow bass line.

'Usual stuff.' Cat caught Mary's expression. 'Well, sort of. My dad walked out—' She corrected herself. '*Left us* when I was a kid. My younger brother has problems. They're his own, not something I want to discuss here. They haven't really affected me.'

Mary opened her mouth to speak, then shut it speedily on receipt of a look, a humdinger of a full-fat look, from Cat.

Sarge wanted to know about Cat's job. Something about the way she phrased the question implied that it couldn't possibly have been as important as delivering yoghurt.

'I produced commercials,' said Cat simply.

'What sort of job's that?' scoffed Sarge.

'A very complicated, stressful one, juggling budgets and personalities and schedules,' said Cat glibly. 'I loved it,' she added, feeling abashed. In front of non-media people, ordinary humans, it felt shallow to love such a job. She had never saved a life, nor eased world hunger. She hadn't even driven a milk float through a hailstorm.

'Do you miss it?' asked Lucy.

'I—' Cat stopped short. Her kneejerk response was wrong, and she said slowly, 'Not really,' then laughed a stunted little snort, amazed.

A hesitant hand clutching a tissue went up. Antonia had a question. 'What is he like, this chap you fell for?'

'Old,' snapped Mary while Cat was still marshalling her thoughts. 'Really really old. Poncey. Snobbish.'

'Whose Group is this?' Cat assumed a haughty look (one she hadn't dug out since London) and said, over-emphatically in Antonia's direction, 'Hugh is mature, and sophisticated, and . . .' She drifted off a little. Conjuring him up was dangerous. She'd assiduously reduced Hugh to a cartoon, all lacy cuffs and nose in the air, but the flesh and blood man she'd lain naked beside was before her now. She sighed. 'He had real *focus*, I felt so noticed by him.' Over a shower of tuts from Mary, Cat appealed to the others. 'We had something, we fell for each other, it wasn't some office thing.' She heard herself protesting, and knew how hollow it must sound. 'Look,' she said, 'nobody knows what goes on in other people's relationships. For four years I lived with the fact that, on paper, my love life was tacky. But what kept me going was the fact that he saw me, really saw me.' She turned to Mary, arms folded. 'You don't know him, not really, Mary.'

'How could I?' asked Mary contemptuously. 'I only met him once. He didn't want to meet your friends, did he?'

Instead of answering, Cat said, waving her hands in front of her, 'Anyway, it's over and I'm doing cold turkey and it's tough and more importantly . . .' She took a deep breath. 'I'm going to find my dad.'

The hall was dark as Cat put the letter down on the table, stroking it before she turned back to the parlour.

'Here,' said Mary peremptorily, clearing a space between herself and Lucy on the hard settle.

'But I . . .' Cat gestured towards the sofa where Jozette was showing photos of Trev to Beulah.

'*Here*,' said Mary.

Conscious of just how much space her behind would take up on the narrow wooden seat, Cat inserted herself between Mary and Lucy, expecting Lucy to pick up the notepad at her feet. She didn't.

'Have you gone nuts?' asked Mary. 'After what your dad did to your family?'

Cat's lips thinned, and her patience did the same. 'I must have missed the memo about running all decisions past you.'

'I'm worried about you.' Mary knew Cat well enough to know that this could only result in even thinner lips. 'Your family's been through so much.'

Pulling a furious face, Cat tried to surreptitiously incline her head towards Lucy.

'Oh, Lucy knows all about your situation,' said Mary breezily.

That took a moment to compute, a moment neatly filled by Lucy's 'We really feel you should think twice about this.'

'*We?*' Cat repeated the word caustically. 'Perhaps Sarge could give us a seminar later on the pros and cons.'

'You said you wanted to share,' Lucy pointed out, maddeningly serene and maddeningly right.

'Yeah, but . . .' Cat tried to nail Mary with a 'how could you?' look but couldn't catch her eye. 'Look, the wheels are in motion.' True, if a one-page letter to her mother asking if she'd object could be called 'wheels'. 'I'm not sure how to track him down, but I'll manage it. And then, well, I'll see if he wants to meet.'

'And if he doesn't?' Either Lucy was unaware that Cat didn't want to talk to her about this topic or she didn't care.

'Then I'll deal with it.'

24

'It brings out the colour of her eyes.'

'Does it?' Cat was doubtful, but Jozette was sure: the vivid pink on the walls of Dave's sty brought out the animal's pinprick dark eyes. 'It looks fabulous!'

Unless Elton John kept pigs there was unlikely to be a more fashion-forward sty in the whole of the world. Thanks to Jozette, Dave had pink walls, a turquoise shade over the light bulb, and a gilded trough.

'*I* want to live here,' laughed Cat. It was surreal, another world. Jozette World. 'You're so creative,' she said, unable to keep the surprise out of her voice. She'd always assumed that personal stylists dicked about with bits of fabric and told rich women they looked fabulous.

'Sure am,' said Jozette comfortably, hands on hips, surveying her work. 'Making things look good. Making people feel good. It does it for me.'

'And me.' Cat was unable to keep the smile off her face. The afternoon had been funny, and feel-good, and all sorts of things she'd underrated back at Percival Cant Jablowski, which seemed glassy and sharp from this distance. The generosity with which Jozette spilled colour over the commune was inspiring.

Strolling back to the house together, Jozette took her arm as she always did. Jozette was always reaching out her long, thin arm to the person nearest to her. Cat squeezed it. She wished she had the eloquence to apologise to this quirkily beautiful, double-jointed black girl. For years Cat had viewed Jozette through the prism of her brother's propaganda.

'Dippy mare,' Trev called Jozette. 'Dozy bird.' Her job had been carefully downsized to a girly nonsense. Cat shrivelled inside: she hadn't stuck up for Jozette when Trev had taken to calling her Brain of Britain. A frustrated man in a traffic warden's uniform throwing rocks at a statuesque beauty draped in silks; funny how a few miles and a few months helped the truth to rise to the surface.

'How are you getting on here?' asked Cat, leaning in cosily.

'It's fabulous,' said Jozette. Most things were fabulous in Jozette World, but somehow the epithet wasn't devalued. 'Older women, younger women, *women*, you know. Man, I don't get enough of women in my day to day life.' She pulled a face. 'I miss my mom, you know. She's a long way away. And I have, like, an army of aunties. But over here in London, it's just me.'

Jozette wasn't 'just' anything. Cat had been blinded by the woman's innate glamour, never thinking of her as lonely, or displaced.

'So,' Jozette carried on, 'this is like a family. A whole new family, of mad Brits. And no guys to hit on me, then bring me down. Take the piss, as you'd say.' She glanced at Cat apologetically. 'Sorry. I didn't mean Trev. He's your brother after all.'

'You did mean Trev,' said Cat. 'Are you in touch?' Cat felt the warmth of Jozette's arm in hers and suddenly hoped she wouldn't split with her brother completely.

'He writes. His spelling!' whooped Jozette. 'He misses me, he says. What am I doing in the country with a bunch of old bats? Vintage Trev.' She let go of Cat as they went through the front door. 'I think about him all the time,' she said suddenly in a twisted voice as if test driving a foreign language. 'But,' she paused, and tried to smile. 'They're not all nice thoughts.'

'Sister,' said Cat, 'I hear ya.'

Mincing at speed, Dave led the way up the hill, the very picture of porcine health. Struggling to keep up, Cat discarded a layer of non-descript knitwear, revealing a jade angora tank top recently filched from one of Jozette's trunks. The quality of the house's communal wardrobe had soared since the American's arrival.

'Dave! Do a left at the rowan tree!' shouted Cat.

The pig obeyed. Evidently its knowledge of trees (not to mention the English language) was as comprehensive as Cat's. Using a book she'd found on a bookshelf in the parlour, whose pages smelled like damp leaves, Cat was educating herself about the leafy landmarks on her route. The rowan in question was handsome and broad, its branches filling out nicely as the year progressed.

'Nettles,' muttered Cat. 'Nettles.' Beulah had sent her out foraging. Nettle soup was to kick-start dinner that evening, and although dubious about how it might taste, Cat felt smugly Head Girl-ish at being asked to help.

After a career in advertising, handling prickly so-and-sos was second nature to Cat. The commune wasn't without its nettles either: living with women meant there were tank tops to borrow, moisturiser to try, and somebody to appraise whether or not your neck had started to age, but with so many disparate characters the element of the unexpected lurked.

Cat preferred certainties. She wasn't a natural off-roader, preferring a well-lit path and a pork pie for the journey. Germaine's social experiment was unfolding in an erratic, crumpled manner: Cat was nostalgic about her worries that she would be bored without television, without the internet, without her phone. Cat didn't have the time to be bored.

Nothing was panning out as she had hoped and feared. By now, Hugh should have obediently faded to a featureless stick man on the horizon. Cresting the hill and feeling the sweet wallop of scented air, Cat recalled with a narcotic rush the feel of his body, the wry rhythms of his speech. Hugh was still defiant flesh and blood, still a pretty blot on her landscape.

If Mary hadn't destroyed those letters . . . Cat never got further with that thought. What, she chided herself, could he have possibly said that would make any difference? Apart from revealing that the scene in Simon's office was an elaborate practical joke involving a professional actress with a pillow up her jumper, there was nothing Hugh could say that would change anything. Nothing could redeem him, or Cat, from her own low opinion of their reckless behaviour.

Except the usual. Hugh could say the usual. And Cat missed the usual. The post-break-up barrage of compliments. The elegantly worded professions of adoration. The careful tour of her best features, lovingly detailed and wittily worded. Cat hungered for Hugh's aftercare. Without his gaze to shape her, she felt formless, as hazy as the ghost who interrupted her sleep.

Exit Hugh stage right, enter Harry stage left. If she could track the bugger down. Wasn't it just as illogical to ask her father to square her circle?

With distance, Cat discerned the whorls of her life in London. She'd trudged the same narrow ruts year in, year out. At least out here she had the reward of pink sunsets, the sudden blast of a frisky breeze, the happy snort of a pig happening on a fungus. Small pleasures certainly, but the sensible side of Cat, the side she'd muted when snuggling up to a married man, appreciated them.

A carrier bag of nettles in each hand, Cat tramped back over the courtyard. Either side of the battered front door stood a pot. One large, one small, both dented, they were home to two scarlet geraniums.

Their colour, their unexpectedness, the fact that one of her cohorts had bothered to plonk them there, touched Cat. 'Nettles! I bring you nettles!' she sang down the hall that the sun never penetrated.

Beulah was alone in the kitchen, concentrating on something flour-related. 'Top class,' she smiled, her Famous Five vocabulary, as ever, tickling Cat. 'Let's not tell the others what's in the soup until they've tried it.'

'Whatever you say, O devious one.' Cat set the bags on the scrubbed table, enjoying the absurdity of her accusation. Beulah looked anything but devious with her lamb's rump of white curls, her button eyes and her soft, sagging cheek.

And yet. Cat knew next to nothing about this woman. She was drawn to Beulah, like a tired tabby to a grate, but if Beulah had gone missing she couldn't have told the search party much beyond 'Probably wearing an apron and smelling of scones'.

'Are you a feminist, Beulah?' she asked.

'Well, what *is* a feminist?' Beulah upended the nettles into a colander.

This was top notch evasion. Beulah was *good.* But Cat was persistent. She hadn't got to where she was today (or rather where she'd been until two months ago) by giving up that easily. 'Couldn't tell you the dictionary definition. Germaine's brand of feminism involves flinging custard pies at men. Mine is more about . . .' She considered for a moment, suddenly wary of being too flippant. 'Equality. Sisterhood. Fulfilment.' That was all rather grandiose, and abstract. 'Do you know what I mean?'

'Do *you* know what you mean?'

'Kind of.' Cat sniffed the air. 'Any biscuits hanging about, getting under your feet?'

'You can have *a* pistachio and white chocolate cookie.'

Not caring for that stressed 'a', Cat picked up the biscuit. If Beulah thought she'd given up, the old lady was wrong: Cat was merely regrouping. 'Was it the feminist ethos of the commune that drew you here?' she asked, hyper casual, as if she used words like 'ethos' all the time.

'You're not so much a feminist,' observed Beulah, full-on ignoring as opposed to evading, 'as a people-ist.'

'I am? What's that?'

'You like people. You're pro-people.'

Cat frowned. 'You might not say that if you knew my innermost thoughts.'

'Possibly not. But many private thoughts are shocking.'

'Are yours?' Cat was enjoying this ping-pong.

'I've watched you. Talking with people. You ask questions. You care, Cat.'

'Or I'm phenomenally nosy.'

'Oh, you're that too.' Cat's harrumph amused Beulah. 'But you're humane.' Beulah paused in her cautious rinsing of the scratchy leaves and looked through Cat. 'Not everybody is.'

'Like who?' It verged on cruel to ask when Beulah obviously had someone specific in mind.

'I've heard you talking to Antonia about her children.' Beulah was all purpose and clatter, filling a saucepan at the tap. 'And she's not the most, how can I put it, *fascinating* of storytellers. You listen to Sarge's derring-do tales. You're the only one who does.'

'S'pose.' Cat squirmed. 'Maybe I'm just a creep.'

'No,' said Beulah placidly. 'You're nice, dear.'

Back at the agency, Cat had warned budding copywriters against 'nice'. Too bland, she'd declared. Too vague. In Beulah's fastidious mouth it was a massive compliment, one Cat felt unworthy of: just that morning she'd fantasised about drowning Sarge in her two inches of tepid bathwater. 'If you say so.'

'And you notice things,' said Beulah contemplatively. Her eyes flickered about her. 'Some people don't notice what's right under their noses.' She looked closed off suddenly.

But not closed off enough to miss Cat reaching out for a second biscuit. 'Now, now,' said Beulah mildly.

Shocked into wakefulness, Cat couldn't tell if the loud bump was part of her dream or ghostly choreography up in the turret. She pulled the heavy quilt up to her nose, its musty smell reassuring.

In the next bed a Mary-shaped lump rose and fell to the rhythm of her noisy breathing. Across the way Jozette snuffled à la Dave and turned jerkily under her covers as if annoyed. Germaine spluttered and scratched her nose.

Good, honest, decent human noises. Cat listened as if they were Mozart.

25

'If it's not one thing,' said Cat, 'it's another.'

Trite, but true. Now that Dave was restored to rude and noisy health, the chickens had decided to be ill.

Mary felt that 'decided' was putting it strongly. 'I'm sure they didn't hold a meeting and vote for their bum feathers to fall out.' She stared down at baldy, bedraggled Maryhen jabbing the earth around her boots. 'Look at the state of her. Frankly, I expect more from my poultry avatar.'

'They've stopped laying.' Cat rubbed her chin. 'Sarge went bonkers this morning when she couldn't have her boiled egg.'

Mary pointed at a scrawny chicken dragging its nude bottom up the drawbridge. 'Look at yours! Must have been some party, Hencat, babe.'

Sarge wouldn't divulge Will's number. '*I'll* call him,' she'd said, treating Cat to a suspicious glare.

'All right, all right, but do it now,' pleaded Cat. 'The chickens will start keeling over if we don't get the vet in.'

'Or you might.'

'Eh?' Cat worked up a furious expression that she hoped would explain the blush. 'What are you saying? Because if you're saying I'm interested in Will then you're mad. Because I'm not. Uninterested, that's me. In all men. Especially vets.'

'Have you finished?'

'Oh shut up,' said Cat.

Her hand looked small on the big iron latch. Cat squared her shoulders. It was just a room. The world was full of rooms and this was just another one. A room in a turret. She lifted the latch purposely.

The oddly shaped room was quiet. Cat had expected something to happen, an eerie laugh maybe, or the reflection of something unearthly in the small panes of the windows. Nothing happened.

She sniffed the air. There was a smell, an acrid smell, of old things, of unloved things. It was just a room with a stained mattress in it, and a wardrobe that was old and battered but not particularly spooky. Just a room. And, thought Cat, scuttling back to the banal safety of the others, for some reason, a sad room.

'Coccidiosis,' said Will, with conviction. 'Nasty, but simple to treat.'

'Good.' Cat looked at Hencat, still and calm in Will's hands. The little traitor. If Cat tried to pick up a chicken they scattered as if she was a convicted chicken murderer. 'How do you do that? Pick them up so easily? Could you show me?'

'Yeah. 'Course.' Will placed Hencat on the ground where she placidly pecked at something that didn't exist, her sole hobby. 'Be direct. Firm. Supportive. Be boss.' He clamped the little bird gently between his hands. 'You have a go.'

Hencat wasn't as thick as she looked. As soon as Will put her down she fled.

'Typical. They know they can take liberties with me,' complained Cat. 'Somehow they know you're a vet.'

'I'm used to handling birds.'

If anybody had said that in Percival Cant Jablowski there would have been howls of fnarr fnarr. He reached for another fowl. It was Chickenlucy: named for its habit of disdainfully lifting its head to stare down its beak at the other birds. 'Look. Place your hands over mine.'

It was, thought Cat wildly, like the pottery scene in the movie *Ghost.* Except with a chicken. 'OK,' she said. Will's hands were warm. Her palms met his knuckles and something very nice happened. She wondered if he felt it too. Going by the expression on his face, that of a man trying hard to control a bucking chicken, he didn't.

'Ooh, she's a wild one!' he laughed, and that wilful lock of dark brown hair that hovered above his eye fell in front of it. 'Can't blame her. We haven't even been introduced.'

Cat removed her hands. She'd been immunised against other men throughout her relationship with Hugh, and was out of practice: she couldn't be sure that she was reading the signs right. Maybe what she felt was gratitude for a veterinary job well done. But if that was so, why was she trying to check out his bum under his Barbour? 'Can you stay for a cup of tea?'

'Am I allowed in?'

'We'll keep you outside the back door, just in case.'

Beulah, whose head Cat had seen bobbing into view at the window every minute or so, placed a tray on the step as they approached.

'This is Will, the vet,' said Cat, as they drew near. 'And this is—' But Beulah had dodged back inside the kitchen, already fussing over a grater and a piece of cheese. 'Oh. That *was* Beulah.'

'Biscuits,' said Will avidly. He was obviously a biscuit man.

Hugh, Cat recalled, was more a Danish pastry man. She hated herself for these trains of thought but they were the only ones she had tickets for nowadays. 'What made you want to become a vet?' she asked, handing him a cup.

'Lack of imagination,' said Will, disappointing his interrogator. 'Dad did it. And his dad. Carlow and Son. We've been on Lyme's high street for decades.' He shrugged. 'There was a ready-made job waiting for me in my dad's practice. Even a ready-made home in the flat above.'

'But isn't it a vocation?'

'Well, yes.' Will seemed reluctant to admit this. 'That sounds a bit pretentious, though. Priests have vocations. I just have the right exams.'

'And chickens trust you,' said Cat. 'Sorry. That's such a weird compliment. But it's true.'

'Well, I trust them,' smiled Will. He had a wonky tooth, perfectly placed to show up the perfection of the others. 'I love my job, that's all. No complicated philosophy. It's, you know, a positive thing to do.' He gave Cat a quick glance, possibly to check if she found this icky.

She didn't. 'I loved my job,' she admitted. 'Really loved it.' Cat had loved her job in a different way, though, the way men love a difficult woman. She'd enjoyed its unpredictable nature, its essentially worthless glamour. And of course its rewards. 'Is it lucrative? Vetting?' she asked.

Taken aback, Will said, 'I get by.'

Cat heard the unmistakable clang of a *faux pas* drop on the gritty yard. It might be acceptable to grade Londoners by status, but here in deepest darkest Not-London folk clearly had other criteria. 'You don't do it for the money,' she suggested ingratiatingly.

'No vet does.' The idea seemed to tickle Will. 'I was born here, and this is the only landscape that makes sense to me. I feel right here. The way the sky meets the hills.'

'Poetic,' said Cat. In her flat accent it sounded terse, and she regretted saying it: Will's face closed up like a bad clam. 'London's my landscape,' she said ruefully.

'Never been there.'

'You what?' she gawped, teenager-like. 'You must have been.'

That amused look again. 'No.' Will shook his head. 'Honestly. Never fancied it.'

'But it's the capital,' Cat spluttered. For some reason it was important to her that Will should have been to London. 'It's the centre of fashion, of business, of, well, *life.*'

'That's where you're wrong.' Will took a long slug of Beulah's excellent tea. 'Dorset is the epicentre of the known universe. Just ask Dave.'

'Why don't you like London?' frowned Cat.

'Noise. Pollution. Graphic designers. Crowds. Theme pubs. Women in stupid clothes.' Will shuddered, as if somebody had walked across his grave in Manolos.

'Those things are good,' insisted Cat, with a twinkle in her eye. It felt good to twinkle at a man. She hadn't done it for a while. 'They make the world go round.'

'Not for me.' Will spoke as if he was sure of every word. 'I like it here. And it likes me back.'

This homily neatly hammered nails into the coffin of Cat's tepid daydream of herself and Will. 'I can only do London,' she murmured. 'I can't really cut it in the countryside. It's too big, or something.'

'That's comforting, though.' Will seemed to understand what she meant, yet he didn't laugh, or throw his tea over her. 'Sometimes it's good to feel part of something big and timeless. As if you're a tiny pebble letting the sea wash over you.' He clocked her unconvinced expression. 'Isn't it?'

Now was not the time to share her fear that she had shed her skin on the M25 and neglected to grow another one. 'Yeah,' she fibbed. 'It is.' She raised an eyebrow. 'So you're a philosopher on the side.'

Will didn't laugh. 'Thought we were talking,' he said.

'Oh we were, I just meant . . .' Cat's flirting techniques didn't suit this man. 'Another cup?'

'No, ta. Things to do. Pregnant cows to see.'

Never before, thought Cat watching his broad back recede, had a man used that excuse to escape her company.

26

'Mmm,' said Germaine.

'Oooh yes,' said Mary.

Cat said nothing: her mouth was too full of gooseberry crumble.

Only Sarge was unseduced. 'Early for gooseberries,' she said sulkily.

'They're quite perfect,' mused Beulah, picking up a hairy little green fellow and turning it in the light. 'Our first crop. Quite perfect.'

Wiping her chin, Germaine said 'Guess what, sisters? I've entered us for the county show.'

'Eh?' Mary excavated seconds from the dish. 'Is there a prize for Most Deluded Feminist, then?'

'Not *us*, per se,' said Germaine, a warning rumble in her voice. 'Our produce, specifically our courgettes, Beulah's cake and Dave.'

Sarge shook her head. 'We won't win,' she said emphatically.

'I rely on you to be positive,' said Germaine, with a disappointed mew.

'That vegetable patch is strange,' Sarge continued. 'It has whims. I mean, look at it.' The others obediently looked. It looked like the Somme. 'Half of what we plant fails. We'll never come up with prize-winning courgettes.'

'You're forgetting my carrot,' snapped Germaine.

Tiring of vegetable-related bitching, Cat broke in. 'Dave will win.'

'Do you think you can turn out one of your wonderful sponges for the show, Beulah?' asked Germaine. 'It's in July.'

'I dare say.'

It shocked Cat that Germaine hadn't checked with Beulah before entering her, as if the old lady was as passive as a courgette or a cake.

Cat had been on washing up duty for two days running and was relishing the fact that tonight she could just walk away from the kitchen with her tummy nicely full of Beulah's crumble. 'The parlour's locked!' she said, nonplussed, rattling the doorknob.

Bossily, Germaine elbowed her out of the way and rattled it too, with a demeanour that said *move over and let a real doorknob rattler at it.* 'Oh. So it is.'

'Yes. I *can* tell when a door is locked,' said Cat rattily.

A shout from the other side of the door halted the jostling. 'Just a minute, you guys.'

Only one person in the commune could call the others 'guys' with any credibility.

'What are you up to, Jozette?' called Germaine.

'Come and see!' Jozette opened the door, and let the little herd in.

'Ooh,' purred Antonia, eyes alight. 'It's like a grotto!'

'It needed a little something,' said Jozette, beaming.

Lamps had been press-ganged from the rest of the house, and their shades wrapped in brilliantly coloured scarves. An emerald green Versace square transformed the corner by the window, and the shocking pink scarf over the standard lamp whisked Beulah's usual seat straight to a bordello. A blanket, soft and striped in dusty pinks and hazy blues, was draped over the sofa, and another one, this time a singing scarlet, covered one of the armchairs. The lumpy old furniture was softened, and sweetened, like sadists who'd been through painful therapy to emerge as better people.

The women walked through the door into Oz. Germaine picked

up a fuchsia cushion, and ran her hand across it. 'Where did you find this?'

'That's an old skirt of mine, wrapped and knotted,' said Jozette, shrugging as if she transformed hellholes into luxury pads every day. 'I replaced the curtains. They were a bit bleurgh.'

Cat couldn't have put it better herself. The nondescript beige curtains of an indeterminate age had been bleurgh enough to provoke thoughts of self-harm (especially on the nights Sarge tap-danced). The multicoloured saris hanging in their place were much more like it.

Plonking herself down with her embroidery, Beulah bounced on her new floral cushion. 'I feel quite spoiled,' she said happily, her white curls tinted a brazen pink by the lamp.

'The fire!' Mary pointed at the grate, where a small pile of logs burned.

'That old thing *had* to go.' Jozette pulled a face at the memory of the monstrosity now languishing in an outhouse.

'Did you check the chimney for nests?' Sarge pointed her face as near to Jozette's as the height difference would allow. 'Or avian corpses?'

'Well, no, but it seems OK,' drawled Jozette. 'The weather's getting too warm for a fire anyway.'

'Hmm,' said Sarge, whose glass was not only continually half empty, but contained wee.

The room buzzed with chatter. 'Budge up.' Cat loomed over Mary and Lucy who were sharing the sofa and leafing through Jozette's copy of *Vogue*.

'We're looking for cellulite,' Mary explained, persuading her ample bottom along the seat. She threw an arm around Lucy's shoulders to lean over the glossy pages as Cat insinuated herself at her other side.

'We're not having much luck,' said Lucy wryly. 'The airbrush is a wondrous thing.'

'Yeah,' said Cat, with a grin that stayed resolutely on her lips and refused to tinker with her eyes. That casually slung arm perturbed her. She and Mary were resolutely non-physical: they only kissed each other on the cheek with heavy irony. They left that kind of stuff to other people with shallower friendships. Cat noticed how right that arm looked, how comfortable. And how it excluded her.

The house whistled and sang as the wind found its way in. Sarge stoked the fire and sparks flew up the chimney. 'Oi!' She shouted, straightening up by the fireplace, turning all heads in the room her way. 'I'm going to treat you ladies to a little seminar,' she told them. 'You might thank me for this some day.' She put her hands behind her back and recited, as if recalling a poem from memory, 'Survival in the wild. How to cling to life in inhospitable terrain.'

Mary's head sank on to Lucy's shoulder. Cat's lips pursed. Beulah let loose the smallest of sighs.

'You!' Sarge pointed at Antonia. 'You're abandoned on the hillside, alone, without food or drink. How will you survive?'

'Oh. Erm.' Antonia's eyes were wide.

Mary twisted round to whisper in Cat's ear, 'I'm not sure if Antonia would survive if she was abandoned in the kitchen. Beside the fridge.'

'Shout for help?' offered Antonia, with a self-deprecating gurn.

'And who exactly would hear?' Sarge seemed pleased with this apparently very wrong answer. She bent forward like a penguin. 'You are alone. With only your wits to keep you alive.'

'Oh dear.' Antonia didn't look as if she reckoned her wits much. 'Would I,' she hesitated, 'drink from a mountain stream, maybe?'

'Only if,' said Sarge, 'you'd traced it to its source and checked for sheep cadavers.'

'Right,' said Antonia weakly.

'You!' Sarge swivelled round to point a finger at Jozette. 'It's below freezing and you are exposed! What's your next step?'

'Sweetcakes, that would never happen,' said Jozette. 'I always wear my fake fur when it's cold.'

'It's obvious to me,' said Sarge with some satisfaction, folding her arms across her neat khaki chest, 'that you civilians would make a tasty snack for the vultures in a life or death survival situation.'

'There are vultures in Dorset?' queried Lucy languidly.

'Metaphorical ones, yes,' said Sarge, with a quelling stare.

'So,' clarified Mary, 'we'd be a metaphorical snack?'

Germaine called '*Ma-ry,*' in a dangerous way from the back of the room.

'You're gonna need shelter. You're gonna need food.' Sarge ticked off their requirements on her stubby fingers. 'And you're gonna need water.'

Jozette raised a hand. 'And hair straighteners. Sister, I'm going *nowhere* without my straighteners.'

'Don't play chess with Mother Nature, my friend,' said Sarge. 'You'll always lose. You!' This time Sarge's terrible gaze fell upon Cat. 'How long could you survive without food?'

'Um, a week?' guessed Cat.

'A couple of weeks,' Sarge corrected her. 'Your mental acuity would be impaired and you'd struggle to make decisions, but you'd survive.'

'She's like that,' confirmed Mary, 'when she cuts out carbs'.

'But you can't survive without water.' Sarge made a slitting motion across her throat to underline this fact. 'And who is your best friend?' she yelled suddenly at Beulah.

'Goodness,' said Beulah, in that fluffy way that had stopped convincing Cat. 'Is it God?'

'Nope. Well,' Sarge looked taken aback. 'It could be, I suppose, in a way, but apart from God, it's your knife,' she said with certainty, back on familiar ground. 'Love your knife, ladies.'

The soft chill of the evening had matured into biting cold by bedtime. Cat stepped out to visit Dave, and was surprised to find Antonia by one side of the front door, hugging herself against the night air.

'Oh! Hello there.' Cat smiled encouragingly. Her habit of treating

Antonia like a dopey child was dangerous: one day she would offer her a sweetie or check her pants for dampness. 'What are you doing out here on your own?'

'Thinking. About . . .' Antonia tailed off.

'The kids,' Cat softly ended her sentence for her.

'Cigarettes,' said Antonia.

Surprised, Cat said, 'Right'. She assumed that Antonia always thought about her children. It was certainly all she could talk about. 'I didn't realise you smoked.'

'I don't. Not any more. But some days . . .' She bounced on her heels, and her face looked grim and tight. 'I had to give up. One vice too many.'

'Yeah, right, Snow White,' laughed Cat. 'You're such a sinner.' Leading her over to say hi to Dave, Cat marvelled at Antonia's capacity to hate herself.

27

Day padded after night, and gentle May evaporated, making way for June, who was a lot more brassy. The hill across the way was furry and luminous, the hedgerows as ebullient as Jozette's Afro.

Cat's bob had long since grown out, and she gathered her shoulder-length hair into a ponytail, gratified by its weight bouncing at the nape of her neck. The lifebelt of fat around her midriff would have propelled her straight to the gym in London, but it felt comfortable in the commune. Within such a disparate collection of shapes and sizes, Cat didn't feel odd for carrying a little spare flesh. This, she told herself, is what women look like, and those hags on King's Road shimmying into size zero bandage dresses didn't know what they were missing as they struggled through life without the consolation of Beulah's strawberry pavlova.

The absence of men had started to feel natural. Cat likened it to dieting: after a week or so, tea without sugar tastes just fine. There was a danger in this analogy: Cat's detoxes were followed by a Krispy Kreme binge.

The closest thing to a Krispy Kreme in these parts was Will. Far too wholesome to be a convenience food, Will was more of a carrot cake. (Cat spent more time than was healthy on her analogies.) Cat had always been wary of carrot cake, adhering to a food apartheid where vegetables didn't stray into dessert and fruit kept away from her dinner.

Cat was honest enough to admit privately that she was drawn to Will, that she would have liked to trail her fingers over that heavy, handsome face of his, but her wires short-circuited if the daydream went any further.

Loyalty to Hugh was one hurdle. It makes no sense to be loyal to an ex who has lied and cheated, but reason has little sway over the human heart.

Lack of confidence was another. Will's interest in her had been semaphored so subtly that the merest contemplation led Cat to conclude that she was deluding herself. Yes, even a vet in a down-at-heel seaside town in the back end of nowhere at all had better fish to fry than Cat O'Connor.

And so the days passed in a gentle rhythm of chores and books and walks and Dave-tending. A blip, a moment of excitement so extreme it made her stand up, sit down, stand up again and do a funny walk around the kitchen came in the form of a letter.

'*Quite right,*' her mum wrote. '*Of course you should look your dad up. Here's his address.*'

'*Here's his address?* Just like that. Here's. His. Address. Her mum had known Harry's whereabouts all these years, yet had never mentioned it. Cat gobbled up the address greedily.

She looked up from the letter. She'd expected somewhere exotic: Capri, maybe Mozambique. Not Guildford. There was no going back now. She had to tap her father on the shoulder and say, 'Hi, remember me? I'm the fruit of your loins.' Cat swallowed hard, and looked mutely at Beulah.

'Biccie?'

'Beulah,' said Cat. 'This is a five biccie moment.'

'Group again already,' said Sarge with a sigh.

'Tonight's subject,' said Germaine, in her special Group voice 'is a real individual. Rare and beautiful like a desert bloom. I met this vibrant, special woman through a friend. Through Cat, in fact.'

The tiny silver bells on a chain around Jozette's ankle tinkled an alarum as she uncrossed her legs.

'She's brought colour and life and inspiration to us all. We didn't even know we needed her until she arrived.' Germaine looked at Jozette with the maternal fondness the woman seemed to inspire in everybody. 'She's a long way from home, and the man she chose to make a life with has disappointed her. Jozette da Costa's story is both unique and very ordinary. Let's hear it.'

Enthusiastic applause sounded as Jozette unfolded her long limbs from her chair, like a sexy paperclip coming to life.

'Oh God,' she grinned. 'Oh God oh God oh God. I don't know how to . . .' She looked to Cat, who blew her a kiss. With Jozette such gestures seemed normal and necessary: Cat would have garrotted herself before she blew Mary a kiss.

'Ohhhhh kaaaaaaay. I'm Jozette and this is my, like, story.' Hand on hip, head bent, Jozette made a pretty shape in the middle of the circle. She studied her long dark toes in their gold sandals. She looked up. 'I'm American, but you know that, right?' She threw up her arms as her audience laughed indulgently. 'I'm the token Yank. Ordinary Cuban-Spanish-West-Indian family. Mom and Dad are still together. Spent my childhood out of doors in the Miami sun. I started out modelling.' She threw a dramatic pose. 'I moved to Paris when I was sixteen. That was a blast.'

Eh? That was news to Cat. The aura of glamour around Jozette fizzed even brighter.

'Modelling was kind of ick, to be honest,' said Jozette, that megawatt grin still in place. 'Girls starving themselves. Drugs everywhere. I came to London, because London's where it's at, right?'

'Right!' said Antonia, surprising Cat.

'Got into retail. High-end stuff. Fashion. Did that for ten years. I was with a guy who used to be a model. Kind of loved himself. Nothing much left over for me. Lost a baby. Lost the guy. Became a stylist.'

Whoah, thought Cat, blindsided. The baby was news to her. She stopped smiling but Jozette's beam endured.

'Styling saved my life,' said Jozette, rueful, as if she knew how odd that sounded. 'Making things beautiful, showing women they can look great, whether they're fat or skinny or a teenager or a grandma. It's so satisfying. And I'm kinda good at it.' She shrugged, evidently uneasy with such flagrant auto-trumpet-blowing. 'I got my own flat. The size of a lift. Big for London. I was clean.'

So, thought Cat, there'd been an addiction. More news. Jozette, she concluded with fearless use of hackneyed metaphor, was an iceberg whose tip Cat had only glimpsed.

'Life was cool. This great guy was chasing me.'

Cat had wondered when Trev would enter the story. She lowered her head, relieved that, for the moment at least, her brother was a 'great guy'.

'But I wasn't interested in him. I'd met Trev.'

Ah.

'Trev was . . .' Jozette exhaled and threw her elegant neck back. 'Oh, he was cool. Soooo handsome.' She lifted her head and eyeballed Beulah. 'Believe me, girl, this man is hot.'

'Good, good dear,' said Beulah, shifting in her elasticated slacks. 'That's nice.'

'Washboard stomach. Biceps. Tan all over. Black black hair. You get the picture.'

Lucy put her hand up and said, 'So appearances are very important to you?'

'I guess so.' Jozette didn't seem to catch anything negative in Lucy's question. 'I think everybody's beautiful, though. It's just that Trev is my type.' She shrugged. 'Physically, anyway.'

'Why are you here?' interrupted Germaine, chin forward, intent on the answer.

'I'm here because I came to a dead end.' The smile was still glued on. 'I was trying so hard, but I couldn't get any further. God, I love that man. I cook, I clean, I respect him. And it's all one way.' She slid her tigerish eyes towards Cat. 'Sorry, girl.' Jozette shrugged. 'Trev knows that his big sis is better than him at most stuff. The big job, the fancy boyfriend, the lifestyle, the brains, the common sense.' Jozette shook her head fondly. 'Fool. He thought he couldn't compete. He says that the women in his family got all the balls. He had this recurring nightmare where Cat and their mom came into his room and whittled away his you-know-what with a cheese grater.'

Along with the others, Jozette chuckled, but Cat was stunned. Her brother was *all* balls. He was the one who got to behave exactly as he wanted while she struggled with the 'big job' he sneered at.

'I've been plodding along, picking up clients, saving a little, but Trev refuses to plan a future. He's all, *oh who knows what'll happen* and I'm all *I do! I know! We'll make babies and be happy!* but Trev won't discuss anything properly.'

'How long have you been together?' asked Sarge brusquely.

'Five years. We've lived together for . . .' Jozette pulled an apologetic face. 'Five years. We kinda moved in the night we met.' She waved her arms at the splutters. 'We met in a club. We're clubby people. We're kinda wild. That's how we are. You move in. You suck it and see. I was crazy about him.'

'And he was crazy about you.' Cat had to say it. 'He couldn't stop talking about this amazing girl he'd met. You weren't like anybody else he'd known. You were sexy *and* grown up.' She sighed at the memory. 'You bowled him over.'

'Really?' Jozette's mouth hung open. 'Aw, that's so sweet. Not helpful, when I'm trying to leave the guy, but sweet,' she guffawed.

'If he's so mad about you,' said Sarge gruffly, 'why give in? Why not stick it out, make it work?'

'I'm running out of steam,' admitted Jozette. She was, it hardly needs to be said, still smiling. 'The issues with his family . . .' She glanced at Cat. 'He feels like a heel because he doesn't help out more.'

'Then why,' asked Mary wryly, 'doesn't he help out more?'

'Trev can't cope with the fact that Jon will never get any better.

There are tears for days after he visits. Watching his mum wear herself out kills him. He really envies you, Cat, for your strength.'

The idea of Trev in tears floored Cat. She had seen him cry just the once, when David Beckham was sent off during the World Cup. Jozette had scrambled her perception of her brother, as if Trev was a jigsaw a toddler had stamped on.

'And then,' said Jozette, taking a deep breath as if about to dive in at the deep end of a not-so-clean swimming pool, 'there are the women.' She grinned, really grinned, as if imparting the best news she could imagine: free HobNobs for all. 'Always the women. Tacky sluts. Girls who think it's cute to socialise in a BacoFoil bikini. Silicone-chested bitches who spend their waking hours in tanning booths. That's the kind of girl Trev betrays me with. TV dinners, I call them.'

'You know about them!' gawped Cat.

'Of course I know!' Jozette pulled a face. 'What do you take me for?'

Cat had taken her for an idiot. She saw that now. 'Yeah,' she said in an undertone, 'of course you know.'

'Trev's not exactly Mr Discreet,' laughed Jozette, with detachment that was both admirable and a touch creepy. 'There are love bites, lipstick marks, and finally that phone number in biro on his ass. So, ladies, that's why I'm here. Because my relationship's a mess and because of that, *everything* feels like a mess.' She held up one long-fingered hand. 'I know that's wrong, that I should be strong and all that. But the truth is I love the bastard, and it's destroying me that I can't make him love me back. I guess I have to decide what I want. Is it fidelity? Or is it excitement? Cos Trev still excites me.'

'Does he make you feel good?' asked Mary.

'Damn, you had to ask that,' laughed Jozette. 'No, he makes me feel like that.' She put her forefinger and thumb an inch apart. 'You know something?' she said, still laughing, but shakily. 'I've kind of had enough of this Group thing.'

Jozette left the room.

28

The women knew the symptoms of Post-Group introspection by now, and let Jozette mooch about the next day, running at half her normal speed.

'Did you hear the hoo-ha?' Mary asked Cat as they sat down for elevenses. Well, half-tenses.

'Hoo-ha? No. Do tell.' Cat loved a good hoo-ha.

'Sarge only forgets this is Antonia's day to go to London,' said Mary, eyebrows waggling histrionically. 'And she goes and takes the minibus to Lyme to buy a new rake and Antonia's in hysterics, snot coming out and everything, because it's one of the boys' birthday and if she misses the train she misses the party and her husband'll say "told you so" and he'd given her permission to stay overnight with the kids so in the end she has to get a lift from the man who delivers Dave's hay, you know, the one with the limp.' Mary drew breath.

'Crikey. Top notch hoo-ha.' Cat inclined her head towards the hall. 'That sounds like Sarge now.'

Met by news of her cock-up, Sarge's expression wavered just enough for Cat to surmise that she was furious with herself for letting Antonia down, even though all Sarge said was, 'Oh. Well. Can't be helped.' She sucked her teeth, looking around for somewhere to park her rancour. Her gaze fell on Cat.

Crossing the kitchen to drink noisily from the tap, Sarge said, 'Saw him just now. In Lyme.'

'Saw who?' asked Cat vaguely, counting the jam tarts: she suspected Mary of perfidy.

'Your vet.'

That 'your' was interesting but Cat didn't take the bait. 'Really?'

'Yeah. Told him about Dave's ear.'

'What about Dave's ear?' Cat sat up, the jam tarts forgotten.

'The seepage.' Sarge pointed at her own ear. 'Discoloured discharge.'

The woman sounded like a textbook. Cat imagined her in the throes of orgasm: *Oh God, oh God, I'm concluding the plateau phase of my sexual response cycle!* 'Dave's ear is fine,' insisted Cat, rattled that Dave might be unwell, and more rattled that she hadn't noticed.

'I think you'll find,' said Sarge, 'that Dave's ear is far from fine. I noticed it last night when I visited.'

'Sizing her up for how many chops she'll yield?' Sometimes when Cat was rattled she wasn't all that nice.

Sarge took a moment replying. 'Will is attending in a professional capacity the day after tomorrow about six,' she said, and left the room.

Cat went out to the sty and discovered that Sarge was right. The inside of Dave's left ear was red and angry looking. 'Will'll cure you,' she cooed into Dave's other ear. Then, more quietly, 'why didn't you tell me she visits you?'

The letter containing Harry's address pulsed gently in Cat's pocket. Neurotically, she patted it hourly. It spent its nights in her shoe, by the side of her bed. Cat had anticipated an internet search when she got back to normality, hours poring over a keyboard with a pencil stuck in her ponytail, knee deep in scribbled notes. This was too easy.

'*All this time,*' she wrote to her mum, '*you actually had his address?*' She didn't add 'and never told us', it felt gratuitous.

It amazed Cat that Harry could live in Guildford, an hour away by car, and never visit them. Never see Jon. Did she really want to hear what such a man had to say?

Yes, she really did. The problem lay in what Cat had to say. The drafts of her letter to Harry sounded wrong. There was the timid version that began *I hope you don't mind*, the bombastic one (*As you obviously have no intention of getting in touch with your only daughter I'll have to be the one to do all the work)* and the weirdly formal one that ended *Thanking you for your time, and looking forward to a prompt reply.*

None of them fitted her brief. She'd have publicly crucified any copywriter who'd produced them. 'I need to be mature, approachable, non-resentful, sensitive, keen.'

That wasn't as easy as it sounded. And it didn't sound particularly easy. Cat screwed up another piece of paper. The sun was setting in the distance, rolling out a faded pink carpet that reached all the way to Cat at the kitchen table. The room felt so comfortable and safe, and yet Cat struggled with her task.

Emerging from the pantry, Beulah caught the tail end of a tut. 'Having trouble?' she asked.

'It's this letter.' Cat hesitated. 'The one, you know, to my dad. I don't know what to say.'

'Be plain,' said Beulah, flouring the marble slab.

'Yeah, well . . .' Cat recalled doling out the same advice to her team: why had nobody thrown a laptop at her? 'That's fine if you know what you want to say.'

'What do you want to say?' Beulah held up a floury, rather fat finger. 'No. No thinking. Just say it to me.'

'Hello, Dad, it's about time we saw each other. If you don't want to I'll understand, but I'd love to meet you.'

'There you go then.' Beulah slapped down a springy dollop of dough and proceeded to pester it.

*

'It'll be better than lying around here like walruses,' said Sarge. She wasn't a natural saleswoman.

'I don't feel like going to meet Antonia,' said Cat. The ghost had been on top form last night, gargling through the small hours: the lack of sleep was catching up with Cat. She guessed that Sarge was trying to make amends to Antonia for forgetting to take her to the station the previous morning.

'Oh come on,' nagged Mary, shrugging on a glittery bolero of Jozette's. 'Antonia will be chuffed to see us. It was her son's birthday. Play nice.' She frowned down at her herself. 'Does this bolero make my arms look fat?'

'No,' said Sarge, 'they *are* fat.' Briskly, she herded everybody like so many recalcitrant sheep into the minibus.

Passing Germaine on the doorstep, Cat chided her to hurry up. 'Sarge'll have your guts for rather messy garters if you don't get on the bus.'

'Not going.' Germaine tried to look disappointed. 'Accounts to do.'

'Never thought I'd envy anybody that,' said Cat in an undertone.

'Is that the letter to your dad?' Germaine nodded at the envelope in Cat's grasp. She narrowed her eyes. 'You all right, Cat? I'm always here, you know.' Germaine ignored the insolent blare of the minibus horn. 'Not as your leader.' Germaine used the word unselfconsciously. 'As your friend.'

'I know,' said Cat.

'Don't think about giving up,' said Germaine, urgently. 'I need you. We need you.'

'Like we said before, we're a patchwork by now.' Cat was uncomfortable with the notion of being more important than any of the others. 'Remove one of us and the design is ruined.' She squeezed Germaine around her middle. 'Nobody's going anywhere, Germy. Well,' she corrected herself. 'We're all going to the station. But,' she winked, 'we'll be back.'

Feeling the need for silence, Cat sat beside Lucy, who said nothing the whole way. Behind them, Mary and Jozette whooped and yowled like prisoners just released from solitary, each hedge cause for comment and hilarity. The van reached the station just as the train was pulling in, and Sarge leapt out like a stuntwoman.

Trailing behind the others, Cat detoured to a postbox. She held on to the envelope for an extra moment, then with a whispered 'Get a grip, Flowerpot' she released it into the wild.

The others were muttering, hen-like, on the short platform when she joined them. A handful of people had disembarked, none of them Antonia.

'Funny.' Sarge strode up and down the platform, her boots cracking out a tango. 'She would have called to say she'd missed it, surely?'

'She's a bit of a flake,' Mary reminded them.

'But,' argued Sarge, her characteristic frown corrugating her forehead, 'she knew I or Germaine would collect her.'

'And,' Cat took up the line of thought, 'Antonia would rather die than put somebody out.'

'Perhaps she'll be on the next one,' suggested Lucy.

'Perhaps she's staying another night in London,' offered Beulah.

'Perhaps she's dead.' Mary, bored, cut to the chase.

Nobody could supply a mobile phone. Cat and Mary shared a look of marvel at this: back in Fulham they'd been superglued to their mobiles, suffering pangs of withdrawal worthy of a crack whore if they left them on the hall table.

There was, declared Sarge, no option but to drive back to the commune, find Antonia's number and call her to see what had gone awry.

'But we were going to have a cappuccino in Lyme!' whimpered Mary. 'An actual *cappuccino*, for God's sake!'

The minibus had a deflated air. Cat was drawn into a game of I Spy. 'Farms?'

'Nope,' said Mary.

'Fronds?' was Lucy's guess.

'Nope,' said Mary.

'Foliage?' tried Beulah.

'Give up? I'll tell you,' beamed Mary. 'Fuck all.'

'You weren't long,' said Germaine, not sounding entirely pleased. A brief confab confirmed that Antonia hadn't rung the house. A call to her mobile clicked straight to answerphone. Germaine was all at sea: she hated it when the world threw her a curveball.

'Call her ex,' said Lucy decisively. 'See what time she left.'

'I don't like to.' Germaine bit her thumbnail. 'The man is such a beast.'

Sighing, Cat urged her to follow Lucy's advice. 'He's just a man. A horrible man, but a man. He's the only one who can tell us when to expect her.' She was impatient with Germaine's preposterous anti-man bias at such a juncture. 'Go *on,* Germy.'

Germy did go on. The others clustered around her as she dialled on the heavy old phone, leaning towards her like felled corn in a field.

After some cool niceties, Germaine asked Paul, 'I'm trying to get hold of Antonia. Is she still with you?'

'Still with me?' echoed Paul irritably.

The women exchanged knowing looks: Paul was confirming his bad guy rep.

'The boys have been crying non-stop since yesterday, asking where Mummy is,' he continued bitterly. 'Pity she had to choose George's birthday for her no-show. If you see her, tell her thanks from me.'

The phone line died to a purr. The kettle went on. Grave expressions were assumed.

'So the last we saw of her,' said Germaine after some input from the women, 'she was going out to the gate at 10 a.m. yesterday to get in the hay man's van?'

'Never liked the look of that hay man,' said Mary darkly.

Beulah shook her head. 'He's a perfectly decent chap,' she declared.

'He has a limp,' said Mary knowingly.

Sarge backed her up. 'Inside every man lurks a—'

'Yes, all right,' said Germaine hurriedly. 'We know, dear, every man is a monster but let's not get sidetracked. I really don't think the hay man kidnapped Antonia, his van has an RAC sticker.'

Uncertain about this logic, Cat agreed that the hay man was no Jack the Ripper. She had a different theory. 'Antonia's very fragile,' she said anxiously. 'It's much more likely that she had some kind of breakdown and couldn't face the birthday party.'

'That does sound likely,' agreed Lucy.

'Yeah,' said Mary, nodding in unison with her. 'The children's expectations could have sent her over the edge.'

'Great,' said Jozette wryly. 'She could be anywhere. Do we call the cops?'

'They wouldn't take it seriously,' said Lucy.

'They might,' countered Jozette.

Putting it to the vote, the women decided to wait.

29

The evening dragged its feet. The days were longer now, and it seemed an age before shadows claimed the kitchen and the oil lamp was lit. It was impossible to settle to anything, and each attempt at conversation around the table inevitably drifted back to a fresh theory about Antonia's whereabouts.

'She could be with friends. Has she ever mentioned anybody?'

'If she was in hospital they'd contact Paul.'

'Amnesia? Maybe she got a bang on the head.'

The only concrete fact was her empty chair. Absent, Antonia made a bigger impact on the community than her presence ever had.

Midnight was the turning point. They all agreed: time to involve the police.

'I for one will *not* be able to sleep while that poor woman is out there somewhere, God knows where,' shuddered Germaine as Jozette put out the light in the dormitory. By the time Jozette's bare soles had slapped along the boards to bed, Germaine was snoring like a grizzly.

Desultory chat broke out among the others who, although they hadn't advertised the fact, truly couldn't sleep. There was a tacit agreement not to mention Antonia, whose various possible fates they'd exhausted. The police officer on the other end of the phone had taken down details in a disappointingly nonchalant manner, advised them not to worry and promised to send an officer along in the morning.

'Let's play I Spy again!' suggested Mary enthusiastically.

'It's pitch black in here.' Cat was bone weary.

Undeterred, Mary ploughed on. 'I spy with my little eye,' she began, a vivid voice in the darkness, 'something beginning with—'

'AAAAAARGH!'

Everybody, even Germaine, sat bolt upright.

'EUUUUURGH!'

Mary leapt like a goat from her bed to Cat's. 'The ghost's never been that loud before,' she gibbered, her elbows and heels coming into contact with various soft bits of Cat.

'It sounds angry,' whispered Jozette. 'Like it's coming to get us.'

'Oh shush,' said Lucy, stuffing her feet into slippers. 'It's time we faced it,' she said, provoking a chorus of 'WHA-A-T?' and 'Are you mad?'

'I'm staying here, sugar.' Even the threat of an unfettered soul bent on revenge couldn't erase the smile from Jozette's voice, but it shook. 'You go if you want.'

'I'll come,' said Beulah, as casually as if a shopping trip had been mooted. She heaved herself out of bed with a groan. 'Some things have to be faced up to. They may not be as bad as you think.'

'Count me in.' Cat disentangled herself from Mary: she wouldn't let Beulah go up there without her. 'It's chosen the wrong night to misbehave. I'm all fired up about Antonia. How bad can it be?'

'WHAAAAAAAARGH!'

'Jesus Mary and Joseph,' shrieked Mary. 'It's the undead. Isn't that fecking bad enough?'

'Maybe if we confront it, it'll move on,' suggested Cat, her *Buffy the Vampire Slayer* addiction coming in handy for the first time ever.

'Or maybe,' Mary countered, 'it'll reach out cold dead fingers to throttle youse all,'

'Ma-*ry*.' Lucy sounded like an affectionate but no-nonsense Sunday school teacher.

'Sorry,' said Mary meekly, a word that Cat rarely managed to wrench out of her.

After much whispered squabbling and goading and prodding, a delegation of four left the dormitory. Cat, Lucy, Beulah and Sarge all tiptoed up the short flight of uneven stairs that led to the turret room.

'NOOOOOOO!'

The quartet stopped dead and looked at each other, their faces pale blurs in the darkness. Cat cursed Germaine's penny-pinching refusal to light the stairs. 'It sounds furious,' she hissed, grabbing Lucy's arm.

'Or sad.' Lucy un-prised her fingers. 'Are we ready, ladies?'

'GO! GO! GO!' roared Sarge, seizing control as a true control freak must. She led the charge, shouldering open the turret room door.

Adrenalin lent Cat courage and she barged in to stand alongside Sarge, feet apart, breathing heavily, taking in the octagonal room.

It stank. Cat's nose processed the bitter, musty smell before she saw their ghost. Antonia lay thrown back across the filthy mattress, her face as white as the spirit they'd anticipated, her ashy hair floating in a tangled halo about her head.

Upended bottles littered the room. Antonia grasped one to her, the dregs bleeding on to the crumpled gingham dress she'd left the house in.

'She's intoxicated,' said Sarge.

'Gee, you don't say.' Cat edged nearer to Antonia, who had started to laugh, a maniacal clucking familiar from many sleepless nights. Cat knelt beside her. 'Antonia,' she said softly.

Antonia leapt as if goosed with a hot poker. 'YOUUUUUU!' she howled, waggling a finger at Cat. 'YOU RUINED MY LIFE!'

'No, no, I really didn't,' said Cat soothingly. 'We're taking you downstairs, Antonia.'

'Yes,' said Sarge, peeved at being usurped. 'We're taking you downstairs.' She elbowed Cat out of the way, and slid her arms under Antonia's torso.

'SHE'S KILLING ME!' bellowed Antonia, spectacularly finding her voice after months of mousiness.

'Let us help,' said Lucy, pulling a face at the spectacle of petite Sarge hoisting Antonia's dead weight.

'No need,' puffed Sarge, rising unsteadily, Antonia in her arms creating a wall of sound Phil Spector would covet.

All those push-ups paid off. Sarge clomped down the stairway and deposited Antonia on her own mattress, ignoring the others huddled like shipwrecked sailors on another bed.

'*That's* our ghost?' Mary sounded disappointed.

The women gathered around Antonia, who was belching and wailing on her catacomb. Suddenly, with one impressive snore she fell asleep as if drugged.

'I think,' said Lucy eventually, 'we may have misjudged Paul.'

'Yeah,' said Jozette, sounding awestruck. 'She's no teetotaller.'

'So hang on. Am I getting this right?' Mary was frowning. 'Antonia didn't go anywhere? She didn't get in the hay man's van? The hay man didn't kill her?' She'd been rather attached to that theory.

'And we don't have a ghost,' said Jozette, softly, bending over to push Antonia's damp, matted hair off her forehead. 'Just as I was getting used to it.'

Germaine turned to Beulah. 'Should we call a doctor?'

'No need.' Beulah had struggled down on to her well cushioned knees and was pulling a thin eiderdown over Antonia. 'If we let her rest, and keep her topped up with liquids, she'll sober up, poor woman.'

'Who would have guessed timid little Antonia could fool us all?' Mary asked wonderingly, staring at the prone woman, impressed and horrified. 'All that *just a water for me thank you* and *oh no I couldn't* if you waved a wine box anywhere near her.'

'She's an addict,' said Lucy, matter-of-factly. 'They're cunning.'

Beulah offered to sit beside Antonia until morning. 'She's in another world at the moment, but when she comes to it'll be reassuring to see a familiar face.'

'Don't you mean humiliating?' Lucy stroked her chin. 'We all know her little secret now.'

'Secrets,' sighed Beulah, taking Antonia's hand as she settled herself awkwardly on a rickety chair. 'Who hasn't got one of those? Luckily for Antonia,' she said quietly and deliberately, 'she's in a feminist commune and won't be judged harshly.'

A memory, clear like a carved cameo, distracted Cat. She remembered seeing Beulah hand Antonia a pill one morning after the ghost's shenanigans. *You knew*, she thought. *You clever old dame, you knew all along.*

Sarge waved the women away, like a police officer at the scene of an accident. 'Can't we judge her a bit?' asked Mary hopefully, clambering into bed. 'I quite enjoy judging.'

Next morning the house was as sombre as a cathedral. Antonia hadn't emerged, although an ear against the dormitory door was rewarded with faint puppy-like whimpers.

Trudging in from the garden, Germaine threw a sweet potato on the table. 'There,' she said, tired. 'Latest offering from the veggie patch.'

'It's fantabulous,' said Cat obediently, noting that Germaine was running on empty. 'Sit down, Germy,' she said, offering her a chair.

'What? Oh. No thanks.' Germaine sat down heavily, her legs apart. 'I can't get my head round this at all,' she said unhappily. 'Why didn't I notice? Too busy—' Germaine cut herself short, a bitter twist to her lip.

'None of us noticed.' Mary was breezy. 'Don't blame yourself.'

Germaine squashed a pea into the grain of the table. 'Sarge has made a suggestion,' she said, drably. 'A new rule.' She hesitated. 'No more wine,' she said eventually.

'What? Never?' Mary's hand went to her throat, genuinely shocked, as if Germaine had mooned at her.

'It's to show solidarity with Antonia.'

'She hasn't shown much solidarity with us,' said Mary slowly, cobbling together a case for the defence: Mary and wine had been through a lot together.

'It's a lovely idea,' said Cat decisively. It wasn't, it was a horrible idea, but it was a decent thing to do.

'Well, whatever . . .' Germaine had sloughed off her authority, her shoulders round and defeated.

Nature abhors a vacuum: Sarge stepped up to the ocky. Now she materialised in the doorway, fresh from bedside duty, barking 'Out, out, the lot of you!' imperiously. She was wearing her Aviator shades, which usually meant trouble. 'I need the phone and some privacy. Important business related to the current emergency.' Her hands went to their rightful place, her hips, when nobody moved. 'OUT!'

30

Holding the shard of bathroom mirror at this angle and that, Cat squinted at her features.

The one blue eye she could see was bright, the white clearer than she remembered. And her cheek was touched with a new pink. Cat looked well.

Even her hair was responding positively to the idiosyncratic rules of the commune spa. Nowadays its shape was as God intended, the expensive bob a memory. Shiny and swingy, it enjoyed fewer washes, less product and less inexpert attention from the hairdryer.

'Not so bad,' concluded Cat, with a sneaky smile. Angling the mirror to see how Jozette's emerald green silk tunic looked over her jeans she gasped at the little roll of happy flesh around her waist. 'Beulah,' whispered Cat. 'Beulah and her scones.' It was hard to dislike a part of her body created entirely by pleasure but Cat made a mental note to hold her tummy in. And her sides. And, somehow, her back.

Creeping to the dormitory, Cat peeked in. Antonia slumbered on, like a marble martyr, albeit one stinking of booze. Her bedside was a place of pilgrimage, the women kneeling at it, asking gently if she needed anything. There was never a reply. Antonia's sore, crêpey eyes were shut, her hands on her chest, her breath stertorous. Lucy stayed away, Mary visited out of duty, but Cat felt drawn to Antonia, who seemed to be under a wicked witch's spell, just out of their reach.

'The vet's here,' called Lucy from the hall.

'Oh? Really? Right. Six o'clock already? OK.' Trying to sound blasé while speeding down bare wooden boards in heels is tricky. Cat scooted out of the front door, into the fading light. At the gate stood Will, in a black dinner jacket and a bow tie.

'Crikey,' laughed Cat, reaching up to unlock the gate. 'Vets in London don't dress up for house calls.'

'It's the Dorset Veterinary Association annual dinner and dance later.' Will curled his lip and ran an awkward hand over his silky lapel. 'Do I look like an idiot?'

'Not at all.' Cat tried not to lick her lips. Will looked wonderful. He'd stepped straight from a fantasy she didn't even know she had. Broad shoulders in dark suiting, crisp white collar against a newly shaved jaw line – most men are improved by a tux, but it helps if the raw material is six foot four with, corny but true, eyes of blue. 'You look very smart.' Cat recalled the dinner jackets in Hugh's wardrobe. Royal blue silk, black wool, ivory merino. Her knees had buckled whenever he'd worn one. 'If men knew how women feel about dinner jackets they'd wear one every day.'

'Right.' Will shot her a slight frown, the sort of look Cat might bestow on a dishevelled woman shouting non sequiturs on a bus. 'May I . . .?'

Jumping out of his way, Cat let him in and tried to match his long stride over to Dave's sty. She'd just experienced, she was fairly sure, a rebuff of some sort. Oh, how she longed for London's horrid nightlife with its well defined rules of flirting. Basically, if somebody gave you a lecherous once-over on the dance floor, then bought you a tequila slammer, he was yours.

Not that Hugh would have been caught dead in a club. He'd opted for the long lunch method, lingering looks over the Cristal and an impassioned declaration over the sorbet.

His black trousers tucked into wellies, Will stopped abruptly at Dave's door.

'What the . . .?'

'Oh yes. Dave's had the decorators in.'

'It's very pink,' said Will carefully, once again treating Cat like the aforementioned woman on the bus. His face puckered. 'I have literally never seen anything like this before.'

'It's just some paint. And some gilding. And some fairy lights.' Cat followed Will's line of sight to the opposite wall. 'Oh, and a watercolour portrait, obviously.'

'The artist has certainly caught her essential Dave-ness.' Will seemed to teeter between laughing and making for the hills. 'Do you usually dress like that –' he gestured at her silken fluted sleeves – 'to tend to animals?'

Cat folded her arms. 'Do you?'

'Good point.' Will's features relaxed into a grin. Each fresh expression transformed his face utterly. He looked about seven as he beamed at her. 'Look, if Dave likes it and you like it, it's none of my business. It's just that it's the fanciest sty I've ever seen.' He shook his head as Dave dipped her brawny head in the golden trough. 'By quite some margin.'

Putting down his bag, Will approached Dave. Familiar with her physician by now, Dave didn't complain as he gently took her under the chin and tilted her head towards him.

'Big do tonight, is it?' asked Cat.

'Yes, unfortunately.' Will squatted beside the pig, intent on her ear. 'Bit gruesome. Not my kind of thing.'

The squat had produced a tension between Will's trousers and Will's bottom that wasn't lost on Cat. She gulped and fiddled with a lock of her hair. 'Really? What is your kind of thing?' She must look away from his bottom or he'd catch her. *Look away! Look away! Or he'll catch . . .*

He caught her. Another funny look, before Will recovered to say, straightening up, 'I'm more of a pub man.'

'Me too. Well, a pub woman.' Cat hated pubs. She'd been relieved that Hugh was a wine bar man. A *champagne* bar man. 'A pint of, erm, best and a packet of pork scratchings and I'm happy.' Cat realised what she'd said. 'Sorry Dave,' she added.

'I'm sure Dave's English is poor,' said Will. 'Her feelings are safe.' He peered into Dave's ear, using a pen-shaped torch. 'Ooh, that was a nasty infection, girl,' he said, in a low soothing voice. 'You're over the worst,' he continued, in a kind of deep register coo that Cat rather liked. 'You're a fine figure of a pig, aren't you?' He tousled Dave's gingery topknot. 'Aren't you, gorgeous?'

'Crikey, get a room, you two,' said Cat.

Will didn't laugh. He laughed, Cat noticed, when she didn't make a joke, but remained straight-faced if she attempted one.

'The infection is waning, and I don't want to prescribe any unnecessary drugs. I'm glad you got me in though, because we should keep an eye on that ear. It's likely to be prone to other infections from now on and some of them can be quite distressing.' He slapped Dave's fat pink back. 'You're looking after her very well. Shall I check the chickens while I'm here? I assume they're responding well to the coccidiosis treatment?'

Will knew the drill. He dashed down the hall that ran from the back door to the kitchen, Cat at his heels. 'Dead man walking!' he muttered, whipping through the kitchen in his finery.

Behind him, Cat nodded at the face that Beulah pulled as they passed her at the sink. It was the same look that Beulah used when she iced a cake or took a tray of muffins from the Aga, a look that said 'Yum yum'.

Scuttling to keep up in her heels, Cat chased Will to the hen house. He'd seen the chickens' whimsical lodgings before and didn't comment, although she spotted the hint of a smile at Jobird wedged in a Gothic doorway.

'Come on, ladies,' he encouraged them. 'The doctor will see you now.'

Naughty fate decreed that he pick up Hencat first. Cat wrapped her arms around herself and slid her palms over the sleek fabric of her top as Will took a firm grip on her namesake and turned her over. He stroked her feathers and murmured, 'Lovely, just lovely,' almost to himself.

A thought, a daring one, occurred to Cat. Her words tumbled out in a juvenile rush: 'I could come with you, if you like, to this do, you know, it might be nice, if it's so awful, to take someone, kind of thing.' She rolled her eyes enthusiastically like a children's TV presenter. 'I mean, God, they can be sooo boring. We could, you know, take the mickey, have a drink, do some gimpy dancing.' Mentally she rummaged through Jozette's wardrobe and stopped at a black sparkling spaghetti-strapped gown that promised the requisite vet-enslaving qualities. 'I could be ready in ten minutes.' *Make-up*, she reminded herself. 'Fifteen.'

Will had moved on to Maryhen. He was gazing deep into the chicken's eyes, like a lover. 'Actually,' he said slowly, concentrating, 'I'm taking my girlfriend.'

'Of course you are. Good. Great. Have a great time. That's great. Great.' Cat's vocabulary had disappeared up her swollen embarrassment gland. 'Great great great. Are the hens OK? Great. You'll want to be off. Mustn't keep the little lady waiting!'

Little lady? marvelled Cat: who used phrases like that? Mortified twats, that's who, she concluded as she led Will at a gallop back up the hall and out into the courtyard.

'I'll . . .' The embarrassment was contagious. Will bit his lip and backed towards his Land Rover, nodding and shrugging instead of talking. 'It would have been . . .'

'Yup.' Cat dug her hands down the front pockets of her jeans, hunched with humiliation. 'See you.'

'Absolutely,' said Will with a shot of energy as he neared his vehicle, the joy of escape written all over his handsome, heavy face. 'See you. For sure.' He jumped in, flung his case on to the back seat and tore off down the lane.

*

'Germaine,' said Cat menacingly, 'I need that wine.'

Backed into a corner of the larder, Germaine wrapped one of the eight shawls she was wearing more tightly around her. 'We agreed,' she averred, as if that ended the matter.

'Wine!' Cat bordered on feral. 'Wine!'

'There was a democratic decision to support Antonia. I've hidden the wine. Rules are rules. Where would we be if we just ignored them?'

'We'd be drinking wine!'

'Do you really think a glass of wine is the best thing for you when you're in this . . . this . . .' Germaine studied her anxiously, 'this strange state of mind?'

'Of course not. I need at least a bottle.'

'I'm sorry but—' Germaine stopped abruptly and looked over Cat's head.

Beulah stood in the larder doorway, the sputtering oil lamp in the kitchen beyond making her outline shift and dance, like an apparition. Her apron was floury and she held a warm pie in an oven mitt. 'You can make an exception just this once, can't you, Germaine?' she said, in a voice that was every bit as gentle as usual, but with a squeeze of lemon. 'It'll go nicely with this pie I baked with our home-grown rhubarb.' If there was such a thing as a cosy threat, Beulah managed it.

After a moment's chewy silence, Germaine muttered 'Just this once,' and barged past them both.

'How'd you do that?' Cat lifted her eyes from her embarrassment. 'Are you a Jedi or something?'

'A what, dear?' Beulah ambled over to the table and set the pie on a cooling tray.

'That was mind-melding.' Cat puzzled over what had just transpired above her head.

'Don't be silly,' chided Beulah gently.

'But . . .'

'Go and enjoy your wine,' advised Beulah.

*

Enjoying wasn't quite the word. Throwing her head back to tip the fruity red liquid down her throat, Cat closed her eyes against the taste. It was vile stuff and she deserved it. She wasn't bothered about the wine's bouquet, nor its base notes, she simply needed its alcohol content.

And Mary. She needed Mary to get drunk with her. Mary would understand.

'I don't understand,' said Mary, cross legged on the sofa, slopping wine into a mug. 'Why didn't you check whether he had a girlfriend?' It felt wrong to be in the parlour before dinner. 'I mean, he's not bad looking, it's not out of the question.'

'He's *good* looking,' corrected Cat with a hint of huff. 'Very.'

'All the more reason to suspect he's spoken for.' Mary sipped the wine and shuddered. 'Oooh, that's revolting,' she said pouring more into the mug. She stared at it. 'Should we be doing this? It feels mean, with Antonia lying up there, sleeping it off.'

'Yes, you're right,' sighed Cat, regarding her glass with a jaundiced eye. She hesitated for a moment, then slammed it down. 'God, Mary, you've even taken the pleasure out of getting rat-arsed. Have I nothing left?'

Awarding a raised eyebrow – quite an unruly one, Mary seemed to have given up the tweezer – to such melodrama, Mary asked, amused, 'Since when did you ask blokes out? You prefer them to do the running.'

'Maybe the feminist ethos is rubbing off on me.' Cat laughed mirthlessly.

'Or maybe you're feckin' desperate.'

'Well, yeah, there is that.'

'Is he a sticking plaster? Over your Hugh wound?'

'Hugh who?' That's not easy to say: Cat needed two attempts.

'You need twice as long as you went out with him to get over him.'

'Eight years!' yipped Cat. 'I'll be forty . . . something by then.'

'Them's the rules.'

'I thought it was half as long as you went out with him.'

The women exchanged puzzled glances about the science of love.

'He's still there, in the background,' admitted Cat reluctantly. 'Like a car alarm going off in the next street.' She slumped back against the cushions. 'I've never smoked but I imagine it's like trying to give up.'

'We all miss somebody but we don't go around asking random fellas out.'

Stung, Cat jabbed a finger in Mary's direction. 'Oi! I'm not *going around* and Will is not random.'

'He's the only man we ever see. Not exactly picky.'

'I thought there was something between us.' Cat executed a perfect Elvis sneer. 'There is: he thinks I'm an idiot. And so do I.'

'We're only here for a few months. There'd be no future in it.'

'It's a here and now I'm after,' moaned Cat. 'What do you think his girlfriend is like?'

'Country born and bred,' said Mary immediately, her complete ignorance of the woman in no way hampering her ability to describe her. 'Perm.'

'Blouse tucked into jeans.'

'*Stonewash* jeans,' said Mary with grim satisfaction.

'Barbour,' said Cat, '*d'accord*.'

'She'll be in taffeta tonight. Lots of ruffles.'

'Too much blusher.' Cat could see Will's other half plain as day, a gauche girl who favoured practicality over fashion. 'I wonder what the "do" will be like,' she said, a hint of wickedness in her voice that Mary instantly picked up on.

'Prawn cocktail to start.'

'Steak and all the trimmings.'

'Black forest gateau.'

'Then a local band.'

'Or Don's Disco.'

Their sarcastic laughter dwindled to a shared sigh.

'Actually,' said Cat, 'it sounds nice.'

'Imagine Hugh at Don's Disco. He'd never knowingly stand within ten yards of a prawn cocktail.'

'He *is* a bit of a snob.' The truth juice was weaving its magic.

'A bit, yeah.' Mary relished the understatement. 'I used to wonder what he saw in you, he was so snooty.'

'Thank you *very* much.'

'I'm not saying you're common,' Mary reassured her. 'But you're ordinary. I . . .' She paused. 'Let's face it, he would never have married you in a million years, wife or no wife.'

'Oh do carry on with the making me feel better,' deadpanned Cat. 'It's going so well.'

'It's not that he doesn't, didn't, oh shit whatever, *love* you. But he's a realist. Hugh is a certain sort of man, a Belgravia type. And you . . . aren't. A Belgravia man marries somebody well connected, with the same accent as him, and an inheritance. It's how come that sort live so well. His heart might choose you, but his head would always choose a Right Honourable. He's no fool.'

'Selfish, you mean.'

Mary didn't contradict her.

'What made me think,' whispered Cat, 'that I could obliterate a man like that with a bloody vet? Will's so *ordinary*. He's a pub man, he said. He'd never take me to the sort of places I went to with Hugh.'

'If you're so fond of those places you could take *him*.'

'Nah. Will wouldn't get it. He's not sophisticated. I'd be bored with him in ten minutes flat.' Cat recalled how Hugh had charmed clients with his idiosyncratic wit. Hugh was unpredictable: talking to him was like taking a freezing shower, it sent all her senses tingling.

'The way I remember it,' Mary said carefully, 'Hugh hardly ever took you anywhere. In case you were seen.'

From upstairs came a shout, a lilting cry of 'Ma-ry!'

'Gotta go.' Mary put her glass down and jumped up. 'Lucy and I are rota-ed to clear out the turret room.'

'Mustn't keep the rota waiting.' Cat looked at the closed door for a long while after Mary had gone through it.

31

Flat and colourless in the centre of the Goddess circle, Antonia resembled a cardboard cut-out that has stood too long in a building society window. Feet together, hands clasped, head down, she was a picture of blameless, toothless femininity.

Group felt more like bear-baiting than ever. Cat noticed the tremble in Antonia's hands, whether from withdrawal or fear she couldn't tell, and hoped the others would be gentle with her.

The preamble over – Germaine had used words like 'afflicted' and 'challenged', avoiding 'blotto' or 'sozzled' – an expectant silence fell over the room. Tea had been sipped, cardigans tugged at, comfortable positions found.

Stock still, Antonia allowed the silence to stretch and swell.

Cat coughed. Mary began to tap her foot against a rung of her chair.

'So,' said Lucy lightly, 'are you an alcoholic?'

'No!' Antonia spoke at last. 'Of course not. Really, no, I'm not.' She shook ratty hair, unwashed and sweaty looking, out of her eyes. 'I just drink at the wrong times, that's all. I can't hold my drink.'

'Mary and I cleared twenty-three bottles of vodka out of the turret room. Rather large bottles.' Lucy put no weight on her words, but they threatened to crush Antonia all the same. 'And a bucket of urine.'

Her face caved in, and Antonia's long hands flew to her eyes, the knuckles red and knotty. 'That's disgusting. I'm not like that.'

Leaning forward, her necklace of stars and moons jangling, Jozette asked, 'Tell us what you *are* like, hon.' She smiled, her slanted eyes sad and wondering. 'Cos we'd like to know.'

'I've been feeling very low. Very depressed,' said Antonia haltingly. She was guarded, not in the least confessional. Cat guessed she was gauging how little she could reveal, not how much.

'Alcohol,' said Sarge, 'is a depressant.'

'Well, yes, but . . .' Antonia sighed. 'This isn't fair. I want to go back upstairs.'

'To drink yourself to death?' asked Sarge.

Germaine was gentler. 'Don't you owe us some insight into your situation? You weren't entirely truthful during the first Group. We understand why, but it's time to be upfront.'

Mary had a two-penn'orth in every situation and she contributed it now. 'How could you let us believe in the ghost?' she asked truculently. 'You made fools of us.'

'I didn't mean to,' said Antonia, petulantly. 'The first time I, you know,' she gestured limply with her hands, unable to describe her noisy hobby. 'Well, everybody just assumed the noises came from the ghost. I didn't actually lie.'

'Oh come now.' Lucy was having none of that.

'We fooled ourselves, guys.' Jozette shrugged. 'Thinking back, why the hell didn't we just go up to the frigging room and check it out?'

Mary groaned. 'We actually took Jamie's word for something.'

There were titters at this, and an 'I wouldn't trust Jamie to find his bum with his hands' from Sarge, which Germaine cut short with a regal, 'Let's not drag outsiders into this, ladies. Perhaps you'd be so kind as to let Antonia speak.'

More silence, before a small 'I missed George's birthday.' Antonia drew a long, scratchy breath that sounded painful. 'I couldn't face it. A house full of people. They all knew about me. They all knew his own mother hadn't organised his party, wasn't allowed to.' She seemed about to dissolve into tears but instead she ploughed on. 'I've always drunk,' she said, animated for the first time. 'I was fourteen when I had my first glass of wine. I've been drunk for all the important moments in my life. When Paul proposed I was woozy. When I got married. When I conceived the boys.'

'But,' Mary was puzzled, 'you're not exactly a quiet drunk, love. Didn't anybody notice?'

'I could handle myself for a long, long while.' Antonia turned to face her, and her eyes were avid. Her voice grew louder. 'Nobody knew. You'd be amazed how secretive I can be, how easy it is to blend into the woodwork. I kept getting worse and nobody noticed.'

'Nobody saw you,' said Lucy quietly.

'I was able to keep things afloat.' Antonia shuddered. 'It was so hard. I couldn't tell Paul. And my mother . . .' Antonia made a helpless gesture. 'I drank on my own, during the day, while the boys napped. When Paul got home I pulled myself together enough to, well, function, I suppose.' She stopped, looking around the room horrified, as if she'd just tuned into what she was saying. 'You don't want to hear this.'

'We do,' said Beulah, surprising everybody. She was generally silent at Group. 'It's time, dear.'

'Things got . . . a little out of control.' Antonia's face suggested a home movie playing behind her eyes that was singularly lacking in heart-warming moments.

'Good old British understatement, I'm guessing,' said Jozette.

'Paul gave me an ultimatum. Him or the drink. And I chose him, obviously, and home and the boys. But . . .' Antonia's scant self-possession vanished. Her voice was a squeak. 'But I couldn't do it. I couldn't keep it up. I'm so weak, I'm so bad. I don't deserve my life, and my lovely family. I don't deserve any of it.' Those long fingers were balled into ineffectual fists.

'You do deserve it!' Jozette was outraged. 'You're a sweet woman.'

Cat wondered about this confident assertion. Antonia was so reserved that Cat didn't feel she knew her at all. The drinking complicated matters, obfuscating Antonia's outline further. Cat couldn't comprehend enslavement to alcohol. Drink flowed like a hiccuping river through all the wild sprees of Cat's past. It was an essential element of her nights out – that first slurp! bliss! – and consoled her when she was blue. But to *have* to drink, to be unable to face a day without its sticky embrace, was unthinkable. 'I hope you don't mind me asking,' she began carefully, when the sobs tapered off, 'but have you been drunk every day in the commune?' She did her best to sound sympathetic.

'No, no.' Antonia blew her nose, wiping it viciously with a handkerchief. 'I thought this place could be my rehab. If I couldn't get my hands on my usual amounts of drink, then, well, I couldn't drink, could I?'

'One would assume so,' said Lucy.

'But I underestimated myself.' Antonia sounded bitter. 'It turns out that the only talent I have is locating booze. I can go a few days, that's manageable, if I grit my teeth and hold on.' Antonia wrung the hanky mercilessly. 'But then it builds and builds and I just have to. Then I'd nick a bottle or two from the house stash.' She looked guiltily at Germaine. 'I didn't think you'd notice and you didn't. You,' she gulped, 'trusted us. But when I went up to London I always brought my big Orla Kiely bag. I can fit three huge bottles of vodka in that,' she confessed, head down.

Cat had always admired that bag. Evidently, she wasn't as perspicacious as Beulah liked to think. 'Do you need a drink now?' she found herself asking, instantly ashamed at her gaucheness.

'Oh yes,' said Antonia passionately, the same light in her eye as when she described her babies' first steps. 'Shall we open a bottle of . . .' She collected herself. 'Sorry.'

'What now?' asked Germaine, elbows on knees, chin in hands.

'Obviously I go home,' said Antonia, wiping her nose.

'What?' Germaine's head flew up.

'Eh?' said Cat over Mary's 'Feck that!'

'I'm a liability,' sniffed Antonia miserably. 'You don't really want me here. It's fine. I'll go.'

'Antonia,' said Lucy, cutting through the brouhaha, 'don't tell us what we really want. I vote that you stay, and that we support you all we can.' Every other hand in the room shot up; Sarge waggled hers for swotty emphasis. 'There. We would prefer you to stay. But it's up to you. You can go if you wish.'

Germaine echoed 'You can go if you wish', giving Lucy a look that clearly said *This is my commune, thank you very much.*

Antonia said quietly, 'This is the only place I feel safe.'

Cat got up from her chair and approached Antonia, taking her hand. The others, with the exception of Sarge, followed suit, braving Antonia's body language to embrace her.

'Tomorrow,' announced Sarge, above them, 'Antonia has her first AA meeting.' She met the woman's horrified gaze. 'Oh yes you have. I rang around and found the nearest chapter. There's one in Lyme. I'll take you there myself.'

'I don't need AA.' Antonia was insulted.

Sarge was resolute. 'Tomorrow,' she said.

32

Opening her eyes the next morning, Cat experienced a moment of idiotic rapture when she had no idea who she was, or even what she was, never mind *where* she was. And then the first thought of the day coagulated.

Since walking the plank at Percival Cant Jablowski, her first thought tended to be a grim one; Hugh featured heavily. Cat was superstitious about her first thought, believing it set the tone for the day. So it was with a groan that she welcomed a novel one: the post. Would there be a reply from Harry?

There was no reason to be optimistic: her father wouldn't suddenly change into a better, nicer person with an urge to meet the daughter he abandoned just because she dropped him a line. She urged herself on to the second thought.

Will.

Damn.

Breakfast was still too early for Cat's liking – 7 a.m. was the devil's own hour – but even through eyes bleary with sleep she could see that her comrades were looking better. Jozette's luggage had marked an upturn in the general appearance of what Cat sometimes thought of as the inmates. Jozette was relaxed about lending her pricey schmutter. 'Easy come, easy go,' she'd grin, with that strobe smile, reassuring them indulgently that so much of her wardrobe was freebies that it was fine for Antonia to muck out Dave wearing a Prada camisole, or for Mary to bleach the toilet in a Dolce & Gabbana cummerbund.

The glorious fabric and cunning cut restored some of the women's atrophied vanity. Hair was washed more regularly, skin moisturised, nails buffed. There was no point aspiring to WAG standards of grooming when there were chickens to chase, but a subtle shift had taken place. The days when Cat had spotted the same leaf in Mary's fringe eight mornings on the trot had gone.

The clang of the jangly bell jerked every head up. 'Post!' said two or three voices, and Jozette sprinted out of the kitchen. Cat shuddered and whistled and swallowed hard.

Beulah was placidly stirring the tea in the pot. Cat had never seen Beulah slit open an envelope or smile over a postcard. Nobody, Cat realised, knew she was here.

Jozette returned, staggering under the weight of a huge cardboard box.

'Who's it for?' demanded Mary, jumping up with her mouth full of boiled egg.

'Me!' sang Jozette, slamming it down amongst the breakfast debris. 'Well, all of us.'

The other women pecked at the jumble of letters like their feathery namesakes in the yard, keeping an eye on Jozette as she tore at the wrapping with her one remaining silicone nail.

Cat knew there'd be nothing with her name on it. She'd had a letter from her mum, her only regular correspondent, a couple of days ago.

I do hope you're not getting your hopes up. Your dad let me down time and time again before I learned my lesson. Grow some armour around your heart, love. Oh, and Jon drank a whole cup of juice on his own today! He sends his love.

The cardboard box was open. 'Fairy lights!' said Antonia with all the delight she could muster, which wasn't much. The recent past was strenuously not mentioned by the commune, and Antonia was valiantly trying to behave as if it hadn't happened.

'Job lot,' announced Jozette proudly. 'You can never have too many fairy lights, that's my motto.'

As mottos went it wasn't really up there with 'Who Dares Wins': Lucy's sardonic lift of an eyebrow wasn't lost on Cat. She surreptitiously checked to see whether Mary was joining in with this sniping at a blameless fairy light lover, but the Irishwoman was engrossed in a letter that had to be from Alun, as nobody else could have managed to cram both a lager stain *and* a spot of blood on to such a small envelope.

Mary looked over. 'Alun sends his love,' she told Cat without a trace of irony.

'Oh *good*,' Cat replied, with lashings of the stuff.

The fairy lights emerged, strand after technicolour strand. 'Some for the bathroom,' Jozette was musing. 'Some for the kitchen, eh, Beulah?' The fairy lights, unlit and hitting the table with a clunk, were already having a positive effect on the commune.

'Can I have some on my bed?' asked Antonia meekly.

'Hon,' said Jozette, curling a length of kaleidoscopic balls around Antonia's neck, 'you can have them wherever you want.'

With a frown, Germaine swept up the rest of the post and flicked through it, sending a postcard and an A4 envelope Lucy's way. 'All the bills are for me, of course,' she said under her breath. There were circles beneath her eyes this morning. She caught Cat looking her way and turned the corners of her mouth up with some effort.

Cat hastily gathered up her plate and mug, detouring on her way to the sink to plant a kiss on Germaine's rowdy hair. 'Beulah,' she said, turning away before Germaine could react, 'I've been wondering.'

'Indeed?' A visor slammed down over Beulah's powdery features. She turned on the hot tap and steam billowed in a mushroom cloud over the sink.

'Where were you passing through *to*?' Cat scraped an eggy plate over the bin. 'When you found us?'

Before Beulah could open her mouth, Jozette twirled a lasso of gaudy lights around Beulah's waist. 'Gotcha!' she squealed.

'Oh, dear, you got me all right,' laughed Beulah, moving to the Aga.

But she had escaped, and both she and Cat knew it. Cat washed her hands and then raised them to catch the envelope which Germaine, with a 'One for you, Cat!' suddenly flung her way. *Harry*! *You hero!* thought Cat, smudging it with her wet fingers.

There was only one place to read this.

Smythson hand-milled envelope in one hand, mouldy cabbage in the other, Cat discovered the hole in the door and the empty sty.

Her screams of 'Dave's gone! She's gone! Dave's gone!' and so on didn't incite the kind of reaction Cat was after.

'She'll come back,' was Mary's placid opinion, as she weeded the spring onions.

'She'll come home when she's hungry,' Lucy asserted, as if she'd dealt with runaway pigs all her life. 'Don't fret.'

Fretting was right at the top of Cat's to-do list. 'I'm off to search for her,' she said in a strangled voice full of tears, dragging on the nearest jacket, which was Antonia's and therefore three sizes too small.

'Calm down,' advised Mary, tugging off her wellingtons as she entered the kitchen. 'It's a pig, not a child.'

'It's Dave,' said Cat, more annoyed with Mary than she'd ever been.

'Look,' said Lucy, in a tone so rational that Cat wanted to throw the grotty cabbage at her shiny hair. 'It's starting to rain. You don't know where to look. She'll come back.'

'But foxes . . .' began Cat anxiously.

Mary laughed, taking a seat beside Lucy at the table to help her with potato peeling. 'It'd be a bloody brave fox that'd take on Dave.'

'Badgers, then,' said Cat, uncertainly. Her knowledge of pig predators was sketchy.

'Actually,' said Mary, eyes wide, peeler halted in mid-air, 'you're right. A pack of marauding badgers could bring Dave down. It'd take some planning and possibly specialist equipment, but they're clever, those badgers.'

Wondering just when Mary had become immune to seeing tears in her best friend's eyes, Cat stalked down the hallway.

'Hang on.' Sarge bustled along the gloomy hall after her. 'Can't have you going out there on your own. You're too weak. Vulnerable. Fragile. I'll come with you.'

Glad of the company, even if it was Sarge, Cat offered a gruff 'Thanks'.

Striding out across the field opposite, following her usual route, she sidestepped potholes and ruts. Cat's feet found their own way, as surely as if she was on a Fulham Road shopping expedition. Behind her, lurching and swearing in the sleet, Sarge puffed 'Hold on!'

'D-A-A-V-E!' cried Cat. Up on the foggy crest of her hill (that's how she thought of it now: Sarge was trespassing) the trees had melted into misshapen blots. 'Oh Dave,' whispered Cat. She had seen women in supermarkets calling toddlers' names in precisely this state, the hot face, the terrorised expression, the feet speeding blindly along.

'I'm trained in tracking,' Sarge told her, a good few feet in her wake. 'If you'll just slow down . . .'

'I can't. Anything could have happened to her.'

'What are her known haunts?'

Cat ignored this question.

'Has she been depressed lately?'

This one begged to be ignored also.

'I'm trying to ascertain if the subject is suicidal.'

That stung. 'Dave is happy,' snapped Cat. 'And fulfilled.' But I, she thought, am quite quite mad.

They trudged on, shouting Dave's name and flinging buzzwords such as 'Dinner!' and 'Carrots!' into the gloom.

Along the stream, past Will's tree, down into the embrace of the rapidly darkening valley, the two women sought their pig. Sarge wielded her torch, symbol of her training and general know-all-ness. Her confidence was reassuring. A bulwark against the night, she said 'That pig can't hide for ever', Bogart-like, as if in a farmyard *film noir*.

'Maybe Dave ran away from *me*.'

'You're not,' said Sarge briskly, 'the centre of the universe.'

Harsh, but spot-on. This meagre Cat, fashioned from the London leftovers, desperately needed to be important to somebody, even if it was a pig. The pathos shook Cat: she poured her discombobulation into a fierce shout of '*DAVE!*'

'What was that?' Sarge cocked her ear towards the trees huddled like hoodies in the valley.

'It's Dave!' Cat would recognise that distinctive oink anywhere. She began to run, with Sarge at her heels.

It was touching, the reunion of a girl and her pig, provided you had no sense of humour. Sarge didn't titter as Cat flung her arms around Dave's neck and scolded, 'Never, ever do that to me again!'

Her wanderlust sated, Dave ambled behind the women all the way back to her sty, where she flopped on to her straw and lowered her albino-lashed eyelids.

Rolling up her sleeves, Sarge fetched the toolbox and repaired the hole. 'That should sort it out,' she said to herself, packing up the hammers and nails and odd-shaped items whose uses Cat couldn't guess at.

'Thanks, Sarge,' said Cat awkwardly. She knew it was vital to avoid sentiment. 'You were the only one who . . .' She shrugged. 'I know you think of Dave as dinner. Thanks for helping me to find her.'

'It's important to you.' Sarge tossed her head, obviously uncomfortable. 'Don't like seeing you upset,' she said hoarsely, kicking the sty door open with a Doc Marten. 'And besides, that pig won't make good meat. I can tell. I've warned Germaine not to slaughter her.' She ducked away across the yard, out of range of Cat's beatific grin.

Cross-legged on a parcel of clean hay, Cat pursed her lips and stared at the unopened envelope. She tapped it on her palm. She drummed her fingernails on it. She stood it on end. From where she sat she could easily launch it on an elegant arc into Dave's slop. And that was tempting. Because the handwriting on it was Hugh's.

Whatever Hugh chose to say on his costly stationery couldn't change one huge, hairy and un-ignorable fact: he was a daddy by now. Hugh was out of bounds to any decent woman.

Cat spread the one creamy sheet of paper on the hay.

Darling Girl,

I should give up. If the news in my last letter didn't prompt you to contact me, then what would?

But I warn you, O'Connor, I'm made of sterner stuff than that.

I won't give up. I love you far too much to even think about it.

Hugh

The sound of Antonia's raised voice was unexpected, wrong. 'I won't go!' she was yelling, from the top of the crooked stairs. 'You can't make me!' She was shrill, wild.

'Come down and get in the minibus.' Sarge was strolling down the stairs as she spoke. 'Or I'll come up and get you.'

Like a French aristocrat approaching the guillotine, Antonia made her sombre way out to the courtyard.

'Good luck,' shouted Cat as the vehicle dragged its sorry carcass down the lane.

'Cheer up,' advised Mary, as they went back to the kitchen and she beat Cat to the last Eccles cake. 'Might never happen.'

'I think,' said Cat slowly, 'it already has.'

'Another Group?' complained Cat, taking a seat. 'We had one last night.'

'That was a special one,' snapped Germaine. 'Oh do hurry up!' she called testily to the women drifting through the parlour door in dribs and drabs.

Jozette had her arm through Antonia's, and one of her soft sweaters was around her companion's shoulders. She asked the question nobody else had dared to. 'So, how was AA.?'

Pretending not to listen, the others all eavesdropped.

'Awful,' said Antonia on a kind of sob. 'Having to stand up in front of strangers. And some of the stories . . .' She shivered, and leaned into Jozette. She hesitated, before saying, a tiny smile prinking her mouth, 'Now I really need a drink!'

The rehearsed line was met with indulgent laughter. Cat noticed Sarge rocking on her heels like a proud stage mother.

Strolling to the middle, Germaine waited for quiet before she began. 'Tonight's speaker is a very talented lady, a writer.' All eyes turned to Lucy, who braced herself, as if expecting a punch to the solar plexus.

'We met,' continued Germaine, 'almost exactly a year ago at a feminist chick lit course: a literary sub-genre where basically the heroine knees the hero in the balls and starts a small business. Lucy said very little, but everything she did say was worth listening to. Even if,' she cast a rueful look at her subject, 'she convinced me to abandon my manuscript involving a bra that squirts nerve gas at any man who calls the wearer "love". We kept in touch, and although she's not an easy person to befriend, I persevered. I felt it would be worth the trouble and I was right. Lucy is a vital part of our community, a sane and rational woman who helps to keep us on the straight and narrow. We're not privy to what she's working on, but it's sure to be ever so literary, because she's rather a culture vulture. Here she is. Our Lucy.' Germaine sank, satisfied, into her chair as Lucy took the floor.

'I'm Lucy and this is—' began Lucy: behind her Germaine had bobbed up and taken one crouched step forward to interrupt.

'Sorry. Forgot to say. This girl puts her money where her mouth is. She's a lesbian.'

'Thank you,' said Lucy, eyebrows raising expressively. '*Was* going to get to that in my own time, Germaine, but thanks anyway.'

'Ahh!' blurted Antonia, as if she'd just solved a particularly frustrating crossword clue. 'So you've given up on men. Don't blame you.'

'It's not a case of giving up,' said Lucy. 'It's the way I am, the way I was born.' She paused. 'The way I love to be.'

'Unbe-fucking-lievable.'

Cat swivelled to check that Mary was joking.

'Pardon?' asked Lucy.

'Nothing.' Mary wasn't joking. Arms crossed, legs crossed, she was glowing with ill humour.

'I'm not just a lesbian,' said Lucy, circling the group slowly. 'I'm a journalist. Freelance. Quite a precarious job. I was brought up in a very traditional home. Traditional insofar as Dad ruled the roost, Mum stayed at home and we were all miserable as sin.'

So, thought Cat, broken homes don't have the monopoly on unhappiness. Still, she would have liked the chance to give normal family life a go.

'My father is an MP.' Lucy waited for the impressed/surprised murmurs to subside. 'Perhaps that's why I have such an aversion to rules, to *shoulds*. I'm a natural rebel, even if my wrapping is very conservative. This commune sounded so fascinating, a real opportunity for women to support and encourage each other, that I had to give it a try.'

Sarge put her hand up. 'If that's so,' she asked, cocking her chin combatively, 'why are you so snooty?'

'Am I?' laughed Lucy, in an undeniably snooty way. Cat could tell she didn't take funny little Sarge's funny little question seriously. 'Perhaps there's more of my dad in me than I care to think.'

'Do you,' ventured Antonia doubtfully, 'hate men?'

'Of course not.' Lucy suppressed a sigh. 'I just don't fancy them.'

'What, never?' said Mary sceptically. 'Not even . . .' She racked her brains. 'George Clooney?'

'Not even the wondrous George.'

'Is it political?' Cat was interested. Lucy was so calculating she wouldn't put such cold-blooded behaviour past her.

'No, but it's made me political,' said Lucy slowly, looking faintly surprised by the end of the sentence. 'Yeah, definitely. But hang on,' she waved her hands in the air. 'This isn't a Q and A on the wonderful world of lesbianism. I'm at this commune because I believe, passionately, that women can live without men, and live well.'

'Is that all, though?' Cat relished the opportunity to quiz Lucy. 'Surely there was some turning point, some event, to make you leave your home and family and friends and come here?'

'If you're expecting to hear my emotional history, you'll be disappointed,' said Lucy baldly. 'I don't have tons of baggage. I'm a loner. I like it that way. I don't need your pity, nor your understanding.'

Well, thought Cat, *that told me.*

'So,' said Mary, a dangerous glint in her brown eye. 'We're all saddoes and you're the sane one. Is that it?'

'No,' said Lucy, gently but clearly. 'That is not it. That's the spin you're choosing to put on it. I'm here for the experience.' She walked back to her chair and her dainty bottom hit the seat with a decisive thump.

33

Fact: late night sandwiches, devoured in a cold kitchen, are tastier than ones eaten during the day.

'It's cos it's naughty,' opined Cat, taking an awkward bite of her messy creation.

'I'm freezing,' complained Mary. 'And this bread is stale.'

'The bread is fine.' Mary complained about everything and anything when she was out of sorts: once, during period cramps, she'd claimed that Tony Blair's hair on the ten o'clock news was making them worse. 'Food'll help you sleep.' Cat couldn't put up with much more of the tossing, turning, sighing and grrrr-ing emanating from the neighbouring bed since lights out. 'What *is* the matter?' She really really hoped that Mary's answer wouldn't be the one she feared.

'Bloody Lucy,' spat her friend.

'Oh come *on*.' Cat's dismay soured the delights of the mingling cheese, mayonnaise, mustard and jam. Chewing hurriedly, she leaned over to move the oil lamp nearer to Mary's face. 'Are you channelling my nana about Lucy being a lesbian?'

'Did you know?' asked Mary, with what Trev would call the raging hump. 'Could you tell? I had no idea.'

'How could I possibly have known?' Cat was baffled. Mary was naturally liberal and laissez-faire. Cat would have betted a fortune on her nonchalance. They had the usual percentage of gay friends and acquaintances. Mary's own cousin Bob was happily married to a librarian called Gordon, a dull man who collected beer mats. 'Have you gone homophobic?' She felt Mary's forehead with her palm. 'Don't breathe on me. It might be catching.'

'You know I'm not homophobic. It's just made me feel differently about her, that's all.'

Cat rapped Mary's head with her knuckles. 'Hello in there! Could you send my best mate out, please! I don't like this KKK bint you've replaced her with.' She paused, weary. 'What's that phrase you use whenever we hear of an unlikely couple? When people gossip and take the mickey you say that love is where it falls. You've always been understanding, forgiving. Well, if love falls between two women, why should that upset you, you Neanderthal?'

Swatting the hand away angrily, Mary said, 'I don't give a toss that she's a lezzer.'

'Lesbian. The word is lesbian.'

'Whatever. But she should have told me.'

'Ah.' Cat wrinkled her nose. 'I see. I didn't realise, you know, that you and she were so close.'

'We're very close.' Mary sounded insulted. 'We get on great. Or so I thought.'

It was hard for Cat to defend a woman she was jealous of. 'She didn't lie to you. It's her business whether she tells people or not.'

'Huh. So I'm just *people*, now, am I?'

Time, thought Cat, *for bed. Again.*

The quote reared up in red behind Cat's eyelids as she struggled to get back to sleep.

If the news in my last letter didn't prompt you to contact me, then what would?

News. News? News! Cat tried saying it a variety of ways in her head. Said jauntily it could refer to something as simple as buying a new suit. Said portentously it could refer to something momentous. Such as leaving your wife.

And your newborn.

Hugh's news had disappeared, unread, down Dave's digestive tract. The only way to find out what his letter referred to was to ask the man himself.

There was much carrot-based joy in the kitchen the next morning. Proudly mucky in the centre of the table, the commune's crop of orange root vegetables were admired and discussed and venerated by the women, like Posh Spice surrounded by paparazzi.

'You must be very proud,' said Antonia to Germaine.

'Oh, I am,' said Germaine, with no debilitating modesty.

Mary held up a large, knobbly, rudely shaped example at an evocative, provocative angle and said casually to Lucy, 'Don't suppose you'd have much use for this one, eh?'

Beulah took it gently out of her grasp. 'Soup,' she said reverently.

'Sooop,' echoed the others, like a cult.

Lucy left the room.

Cat gave Mary a penetrating stare.

Mary poked her tongue out at Cat.

And there was no letter from Harry.

'Shall I look for Antonia?' asked Jozette, putting down her spoon. 'She really should try this soup.'

'Leave her,' said Germaine dismissively. 'If she doesn't want to join in we can't force her. Move the lamp, someone,' she added imperiously. 'It's in my eyes.'

Sarge's hand shot out to reposition the trusty old lamp.

'Antonia disappears when she's drinking,' said Mary. 'And she disappears when she's not. Some women just can't hack it.'

'Hack what?' Lucy broke a piece of Beulah's excellent bread. 'Addiction? Heartbreak?'

'God, we're all spiky tonight,' said Cat lightly.

Sarge said, as if delivering the final word, 'Erratic behaviour is to be expected while undergoing the AA process. I've been reading up on it. It's all part of her recovery.' Underlit by the lamp, Sarge's features were demonic. 'Antonia expected a man to make her life work. Me, I answer to no one.'

'Sarge,' said Germaine, in her 'migraine' voice, 'that's enough.'

'Sure thing.' Sarge's head dropped over her soup plate which didn't match any of the other soup plates.

'I'll, er, be going out later,' said Germaine with atypical diffidence.

'Where?' 'Whaddayamean?' 'Can I come?' A volley of responses bounced off Germaine's raised hands.

'I knew,' she said thickly, 'that you'd make a fuss. I am allowed out after dark, you know. I'm not a teenager.'

'But we never go out at night,' Cat pointed out, hoping she wasn't whining. A vision of a pub, with horse brasses, crisps and possibly a Will in it had sprung fully formed into her mind. 'It's not fair.'

'What are you up to, Germy?' Mary was suspicious.

'I'm not *up to* anything. There's a problem with the lease. I have to visit the owner. Believe me, I won't be having fun.' Germaine looked burdened. 'But don't worry!' she said hastily as Cat's face fell at the mention of a problem. 'It's nothing. Really. I'll sort it out.'

'Is it money?' asked Mary, pained. 'Is that the problem?'

'Oh good Lord, there is no problem. I wish I'd never mentioned it. Everything's fine.' Germaine banged her spoon on the table. 'Will everybody just eat their fucking soup!'

After an interlude of slurping and sipping, Germaine said, huskily, 'Oh all right. Let's all go out for a meal one night soon.'

If Cat stopped to think about it, it was pitiful that the expectation of one night out should induce such euphoria. So she didn't stop to think about it.

Her hands slowed and stopped, enjoying the sudsy warmth of the washing up water. Cat stared out at the night, tangled in thoughts.

'Get a grip, Flowerpot,' she murmured: there wasn't a lot of washing up getting done.

'Want some help?' Mary wandered in, slamming the larder door with one foot and grabbing a tea towel.

'You? Offering to help when it's not on the rota?' Cat looked sceptical. 'Is there a mad dog in the parlour?'

'Nope. Just a lezzer, a weirdo in fatigues and a snoring stylist.'

'Mary . . .' Cat shook her head. At this time of the evening, Mary and Lucy were usually side by side on the sofa, swapping private jokes. 'The L word? You promised?'

'I lied.' Mary gave a mug the wiping of its life.

Too tired to take her friend to task, Cat asked abruptly, 'Am I turning into one of *those* women?'

'Which women are they?'

'The sort who get upset all the time. Who show all their emotions.' Cat remembered how her face had buckled at the dinner table when Germaine had hinted of trouble at t'mill. 'I used to be self-contained, cool. Now I'm all over the bloody place. The old me would never have run after a pig, crying.'

'The old you would have told Marian to look up Pig Chasing Services in the Yellow Pages and got on with frightening copywriters.'

'Exactly. This place is stripping me bare. I'm turning to mush. I'm becoming one of those women.' She dropped her voice. 'By the end of the six months I'll be Antonia.'

'You've always been one of those women.' Mary attacked a plate with her cloth.

'I have *not*.' Cat rinsed the soupy pan.

'You've always felt deeply. I wouldn't bother with you if you didn't. You've always . . .' Mary pulled a face and said gravely, 'I apologise for the soppy language coming up.' She took a deep breath. 'You've always *been there for me*.' She fanned her face. 'There. I've said it.'

'Well, yeah,' muttered Cat, unwilling to admit to *being there* for Mary but certain that she always had been. Cat would never describe it that way.

'You're one of those women whether you like it or not, but you've pretended to be one of *those* women.'

'You've lost me.'

'You pretend your heart is as organised as your desk. You present a perfectly composed front to the world, as if you put work before everything else and diarise nervous breakdowns for next summer.'

'I wasn't pretending. That was me.' Cat upended the pan on the drenched draining board. '*Is* me.'

A scream ripped through the kitchen. It was horrible, like a trapped creature.

Mary dropped a plate.

The howl carried on, weaving up and down the scale, drawing the others from the parlour.

'What the . . .' Even Lucy was rattled.

'That,' Jozette was saying fearfully, 'really is super-fucking-natural.'

Clustered together, the women jumped in unison at a fresh sound, a demented scratching, as if something was trying to break through the walls.

'The larder,' whispered Cat. Ignoring the heartfelt 'Don't!'s she tiptoed over to wrench the door open.

Beulah hurtled out, still howling. Her body was bent, misshapen, like an animal after a whipping.

'No! No!' shrieked Beulah, sinking to her knees on the hard kitchen floor.

'Beulah,' murmured Cat helplessly, at a loss for anything more pithy. 'Beulah.' She knelt awkwardly beside the old lady and tried to wrap her arms around her. But there was a lot of Beulah. 'Mary!' she waved her over.

Mary put her head close to Beulah's. 'It's all right'. Her accent warmed the platitude. 'It's all right, love.'

The sobbing ebbed. Beulah was helped to a chair. Sagging as if her bones had melted, she accepted the water Lucy offered.

With gentle hands laid on her, Beulah was put to bed that night like a Tudor monarch.

The consensus of a late night council was that the women would take their lead from Beulah.

The next morning Beulah was up especially early, and there was an oven-warm roll on each plate. She spoke of the Aga's contrary nature, the blue of the sky and the chatter of the chickens. She didn't mention the night before and neither did anybody else.

They didn't need to. It hung over the breakfast table like a dour fog. Cat conjectured pointlessly about what had triggered Beulah's panic, while the others talked of this and that around her. Their banal conversation had a subtext: it was a warm and elastic safety net for Beulah. Cat wondered if she'd ever need it herself.

34

There was an outbreak of yoga in the back garden. Beyond the palais de hen, Lucy had laid out her mat and a select band faced her, alert and ready and just a touch self-conscious.

Cat stood in the front row, relishing the sun on her bare arms. June was proving to be a profligate month, spending its sunshine like a sailor on shore leave.

'And exhale . . .' Lucy led them through the breathing exercises.

Feeling ridiculous, Cat did as she was told. She needed to clear her mind, to forget the stack of letters that, once again, held none for her.

'We'll just do some light exercises, warm us all up,' said Lucy with a smile that teetered on condescension. 'Nothing too challenging. I know we have all levels of expertise in our group.'

Unsure if she could trust that 'nothing too challenging', Cat sat down on her mat. These yoga classes scared her. They were too revealing. Cat didn't want every Tom, Dick and Germaine knowing she fell over if she balanced on one leg. Today she felt the fear and did it anyway, only to regret her brio when she saw the elegant way Lucy folded herself down into a seated position. Out of the corner of her eye she could see Jozette, whose arms, legs, hair and teeth all seemed to be double jointed, sitting poised and upright.

Saluting the sun was, apparently, a doddle. If you were Lucy. If you were Cat it was hellish. Her own legs were laughing at her. The Downward Dog almost undid her.

'Try it like this,' said Jozette kindly.

That was the worst bit, the kindness. The kindness of women who are thinner than you is a terrible thing. 'Oh. Right,' said Cat as if it was all clear now. How she wished one of the chickens would explode or something. Anything to distract the class.

Behind her Germaine was panting like a pug. 'I'm too old for this,' she moaned, but when Cat risked a look over her shoulder she saw that Germaine was doing better than she was. Cat toppled noiselessly on to her side.

'That's fine,' said Lucy. 'We're learning. We never stop learning in yoga.'

Antonia turned out to be surprisingly supple, although she had no stamina and couldn't hold the poses. Beulah, at the back, was still in her apron and nobody would have described what was happening on her mat as yoga.

It was Sarge who stole the show. Lithe and graceful, she was used by Lucy to demonstrate the correct way to ease into positions.

And Mary was indoors, out of the sun and as far away from Lucy as possible. Cat had scolded, cajoled and resorted to insult. 'You're an idiot. A big one,' she'd said as she dragged on her leggings. 'Are you the new Bernard Manning or something?'

'For the eight hundred and eighty-fumpth time, this is not about Lucy being a lesbian, it's about—'

'Yeah, yeah,' Cat had interrupted. 'It's about her not telling you. We know, we know. And yet . . .' she'd paused in her tussle with grey lycra, 'we don't believe you. No, hang on,' she'd raised her voice over Mary's aggrieved grunts, 'you've been making sarky remarks, and off-colour comments, ever since you found out. Admit it.'

'They're just jokes.'

'I'm not even going to answer that.' Cat had left Mary ostentatiously pretending to tidy the dormitory. The two women had never made jokes about lesbians before, and they wouldn't have laughed if somebody else had. Pounding down the stairs, enjoying the feel of the wood on her bare feet, Cat had been grateful to leave Mary behind.

Now she longed to have Mary by her side. At least that would guarantee there'd be one person crapper than her at pleating her body into a pose called, possibly, 'The Pillock'.

By the time the promised trip to Lyme Regis rolled around, Antonia had been to her second AA meeting. AWOL when Sarge started the minibus, she'd been discovered hiding behind Dave and escorted to the passenger seat by the whole commune. Antonia was silent on the subject, but Sarge filled everybody in about the twelve steps, and the mentor that Antonia could call if she needed to.

'And,' continued Sarge, sitting on the bed as the others got ready for painting the town red, 'she's not going to visit her kids until the end of the experiment.'

'But that's a whole three months!' Mary was shocked.

So was Cat, but for a different reason. When she'd arrived, six months had seemed an eternity. She ran her hairbrush through a tangle and squealed. She hated endings, she'd had enough of them.

'Antonia wants to be further along in her recovery when she sees them again,' explained Sarge. 'She wants to have more confidence.'

It sounded as if Sarge and Antonia talked on the drive home after the meetings. Cat was touched by the way Sarge waited outside the church hall for her charge. She smiled over at the little milkwoman. 'What are you wearing tonight? You'd better get changed. We're off in ten minutes.'

'I'm wearing this.' Sarge seemed baffled by the question.

'Oh. Right.' *This* was a pair of camouflage dungarees over a tee the colour of silt.

Slipping into the room, Antonia tugged at Cat's sleeve. 'I'm not going,' she said apologetically.

Cat curbed her disappointment at losing one of their coven. 'Aw, OK. But why?'

'Well, I would find it hard. You know. Drink. Seeing you all drinking. It would . . .' Antonia shrugged, her eyes elusive.

If Cat hadn't been wearing a pair of Jozette's platforms she would have kicked herself. 'I didn't think. Sorry.'

'No, don't be.' Antonia waved the apology away, embarrassed. 'It's me who should . . .' She rallied. 'Anyway, have a great time. Get slaughtered!' she said, raising a weak fist.

Beulah was lowering her comfortably upholstered behind into the minibus seat in front of Cat and Mary. She had added a hand-knitted waistcoat to her brown terylene zip-fronted dress in honour of the occasion, and pinned a hair clip to her curls. Somebody had forgotten to tell her face about the night out, however: it was arranged for a wake.

'Get a move on!' With Sarge, impatience came as standard. She gunned the feeble engine. 'Stop bloody chattering and get on board,' she ordered the stragglers.

'All right, all right,' laughed Jozette, looking both understated and amazing in lots of little black bits and pieces. She glittered and shone, carrying off the tiny black shorts over black lurex tights blithely. Somebody, Cat thought fondly, had forgotten to tell Jozette she was stunningly beautiful: her gawky insouciance was at odds with her looks.

Seating herself beside Jozette, Lucy made quite a contrast. Chic, conformist, she was highly self-aware. Cat studied her as Lucy smoothed the sleeves of her linen blazer and tweaked the crisp cotton collar of her white shirt just so. That, she concluded, was how you got to look so groomed – you *bothered.* You didn't think 'Oh this'll do' and decide not to get the iron out because you couldn't be arsed. Cat wondered if Lucy took as much trouble with the emotional image she presented to the world. Seeing Lucy's carefully composed face, smiling at Jozette's squawking excitement, Cat guessed that she did. Maybe there was a rumpled, chocolate stained, hot-blooded woman inside there trying to get out.

Feeling a dig in her side, Cat turned. Mary was waggling her eyebrows in a way that meant trouble. Looking down, Cat snorted at the bottle of wine Mary was pressing against her.

'It's not a school trip,' laughed Cat. 'We can drink if we want.'

'It's more fun if we keep it secret.'

'Where's the corkscrew?'

'Um . . . bollocks.' Mary stuffed the bottle back into her bag.

'Wagons roll!' roared Sarge, taking the handbrake off. The minibus farted extravagantly and the commune struck out for Lyme Regis.

Seven women, of varied shapes and sizes, proved a tall order for Nelson's. Two tables were pulled together, with much exaggerated heaving, by the teenaged waiter, who informed them as they took their seats that the pollock was off.

'Say nothing, Mary.' Germaine nipped the inevitable double entendre in the bud.

Choosing starters and a main course from the laminated menu made the Middle East peace process look straightforward.

'The prawns,' said Mary. 'Hang on, no, the soup. No, the prawns.'

'Are the eggs in the egg mayonnaise organic?' Germaine questioned the waiter who was ready with a question of his own: 'How would I know?'

'No, the soup,' said Mary.

'Can I have two starters and no main?' Jozette's query gave the waiter a migraine.

Beulah didn't want a starter: when pressed she agreed to have a taste of Cat's. Cat ordered bruschetta.

'Bruschetta's off,' said the waiter.

'No, prawns,' said Mary.

'You said the pollock was off.'

'It is.' The waiter sighed, a long sigh redolent of regret for not listening in class, the unlikelihood of his ever playing for England and his deep abiding hatred for women old enough to be his mother who hassled him about bruschetta.

'No, the soup,' said Mary.

'What if I had three starters and no dessert?' asked Jozette.

'No, the prawns,' said Mary.

'My compliments to the microwave,' muttered Cat to Lucy as the waiter cleared away their main courses.

Lucy giggled. It suited her to giggle. Maybe it was the effect of the white wine spritzers, or the company. The women ate together three times a day, but the addition of place mats, candles and other human beings dotted about the room lifted the atmosphere.

Germaine, a little pink about the cheeks, was meandering through a half-remembered joke. Beside her a smitten Sarge gazed up at her, patiently awaiting a punchline that would never arrive.

'You bitches had better be having afters,' proclaimed Mary.

Handing her menu to the waiter with a 'Just a sticky toffee pudding for me' (Cat liked to add 'just' to any request that involved more than the advised daily intake of calories), Cat eyed Beulah covertly.

At the far end of the table, sandwiched between Sarge and Jozette, Beulah sat impassive, like a well-trained hound tied up outside a supermarket. Cat knew that she had picked at her food and sipped at her wine. Beulah had made no attempt to join in with the freefalling conversation, which ranged from Jozette's tattoo to Sarge's six-pack to American foreign policy.

Quite still, and almost silent, Beulah's body language was eloquent. Cat read her unease as she pushed her food around the plate and cleared her throat anxiously.

In between the raucous laughter and the teasing of the irresistibly tease-able waiter, Cat regretted insisting that Beulah join the charabanc. Just because Cat missed the loud warmth of the outside, night-time world, it didn't follow that everybody else did.

'Oi!' Mary waggled a gooey spoon in her face. 'You're musing. Stop it! I won't tell you again.'

'I wasn't. Well,' conceded Cat, 'not about Hugh'. Her ex was trussed in yellow and black crime scene tape. She didn't dare contemplate any further what his news was, in case it exposed him as a heartless fraud who had deserted his newborn child. Which exposed her as the ex-mistress of a heartless etc. etc.

'Will?'

'When I muse,' said Cat, scaling her high horse, 'it's not *always* about men.'

'D'you know what bothers me about leaving Trev?' ruminated Jozette, licking her spoon in a lazy but thorough manner that made the waiter's night. '*If* I leave him, I mean,' she corrected herself. 'It's the starting again. In my thirties. Do I have the energy?'

'I hear you,' said Cat, who had a lamentable habit of lapsing into Americanisms around her almost-sister-in-law. 'Another naked body to get to know.'

'Foibles,' said Mary sagely, 'to navigate.'

'Quirks,' said Lucy darkly, 'to accommodate.'

'Vanities,' sighed Jozette, 'to pander to.'

'What if,' posited Germaine gravely, 'he didn't like my toad-in-the-hole? Am I going to change the recipe after all these years?'

'Quite,' said Cat. 'I'm not malleable any more. I is what I is.'

'Too right,' whooped Jozette. She was even more prone to whooping when tipsy.

'Could I,' asked Mary, 'put in the hours with his family?' She shook her head a gloomy *no.* 'Another putative mother-in-law to impress? I'm sick of washing up in other women's kitchens.'

Nudging Lucy, Germaine asked, 'Are you looking for love, Lucy?'

Her handsome face reflective, Lucy took a second to answer.

Somebody else got there first. 'Aye aye,' grunted Mary. 'Watch your backs, ladies. Or should that be your fronts?' Proud of her joke, she chortled. Nobody else laughed.

Lucy put her knife down deliberately, the silvery clatter it made the only sound at their table. 'Mary, as you seem to glean all your information about lesbians from Benny Hill, I should let you in on a couple of secrets.'

This, thought Cat, is going to smart.

'Go on,' said Mary, so utterly laidback that Cat knew her innards were churning like a washing machine.

'Lesbians,' began Lucy in a clear voice, resting her chin on interlaced fingers. She had the waiter's full attention. 'Lesbians do not fancy all women. Lesbians are not always *up for it.*' The phrase received a full raise of both circumflex eyebrows. 'Lesbians fancy some women, some of the time. They are all different. They are not a "they" at all.' Her mouth grew tighter, her diction pinched. 'Speaking for the only lesbian I know intimately, i.e. myself, believe me, Mary, you are safe from my attentions.' She picked up her knife and sliced the dollop of Brie on her cheese platter. 'I like my girlfriends lean.'

Cat sensed Mary pulling her tummy in.

From the other end of the table Beulah spoke for almost the first time that evening. 'Could we go home now?' she asked.

'PUB!' roared Jozette.

'Yeah, pub,' agreed Mary, showing all her teeth in a very unconvincing smile.

35

Standing at the teeming bar of the Fisherman's Rest, trying to catch the barman's eye, Mary finally surrendered to Cat's searching look. 'Don't,' she winced. 'Don't give me that *do you want to talk about it* stare.'

'Do you?'

'No. There's nothing to talk about. Lucy is a bitch. End of.'

Silently vowing to take Mary to task for saying 'End of', Cat waved a twenty pound note at the overwhelmed barman. The old men of their last visit were invisible in the throng: the pub was heaving with a younger, mixed crowd. 'Don't blame Lucy,' she said. 'You've been asking for it.'

'And she made sure I got it when everybody was listening,' said Mary bitterly.

'If you can't take it, don't dole it out.' Cat regretted her tough love when she turned and saw Mary's mottled, confused face. 'Aw, Mary,' she said, instantly softer. 'You can't really blame the girl.'

'I know. And that just makes it feckin' worse.' Mary leaned over the beer-spangled bar and bawled 'CAN I HAVE SOME SERVICE PURLEESE THANK *YEW*!' at the barman.

It worked. As Cat ferried glasses to and from the inadequate table

Germaine had commandeered, she felt eyes upon her. She looked nervously around at the gaggle of people at the bar as she returned to collect Beulah's elderflower cordial, and caught the gaze of a young woman.

'Sorry. Am I staring?' the girl giggled. She really was just a girl, perhaps a smidgeon over twenty.

'Well, yeah,' laughed Cat, shrugging. 'Am I just too beautiful to take?'

'Eh?' The girl's smile slipped. Irony had not reached her neck of the woods. 'No, well, I mean . . .'

'Do I know you?' Cat rescued her, with a quizzical look. The girl was slender, tall and wearing the kind of jeans that constituted the Holy Grail for Cat. They slimmed the hips, elongated the leg and flattened the tum. Or perhaps the girl's body did that all by itself.

'Kind of.' The stranger shook a hank of thick blonde hair out of a sea green eye. 'I'm Will's girlfriend. Will the vet?' she added helpfully.

And crushingly. 'Oh. Right. Yeah. Good. Wow.' Cat's face performed an acrobatic sequence of ecstatic expressions. 'I've heard a lot about you. Well,' Cat corrected herself. 'I've heard about you. Great to meet you . . .?'

'Lisa. Will's fascinated by your, er, commune, is it?' Lisa was evidently treading carefully. Her friends, all several leagues behind in the hot/gorgeous/could-be-a-Calvin-Klein-model stakes, were listening intently. Cat felt like a performing bear they expected great things of. 'No men, apparently?' Lisa dug the boy nearest her in the ribs when he sniggered.

'Nope. No men.' Cat told herself to stop staring at Lisa's twenty-year-old breasts. 'We've had enough,' she said theatrically, bowdlerising Germaine's carefully reasoned theories. Lisa really did have quite the best breasts Cat had ever seen.

'I might just join you,' laughed Lisa, and her friends all giggled in a wholesome, *young* way.

A girl with skin that looked like Cat's might look if she'd been born fifteen years later and never lived on a bus route poked her head over Lisa's shoulder. 'Except she's in lurve,' she said teasingly. 'She'd never go anywhere without Willy-Billy.'

'Yeah, but if he ever chucked me,' said Lisa in a tone that underlined the absurdity of such an idea, 'then I might consider it.'

'Ain't gonna happen, babe,' cooed the girl with good skin.

'If it does,' smiled Cat, showing off teeth she didn't even know she had, 'give us a ring and I'll save you a bed.'

'What about me?' The boy who'd sniggered earlier looked eager. 'Will you save me a bed? Or is it all les-be-friends up there on the hill?'

'Christ, you're so not funny.' Lisa pushed him.

'Lisa's right,' smiled Cat, turning with her precious cargo of elderflower. 'You're so not.'

'Saw you getting down with the kids, dude.' Mary budged up on a sticky bench to make room.

'That ain't no kid, that's Will's girlfriend.'

'The young one? With the great hair? And the killer figure?'

'May I stop you there?'

'Ohhhh dear.' Mary sucked on her straw. 'Is she thick?' she asked hopefully.

'No.'

'Horrible?'

'Friendly. Pleasant.'

'Let's murder her.'

'We were wrong,' said Cat wryly, 'about the perm.'

'Isn't she,' Mary squinted over at the bar, 'a bit young for him?'

'In my bitter, twisted, envious opinion, yes.' Cat flipped a beer mat. 'In Will's opinion, she's obviously just right.'

'God, she's slim.'

'Probably doesn't eat.' Cat braced herself. Lucy's comment about preferring lean women would have repercussions. Cat would need all her strength to withstand the next few weeks of Mary's loathing for her soft, curvaceous body. There would be eulogies to stick-thin celebs, ruthless self-criticism, endless unhappy mirror gazing with lots of tummy grabbing, thigh slapping and midriff poking. It would eventually peter out: in a straight fight, cake would always triumph over the gym. And Cat's mantra that Mary looked great just the way she was would get through.

Germaine stood up and grabbed her bag. 'I'm off to the loo, ladies, and then I think we should get home.' The smattering of disappointed noises tapered off when Germaine coughed and gave a discreet nod in Beulah's direction. Beulah was hunched over on her chair, staring into her cordial as if God, at the very least, was in its flat depths.

'Yeah, let's call it a night.' Cat even added a yawn.

'Time to go,' said Mary over-loudly.

'Must just powder my nose.' Germaine made for the sticky door bearing a jagged silhouette of a woman. She bumped into a man in a leather jacket. 'Sorry,' she murmured, pressing on.

'Germy!' sang the man. 'All right?'

'Er, yes.' Germaine's brows knotted and she disappeared into the sweaty crowd.

'How,' asked Cat, slipping her arm through Germaine's as the women straggled back uphill towards the car park, 'do you know that guy in the pub?'

'I don't,' said Germaine, looking puzzled.

'But he knew your name.' Cat corrected herself. 'Your nickname. And it's not exactly common.'

'I wondered about that too,' said Germaine. 'We're a little more famous around here than is entirely comfortable, don't you think?'

'S'pose.' Cat remembered her surprise when Will had known where she was from before they'd introduced themselves. 'But Germy, he knew your *name*.'

'Creepy.' Germaine pulled a face. 'I hope they don't storm the house one night, with pitchforks and flaming torches.'

Catching up with them, Mary took Germaine's other arm. 'How come this place is all uphill?' she wheezed. 'Surely it stands to feckin' reason that *some* of it must be downhill?'

36

The toast was burnt. The eggs were runny. Even the cornflakes looked miserable. Beulah was still in bed leaving Mary, and her hangover, in charge of breakfast.

'Oh, just eat it,' she growled, as Antonia dissected her eggs with a timid fork.

'I'm not hungry,' said Lucy brusquely, striding through the kitchen.

'Good,' said Mary.

An effusive letter from Cat's mum carefully avoided asking about the quest to find Harry.

I'm having Jon's room decorated. Something more masculine. What do you think of blue? I had a right to-do in the electrical shop over the faulty pressure cooker. Ended up with a credit note. Jon's sleeping much better. That new medication is brilliant.

Trev was glaringly absent from the pages.

'Ladies,' Cat addressed the chickens, whose ordure she was removing, 'it must be karma. What did I do in a former life to deserve such godawful men?'

'Sorry I'm late!' Antonia was out of breath, jogging down the cinder path. 'I just got back from AA and I looked at the rota and thought oh dear, Cat's out there on her own, cleaning up the poopoo.' She took the shovel from Cat's hand.

'How was it?' asked Cat tentatively, feeling she should show an interest but not wanting to intrude.

'Fantastic!' Antonia's wide grin was as unexpected as the adjective. The erratic behaviour Sarge had forecast meant that nobody could be sure how Antonia would react to ordinary questions. This afternoon, evidently, her mood had swung buoyantly up. 'This woman spoke, she was so inspiring, she's been through so much and yet she's . . . thriving!' Antonia flung her arms, showering the vegetable patch with hen excrement.

'Good,' said Cat, slightly at a loss. 'Excellent.' She didn't know much about AA. 'How long do you have to go for, before you're, like, cured?' It sounded like the wrong term, and it was.

'I'll never be cured,' said Antonia. 'I'll always be an alcoholic.' The word was no longer volatile. 'But if I use the tools I can handle it.' Antonia bent over to scoop up some dark dots: Cat noticed how pert her bottom looked in well-cut jeans that were recognisably Jozette's. Cat had never noticed Antonia's bottom before. The woman was fleshing out physically as well as emotionally.

'I mustn't rely on PPT any more.' At Cat's baffled 'Eh?' Antonia explained. 'People Places Things. It's an AA acronym. I'm learning to rely on me to make myself happy. People, places and things didn't do it so I turned to booze.' Antonia sighed, a light sigh, a feathery one, not her style at all. 'Tonight I have to make out my gratitude list.' She explained again, clearly enjoying sharing the arcane knowledge. 'A list of all the things I'm grateful for, that make life worth living. You're on it,' she said, shovelling up a noisy little cache of pellets.

'Really?' Cat was warm with pleasure.

'Yeah. The whole commune is,' said Antonia.

'Ah. Good,' said Cat, less warm.

Straightening up, Antonia groped in her smock pocket. 'Oh goodness I'm such a fool,' she said. 'This has been in my pocket since this morning. It's from your dad.' She handed over a postcard, creased in two. 'Sorry. Couldn't help but see the signature.'

'No, that's all right.' Cat's hand reached out in slow motion, possibly soft focus too. She took the card. 'Thanks.'

Each detail was precious. Alone up in the dormitory, Cat unfolded the card like a curator with a medieval document. Slowly, she read the address. Blue biro, she noted. The handwriting was courtly, lots of flourishes and curlicues. Very neat. It didn't slope. The stamp was first class, and she chastised herself for feeling grateful.

Turning it over, Cat read the date, all properly spelled out, no numerics. The scant copy disappointed her, but the first word after *Dear Cat* sparked a deluge of adrenalin.

> *Yes, of course we can meet up. I know Lyme very well. Give me a ring or drop me a line and we'll arrange something. It made my day to hear from you.*
>
> *Love, Dad.*

Cat couldn't read the number at the foot of the card because her vision was blurred.

With everybody tucked up, Cat stole away from her bed. Antonia was right: it was easy. Down in the parlour, she shut the door and lit one sherbet-coloured lamp.

Settling down on the least uncomfortable armchair, Cat curled up against the cold and stared at the blank page of her pad. She had decided not to ring Harry. This was too delicate a process for a call that might catch him at the wrong moment. A letter was safer, easier to control. She closed her eyes, the better to think.

With a grunt, Cat came to. A comma of saliva sat frozen on her chin. She might have been asleep for a moment or an hour, it was impossible to say. The noise of the back door closing had woken her. Or had it been part of her dream? She slid off the chair and groped her way along the dark room, from settle to dresser. Easing the door to stifle its Chewbacca groan, Cat tiptoed out into the pitch-black hall, her bare feet noiseless on the stone.

There it was again! The back door opened. Cat drew back, craning to peer into the kitchen as a figure slipped in from the garden. Not at all ghostly, it was Germaine. She was rolling something up, something that crinkled and rasped. Germaine looked about her, furtive enough to convince Cat to stay still. Germaine disappeared into the larder and Cat heard the familiar metallic clang! of the pedal bin.

It would have been natural to say 'wassup?' or a variation of the same, but instinct sent Cat bolting for the dorm. By the time Germaine sank into bed Cat was bundled up and pretending to be asleep.

Some people meet trouble halfway: Cat picked it up from the station. On evenings out, she considered midnight to be nearer 2 a.m. than 10 p.m. It was a party-pooping outlook but she was stuck with it. Thus, with two and a half months left of the social experiment, Cat felt that it was winding down. 'Soon be September,' she said, Eeyore-like, slicing a doorstop of crusty breakfast bread.

'How can early July be nearly September?' asked Mary rattily.

'Just saying.'

'Well, don't. Here.' She handed Cat a greasy gobbet of used kitchen roll. 'Bung this in the bin.'

'What did your last servant die of?' asked Cat.

'I locked him in the Aga when he answered me back.'

The cold clank of the bin's mechanism reminded Cat of the night before. The ball of kitchen paper dropped noiselessly on to a crumpled Waitrose bag. Before the lid of the bin had stuttered shut, Germaine threw open the back door, magnificent in a shaft of sunlight, a menopausal valkyrie.

'Look, ladies!' she roared. 'Mother Nature has smiled on our sisterly endeavours once more!' She tipped a selection of muddy vegetables on to the table. 'These courgettes are good enough for the county show.'

'Mm, shallots,' said Lucy.

'But the courgettes,' said Cat admiringly. 'The courgettes are unbelievable.'

The letter to Harry was on the hall table, waiting to be posted.

Dear Dad,

Thanks for getting back to me. Do you know the Lyme Majestic Hotel? It's at the top of the hill. How about the 18th of July, about three? We could have afternoon tea.

Love, Cat

She'd longed to sign herself Flowerpot, but jettisoned the idea as too childish: might as well write the letter in crayon.

37

'What do you people find to do when you're called?' kvetched Germaine from the parlour.

What, wondered Cat, *do you find to do out in the garden when we're all asleep?* She wondered it quietly however, and found her place in the circle, pocketing the reply from Harry that she'd read and reread all day. In a few days she'd see him in the flesh. It was terrifying, and wonderful, and very distracting.

'At last.' Germaine strode to the centre. 'Well,' she said on an exhaled breath, as if she was worn out before she began. 'There are only two of us left to share, so as one amongst us refuses to do so,' she shot a baleful look Beulah's way, 'it looks as if *I* must—'

Beulah was on her feet, interrupting. 'It's about time,' she was saying, 'that I did my duty.'

'Hang on, Beulah,' gabbled Cat, Harry chased efficiently from her mind. 'You don't have to!'

'It's time,' she insisted, with a look just for Cat that was part warning, part plea.

'If you insist.' Germaine put a hand on the old lady's shoulder and squeezed. 'Ladies: Beulah,' was her only introduction.

'My name is Beulah,' said Beulah, 'and this is my story.' Her voice was as period as her clothes, clipped and upper class, straight from the soundtrack of a Miss Marple film. 'It seems to me that I have led a dull and uneventful life. That nothing ever happened to me,' began Beulah, flat feet planted apart, eyes on something far beyond the end of the room. 'But that's not entirely true. Something horrible happened to me. Or did I do something horrible? It depends on who you listen to, and I'm not sure what the truth is, but I've gradually become aware that I owe you ladies my history. Friends share their truths. It took a while for that to sink in, because I've never had a friend before.'

Beulah had everybody's attention. Mary frowned across at Cat, who returned her expectant puzzlement with more of the same.

'I was born, quite a long time ago, in a big house in Surrey. My mother died almost straight away. She's just a photograph to me, a black and white picture of a lady with a very nice face. But scared eyes.' Beulah licked her lips. Cat longed to offer her a chair, but she guessed Beulah would prefer to stick to the rules. 'Her death was sudden, unexpected. When I am feeling generous, I can make an intellectual leap and suppose that this tragedy made him what he was.'

A quiet 'Ah!' seeped from Germaine, gratified that a 'he' had appeared so early on.

'He was a man of God. His God. Not mine, certainly,' said Beulah. Cat intuitively knew that this tale was freshly minted: Beulah had never said all this out loud before. 'He raised me conscientiously, sending me to private school, policing my playmates, correcting my childish mistakes.' She faltered. 'Brutally. He brutally corrected me, according to his beliefs that a child's sin must be beaten out of them.'

'Beulah,' interrupted Lucy gently. 'Was this man your father?'

'Yes.' Beulah choked slightly. 'That is the word. For who he was.'

Cat suddenly knew she'd never hear Beulah call him Father.

'I was very protected. I knew little beyond the vicarage, I knew nothing of the world. It was suffocating at times, hard, but I loved him,' said Beulah, a little mist of wistfulness trailing that admission.

'I looked forward to the day when I could strike out on my own. Make my mark.' She sighed knowingly. 'What as, I can't tell you. But the ambition was there. And the need to explore.' She looked from face to face, suddenly desirous to correct herself. 'Not that I wasn't grateful. I would never have cut my ties with home, but I wanted some adventures.' She shrugged. 'Small ones. Manageable adventures,' she smiled to herself.

A silence fell, broken only by Antonia's slippered foot knocking against the leg of her chair.

'And . . .?' Germaine's kindly nudge started Beulah's motor again.

'And then everything changed.' Beulah altered, in front of their eyes. Her face turned a queasy grey.

Cat bolted forward and put her arms around the woman, but found herself pushed gently away.

'I'm all right dear. This should finally see the light of day.' Beulah coughed, as if giving evidence in court, and then raised her chin and her voice. 'At the age of fifteen I conceived a child. Like countless innocent, ignorant girls before me. If I'd been a little more worldly, if I'd known I was being taken advantage of it might never have happened. He was horrified. He fumed and raged and began calling me the names he used for the rest of his life.' She swallowed. 'Whore. Slut. Harlot.' She nodded, accepting the women's empathetic murmurs. 'Terrible words. Terrible, terrible words. It surprised me,' she said contemplatively, 'the power they had over me.'

Another pause. What had taken a lifetime to air needed a few moments more to ripen.

'I had the baby,' said Beulah in a rush. 'I never held her. She was taken away. I don't know what shape her face was, or if she had hair. She was taken from me and given away.'

Cry, thought Cat. *Please cry.*

Beulah's eyes were dry. 'I know how she sounded, though. Like a lamb. It was a lovely noise.'

Noses were being blown. Mary looked shipwrecked. Jozette was still, her face drained.

'And the child's father?' Germaine's voice was colourless.

'Didn't care,' said Beulah, shutting out some unwelcome memory with a lowering of her eyes. 'Not a jot. So.' She squared her shoulders. 'Life went on. Life always goes on, ladies, even when you don't want it to. The baby was never mentioned.'

Your baby, Cat corrected her in her mind, then out loud. '*Your* baby, Beulah,' she said, her voice shaking.

'Yes, dear,' nodded Beulah, seeming surprised. 'My baby. My little baby was never spoken of again. My life story was rewritten, its beginning, middle and end all dictated by him. I was to stay close to him, where he could keep an eye on me. I was to keep to the straight and narrow, bring no more disgrace on his name. It was a highly respectable name, he meant something in our community. And I . . .' Beulah shook her head almost imperceptibly. 'I meant nothing. I was snuffed out like a candle. I couldn't leave the grounds without his permission. And he rarely gave it. The staff were let go, one by one. I looked after the house, and the garden, and him. And his parishioners, such as they were. His flock dwindled as his hellfire and brimstone spirituality fell further and further out of step with the world.'

'You were,' interrupted Lucy, in an angrily cold voice, 'a prisoner?'

'Yes and no.' It seemed important to Beulah to be fair. 'I could have walked out at any time. He didn't lock me in. But I was his creation,' she squinted, trying to explain. 'I didn't have any meaning, or purpose, outside his house. I only knew what I was so long as he was there to tell me: I was a low thing, a vile thing that wouldn't last ten minutes on my own. And the years passed. I grew older and he grew old. I cleaned, and cooked, and listened to his sermons echo around the chapel.' Beulah giggled, a noise so unexpected that her audience followed suit. 'Then I discovered *Coronation Street*!' she said, in a delighted voice. 'The old lady next door to us was one of his last followers, a tired, sick old girl who had nobody. He would send me in to check up on her, make sure she was coping. And she had a television!' Beulah's amazement was more suited to the discovery of a polar bear in her neighbour's sitting room. 'He never knew, of course, but we would settle down, this dear old creature and I, to watch *Coronation Street* twice a week. The stories were so fascinating, and the people so . . .' Beulah spread her hands as she sought to express herself. Her demeanour had shifted from hunted to zealous. 'So bold, so *alive*. They taught me so much.'

Cat caught Germaine's eye and they shared a small smile.

'It was Ken and Rita and Bet and the rest of them who showed me that people could be kind to one another. That an individual could do something wrong, atone for it and be accepted. They were funny and they got into muddles and they lost dear ones, but it all came out in the wash. Sometimes, when it was dark and he was shouting for me to bring him something, listing all my faults, prophesying Hell for me, I would imagine myself in *Coronation Street*, where Rita Fairclough could come along and give him a piece of her mind.'

For a moment, Beulah seemed lost, back on the Weatherfield cobbles maybe. She rallied for the next part of her tale. 'He fell sick. He needed a lot of care. I did everything I could, made him comfortable, but he knew. He knew how I longed for him to go. May God forgive me,' muttered Beulah.

'*We* forgive you,' said Lucy. 'If that's any help.'

'It is,' said Beulah. 'He took a long time dying. He would have taken me with him if he could.' She acknowledged the shocked tutting. 'Oh, he said as much. He slipped away one night, the first night in an age that I had a full night's rest. When I opened my eyes I knew.'

'You were free!' breathed Cat.

'I was terrified,' said Beulah, as if she hadn't heard. 'I ran to his bed and tried to shake him alive.' Beulah's lip curled at the memory. 'I didn't know what to do. How to be. I was nothing. I had listened to him for decades. Then I found that there are people who step in, who sort things out. An odd impetus took over and suddenly the house was sold and I had a bank account and there I was, out amongst strangers.'

'How long ago was this?' Germaine pushed her glasses back up into the nest of her hair.

'About a month before I found you. I tumbled about the country like a loose billiard ball, from B&B to B&B. Buying toffee in Lyme Regis I heard about this commune and I didn't question the voice in my head that told me to find you.' Beulah sagged. 'That's all,' she said, and shrugged. 'The end.'

Sitting on the back step, as a moody sun sank in a bath of pinks and oranges across the fields, Cat and Mary were squashed close together. Leaning against the hen house, Germaine's exuberant hair gave her the silhouette of a lollipop against the dramatic backdrop. 'Who'd have thought?' she was saying contemplatively.

'Me,' said Cat. 'I'd have thought. Not the detail, obviously, but I've always suspected there was something odd about Beulah's background. She doesn't react the way other people do, she's a one-off. Remember the pub? She can't cope if she's too far away from the commune, from, well, home I suppose.'

'That father of hers stunted her emotionally,' opined Germaine.

'Ye-es,' agreed Cat slowly, feeling that the theory didn't do Beulah justice. 'But she's wise, you know. She has depth. Sometimes I look up and find her watching me and I get the notion she knows exactly what I'm thinking.'

'Empathy,' nodded Germaine knowingly. 'It's a gift. Not many people possess it, but Beulah and I have it.'

A hurried glance passed between Cat and Mary: they'd pore over that little gem another time.

'Her father sounds a right head-the-ball.' Mary cut the preacher down to size. 'I reckon he locked her up, you know. Remember her freak-out in the pantry?' Mary looked furious. 'Why didn't she just tell him where to stick his opinions? I know, I know,' she said, as Cat and Germaine drew breath for howls of protest. 'He brainwashed her, yeah, I get it. But all those years?' She looked incredulous. 'I'd have killed him. Put rat poison in his gruel, or whatever the old feck ate.'

'Once the baby was born,' said Cat, feeling her way along, 'he had her just where he wanted her. She was full of shame. She felt worthless. The child's father was obviously no help.'

'Perhaps it was rape,' said Germaine, wincing.

'Oh God, I hope not.' Cat shuddered. She hadn't thought of that. 'Shit.'

'Her father sounds the type who would blame Beulah for getting raped.' Mary stuck out her tongue as if she'd tasted something foul. 'Humans stink sometimes.'

The last to climb the stairs, Cat tiptoed to bed in a dark room papered with gentle snores and sighs.

A quiet voice drifted out sleepily from under Beulah's patchwork quilt. 'Are you stealing about in bare feet again?' she asked gruffly.

'No,' lied Cat, making a leap for her bed.

'I've told you.' Beulah's voice tapered off into sleep. 'You'll catch your death.'

Maybe it was then, or maybe it was later, as Cat drifted off, that she decided never to let Beulah stray far from her again.

38

Everybody jumped. A jam tart hit the floor. The ring of the big vintage telephone was both unexpected and damn loud. Cat, Mary, Jo and Beulah all stared at each other, uncertain what to do. Beulah took charge.

'Good morning, the commune,' she said crisply, perfect casting for 'cosy housekeeper', no sign of yesterday's drama in her demeanour. 'Hold the line a moment, please.' She held the receiver out to Cat. 'It's for you. Trev.' The modern name was jagged in her mouth.

Cat looked at Jozette, and Jozette looked at Cat, motioning her to take the phone. The others slipped discreetly away, leaving the two women alone with the man they shared.

'What is it? What's happened?' said Cat.

'Nothing! Nothing's happened. Crikey, you don't change,' laughed Trev.

The laughter vexed Cat. 'Something must have happened. You never ring me for a chat.' Cat wound her neck in: Trev couldn't possibly know how momentous a phone call was in this outpost. 'Oh, sorry, Trev. It's nice to hear your voice.'

'That's better. I hate to disappoint you but everybody's coping without you, sis.'

That stung.

'It's you,' said Trev, 'I'm worried about. You've gone mental.'

Even a brother with cerebral palsy couldn't stop Trev using that term. 'It's a bit late to have a go at me about the commune,' sighed Cat.

'No, not that,' said Trev impatiently, 'although that *is* mental. Bloody mental. It's this Dad business. What are you on?'

Cat couldn't answer. Trev was trampling his muddy boots all over something precious.

'I read your last letter to Mum and I couldn't believe my bloody—'

'Hang on. That wasn't addressed to you.'

Trev quoted her words in a fluting, girly voice that sounded nothing like Cat. *I can't believe this is happening, that I'll really see him again.* For fuck's sake! *Thank you for giving me his address, it can't have been easy. This could be a new beginning for all of us.* You sound like a character in an American soap.'

'If I want to meet Dad it's nothing to do with you,' said Cat, with semi-skimmed conviction.

'Nothing to do with . . .?' Trev subsided, frustrated. 'He's my dad! He dumped me too, remember. And Mum. And Jon. How can you even consider talking to the old goat?'

'It's all arranged. I'm meeting him tomorrow, it's too late to back out now. Beside, perhaps it's not so simple. They were having problems—'

'And his answer was to walk out.'

'Apparently he didn't just walk out. It'd been brewing.'

'Look, Catrina, he walked out on you. And if that doesn't make you angry, remember he walked out on Jon. A defenceless baby with all sorts of things wrong with him.' Trev never named Jon's condition.

'Of course that makes me angry.' Cat struggled to control her volume and her tone. She was keeping one eye on Jozette, who, head down, was trying to look inattentive. 'But maybe it's time we grew up and saw Dad from an adult perspective. Relationships break down all the time.'

'Adult? This is about you still being a kid,' spat Trev. His animation was unexpected: Trev prided himself on sangfroid. 'Running back to Daddy to make it all all right, because her replacement Daddy let her down.'

'That's rubbish, Trev. You're talking crap.'

'Am I? I don't think so. Don't expect your real dad to kiss it better. He's a stranger. Just some bastard who broke your mum's heart. Are you proud of yourself, Cat? Raking all this up again?'

Cat was breathless with outrage. 'All of a sudden you're the big brother?' she goaded him, incredulous. 'Trev, you have no right to tell me what to do. You're never around, you're never interested and suddenly you're ordering me about!'

From across the kitchen Jozette gave up pretending not to listen and leaned against the big old sink, long arms folded. Her face was a question mark of anxiety. Cat shrugged at her, wild eyed.

'I'm the man of this family,' said Trev.

'You what?' spluttered Cat. 'What century are you calling from?' She hesitated. 'Mind you, you are rather like Dad. Neither of you are big on responsibility.'

'Thanks for that,' snapped Trev. 'I'm calling from Mum's, actually.'

'Oh.' Cat was deflated slightly. 'Is she all right?'

'She says she is. But I can tell she's upset about you and *him*.'

Cat sighed. Trev was a ruthless blackmailer. She felt stuffed with emotion, choked with it. O'Connor voices were rarely raised. 'You're forgetting that Mum and I write to each other,' she said, calmly. 'Mum is wary but she accepts that I've got to do it.'

There was silence for a while between the siblings. Cat locked eyes with Jozette and saw the need in the other woman. Her name hadn't even been mentioned. 'Listen, we can't agree on this. I'll meet . . .' she faltered. Bandying the word 'Dad' about was foreign to them both: it sounded false. 'I'll meet him and let you know how it goes.' She reconsidered. 'If you're interested.'

'Of course I am,' said Trev dourly.

'Well, OK . . .' Cat gripped the receiver hard. *Please please ask to speak to her.* She willed the thought down the wire.

'I'd better get off.'

'Right.' *Please!*

'See ya.'

'Yeah. See ya.'

'Hang on!' Trev blurted. 'Is Jo there? Could I have a quick word?'

Relief botoxed Cat's face. 'She's right here. Hold on.' She held out the phone.

Jozette pushed away from the sink, her long feet in their glittering flip-flops speeding up, then stopping. She sucked in her cheeks, holding Cat's gaze, then flapped her hands to shoo the phone away. *No,* she mouthed, shaking her head.

Cat waggled the phone, her face pleading.

Jozette walked out of the kitchen, leaving Cat to say, 'Actually, she's not here. I thought she was. But she's not.' She grimaced at her own ineptitude at lying: Trev would have handled that much more smoothly.

'Ah.' Trev understood. 'Tell her I called.' He coughed. 'How is she?'

'She's good. Not great, but good.'

'Excellent. Well, tell her I'm managing on my own. Another man would have sodded off, you know.' Trev was obviously aiming for breeziness but fell far short. 'I'm still here. Mug.'

'You're not a mug.' Cat felt her brother's paucity of emotional expression keenly. 'You're doing the right thing. That's what people in love do.'

'Whatever.' Trev was having none of that soppy stuff. 'See you, sis.'

'Bye, Trev.'

Out in the hall, Jozette lurked. She really was lurking, Cat noticed, head bowed, shoulders drooping.

'Sorry, Cat.'

'No, don't be. It's complicated.'

Jozette nodded, and stretched. The lurk was over. 'You got that damn right.'

The house was subdued that evening. No Group. No seminars. Cat, listlessly washing up mugs at the deep sink, was distracted by a small dot of red light in the garden. Squinting through the leaded window she made out Antonia, standing alone in the dark.

As Cat approached, Antonia ground the cigarette under her heel.

'Nice night,' said Cat casually.

'Is it?' Antonia sounded bored already. 'Hadn't noticed.'

'Right,' said Cat, rather regretting her altruism in coming outside.

'They said, at AA, they're always saying' – Antonia stumbled, like somebody who'd just learned to speak – 'to expect mood swings.'

'This'll be one of them, then,' grinned Cat, taking a chance.

'Yeah.' Antonia groaned and smiled too, a wan reflection of Cat's. 'Sorry. I'm not myself. It's like they unlace you and you're all over the place and you have to slowly lace yourself back up again. Coming clean about your pitiful life in front of people . . .' She screwed up her colourless face. 'It's not easy.'

'No,' sympathised Cat. 'I bet.' They stood in companionable silence for a while.

Antonia was biting her lip, making it bleed. 'It's the first time anybody's ever really listened.'

Cat took that personally. 'Oh Antonia, we lis—'

'But I wasn't telling you the truth,' interrupted Antonia. 'I was giving you the made-up Antonia, the acceptable one. At AA I talk about the other one.'

'What's she like?'

'A blooming nightmare, pardon my French.'

'Potty mouth,' laughed Cat.

'I wasn't at school the day they had lessons in how to be normal.' Antonia was lighting another cigarette, her face a demonic orange for a split second as the tip flared. 'I envied everybody, *everybody*, the way they just floated through life, dealing with the changes, the experiences. I wanted to run and hide. Growing up, leaving home scared me. But then again,' she laughed drily, 'home scared me too.'

'You know, we don't all float,' sighed Cat.

'I'm learning that. Now I've started noticing other people for the first time. Drinking wasn't partying for me, it wasn't fun, it was numbness. It was the utter pleasure of not being Antonia for a few hours.' She grimaced. 'And now I'm Antonia all day every day.' Her voice had risen. The original Antonia would have apologised; instead her mood swung again. 'Will you do something for me?' she asked urgently. 'And say nothing about it?'

'Ye-es,' said Cat cagily.

'There's a small bottle of vodka in my washbag. Will you pour it down the sink?'

'Of course I will.' Cat turned to go, then stopped and said awkwardly without looking at Antonia. 'Well done, for, you know, not drinking it.'

'Hah!' said Antonia. 'Yeah. Well done me.'

39

All days roll around eventually, the dreaded and desired alike: the eighteenth of July managed to be both these things.

Settling herself into a wicker chair in the conservatory of the Lyme Majestic Hotel, Cat couldn't get comfortable. Trev's words rattled around her brain as she fidgeted and fussed with the cushions. The stately surroundings, all aspidistras and starched doilies, were fusty and middle aged: a condition just around the corner if she squinted at her future in the wrong way.

Turning her attention to the view through the expanse of glass at the back of the room, Cat was rewarded with the swooping curve of Lyme Bay. Outside the hotel, lawns sauntered down to the seafront, and then wild nature took over, with a choppy sea the colour of a Persian kitten's eyes. The tide was in, flooding the flat sands of the bay.

Crossing and re-crossing her legs, Cat bemoaned her instinct to dress demurely. Jozette's crisp navy cigarette pants and white blouse struck a bum note of feminine purity: she was a wimple away from being a nun. Was this some insane ploy to please a Daddy she didn't know? An attempt to rekindle her virginity before meeting Harry?

And she was early. How craven. How *needy.* Cat positioned herself facing away from the door so that she couldn't stare at it: the fear that Harry wouldn't turn up had kept her awake until the small hours. 'Get a grip, Flowerpot,' she told herself. Soon the man who'd coined that useful phrase would be sitting opposite her.

Hopefully.

Risking a peek, Cat was rewarded by the sight of a tall man in a white linen suit saying something to the manager over by the door. *Too young,* she dismissed him.

The man turned to follow the manager's pointing finger and his eyes met Cat's. They were Jon's eyes, brown and bright and doggy. 'Darling!' bellowed the man, charting a weaving course through the sea of small tables.

'Da—' Cat had to cough to get the whole word out. Absurdly, she found herself saying 'Daddy!', the childish title emerging as a tearful squeak.

There was no shaking of hands, no formality, Harry swept his daughter into a bear hug that muffled her 'It's you!' and filled her senses with his smell of coffee, tobacco and mint.

'Look at you,' said Harry, taking a step back. 'You're a knockout, Cat. My little girl, all grown up, well, well, well.' He sat down abruptly and Cat did the same.

Still reeling from the hug (her wildest dreams hadn't anticipated that), Cat drank him in. Her 'You look well' was an understatement. Her father looked a decade younger than his years. She saw the gleam of cufflinks at his wrist and clocked the buttercream silk tie: her mind made associations she would rather it didn't, and Hugh flashed across her vision. 'How are you?' she asked inanely.

'All the better for seeing you!' There was no awkwardness about Harry, no doubt about how he should be. He was gushing, excited. 'God, you're like your mum,' he said suddenly, with a broad beam.

'Oh,' said Cat, who had presumed that her mum would be off limits. 'Am I?' Successive rugs were being pulled out from beneath her: Harry was hurdling over the sticky moments of a father/daughter reunion as if he tackled one every day. His blitheness was impenetrable as he beckoned a waitress like an old friend.

At first Cat couldn't countenance the tempting little sandwiches and the warm scones, but she found her appetite as she relaxed. Harry was full of questions: about her work, her life, her ambitions. She answered with enough detail to satisfy him, but held something back. Hugh was not up for discussion, and she neglected to tell him about losing her job: best to tread warily for now. The commune became 'the house I'm staying in'.

Her suspicion about what Harry might do with her secrets – how they would sound in his mouth – pricked Cat with shame. He was a garrulous, expansive man, with the same broad smile she remembered from the massacred photographs. 'You lost the moustache, I see,' she teased, trying to lighten up.

'Good Lord yes,' laughed Harry, stroking his nude upper lip. His mouth curved just like Jon's. 'And the old hair's starting to go.'

'The touches of grey suit you,' said Cat. She was astonished at how handsome he was, how healthy, as if he was bursting through his outline to get even bigger and more 'there'. She thought of her mother, thin and diminished, a watercolour. 'What do you do these days?'

'Antiques at the mo,' said Harry, in a lower tone as if confiding. 'I got out of yachts.'

'Yachts?' yelped Cat. She tussled with that for a second: her father was dealing in yachts while her mother was arguing with social services about a grant for Jon's specialised bed? 'That's fancy.'

'But no fun,' declared Harry. 'I love going around auction houses, sniffing out the bargains, bidding. It's all a game really.' He looked over the rim of the teacup that was nonsensically dainty in his grip. 'I thought you might come with me one of these days. There's a cracking house contents sale just up the valley next month. The eighth. You up for it?'

'God, yes, hmm, yeah, great,' stammered Cat. Another meeting, so casually arranged! Harry wanted to be part of her life. 'I love antiques,' she claimed, craven again. She couldn't tell an armoire from a bidet, but she had a sudden image of the pair of them,

O'Connor and daughter, careering down country lanes with a Louis Quinze side table they'd bought for a fiver strapped to the roof rack.

'So, you bagged yourself a husband yet, Cat?'

'Er, no, actually,' said Cat, casually, as if it had just occurred to her.

'Really?' Harry seemed surprised. 'Bet that old biological clock is ticking, eh?' he laughed.

Cat managed a smile. These ham-fisted comments were ballast for his charm: Harry had already described her ankles as 'like your mum's, you know, thick'. The alternate punches and tickles were dizzying. The next left hook came in the form of a casual reference to a woman Cat didn't know existed.

'My wife wanted to come today,' said Harry, with a happy shrug at the funny ways of women. 'Maybe another time, I told her. She's very curious about you.'

'Well, yeah,' said Cat. 'She would be.' She hesitated, feeling exposed. Ideally she'd have Trev and Jon and her mum beside her to hear the answer to 'Do you have kids? With her, I mean?'

'Three,' said Harry immediately. 'Two girls. One fella.' He halted, unnaturally, as if he'd reconsidered what he was about to say: Cat guessed it had been some sort of proud parental comment and she was grateful to him for holding it back. 'Carol's younger than me, I'm a lucky dog. She's, let's see . . .' He totted it up on his fingers. 'Three years older than you!'

The equation delighted Harry, but left his daughter reeling.

'The kids are all under ten. They keep me young,' said Harry, patting where his paunch should, by rights, have been. 'I swore no more kids after I had you and the boys,' he said, 'and my second wife was happy with that. But Carol's very maternal.'

'So,' said Cat slowly, 'Carol's your third wife?'

'Yup. What am I like?' asked Harry happily.

Preferring not to answer that, Cat said, uncertainly, 'Dad, may I ask you something? Something you might not like?'

Harry sat back, hands on his knees. 'You can ask me anything,' he said, drained suddenly of vim.

'Why . . .' Cat coughed. The question lodged in her throat. 'Why did you stay away? Why didn't you . . .' She wanted to say 'care', but discarded the word as brutal. 'Why didn't you keep in touch?'

The air went out of Harry, and his shoulders drooped in his white suit. 'I can understand why you ask me that,' he said. 'Absolutely.'

The forgiving tone irked Cat, and she tweaked her bra strap unnecessarily: there was only one person at this table who had something to forgive and it wasn't Harry.

'It was awkward, darling,' said Harry, splaying his hands as if to concede the inadequacy of his response. 'I didn't know how to. Things were so frosty with me and your mum. Which was my fault, of course,' he added hastily. 'She was devastated, and I couldn't face her. It was a terrible time.' He looked at the carpet, as if seeing some dread pattern in the pile. 'I took the easy way out,' he admitted.

'I missed you,' said Cat, in a tiny voice.

'But look at you!' Harry held his hands out as if to show her off. 'You're a belter!'

'I really missed you,' said Cat, her face growing hot and her breath catching on the rusty nail of her father's insouciance.

'That's all in the past, darling,' said Harry, his eyebrows contorting in sympathy. 'I'd change things if I could.' He clapped his hands together. 'But we won't let it spoil today!'

Watching Harry pour them both more tea, and swear at the fiddly tongs as he dropped a scone, Cat composed herself. This showboating, freewheeling man would never realise what he'd done. Harry skated on the surface of things and Cat didn't feel up to wondering whether this was a deliberate ploy to simplify his life, or if her father really was incapable of depth.

'Cream? Jam?' Harry piled her plate.

Sitting back, Cat experienced a mini-epiphany on her wicker chair. It all slid away, the anger, the curiosity, the expectations now exposed as naive. This was a man like any other, no superhero but no villain either. He was Harry O'Connor, good for a laugh but for God's sake, don't rely on him. Fallible, handsome, lively and a dead loss, he wasn't the answer: Harry had no magical solution to the knots of Cat's tangled life.

Unexpectedly, it was a relief.

'So,' asked Harry, licking his fingers. 'What do you make of your long-lost dad?'

Cat winced at the soap opera terminology. Looking around her in an exaggerated way, she said wryly, 'Well, you seem to have left your white steed outside.'

An appraising look glittered in Harry's eyes, as if weighing up what his daughter meant. 'Don't own one of those.' He paused. 'Not many men do.'

'I'm learning that.' Somewhere in Chelsea a desirable, bijou apartment with a For Sale sign outside folded in on itself like a deck of cards. If – and Cat could finally admit this – Hugh had been Daddy Lite, she now knew that her actual Daddy was pretty Lite too. 'As you're not going to ask me about Jon,' she said, with deliberate brightness of tone, 'I'll just go ahead and fill you in.'

'OK.' Harry put his cup down and assumed a listening position, like a bad actor in an am-dram production.

'Don't look so serious!' teased Cat. She was accustomed to people reacting to talk of Jon in this self-consciously grave way: people outside the family. 'He's doing well, amazing all the doctors. Mum turned the garage into a room for him, and all the equipment he needs is in there.'

'So he's all right, my boy?' asked Harry, looking his age.

'He's more than all right.'

The conversation skittered this way and that. It grew less portentous, more frothy. Cat giggled at Harry's turn of phrase, his merciless impressions. As the light changed over the bay, Harry looked at his watch. 'Ah. Have to shoot, darling.' His eyes became sadder and doggier. 'I could sit here all day with you.'

'Me too,' smiled Cat.

'I'll just . . .' Harry nodded his head in the direction of the toilets. 'Back in a mo.'

Cat didn't watch him go, she was staring out at the sea, admiring the hazy violet sky. Her father was 3D now, real and as flawed – *only* as flawed – as the next human. She suppressed a giggle. He was a bit of a fool, really: three wives? That was downright messy. For now Cat preferred to shy away from the boat-rocking realisation that she had half-siblings. Hard though it was to admit, she was envious of those kids: they had a daddy who would be around for their teens.

But there was only one Flowerpot. Cat silently thanked Harry for bequeathing her that mantra: Flowerpot had got a grip.

'So, darling, have to fly.' Harry came back, all movement and bustle, patting his pockets and holding his arms out.

Pressed to his chest, Cat heard him say, discreetly, 'I took care of the bill.' He relinquished her and held her at arm's length, beaming. 'And that's a date for the eighth, yes? I'll call the number you gave me.' He looked at his watch again. 'Carol'll kill me if I'm late picking up our youngest. She's on a play date, or whatever they call them now. You never had a play date, did you, love? They're new things. You'd love my youngest,' he smiled. 'But she'll be very cross with her old Dad if he keeps her waiting.' Turning, he laughed, 'Got a temper on her, has my Flowerpot.' He waved extravagantly, and blew a kiss from the door. 'Goodbye, Cat!'

Cat missed the kiss. She was staring at the sea as it turned its back, preparing to drag itself out towards the horizon, a bright line very far away.

40

Swinging her legs on the kitchen table like a four-year-old, Cat asked, 'Beulah, when are you making more of those flapjack things?' Those flapjack things were chewily sweet and as yielding as a drunk lap dancer. 'I love them.'

'Not today, I'm afraid.' Beulah wiped her hands on her apron. 'Soon, dear.'

Cat needed distraction. Flowerpot had lost her grip. She astounded herself, a woman in her late thirties crying over her daddy, but maybe, as Mary reckoned, it was backdated. 'Need any help?'

'No, thank you.' Beulah was self-sufficient in the kitchen. Placidly she moved through her day, the pace belying her output. She never stopped, and she never sped up.

'Sweet potato and pork casserole,' said Cat, watching the ingredients follow each other into a cast-iron pot. 'Antonia's favourite.'

'She needs feeding up.'

'You're so good to us all,' sighed Cat. 'You'd make a great mum.' Cat's legs stopped swinging. 'Oh, that was thoughtless of me, Beulah. I'm sorry.' She twisted around to get a look at Beulah's face as the old lady passed her with the pot in her hands. 'Sorry. Sorry. I didn't think.'

'Oh hush,' said Beulah, softly. She wrinkled her nose at Cat. 'No harm done.'

Mired in shame, Cat was silent, listening to the soothing clanks and splashes of dinner being put together. 'Have you ever,' she began carefully, 'thought about trying to find the baby? How old would she be?' She looked over at Beulah's broad back at the stove. 'Beulah?'

'Surely,' said Beulah without turning around, 'you have something better to do than buzz around me like a damn bluebottle?'

'I'll . . .' Cat jumped off the table, smarting as if Beulah had slapped her. 'I'll see if Germaine needs any help with, er, anything.'

The noise of the casserole lid being banged into place followed Cat out into the garden.

The windows of the parlour were thrown open that evening, and the powdery air was heavy.

The game of Hangman that Jozette had instigated with Sarge ran aground on a bad-tempered 'Gabbana? What kind of word is that?' Mary was reading a copy of *Country Life* from November 1983 with such concentration that her mind simply had to be elsewhere, while Lucy scribbled in her notepad.

Flopping down beside Cat, Jozette produced a tube of moisturiser. 'Hands,' she ordered.

Stretching out her paws, Cat waited for and got the indignant 'Lordy Lordy' that Jozette always felt necessary. Rubbing the cream firmly into red fingers and neglected nails, Jozette said wonderingly, 'Did you know that Sarge has never been to Selfridges?' She shook her head. 'Poor woman.' She leaned back and scrutinised Cat's face. 'Your hair is getting too long. I'll take the scissors to it tonight.'

'Hugh was always on at me to grow out my fringe.'

'That man has taste,' said Jozette approvingly. 'I only met him once, but girlfriend, the suit!' She licked her lips as if recalling a delicious meal. 'Those swanky English guys have it all worked out. Probably goes to his grandpa's tailor. Velvet, wasn't it? Soft as butter.' She redoubled the massage. 'Hard act to follow.'

Nobody ever said that about Hugh. Cat bunched a bit nearer to Jozette. 'He is,' she agreed enthusiastically. 'Other men are kind of pale, you know? He put so much thought into living. And it was all so de luxe.'

'He was Harrods,' suggested Jozette, 'and other guys are TKMaxx?'

'Exactly.' Cat relished the guilty pleasure of praising the man she'd left behind. 'I mean, Will, he's nice and everything . . .'

'The vet?' Jozette looked up sharply, her teardrop-shaped eyes alert. 'You've got the hots for the vet? Good call, good call,' she said contemplatively, ignoring Cat's sudden backtracking expostulations of *Not the hots exactly, I wouldn't say that, I just like him, you know, as a friend kind of thing.* 'That guy is all guy, you know?' Jozette pulled a saucy face, at odds with her haughty bone structure. 'Could do with sharpening up, but the raw material is kinda juicy.'

The word caused a tremor. Jozette had hit the sexual nail on the head. Will was indeed juicy. Cat blew a smokescreen over him. 'If you like that kind of thing,' she said airily. 'But compared to Hugh. . .' Cat shrugged. Even if Hugh had done something unspeakable to win her back she couldn't forget his style, his wit, and his lust for life.

'Why compare?' Jozette sounded puzzled. 'They're so different.'

'I can't go straight for a Cornish pasty when I've been dining on foie gras all these years,' protested Cat. 'Will's a yokel. He's rooted in this countryside, like the trees. Or Germaine's carrots. He'd think my life was pretentious, shallow.'

'*This* is your life now, hon.'

'No, no, no, this is a holiday. A retreat. A sojourn.'

'If you say so. I prefer to live in the moment.'

'Does that mean Trev's in the past?'

'Right now he is.' Jozette blew out her cheeks. 'I don't know what your parents were up to when they made your brother. He's the most infuriating, adorable person in the world.'

Letting that pass – it would be the twelfth of Never before Cat could describe Trev as adorable – Cat smiled in sympathetic support.

'I know the guy is bad for me. Like, really really bad for me.' Jozette's voice sank an octave or two to demonstrate Trev's essential badness. 'But leaving him behind would break my heart.' Jozette sighed. 'I assumed that was just a saying. Until now.'

Seeing Jozette's face cloud over was like watching a power cut hit New York. At that moment Cat would have cheerfully sucker-punched her dopey brother for putting a good woman through such pain. And for what? For the Pernod-fuelled attentions of a procession of dozy bints in pelmet skirts. Even the new, rounded, human Trev (he cries real tears!) that Jozette had revealed at Group couldn't be forgiven. 'I hope he learns something from all this.' Cat caught Jozette's eye and understood the expression there. 'Naw. You're right. He won't.' She drew back her hand and looked at it admiringly. 'It looks slightly less like a hand that spent its morning down the bog. Thank you very much.'

A tray was set on the coffee table in front of them. Beulah stood back.

'Oh,' said Cat, looking from tray to woman and back again.

'Flapjacks!' yelled Jozette, back to full power.

Dave had never been so clean. Her trotters could take out an appendix: not a great idea, admittedly, but there'd be no risk of infection. The county show, once safely in the future, was a day away and the commune was given over to preparation.

'So it's a show?' Jozette was asking, as she rubbed Prada hydrating body lotion into Dave's ginormous behind. 'But with animals?' She pulled her chin in. 'Do they, like, dance and stuff?'

'That would be worth seeing, but no.' Cat was massaging Dave's neck. 'It's a competition, really. The best pig, the best cow, the best, erm, goat, I suppose.' She rested on her haunches. 'I've never been to one, but I think they have traditional music and a funfair and stuff.'

'Sounds like a blast.'

In the kitchen Beulah baked cake after cake after cake. After much debate, the commune had voted for her toffee sponge as the strongest contender in the 'Home Baked Cake (misc.)' section. An unforeseen competitive streak had emerged in their cook. She was making notes, licking spoons, beating frosting at three times her normal speed. By the time Dave was snoring on muslin carefully laid over her hay, there were four lofty sponges standing like Olympian heroes on the kitchen table.

'Well?' There was a neurotic edge to Beulah's query.

'Bloody hell!' laughed Cat. 'Have I died and gone to heaven?'

'Everybody has to taste them and decide which recipe is the best.' She struck Cat's outstretched hand with a wooden spoon. 'Wait! It has to be scientific, dear. The cakes are numbered one to four and there is a form to fill in about each of them.'

They were long forms. Beulah ignored their complaints and started slicing.

'We're not all here,' said Beulah, looking around.

'Sarge and Antonia are in Lyme. AA,' said Mary through a mouthful of frosting.

'Again?' queried Lucy. 'She goes rather a lot.'

'She told me,' said Cat, between bites, 'that she'd go every day if she could.'

'Rather her than me,' said Lucy with feeling. 'I couldn't expose myself to a bunch of strangers like that.'

'Maybe,' suggested Mary, a toxic edge to her tone, 'some people don't have scuzzy little secrets.'

Cat saw Lucy's eyes slide downwards, before she put her plate down with a sharp clang.

'I've had enough, thanks.' Lucy left the room.

'What?' said Mary innocently to the unspoken accusation hanging in the air.

'You—' Cat began, but Mary was saved by the bell, or rather the scrape of feet in the hall. Antonia and Sarge were back.

'Cake!' said Antonia with undisguised lust. She took a small piece and a form from Beulah.

'Was AA fun?' asked Mary.

'Fun?' Antonia, more vivid these days, pouted. 'It's not fun, Mary. It's arduous.'

'It's tough,' said Sarge, using a word she felt at home with.

'Sorry,' said Mary wryly. 'It's just that you seem high.'

'On life, thankfully!' laughed Antonia. The sound was sunny and unforced. 'Hmm.' She looked loftily at Cat's plate. 'That's quite a hunk of cake. There are many sorts of addictions, you know.' She bent closer, stooping. She was getting taller too: Cat guessed this must be an illusion. 'Filling an emotional hole, are we?'

Just for a moment, Cat mourned the old Antonia, the one who wouldn't say boo to a goose, or a Cat.

'You have to suffer for beauty,' Cat told Dave. 'No walk tonight. You're under house arrest. Stop kicking the door! You'll ruin your manicure.'

A poor replacement for Dave, Mary accompanied Cat through the gates.

'You were mean to Lucy, earlier,' began Cat as they scaled the hill.

'Can we not talk about how vile I am for a while?' asked Mary archly. 'I'm getting a leetle tired of the lectures. Saw you chatting to her last night. After dinner.'

'Mm-hmm.' Cat recalled the conversation. She and Lucy had discovered a mutual friend who neither of them knew all that well. It hadn't been fascinating, and was memorable mainly for the fiery holes Mary's eyes had bored in the back of Cat's head.

'What did you talk about?'

'It wasn't really a chat. Me and Lucy don't do chats.' Cat raised an eyebrow. 'It wasn't about you, if that's what you're worried about.'

'All lovey dovey one minute. *Oh Mary* this and *oh Mary* that. Then nada.' Mary exhaled noisily. 'She never talks to me any more.'

'Are you surprised?' Cat gaped at her friend. 'I don't know what's come over you. You would never taunt me the way you're taunting Lucy.'

'I like you.'

'You like Lucy,' Cat reminded her.

'I did.'

It wasn't really a lie. It just wasn't very accurate reporting.

Dear Mum (and Trev, you nosy bugger),

The meeting with Dad went OK. He's the image of Jon, very smart, very youthful.

She hesitated. The next line *would* be a lie. A lie they all needed.

He asked me all about Jon.

No need, thought Cat, to itemise the wives and the children, nor to tell them how she longed to be standing in her mum's kitchen that smelled of toast, drinking tea out of a mug with her name on it.

41

'Look! Actual people!' breathed Cat, as they piled out of the minibus.

'And mud!' complained Mary.

The county show car park was a field so churned up it looked like a First World War battleground dotted incongruously with Range Rovers.

'Make way for Dave.' Sarge threw open the back doors. Contrary to dire predictions, Dave had not attended to her toilette during the drive and was sweet smelling and ready for her close-up. The mud held no fears because Jozette had fashioned pig bootees out of polythene, tied up with velvet ribbon. Walking behind the women, the pig attracted some comment as they made their way towards the entrance: Cat discerned the words 'townie,' 'crazy' and 'old bags'.

'Careful!' snapped Germaine when Cat veered too close. She was cradling a basket of courgettes as if they were Semtex. 'We don't want them bruising.'

The sacred toffee sponge made its stately progress on an improvised litter made from a tea tray, carried by Lucy and Antonia. The mood was tense, thanks to Germaine's competitive nature. Her persistent use of such phrases as 'we'll show them' and 'this is it' had demoralised the little band: none of them particularly wanted to 'show' the nebulous 'them'.

Lucy had reckoned, sotto voce, before Germaine boarded the bus, that Beulah had a chance of a placement, but that the courgettes were doomed. 'I covered one of these shows for a Sunday magazine once. The standard is incredibly high. People who have been growing vegetables for years employ all sorts of techniques for producing, well, *monster* vegetables.' She'd mimed a whopper of a courgette with her hands.

'Wouldn't have thought you'd have much use for an enormous courgette,' Mary had said, not sotto voce at all.

A fartily exuberant brass band grew louder as the women filed under the entrance banner. A small, rather sedate funfair showed its lurid head above the stalls of local organic produce, local handmade jewellery, local this and local that. Flags fluttered above stripy marquees and a PA system droned non-stop in a languid language that was recognisable as English only at odd moments. Cat strained but all she could make out was 'would the shinkle shankle bankle cauliflower shonkle wonkle immediately'.

'Mmm, the smell of the farmyard,' said Antonia enthusiastically, wiggling her long, thin nose.

Mary gave an 'eeyew' at the mingled odours of countless large, hairy animals, all sweating and defecating to, quite literally, a band playing. 'And *what* tune are they murdering?' she asked, screwing up her face.

'*Hey Jude*, but not as we know it.' Cat had slowed, and was on the fringe of their little crew. Her heart thudded in her throat the way she remembered from fairs when she was little. After so long in the house, such noise and colour was overwhelming. She picked out the back of Beulah's head. The old lady seemed calm, staying close to her cake.

'It's all so feckin' wholesome,' complained Mary. 'Isn't there anywhere to have a drink? Oh.' She put her hand to her mouth. 'Sorry, Antonia.'

'S'all right.'

'This hubbub is ruinous for my courgettes.' Germaine was looking about anxiously. 'Ah! The vegetable tent.' She strode off, alone, as the others had spotted the cake tent, a much more agreeable prospect.

'Oh dear,' said Beulah eloquently as she drew back the curtain.

It was cake Eden. Having tethered Dave outside, Cat swayed slightly at the sight of rows and rows of towering, majestic, fuck-off-fabulous cakes. Some were iced, others jewelled with dried fruit like Plantagenet crowns. Women in dreadful clothes, wearing orange tights despite the heat, primped their creations. An altercation raged over the blameless head of a battenberg, a chiffon tank of a woman shouting 'Maureen, you're breathing on my fondant and not for the first time!'

Despite the heavenly aroma, the atmosphere was strained. The women found Beulah's spot, and laid the cake down as reverentially as a Soviet Leader's embalmed body.

'It's twice the height of the one next to it,' Cat hissed in Beulah's ear.

'It's the taste that matters.' Beulah had dug out a straw hat for her big day. It was comically small for her leonine head, but Cat thought she looked beautiful.

'Then you'll win hands down.'

From the PA a sleepy voice crackled 'Would bink owner snonkle bankle pig bonkle bock cake tent please shinkle shoo.'

'Back in a mo.' Cat slipped away, leaving her friends turning Beulah's masterpiece this way and that.

Outside the tent, a bad-tempered man in a brown overall and a badge gestured at Dave. 'This yours?'

'All mine,' said Cat proudly. And erroneously.

'Then get her to the swine section with the other pigs, pronto.'

The fair was a multi-layered event: at the top were chair-o-planes and morris dancing, beneath that the ruthless matrons with machine guns under their matching separates, and below that again, a strata of officious men in overalls marching around being disrespectful to pigs.

'Swine section indeed,' muttered Cat under her breath, leading Dave through the crowd. People, she noticed, got out of the way for a pig.

Just past the radio road show, where a DJ in a colourful handknit who'd never had a girlfriend was whipping his audience of three OAPs into a frenzy, and just before a baffling stall which offered only a ferret sitting in a drainpipe, Cat found the swine section.

She also found Will, in an overall, brandishing a clipboard.

'Hello,' she said, for all the world like a normal person.

'Hi,' said Will, with a wide smile that shunted his dimples up towards his eyes. 'What are you – oh.' He looked fondly down at Dave. 'Is this an entrant?'

'Yes.'

Scanning the list, he tapped the page with a chewed biro. 'I see. She's in Pig of the Year?'

'Yes,' said Cat, guesstimating just how hard her advertising colleagues would laugh at her right now.

Will raised his eyes. Surrounded by short sooty lashes they looked deep into Cat's.

This made Cat clear her throat. She'd never been one to swoon: throat-clearing was as far as she'd go. Will looked as if he had something momentous to say.

'Please,' he said, in a low voice, sexily laced with urgency, 'don't put Dave in for Pig of the Year.'

It was a poor second to *take me now*. 'Why not?'

'She can't win.' Will leaned in, and she could smell him: he smelled of shampoo, and soap. 'There are pigs in there with fancier pedigrees than Prince Charles. She'll be humiliated.'

Dave was devouring a dirty nappy at Cat's feet. 'What'll I do?' Cat handed the reins entirely to Will. It was comforting: Cat usually held her reins tightly, but Will was so tall and so calm, and possessed the rare talent of looking hot in an overall.

'The only section Dave has a hope in is Pig with the Curliest Tail,' said Will sombrely. 'But the rules disallow any last-minute changes to the entries. They're extremely strict about it.'

'Darn.' Cat's shoulders slumped. Dave oinked.

'But . . .' Will looked about him, bit his ripe bottom lip, and scribbled furtively on the clipboard. 'There. It's done. Go.' He caught her eye, and must have clocked the twinkle there. 'And if anybody asks, we never spoke.'

With Dave safely shackled amongst the other Curliest Tail hopefuls, Cat wandered about, savouring the tame motorcycle display laid on by the local Cubs and treating herself to a free sample of malt loaf, before pulling aside the curtains of the vegetable tent.

Spotting Germaine, Cat made her way over, passing cabbages the size of space hoppers.

Beside her long, green pride and joy, Germaine looked diminished, as if somebody had thrown a bucket of freezing water over her. She glowered at Cat as she approached. 'Have you seen that man's marrow?' She stabbed a finger in the direction of a genteel old gent in a panama. 'It is fucking phenomenal.'

'I'll take your word for it.' Cat compared the commune's entry with the courgettes either side. 'Damn,' she said.

'Quite,' said Germaine.

And then they both laughed, very hard and for rather a long time.

'That's more like it,' said Cat approvingly as they calmed down. 'That's the Germy I know and love.'

'Am I being unbearable again?' asked Germaine regretfully.

'You've been worried, I can tell.' Cat drew closer, leaning over their shameful courgettes. 'Is something wrong?'

Perfectly still, Germaine held her gaze, turning something over in her mind. She shook her curls, finally, and said, 'Of course not'.

Unconvinced, Cat probed on. 'Is it money? Something to do with the lease?' She pulled a face. 'Not your health?'

'All right, ladies?' Jamie interrupted them, beaming. 'All well up at the commune, I 'ope?'

'Yeah, great,' smiled Cat, hoping he wouldn't linger. He was strictly for display purposes only.

Nobody had told Jamie that. 'That's a lovely courgette you have there,' he said gallantly to Germaine, placing his thumbs in the belt loops of his jeans.

'Thank you,' said Germaine meekly. She too seemed to be willing him away.

'Although,' he confided, trilling his Rs, 'I daresay you've had bigger.'

Cat gawped at him and Germaine was stonily silent as Jamie backed off, guffawing his helium laugh and saying, 'All right, all right, girls, just a bit of fun.'

'That guy's a throwback,' sighed Cat, hating herself for watching his bum retreat through the crowd.

Twelfth in a field of twelve, the courgettes were in disgrace. The cake did better. Beulah had her photograph taken standing stiffly with her silver medal for the local paper.

On hearing 'pig judging bonkle shankle now', the women scurried over to the swine section.

Mary was queasy from abusing the free samples of malt loaf, and Antonia had wandered off by the time the judges reached Dave's pen. Straightening up, Mary whispered slyly to Cat, 'Well, well, well, we might just pick up another medal here.'

Shocked that Will hadn't disclosed his status of chief swine judge, Cat watched him peer carefully at Dave's tail. With the eyes of the crowd upon him, he tugged to test for springiness. Dave made an aggrieved noise that might be spelled as 'uurghruh' and Will made copious notes. At no point did he meet Cat's eye.

Clapping with the rest of the crowd, Mary hissed, 'I'm calling the *Washington Post.* This is PigGate,' as a winner's rosette was pinned to Dave's leash.

'Very well done,' said Will, shaking Cat's hand.

'Why thank you,' said Cat, doing her best not to laugh. He

turned away and Cat felt the wrench, watching his broad back until Mary announced 'Booze tent,' in a decisive way.

Sitting on a bale of hay in the open air, Cat nursed a warm local beer and tuned out of her surroundings. Lucy and Mary were sitting opposite each other, apparently in different universes, leaving Beulah, Jozette and Sarge to keep the conversational ball in the air. Germaine had gone to look for Antonia, despite the others' assertion that Antonia was old enough to look after herself. Germaine had insisted, her subtitles clear: if Antonia was drunk in a ditch somewhere she wanted to find her sooner rather than later.

The day was fraying. Stalls were being dismantled, the brass band had tooted their last, and lowing animals were being persuaded into trailers, their huge, heavy feet making clumsy music on the ramps.

The ale fizzed straight to Cat's head. She scanned the thinning crowd, mistaking every other man for Will. After her first half pint, she mistook a few women for him as well: that stuff was strong.

At her feet sat Dave, pinkly comfortable, her rosette drawing the odd congratulation from passers-by. Cat tweaked the winning tail, and wondered if Will had gone home. Or been called away to some Yorkshire terrier emergency.

Stealthily, Will had become one of Cat's unholy male trinity. He joined Harry who loomed, King-Kong-like, over the landscape: part of Cat was gloomily convinced that he wouldn't keep their auction date. Hugh, neatly catalogued as 'Fucked-up Father Substitute' was no longer mourned, but refused to leave the building. And then there was Will. Sturdy, comfortable, country boy Will.

And then there really was Will, leaning over Dave, and looking up into Cat's troubled face.

'Smile,' he prompted. 'You won.'

'Well, *she* won.'

'It was a fix, you know,' said Will, flashing his eyes. 'For my favourite girl.'

Cat went an immediate and whole body fuchsia, sitting up straighter on the hay bale. 'Really?'

'Oh yes,' smiled Will. 'Dave is far and away my favourite patient.'

Willing the blush to recede, Cat fanned herself. Behind her, the other women chattered musically, their voices hanging in the close early evening air. 'How's Lisa?' she made herself ask.

'She's fine. Her granny came third in Cakes Miscellaneous.'

'Oh.' Cat was smug that her pseudo-granny had whupped Lisa's granny's ass.

Will sat beside her on the hay, forcing her to budge up, and causing a momentary but distinct cessation in the chatter behind them. Cat could sense Mary pointing and 'oooh'ing. 'You seem preoccupied,' he said, in a quieter tone that closeted them from the hoi polloi.

'Do I?' Cat sensed a prickle of danger in the air. Will was too close, and she was too tipsy, and he meant too much. 'Shouldn't you be looking for Lisa?'

'I said I'd wait by the gates.' Will didn't move.

'Lucky Lisa.' She was off, off on a reckless route that the beer was mapping out for her. 'To have somebody waiting for her.'

'Don't you? Back in London?'

'I did.' Cat's attempt at a knowing chuckle fell flat. 'Not any more. It was a bit of a mess. Innocent bystanders mowed down, that sort of thing.'

'Sounds grim.' Will was interested, she realised. He was looking at her, really looking.

'Let's just say I don't want him to wait for me.' A sudden vision leapt into Cat's mind: a hotel suite and a bright-eyed, bushy-tailed new girl. 'He's not the type to wait very long, anyhow.'

Will's skin looked cool, like an ice cream, close enough to lick. 'Do you know what?' he said. 'If I loved a girl I'd wait for her to sort herself out. Men don't always let women down. I'd wait. If she was worth waiting for.' He swept a glance down to Cat's chin, and up again to her hairline. 'I'd wait.'

Cat, besides wishing she'd exfoliated that morning, said nothing, prolonging the oddly meaningful and maddeningly ambiguous moment.

'I should . . .' Will stood up abruptly, his height taking him a long way away again. 'Bye-bye, Dave.' He bent to fondle his favourite girl one last time and marched away quite literally into the sunset.

Cat had experienced a meaningful moment all on her own, it seemed.

42

The show was well and truly over, it was time to go, but 'Two of us are missing.' Mary's hands were on her bouncy castle hips. 'Great.'

Sarge struck one palm with the other fist. 'I told Germaine to let me carry out the search for Antonia. I have the requisite skills.' She was on a high after beating all-comers in the arm wrestling tent.

'Whatever.' With three pints of local beer inside her, Mary was in no mood to pander to Sarge's GI Joe fantasies. 'Shall we go without them?' she asked hopefully.

'No!' the others chorused.

Jozette pointed a long brown finger across the twilit field, almost empty now and denuded of marquees and cattle. 'Look! There's Antonia!' She jumped up and down, hallooing through cupped hands, then stopped abruptly. 'Jeez,' she muttered. 'Looks like she's busy.'

Busy locking lips with a long-haired local who had yet to get the key of the door.

'Good Lord,' said Beulah, clasping her cake tin to her chest.

'WHOO WHOO!' Jozette let out a Jerry Springer audience roar and punched the air. 'GO, GIRL!' She shrugged at the others. 'She's single. It's summer. Cut her some slack.'

Lucy didn't have any slack on her, apparently. 'It's extreme behaviour. It's a symptom. She'll regret it.'

'She's having fun,' said Mary, predictably taking the opposite stance, although she couldn't help grimacing at the prolonged and graphic public smooch.

Sarge was openly disgusted. 'That is a minor she's assaulting,' she asserted, chin out.

'He's not a minor.' Even as Cat insisted 'he looks about seventeen,' she felt it to be scant defence.

'He doesn't look *too* unhappy about it.' Lucy raised her eyebrows as the boy's right hand found Antonia's left buttock. 'Bloody hell,' she said, to herself.

Even Jozette was looking away, shielding her eyes. 'Wow,' she said. 'Antonia's a dark horse.'

'Tomorrow she'll be mortified about this.' Unsure why she should feel responsible, Cat took action, striding across the litter-strewn grass. 'Antonia!' she called, as she approached, feeling awkward but unable to stop. 'Come on, we're going home.'

'In a minute.' The words were snatched as Antonia came up for air, her face dragged back to his by her juvenile *amour*.

'*Antonia*,' hissed Cat, pointedly. 'Everyone's looking.'

Twisting away from her admirer, Antonia was unrepentant: she seemed to have borrowed Mary's personality for the afternoon. 'So let them look!' she spat. 'I'm allowed to have a good time, aren't I?'

'Of course, you are,' said Cat, feeling ridiculous now, the third unwelcome wheel. She smiled hastily at the boy's bleary, punch-drunk face, but, lost on Planet Snog, he didn't register her. 'But this isn't *you*, Antonia.'

'And how would you know what's not me?' enquired Antonia, in a very unfriendly tone. 'If you'll excuse me, I've got catching up to do.' She half turned back to her new friend, but decided to lob a grenade at Cat instead. 'Why not sort your own issues first, before poking your nose where it's not wanted? Just because you cocked up back in London and now you're cocking up down here, don't try and make me feel bad.'

Swallowing hard, Cat strode back to the others, her head down. 'She's not . . . receptive just now,' she said, her eyes sparking. Too busy hating Antonia to listen to the excited twittering of the others, Cat thought self-righteously *I was only trying to help.*

Never comfortable on the moral high ground, she soon slithered back down. Antonia was right: Cat should have addressed her 'issues' (how she hated that word) instead of scampering off to the countryside to sidetrack herself with a vet. A vet with a significant other.

Like a bracing wind, Germaine suddenly blew up, assessed the situation, growled deep in her throat and ordered them all to follow her. Grabbing Antonia by the arm as she passed, she detached her efficiently from her boyish suitor with a 'That's *quite* enough of that, thank you.'

'This way,' said Lucy confidently, as they dithered, disoriented, on the fringe of the car park. The messy field looked different stripped of vehicles, with bunting trodden into the mire. 'We parked near that tree stump.'

'Clever clogs,' muttered Mary.

'No, no, we're over here.' Germaine led her band to the opposite side of the field.

'Lucy's right,' said Cat, tugging at Dave, who was tired after her day of glory.

'Lucy is not right,' said Germaine crisply. 'There's the van.'

'Oh,' said Cat, surprised. 'So it is.'

'Not so clever clogs,' said Mary. 'In fact, stupid clogs.'

'I know what you're doing, Sarge.' Antonia sounded irked in the darkness as Germaine struggled with the key of the front door.

'Not doing nothing,' claimed Sarge.

'You're trying to smell my breath.' Antonia sounded tightly wound, her volume knob out of control. 'I'm not drunk. I didn't have a drink. Even though I . . .' She gulped, and elbowed her way to the front as the door gave. 'Even though I wanted to.' She was crying as she took the stairs two at a time, but they weren't the soft snuffles the women were accustomed to.

'Home sweet home,' sighed Mary, lighting the gas lamp in the kitchen as Antonia's banshee wails drifted through the ceiling. 'No, *down*,' she commanded Beulah, who was reaching for the kettle. 'You're the all-conquering cake goddess: tonight you put your feet up.'

Without even a token 'oh I couldn't', Beulah sank into her usual chair, and Cat noticed how jaded she looked. A workhorse of a woman, any endeavour that involved crossing the threshold depleted her in a way that domestic labour couldn't.

When Antonia appeared in the kitchen at midnight, looking sheepish, only Cat was still up.

'Oh,' said Antonia flatly. 'I planned to apologise to everybody.'

'What's a snog between friends?' yawned Cat, unwilling to open another of Antonia's inexhaustible cans of worms so late in the day.

'No, I *need* to apologise.' Antonia must have guessed from Cat's expression how that sounded. 'God, therapy makes one so self-obsessed,' she tutted. 'Sorry.'

'So now you're apologising for apologising?' smiled Cat. 'Oh, come on, Antonia.' She gave in and pulled out a chair. 'Sit down and I'll make us something hot and milky.'

'I snapped at you, didn't I?'

'Yup.' Cat spooned cocoa into two striped mugs, enjoying the soft noise of its landing.

'That was uncalled for.'

As apologies went, it was stiff. 'What made you pounce on that whippersnapper?' Cat trotted out a pleasingly Beulah-style word.

The cocoa was ready by the time Antonia replied. 'It's hard being watched all the time,' she said deliberately. 'I've had years of it. My mother watched me, terrified I was too highly strung to nab a suitable husband. Then Paul watched me, to make sure I toed the party line, keeping the big house clean and bringing up his sons to be "men".' She shut her eyes. 'And now, I'm sorry but it's true, you're all watching me, waiting for me to slip up. Smelling my breath. Gauging my mood. Wondering when I'll crack.'

Cat wasn't watching her now, she was gazing down at the table, wondering if Antonia realised how accusatory she sounded. 'We're trying to help,' she said. 'If you do crack, we'll support you.'

'But the watching will *make* me crack!' Antonia's teeth were gritted, her cheeks pink: she could have been the assertive, impatient twin of the wan waif Cat had met in the minibus all those weeks ago. 'Christ, all my life I've been living up to other people's expectations. I've been mute. Too polite to have an opinion. And this is where it's got me! Alcoholics blooming Anonymous!'

'I get it,' said Cat. 'I really do.'

'I never broke out, never rebelled. Never put a foot wrong.' Antonia was angry: Cat wasn't sure who with. 'So today I thought, right! I've never kissed anybody except Paul. I imagined your faces if I did something wildly out of character. So I grabbed that boy.' She stretched her neck back, her head lolling as she groaned, 'I thought it was daring. But then on the way home I just felt embarrassed.' Antonia straightened up. 'And before I knew it, there I was crying again.'

'You know what I think?' Cat laid a hand on Antonia's long forearm. 'It's just as well you're going through all this AA-related madness while you're here with us. We've all got problems, nobody is judging you.' She ignored Antonia's raised eyebrow. 'We care about you.' She went a little pink. 'I'm not great at these speeches, Antonia, but honestly, you're amongst friends. Be as moody as you like. Snog every second pubescent. Swear, even! We're not going anywhere. And neither are you.'

'I wish I was more like you,' said Antonia in a small, grateful voice.

'No,' said Cat, in a loud, definite one, 'you don't.'

*

Germaine was brushing her teeth when Antonia and Cat climbed the stairs to bed. Cat crept into the bathroom and shut the door softly. Germaine turned, toothbrush poised.

'Courgettes,' said Cat quietly, leaning against the dressing gowns crowded on the back of the door.

'Er . . .?' Germaine stooped to spit out the toothpaste. Her curls quivered as she shook her head questioningly. 'Courgettes?'

'We didn't plant courgettes.' Cat folded her arms as Germaine's eyes moved to the floor. 'But Waitrose did.'

In the short, electric silence that followed Germaine looked capable of beating Cat to death with the nearest loofah, then she hissed, 'Who have you told?'

'Nobody. It's so stupid, Germy. They'll cotton on. You can't just plonk supermarket produce in the vegetable plot and pass it off as our own.'

'Nobody's noticed up to now.'

'The courgettes were your Achilles heel.' Cat regretted the bizarre metaphor. 'And Beulah knows, doesn't she?' Cat clocked the cloud skittering across Germaine's features. 'That's how she blackmailed you into giving me the wine by waggling a rhubarb pie in your face. Be more careful in future.'

'You're not going to squeal?' Germaine looked astonished.

'It would depress them. Better to let them believe they have green fingers.'

'You think me absurd, I can tell, but I'm doing it for the best. Being the leader means you have to make some tough decisions.'

'You're not Napoleon, Germaine.' Her friend's arrogance suddenly irritated Cat. 'Don't treat us like teenagers just because you pay the bills. Which was your idea, by the way. We can cope with the dreadful realisation that our onions are below par.'

'Our onions,' Germaine said sadly, 'turned to mush.'

'You must be spending a fortune.'

'Too bloody true. I have to get organic. The ordinary stuff isn't nobbly enough.'

They caught each other's eye and giggled furtively, hands to mouths like squirrels. When they'd recovered, Germaine whined, in an undertone, 'I'm doing my best.'

'We all are,' said Cat.

43

The design Sarge sketched on the back of a pig feed supplement bag didn't look like a 'poultry shallow wallow area' to Cat. 'That's a swimming pool.' She jabbed a finger at it. 'For chickens. Admit it, you're building a swimming pool for Chickensarge and Hencat and Hentonia and the others.'

Rolling up the drawing, Sarge pursed her lips. 'It is a shallow wallow area,' she said grimly.

'Swimming pool!' sang Cat, enjoying herself. 'Own up. You *love* those hens. You could no more dispatch them with a chair leg than I could.'

'Shallow wallow—' began Sarge, before giving up with a sigh. 'Look, I'm not going to argue with you. Can you take Antonia to AA while I make a start with this?'

'Of course I can.' Cat held out her hand. 'Keys please.'

Racing to the parlour, Cat waggled the keys noisily at Mary, who was on the settle reading a bonkbuster. 'Freedom!' she hissed seductively.

Barely looking up, Mary said 'Nah'.

'No, not *nah*,' admonished Cat, surprised. She spotted Lucy on an armchair, her pen moving fluently across a pad. She looked from

Lucy to Mary and back again. 'OK,' she said slowly, 'see you later', closing the door and allowing the thaw to continue.

'Why don't I teach you how to drive?' Cat suggested to her passenger as the van hiccuped down the main street. 'It will help you to be independent back in London.' Cat admired the neatness of her idea, anticipating in an unattractive Teacher's Pet way how it would please Germaine.

Fingers plucking at her bottom lip like a cellist, Antonia revealed that she already had a driving licence. 'I was banned. You can guess why.'

'Ah.'

'The boys were in the car.' Antonia's voice was dull. 'It was a bad day.' She shook herself, quite literally. 'No need to wait for me,' she said, as they drew up on the forecourt of a church hall. 'My mentor will give me a lift.' She jumped down, offering a small 'thank you' that Cat could easily have missed.

As the day petered out in the sky, Cat was alone. Accustomed to being within gossiping distance of another woman, she hummed to keep herself company as she followed the twisting road.

In the gathering gloom ahead, a figure stuck out an arm, a thumb hopefully cocked. 'Lisa . . .' Cat recognised the girl just as she began to slow down. Her foot almost stepped off the brake, but then she scolded herself. Lisa was a perfectly nice girl in need of a lift. She couldn't just leave her at the side of the road with night approaching. *Behave*, she told her errant childish self.

'You're a lifesaver!' Lisa jumped into the front seat. 'Ow!' She twisted her body to accommodate the malevolent spring sticking out from the padding. 'Are you going back to your place?'

Grinding the bus into gear, Cat nodded. 'Where are you headed?'

'Uplyme, but anywhere along this road will do. My dopey mate was supposed to pick me up but her car's always kaput, so I started walking. Bad move,' she smiled. 'It's further than I thought, and all uphill.'

Cat smiled back toothily, over-compensating in the hope that her envy wouldn't manifest and hunker down between them in all its green glory. 'You youngsters and your japes,' she said.

'Yeah.' Lisa gave her an uncertain look. 'There's a gig tonight. One of my mates is in a band.'

Well of course they are, said the sardonic jealous voice in Cat's head. 'Any good?'

'Crap.' Lisa shrugged. 'I have to go though or they'd kill me.'

She was nice, this Lisa with the skinny jeans and the on-trend tartan shirt. On Cat that shirt would have looked like she'd borrowed it from a lumberjack friend: on Lisa it looked like she'd borrowed it from Kate Moss.

'Why don't you come?'

Taken aback at the invitation, Cat smiled a little more naturally. 'But you said they're crap!' she laughed.

'Oh, that's not the point.' Lisa waved her hands as if to shoo that unfortunate fact out of the rattling window. 'Go on. It'll be fun. You could meet some of the locals. They're dying to know what goes on up in your commune.'

'Oh, they don't want to know the banal details of our lives,' said Cat. 'How we drink cat's blood with our meals, and worship a pagan goddess who demands the sacrifice of a local virgin every full moon.'

Hooting with laughter, Lisa asked, 'Do you weave your own tampons as well?'

Damn, thought Cat, *I like you.* There was a worse thought to come: *I get what Will sees in you.* Denied the base pleasures of hating Lisa, Cat chatted with her instead. She was funny, warm and interesting: Cat was tempted to ask her out herself. 'Is Will going to the gig?' she asked, proud of her insouciance.

'Nah. Not his thing.' Lisa picked at a hangnail, suddenly looking about twelve. 'We split up, as it goes.' She grasped the dashboard as the minibus veered over the verge for a few yards. 'Just wasn't working out, so . . .'

'I'm sorry,' said Cat. It was, on one level, true. 'How is it? Are you OK?'

'The show must go on,' breezed Lisa with a watery smile. 'He didn't break my heart or anything.'

'So, it was his idea . . .' Cat hungered for detail, but she had to be diplomatic: this girl's unhappiness was real.

'Oh yeah,' said Lisa ruefully. 'All him. Came out of the blue. Just didn't see us going anywhere apparently.'

'That's hard.'

'He's right, that's the worst bit. He's too old for me, really. Oh. Sorry.' Lisa was flustered.

'I know what you mean. It's OK.'

'And he's, you know, a bit weird. You probably noticed.'

'Yeah,' said Cat automatically, her mind racing. 'Actually,' she went on, 'no, I didn't notice. He seems resolutely normal.' Especially when compared to the mercurial Hugh.

'Will?' Lisa sounded amazed. 'He's great, don't get me wrong, but the girls used to wonder why I put up with it. The moods. The *thinking*. They all thought he was boring.' She leaned urgently towards Cat. 'Don't tell him that, will you? I mean, *I* don't see him like that. That's just what my mates said.'

'No, no, of course not. I'll probably never see him again anyway.' It took an effort to say that out loud. 'Unless one of our animals gets sick.'

'Well, in case you do. The break-up's been very friendly so far and I don't want him to think I'm badmouthing him.' Lisa sighed. 'Four months. A huge chunk out of my life, man.'

'Hmm.' It was the blink of an eye for an old codger like Cat. If she and Hugh had parted after four months she'd be stronger and happier and somewhere else entirely today.

'My ex has asked me to go back to him.' Lisa pulled a wry face. 'I might have to. There's no talent in Lyme.'

It didn't sound as if Lisa's heart was broken. 'There's no law saying you have to have a boyfriend. Give yourself time to heal.' Cat liked how that sounded: wise, experienced.

'I like having a boyfriend.' Lisa's feminism was newer minted than

Germaine's. 'It's handy.' She looked at Cat and they shared a complicit laugh. 'Lifts, for a start.'

'I suppose men have their uses.'

'Mmm,' said Lisa with a leer. 'Some stuff you need them for. I'm gonna miss Will for *that.*' She stretched lazily, savouring some X-rated memory. 'Man, he was *good.*'

'Really?' Where did that high-pitched voice come from? 'Really?' repeated Cat, attempting to normalise her tone and sounding like Russell Crowe.

'Oooh yes,' said Lisa. 'One benefit of the older man, I guess.'

'I guess.' Cat was hurriedly computing this information. Will as sex god was a surprise. Even when lingering on thoughts of his pout, she'd assumed he'd be the sexual equivalent of his Barbour jacket. Reliable. Traditional. No frills. But apparently he was, to quote Lisa, italics and all, '*good*'.

'Just here is fine,' said Lisa suddenly. 'I can walk up this lane and then I'm at the pub.' She gathered her stuff together as the minibus slowed. 'Come with me. Go on!' she prodded Cat playfully. 'We need some new faces.'

Flattered by the girl, Cat almost said yes. 'I'd love to,' she said with longing, 'but I have to get back for a seminar on how to survive on your own wee if you ever get stranded in a post-apocalyptic landscape.'

'Lovely,' said Lisa, weakly.

So, Will was single. He was Single Will. Bachelor Will. A footloose and fancy-free vet about town.

The news promoted Will up through the ranks from 'don't go there' to 'you just might have a chance if you manage to be completely different to how you usually are'. The smile on Cat's face threatened to swallow her ears all through Sarge's seminar, only fading during the too-graphic demonstration of how to strain urine through your tights.

44

'Any tea going, Beulah?' Cat wandered into the kitchen.

'Isn't there always?' Beulah smiled absent-mindedly. New lines marched from her nose to the sides of her mouth.

Unhappy to see Beulah look her age, Cat set about pouring a cup of tea just the way she liked it. 'There,' she said, placing it in front of her.

'Have you a moment or two to sit with me?'

The simple question was unusual. Beulah never made demands on Cat. Or the others. Beulah was an independent satellite in an apron, circling them endlessly, never dragging them into her gravity. 'Of course. I love the kitchen at this time of the day.'

'So do I.'

The shadows were lengthening, seeing off the last of the sun. The kitchen belonged to the lamp now. It was quiet, with only the elemental grumbles of an old house to disturb them.

The silence unrolled. Beulah didn't seem about to say anything. Cat wondered if she was expected to speak. Just as she opened her mouth, Beulah said 'The baby. The baby would be a grown woman now. Older than you, dear.'

'Your baby,' said Cat.

'Yes. Matilda.' Beulah tilted her head to the side. 'My Matilda. That's what I called her in my heart. I never found out what they christened her.'

'That's a lovely name,' said Cat, feeling it too meagre a compliment. She trembled with the urge to make things right for this meek, mighty woman. It was vital to listen. Beulah, she sensed, was after an ear, not platitudes.

'Matty, I would have called her. For short.' Beulah didn't look sad. She had a stoic expression, but her eyes were sparkling. 'Whenever I knit, I fancy I'm making her a little hat with a bobble on it, to keep out the cold. I'd pull it over her eyes to make her laugh. And mittens to match. I'm very good at mittens.'

Cat sipped her tea. Eventually she risked a bland 'I can't knit'.

'I'll show you how, if you like,' said Beulah.

It seemed that the porthole to the past was closed again. Cat felt heavy with her own impotence. 'Beulah . . .' she began, not sure where she was headed.

'The baby's father,' said Beulah abruptly in a voice no longer gentle, but raw, 'was my father. Incest. That's the word for it. He made me do terrible things. So perhaps there was something wrong with Matilda. But I don't think so. I think she was probably just a normal, beautiful little baby like any other.'

When Cat came home from school to find her mother crying at the kitchen table over Harry, she'd felt this same weightlessness. Then, as now, Cat felt that if she just hung on for a second or two the universe would rewind, and things would return to normal.

But cats out of bags are averse to being bundled back in. Beulah, sitting in her pastel separates on the other side of the table, was crying.

Cat leapt up and curled her arms around the old lady's bulky frame as it shook.

'Oh, he was bad!' sobbed Beulah, scrabbling in her pocket and producing a handkerchief.

'You're free of him now,' whispered Cat, knowing it to be feeble, and furthermore, untrue. The dead man was in step with his daughter, poisoning the well of her fresh start. 'You've got us now,' she said.

'Do you think badly of me?' hiccuped Beulah.

'Badly?' Cat jumped away from Beulah as if scalded. Dragging a chair close to her she sat down and looked into her face. 'I could never think badly of you. Him, I could throttle. I think very very badly of your father, Beulah, but all I see when I look at you is a dignified woman who deserved better. Times have changed. Nobody would blame you. This type of thing is out in the open now. You have nothing to be ashamed of.'

'I didn't fight for her.'

'How could you?' Cat was having none of that.

'He scared me. Right up until he died.' Beulah pressed the hanky across her eyes, like a mask. 'He still does.'

'No, no more.' Cat pulled down Beulah's fingers, still spattered with tomato sauce from the ratatouille she'd made for dinner. 'He's gone. He can only hurt you now if you let him.'

'Maybe Matilda is like you,' said Beulah, leaving her hands in Cat's. 'I hope she grew up like you.'

'That is absolutely the nicest compliment I have ever had.'

Silence returned. Cat didn't trust her voice, and Beulah seemed to have used up every ounce of her spirit. In time, others drifted into the kitchen, boiled the kettle, ransacked the pantry, talked of this and that.

Sitting in their midst, Beulah and Cat accepted hot chocolate and shared the biscuits. Finally, under cover of a rambling anecdote of Germaine's, Cat leaned forward and whispered, 'Time you were in bed, Beulah.'

Cat went as far as the foot of the stairs with her. 'Get a good night's rest,' she said, kissing her on her papery cheek. 'And thank you for telling me.'

'Thank you,' said Beulah gravely, 'for listening, dear.'

Another secret. Cat longed to tell Mary, to hear the gasp of disbelief, and sigh of empathy. It was non-negotiable, however: Beulah had told Cat, nobody else. Beulah's secret would remain just that.

Such a Gothic revelation demanded glowering clouds, and claps of distant thunder, but nature was unperturbed by footling human goings on and the next morning drenched Dorset with the kind of glorious sunshine Cap Ferrat would envy.

'Good morning,' said Cat to Antonia, dragging her slippered feet into the bright kitchen.

'Norman is dead,' said Antonia.

'Oh.' Cat frowned. 'Oh dear. Poor Norman.' She hesitated. 'Who *is* Norman?'

'My great-uncle,' said Antonia impatiently, as if everybody in the UK should know him. 'He's dead,' she repeated.

'Were you close?' asked Cat dutifully.

'God no, he was vile,' said Antonia.

'Oh. Right.' Antonia's new honesty could be abrasive. Poor vile dead Norman, thought Cat, yawning.

'I'll have to go to London tomorrow for the funeral.' Antonia's face was closed. She was probably conjuring up the same equation as Cat: London = booze.

The letter, started in the morning, took all day to compose.

PS, wrote Cat, after two pages of commune gossip and asking after Jon.

> *Please send help – I think I like a man, Mum. Turns out it's not like riding a bike, you can forget how to do it.*

The ground floor was quiet, lit only by the nosy midnight moon. Tiptoeing about in just a baggy T-shirt, Cat shouted 'Oi! Anybody!', shoulders hunched and feeling absurd.

Asleep as soon as her head had hit the lumpy pillow, Cat's dreams had been disrupted by distant noises. Slowly, unwillingly, she'd been dragged back to wakefulness by the muted babble that seemed to be coming from somewhere within the house, within the walls. Cat had sat up, fully alert, and hissed, 'Can you hear that?'

Nobody answered. The dormitory was empty. Cat was alone, something she often wished for at the commune. With a smothered yelp, she'd thundered down the stairs. 'Guys?' she half whispered, beetling through the dark parlour and the slumbering kitchen. 'Ladies?'

Nobody answered. Cat stood in the middle of the kitchen, baffled by and loathing the solitude, as the noises seeped from the fabric of the house. She heard a bleating, then a dull rumble, then silence, then a loud explosive sound like glass shattering. Cat shivered, irresolute.

Later, looking back, Cat was impressed that she hadn't screamed when the kitchen floor suddenly opened up in front of her. Perhaps it was because the apparition that arose through the trapdoor wasn't a headless horseman but a highly disgruntled Beulah with curlers in her hair.

'They're all under the influence down there,' tutted Beulah, negotiating her girth through the narrow trapdoor. 'I'm away to my bed.'

'G'night,' said Cat, distracted, goggling down the wooden stepladder the trapdoor had exposed. It led below the kitchen, and a flickering glow betrayed candlelight. Cat put a bare foot on the splintered top step, then retrieved it hurriedly, as Sarge appeared at the bottom.

'It's a disgrace!' she hissed, pounding up the ladder. 'And to think of poor Antonia doing her best to stay sober up in London.' She stamped off, her boots incongruous under her flowing white nightgown, muttering that Germaine 'should know better'.

A snatch of cackling laughter (easily mistaken for shattering glass) that could only be Mary's drifted up. Cat scrambled down the ladder and found herself in an underground storeroom, lined with dusty shelves, the brick floor uneven and tactile under her toes.

'Cat!' shrieked Mary, from where she was arranged untidily on a rug-covered old sofa in the corner. 'We found Germaine's stash!'

'And then I found them,' said Germaine darkly from her throne of a cobwebby barrel.

'Join us,' said Lucy, her face pink, and softer than Cat had ever known it.

'Yeah, girlfriend, pull up a . . .' Jozette hesitated and then spluttered '*a piece of junk!*'

All four laughed uproariously. Mary even kicked her legs in the air.

'Didn't get my invitation,' murmured Cat, pulling up the nearest piece of junk, a surprisingly comfortable wooden box.

'Oh don't be like that,' spluttered Mary. 'I was going to come up and get you. Wasn't I?' She turned to Jozette for corroboration.

'Of course.' Jozette was naturally inclusive: she couldn't guess at the way Cat suffered if she felt left out. 'We just kept having one more little drinkie,' she laughed. 'You know we wouldn't party without you.'

Struggling to hang on to her huff, Cat relinquished it when Mary squinted and said, warningly, 'Face, Cat O'Connor!' She waggled a finger at Cat. 'I know that face and I don't like it. Nobody left you out. Everybody loves you. *Face!*' she bawled.

'Is this better?' Cat grinned cheesily, and Mary shielded her eyes.

'Aaaargh! Give her wine, make it stop!'

The women laughed, and Lucy yawned. 'I'm getting used to early nights here. At home I stay up late every evening.'

'A night owl?' asked Mary, looking into her mug. Definitely not looking at Lucy.

Cat smiled to herself. This was the first polite comment Mary had aimed Lucy's way since Lucy was outed.

'Yeah,' said Lucy casually, picking at a stray thread on her striped nightshirt. 'On the computer, or listening to music. I miss the internet more than I thought I would.'

'Know what you mean.' Mary turned her body slightly so that she was facing Lucy. 'I certainly miss it more than I miss Alun.'

'Poor old Alun,' laughed Lucy, who seemed to have taken a chill pill along with the wine.

It was a delicate thing, this rapprochement. All the women could feel it being spun between them. Jozette's lips were pursed happily, her Afro bent over her mug as she pulled her pyjama'ed knees up to her chin. Cat could shatter the atmosphere, she knew, with one expertly timed sarcastic comment.

It was tempting. She'd enjoyed having her friend back since Lucy's banishment to the wilderness. Cat gulped down some wine, enjoying the heady, bitter rush. It was cruel to consider it. She did the decent thing and helped the peace process along by laughing appreciatively and not getting in the way.

'This is like the old days!' beamed Jozette, throwing an arm apiece around Germaine and Cat. 'The four desperados together again, getting, what's that expression? Pie faced?'

'Eyed!' Mary corrected her loudly. 'Pie *eyed*.'

'It feels good, doesn't it?' Jozette canvassed her cronies.

'It does,' admitted Cat. 'We're not the same people out here, though.'

'Really?' Lucy, the only non-musketeer, seemed intrigued.

'Nah.' Mary nodded. 'Jozette is much more relaxed without Trev.'

'My God!' Jozette put both hands to her face, a vision of drunken realisation. 'That's right! I'm mellow again.' She hooted. 'I was born mellow, I grew up mellow, then I got involved with Trev and my ass clenched so tight my hotpants nearly fell off.' She shrugged. 'Do you still like me now I'm mellow, ladies? Or do you prefer the London version?'

'I like you, *love* you,' Cat corrected herself, 'however you are, mellow or, err, clench-assed.'

'As for you,' Jozette waggled a finger at her. 'You've gone introthingy. Spective. You don't spill like you used to.'

'I don't have much to spill,' fibbed Cat, acknowledging privately that Jozette's observation was spot on. Spending all her time with her closest friends had opened up some space between them. 'Besides, we're together so much there's no need to catch up. It changes things.'

'True,' mused Mary. 'I used to store stuff up for our get-togethers, but now we all know everything about each other.' She frowned. 'We're more like family these days, aren't we?'

'That's a good thing, right?' Jozette double-checked.

'Ye-es,' said Cat slowly, examining the new thought. 'So long as we don't lose the habit of confiding in each other.' She hesitated but forced herself to say it, to sound vulnerable. 'Because I need you women.'

'And we need you,' said Germaine gravely.

Cat shot her a look, grateful to be taken seriously.

'Pack it in, you sentimental eejits,' admonished Mary, not yet drunk enough to 'do' sentiment. 'Of course we all need each other. We were a gang long before this godforsaken experiment and we'll be a gang long after it's finished, in the old folks' home: Cat'll be the one wetting the bed.' Abruptly she turned to Lucy. 'Sorry. Didn't mean to leave you out.'

Unperturbed, Lucy said, 'I've never been keen on gangs anyhow.'

'You should try it,' laughed Jozette. 'It has benefits.'

'Somebody to split the bill with,' said Mary.

'Somebody to listen to your fears,' suggested Germaine, unexpectedly, to Cat's ears at least.

'I'd save them,' said Lucy, 'for my partner.' She looked down as if remembering something bittersweet. 'And only my partner.'

There was nothing coy about Lucy: Cat could tell that she didn't want to be drawn out. Germaine, on the other hand . . . 'Germy, is something worrying you?'

'I'm not as good at sarcasm as Mary, but I'll give it a go.' Germaine took a deep breath. 'No, of course not, why would I be anxious, with all the expense and responsibility of running a commune on my shoulders?'

'A commune is made up of the people in it,' said Cat gently. 'We're all responsible for its success.'

'Or,' said Mary, leaping straight in with both bare feet, 'do you just think of us as prawns in your social experiment these days?'

'Hey, hey, hey.' Jozette raised her head, perturbed. 'Germy's bossiness comes from a good place.'

'We know that!' Mary slapped Germaine's knee. 'Nothing could change our friendship.'

'I hope not.' Germaine looked into the depths of her drink.

'The Brits are getting maudlin! I'm done!' Jozette stretched her arms above her head, managing to look like a *Vogue* cover despite her exhaustion. 'Goodnight, you goddamn alkies.' She stumbled up the ladder, back to the sober world above ground.

Tilting her shoulder away from Mary and Lucy, who didn't notice, Cat simultaneously poured Germaine another mug of wine and nudged her, resulting in damp laps for both of them. 'Germy, now that you're pie eyed I've got the nerve to ask. Where do you go?'

'When? How go?' Germaine shrugged her shoulders like a foreigner who can't speak the lingo.

'You know.' Cat nudged her again; they'd have to change their nightwear. 'All these errands. Urgent business meetings. They're made up, aren't they?'

'Are you calling me a liar?' Germaine reared up like a dragon. A tipsy one.

'Stop blustering,' commanded Cat, a few drinks behind and enjoying the upper hand it gave her.

'You'll judge me,' pouted Germaine. Sober, Germaine never pouted.

'I won't,' promised Cat. 'Look, if it's because you want to be alone, to get away from us now and then, I understand.'

'You do?' said Germaine warily.

'I do. I just wish you'd be frank with us.'

'Frank. I remember frank. Being in charge,' stumbled Germaine, her hand to her head as if it hurt, 'it's not easy. I thought I'd take to it like a duck to, you know, that stuff, the wet stuff,' she grimaced. 'But it means I have to be perfect and I'm not.' She shook her head gingerly, as if it might break. 'Not at all.'

'And thank gawd for that,' said Cat.

'So yes, I do need to get away now and then, you're right,' said Germaine apologetically. 'I go to Lyme, look at the sea, have a coffee.

Or to a pub for a glass of something. So I'm not the boss for a moment or two. I'm me. I need to be . . .' she gulped, as if sipping poison. 'To be alone.' She eyed Cat anxiously. 'I'm not really playing the game, am I?'

'You're too hard on yourself. At least now I know how that guy knew your name in The Fisherman's Rest. Come on.' Cat stood and started to clink the bottles into order. 'Let's tidy up and get out of here.' She held out a hand and heaved Germaine up. 'And don't justify your actions: if you need to be alone, Ms Garbo, then you need to be alone.'

Mary and Lucy, the détente still thriving, followed them up the stepladder out of the black hole the cellar had once again become.

'Just going to check on Dave.' Cat shoved Germaine towards the stairs. 'See you lot up in the dormitory.' The cellar had been musty: she needed to see the sky over the commune.

The stars glittered reassuringly as Cat trotted over the cobbles. A perfunctory glance at Dave was all she planned, but when she peeked in she gave a little lovestruck 'Aw'.

Dave looked so peaceful, toppled over and snoring like a walrus on the far side of her boudoir. 'Aw,' repeated Cat, her ability to find beauty in Dave enhanced by bad wine. 'Aw, Dave.' She knelt beside her and stretched her arms around the creature's pink abdomen. The rise and fall of Dave's sleeping body was soporific: the smell, stimulating. 'Goodnight,' whispered Cat.

Outside again, the yard felt different. Cat clutched her collar and looked about her as the trees whispered scratchily above her head. Over on the far side of the front door, past the unruly climbing rose, were two figures, waxing and waning with the moonlight.

Snatches of conversation drifted Cat's way. It was, she realised with relief, Mary and Lucy. Wouldn't it be funny, she thought with wine-fuelled confidence in her plan, to creep up and scare them.

Hugging the outbuildings, Cat crept, as quiet as her namesake, around the perimeter of the courtyard. The muted talk became clearer.

'Stop apologising,' she heard Lucy whisper urgently. 'Honestly. It's over. You had a meltdown.'

'It's not as if I really think that way, I—'

Lucy cut Mary off. 'I know, I know,' she said soothingly. 'Listen, I—'

'No, I—'

'The thing is—'

'I just—'

'The thing is—'

This exchange covered the soft sounds of Cat's approach on the mossy ground. Sliding past the front door like a spy, she pulled back the creeper in preparation for a blood-curdling 'boo!' to break the silence: Mary and Lucy had stopped talking.

The boo died on her lips. Mary and Lucy were kissing.

Fingers splayed across each other's faces, hair mussed and mingling, the women's eyes were shut, their mouths glued. As if they both heard a distant alarm, they suddenly pulled far enough apart to stare each other in the eye. They didn't speak, although Cat heard Mary moan, and their lips rediscovered each other.

Flattening herself against the door, Cat inserted herself back into the house, and flew up the stairs.

45

There was no polite way to say it, so it went unsaid, but the real answer to Mary's puffed, out-of-breath question, on the hill opposite the commune was no, it wasn't all right for her to join Cat and Dave on their daily walk. Instead Cat tried a lame, 'Aren't you supposed to be cleaning out the hens?'

'It'll wait,' said Mary dismissively, sounding like a woman who had more than hens on her mind. 'There's something I have to tell you.'

Now was the moment for Cat to pipe up, to say that she knew, but she said only 'Mind your footing by the stream here.'

'I kissed Lucy.' Mary bit her lip, angling this way and that to see Cat's expression. 'Or maybe she kissed me. Damn. Which was it?' She stamped her foot in exasperation, and slithered a few inches down the bank. 'Whatever. We kissed each other.'

'And did you like it, Katy Perry?' Cat held out a hand to tug Mary back up on to the path.

'Yes,' whispered Mary miserably.

'Then why the sad gob?' Cat was brisk, her mind darting all over the place. 'Kisses are good. Kisses are nice. Lucky you, finding a kiss in this place.'

'It was a girl,' hissed Mary, as if Cat had missed this detail. 'I'm not a lesbian, for God's sake.'

'You're not really going the right way about convincing anyone of *that*, are you?'

'It was, oh, it was soft and warm but it was sexy, don't get me wrong. God it was sexy and I can't believe I'm saying all this.'

Cat sighed. 'What am I meant to say? That you aren't a lesbian? Or that you are? Because I don't have a fucking clue.'

'You sound angry.' Mary looked at Cat as if she was an exhibit in a dull museum. 'Are you? Are you angry with me for kissing a woman?'

'No,' barked Cat. 'This isn't about me.'

'Hang on. Answer the question. Are you? Angry, I mean?' Mary looked hurt but punchy. 'Why should you be angry?'

'Yeah, right,' Cat was building up a head of steam. 'Why should anybody have feelings except you, Mary? You can be worried and fearful and . . . and . . . kissy and anything you bloody well like but I have to defend the fact that actually, sometimes, I am actually a bit actually bloody jealous, all right?'

'Jealous?' Mary's voice was soft. They had stopped by the tree. Will's tree. 'Of me and . . .' She looked at the sky. 'Ah,' she said, to herself. Folding her arms, she nibbled at her lips for a while before saying, 'I kind of knew and I ignored it. I'm sorry. I would have felt the same.'

'Would you?' Cat's volume was under control now. 'You're not a jealous woman.'

'Not with Alun. Obviously.' Mary smiled at her, a tender smile a mum might bestow on a toddler who's wearing her out and amusing her at the same time. 'But you, hey, you're *mine.* My bestie. I'm not having any bitch muscle in on my Cat.'

'I thought you . . .' Cat groaned. 'I'm going to sound as if I'm eight years old, but I thought you liked her better than me.'

'Listen, you and I are best mates. It's a contract. Airtight. OK?'

'OK.'

'We're OK?'

'We're OK, Mary,' said Cat. 'So feel free to go ahead and bore me stiff with your am-I-aren't-I-lesbian shtick.'

'Cheers.' They began to walk again, Mary not noticing the light-fingered touch Cat trailed over the bark of the tree. 'She's been sort of off with me this morning.'

'How did you leave it last night?'

'We were both a bit shell shocked. It came out of the blue.'

'Did it?' Cat was doubtful. 'You sure of that?'

'Yes.' Mary rubbed her eye. 'And no. It's always been different with Lucy. I wanted to impress her. Live up to her, or something.' She exhaled heavily. 'My over-reaction to finding out she was gay wasn't really about feeling let down that she hadn't told me.'

'You were upset in case you'd known about her sexuality on a deeper level, and had responded to her in a sexual way.'

'Christ, have you been reading a manual?' Mary frowned. 'Do you think that's true? That I've always . . .'

'Fancied Lucy.' Cat supplied the phrase that Mary was evidently having trouble with.

'Mm-hmm.' Mary looked shifty, as if she'd been caught with her hand in the biscuit tin.

'Only you know that.'

'I wonder if I did it right.'

'What, being a lesbian?' puzzled Cat, slapping Dave's bottom as the pig passed. 'Is there a right way? How wrong could it go? You didn't kiss her elbow by accident, did you?'

'Maybe there's some weird technique to kissing another woman.' Mary looked horrified. 'Oh God. I should have done some research. Asked Alun how he approached it.'

'Is Alun really the best person to ask?' asked Cat. 'Go to the top. Ask a Frenchman. Not,' she repeated, 'Alun'.

'That could be why she's being so off.'

'It's only been half a day. She has feelings, too. Lucy is probably trying to compute what's happened, just like you are.'

'Well, maybe,' conceded Mary, her feet Frankenstein-heavy as the downhill path sped them up. 'But at breakfast I was all open and friendly and she was, you know,' Mary pulled a very Lucy-ish face, all regal aloofness. 'I've fucked it up.'

'Fucked what up?' Cat studied Mary's face, whipped pink by the breeze. 'Is it the start of something?'

Ignoring her, Mary fretted on. 'I fucked up with a man. I fucked up with a woman. What next? Am I going to fuck up with the plant world?'

This kind of runaway reasoning was exactly why Cat had wanted to leave Mary behind at the house. 'Yes, I noticed you undressing the geraniums with your eyes.' Cat slipped an arm through Mary's. 'Baby steps. They'll get you through. Baby steps.' Something more was called for. The spoonful of sugar that had always worked in production meetings. 'I bet she's mad about you. What's not to be mad about?'

'Yeah.' Mary blew her nose on her cuff. 'You're right.'

Dear Cat,

Only time to jot down a couple of lines as I'm waiting for Jon's health visitor to ring the doorbell but I wanted to catch the post and tell you that you're allowed to fancy men, love! About time! Hurray! Oh God there's the door.

Love,

Mum

The phone rarely rang, and when it did, it wasn't Harry. August, blindingly self-confident, like Peter Stringfellow in a thong, was strutting about the commune. Antonia, back from the funeral without incident, was looking bronzed and freckled. No layers were needed now, the women went about their work in strappy tees and halternecks. Cat noted her arms' healthy golden glimmer and flexed them: those were biceps, if she wasn't very much mistaken.

There were only a few days before the house contents sale Harry had spoken of. If he didn't call, then Cat had to face the fact that her own father had forgotten her. Again. She mentally pixelated the phone whenever she passed it.

A chance to escape the house and its pointedly silent phone arose when Germaine announced that she was too busy to drive into Lyme to collect Dave's hay. 'I'll do it!' bayed Cat, grabbing the keys and shooting off into the courtyard. Mary was reading, demure as a nun, in the parlour, a few feet away from where Lucy typed on her laptop: Cat knew better than to invite her this time.

Lyme Regis was packed with holidaymakers, trolling from ice cream shop to fossil shop to beach. There was what passed for a traffic jam on the main street, and the minibus idled, its engine yodelling, outside the Majestic for longer than Cat would have liked. She wondered if her afternoon in there had been a one-off, and was relieved when the jam eased and she could move off.

Midway down the hill, the traffic slowed again. A piercing beep came from a reversing juggernaut, incongruous in this low-rise town. Cat sighed and tapped the steering wheel, looking out at the shopfronts without much hope of distraction.

The dewy eyes and chipped noses of the porcelain dogs in the charity shop didn't pique her interest; the mobility shop did its best but Cat wasn't seduced by the special offer luxury scooters promising speeds of up to four miles per hour. The electrical goods shop was a different matter. Cat put her hands to her mouth and cheeped with shock.

Inside, on eight television screens ranging in size from teeny tiny caravan portable to Alun's wet dream of a plasma, was an advert for Toilet Pigeon. It was garish, bold, eye-wateringly colourful. At the end of thirty seconds of cheesy mayhem, the strapline was emblazoned across the screen in a retro font: 'Toilet Pigeon – your toilet will love you for it'.

On the screens the commercial was replaced by another one. The odious child actor eating an organic cheese sandwich munched unseen by Cat, who sat stock still, oblivious to the symphony of car horns sounding behind her. Thoughts click-clacked along corridors in her mind which had lain empty since March, then she abruptly swung the minibus into a parking space with centimetres to spare.

Barging into a phone box, Cat banged out a number she hadn't used in a long time. A bored, unfamiliar voice announced 'Percival Cant Jablowski, good morning.'

'Marian Miller please.'

'Putting you through.'

'Marian,' said Cat, breathy with excitement. 'It's me, Cat.'

'Hello there,' said Marian in the same unhurried tone she used for everything from offering a Rich Tea to announcing a fire. 'How are you, love?'

'Marian . . .' The lump in Cat's throat surprised her. She imagined Marian, in all her permed, Crimplene glory in the same chair at the same desk outside what was no longer Cat's office. 'I'm great. How are your legs?'

'Much the same,' said Marian philosophically. 'It takes me ten minutes to fetch Liz's redbush organic tea.'

'Liz?' Cat gripped the phone tighter. 'Is she doing my job?'

'Oh dear.' Marian sounded flustered. 'Sorry, I should have broken it to you more gently. Yes.' Her voice dropped to a whisper that Cat knew could be heard at the other end of the vast office. 'Not half as good as you. I mean, *organic tea*?'

'Liz is all right,' said Cat, un-gritting her teeth. Liz was not all right. She was emphatically un-all-right. 'I hope she's treating you well.' Liz was a wisp of a woman who followed a macrobiotic diet and talked about herself in the third person. Liz had long been breathing down Cat's neck: Cat could imagine the glee as she moved her files and her organic tea into the small glass office.

Marian's sniff was eloquent. 'Not my type,' she said. 'She's off in the Maldives for a couple of weeks.'

Never big on vacations (she'd routinely worked bank holidays) Cat didn't care about Liz's whereabouts. She cared about the Toilet Duck campaign but Marian's next comment pre-empted her question.

'The holiday's a freebie from Simon. For winning a D&AD Yellow Pencil award for that pigeon thing.'

Never had Cat's flabber been so thoroughly gasted. A D&AD Yellow Pencil award was an advertising Oscar, guaranteeing a pay rise, the envy of your colleagues, and, it transpired, a free holiday. 'Great. I'm glad for her.'

'I read your notes on the campaign,' said Marian. She paused, expertly. 'So did Liz.'

'It doesn't matter,' said Cat briskly. 'The client got their money's worth.'

'They're over the moon. What are you doing these days?'

'You wouldn't believe me, Marian, if I told you.'

'That ad would have been the making of you.'

'I know.' A canny old moggy like Marian knew exactly what a D&AD on Cat's CV could do for her. Now that Cat's CV was written in invisible ink, it didn't matter much.

'This place isn't the same without you,' said Marian kindly. 'And now that Hugh's gone, we—'

'Who's gone?'

'Hugh's gone.'

'Hugh's gone?'

Rescuing the conversation from Dr Seuss, Marian sounded puzzled. 'Don't you know? Didn't even work his notice. Cleared his desk and walked out. Months ago. Simon was unbearable for days.' She paused, and Cat sensed a metaphorical fishing rod being unfurled. 'So, you're not in touch, then?'

'Well . . .' Teasing Marian was as much fun now as it had been in the old days. 'No. The hanky-panky is over. Lesson learned.'

'Really?' Marian sounded sceptical. 'You had something special, you two.'

This was almost as surprising as the award. 'I thought so once. Why did he leave?'

'Oh, you really are behind the times.' Marian seemed disappointed in Cat. 'He left over *you*, silly. When your commercial was nominated for the award, he insisted that Simon give you your old job back. I saw Liz put a drop of rum in her redbush. Simon wouldn't budge. So Hugh walked out.' An odd clacking noise signalled the decampment of Marian's omnipresent Werther's Original to the other side of her dentures. 'I'm surprised he didn't tell you. Hugh's not the sort to hide his light under a bushel.'

'Marian, my money's about to run out, take care of—'

The phone buzzed like a wasp in her ear, and the connection to London was severed.

46

The hay bounced in the back as the minibus took corners on two wheels. The tired old vehicle was a blur, gobbling up the narrow lanes as Cat pressed the pedal to the floor. She needed to see the commune's wonky gates, to escape the reach of her old life.

Hugh was dead but he wouldn't lie down. Cat bumped along the grass verge as she recalled Marian's words. *He left over you, silly.*

And then he'd sat down and written to Cat about it. And the letter had made a tasty pig's hors d'oeuvre.

Hugh had become a minor discordant note in Cat's inner music. Now here he was, clanging away on the cymbals. How dare he suddenly sprout principles? She'd grown accustomed to him as the Monster Who Had Possibly Left His Pregnant Wife: now suddenly he was the Gent Who Gave Up His Job For Me. My God, she thought furiously, flying over a molehill, these days a woman couldn't even rely on a man to be unreliable.

Men. What with Harry's cavalier attitude and Will's is-he-isn't-he flirting, they were giving her gyp of the highest calibre. 'I came here to live *without* bloody men!' Cat reminded the empty minibus loudly, as it squealed into the cobbled front yard, narrowly missing Jozette.

'Hey, lady, cool down.' Jozette pulled open the driver's door, her full lips pulled back in a grin. 'Why the speed? It's as if you knew.'

'Knew what?' asked Cat as she jumped to the ground.

'Will's here!' mouthed Jozette.

'Will? Why?' Cat felt ambushed. Why would none of the men in her life *behave*?

'The sisterhood is looking out for you,' Jozette grinned. 'Sarge and me, we called him. Told him Dave was poorly. We reckon it's about time you made your move.'

Such timing suggested the existence of God: a sarcastic, giggling God with time on her hands. Earlier, Cat would have been thrilled to see Will, but right now the only man she wanted to see was Hugh, so she could punch him comprehensively and yell '*Why now? Why be decent now? When I'm getting over you at last? When it's too bloody late?*'

The news about Hugh changed nothing. She could never return to him: Cat's conscience had woken up after four years of slumber and wasn't about to nod off again. But Hugh's sacrifice subtly altered how she felt about him. At the eleventh hour he'd suddenly grown a scruple.

'Go get him!' Jozette gave her a gentle shove.

How typical of Hugh, thought Cat resentfully, to agitate her long distance. She kicked the door of Dave's den. All that adrenalin had to go somewhere: Will looked up, innocent of his position in the firing line.

'So, what's the trouble with Dave?' asked Will. 'The others were a little vague.'

Cat folded her arms in a bid to stop herself pacing. In this warm half-light, out of the sun, Will looked good. He wasn't looking at her, he was squatting down to examine Dave. 'She has period pains.' It was all she could come up with, and given her state of mind, Cat thought she'd done quite well.

'Period pains.' Will looked at her now. His eyes were polar in a shaft of sunshine. 'And you know this how?' Either he was struggling not to laugh or he was trying to pass a coconut.

'I'm very attuned to Dave's needs.' Cat spoke low, not trusting herself.

'I see.' Will was studying her, but his interest wasn't flattering. 'I'll take a look. Can't have my little prizewinner suffering.'

Fidgeting on the threshold, Cat wished herself away from the sty. She needed time to calm down, to assess Hugh's gesture with a level head. In marked contrast to Cat, Will was focused, self-possessed. He was a round peg in a round hole, and Cat envied him.

'Nothing much to worry about.' Will bounced to his feet. 'A slight rash behind one ear. You haven't . . .' He shook his head. 'No. Silly idea. Of course you haven't.'

'Haven't what?' pressed Cat, her right foot beating a tense tattoo on the stone floor.

'Been dabbing perfume on Dave?' Will shrugged apologetically, as if aware of how ridiculous that sounded.

'As if!' laughed Cat, over-loudly, surreptitiously checking that Dave's Chanel No. 5 wasn't peeping out from behind the pig's gilt-framed mirror.

After a moment's contemplation of the folded arms, the tapping foot and the rather pink face, Will said, 'Good. Cos if you were, I'd ask you to stop as it's aggravating her skin. But you're not, so I needn't say that.'

'No.'

'I should get on,' said Will, looking slightly at a loss. 'Look, are you OK?' he frowned.

'Yes. Of course,' snapped Cat, with the awful feeling that this afternoon was a runaway horse and she was lashed to the saddle. Making a conscious effort to act normal, Cat took a deep breath as he passed her, and fell into step with him. 'I bumped into your ex,' she said conversationally. 'She told me you'd split up. How is it?' she asked, scrutinising his face as they came out into the sun.

'Is it ungallant to be relieved?' asked Will, shamefaced. 'Lisa's a great girl, don't know how I nabbed her, to be honest, a creased old bugger like me, but she's too . . .'

'Beautiful?' offered Cat ruefully. 'Vicacious? Hot?'

'I was going to say young.' Will stepped back to survey Cat. 'Look, are you really all right? Only you seem a little hyper.'

'Me? I'm fine.' *As fine as any woman consumed with impotent fury at being forced to re-examine her reassuringly low opinion of the man she once loved.*

Cat stopped walking, and Will stopped too. *As fine as I can be when you're about to walk out of those gates and out of my life because all the animals around here are so fucking healthy and I think you might like me and I really really like you and I want to tell you that you do something to me, that your eyes are both kind and sexy which is something I'd have thought impossible, but I won't say any of that because thanks to Hugh I'm all over the place and these stupid lips of mine will only mouth inanities such as* 'So, you and Lisa: no hearts broken?'

'Not mine, no.' Will laughed abruptly. 'And certainly not Lisa's. Shouldn't think she cries herself to sleep because the old bloke who smells of horse medicine isn't around any more.'

'You're not old.' Cat regretted that as too revealing. 'Well, not to me. Which possibly makes me old,' she conceded.

'We're just right, don't you think?' said Will softly.

Cat liked it when his voice changed gear like that. It drew them closer. And panicked her, so that she said stuff like 'My ex is old. Properly old, I mean. He didn't smell of horse medicine, though.'

'Some London toipe, I reckon.' Will attempted a yokel accent which didn't quite come off.

'The quintessential London type.' Cat's voice was bitter. 'And he had to go and do something wonderful, really fucking wonderful, just for me, and I never thought he had it in him and now I'm confused and I could cheerfully murder him but I'd quite like to speak to him first.' She drew breath, feeling naked. Suddenly she wanted Will to go. Exhausted, she was a ping-pong ball who couldn't stop bouncing. In this state, it was dangerous to be near him.

'He probably wants you back,' said Will conversationally. 'I would,' he added, staring out across the yard.

Cat turned sharply to look at him. His face was unchanged, that lock of disobedient hair still dangling over his eye, a faint healthy flush on his cheeks. 'Would you?' she asked carefully, a calm descending over her as she tried to work out if they'd swerved off the path and into some lovely undergrowth.

'You know, you didn't have to manufacture a pig ailment to get me here,' said Will, still maddeningly placid despite the news, the big news, he seemed to be giving Cat. 'I'd have come if you called.' He still hadn't turned to look at her.

'I didn't dare,' said Cat slowly. This was an excruciating game of poker. Will hadn't said anything that would stand up in court: he could still claim she'd misunderstood.

'Truth is, I'm falling for you, Cat O'Connor.' Will finally turned his head. His eyes seemed almost melancholy, but his ripe mouth was turned up at the corners.

Cat gasped: a girlish sound she wouldn't have thought herself capable of.

'Well?' Will nodded encouragingly.

'Well indeed,' said Cat, taut as a drum and unable to return his broad smile. 'Maybe it could work, Will. I thought it would be impossible after Hugh. You're so different. He's so worldly . . . and you're so . . . you know!'

It seemed that Will didn't know. His dimples deflated.

'I mean, I didn't mean that you're not as . . .' Cat's vocabulary imploded. There was no way to claw back the last few moments and rewind to the bit where he was looking into her eyes. If only she'd taken a moment to organise her thoughts but now she was committed to this very, very poor strategy. 'He was so rich and flash and smooth and you're so . . .' She petered out again. 'You're so different. Good different, on the whole. I mean, completely, I mean I don't mind the Barbour, you can't help being . . .' She'd lost him. Will's face was so cold it was almost unrecognisable. It was at this point that common sense packed its bag and completely deserted her: 'Will,' she said in a determined, workmanlike way and rocked up on her toes to place her lips against his.

That sensual mouth of his promised endless fun but Will didn't want to play. Grabbing Cat's shoulders, he rammed her back down on to her heels before managing a curt goodbye and striding off across the yard, Heathcliff-like. Even tripping over Dave didn't hamper his escape, and Cat could still taste his lips as he slammed his car into gear and disappeared in a cloud of dust.

47

Word got round that there had been a kiss, and that said kiss had been rebuffed: pointing and laughing would have been easier to bear than the women's pity.

'You win some, you lose some,' was Jozette's take, but there was sisterly concern in her eyes as she watched Cat pick at her dinner.

'Yeah. No biggie,' agreed Cat airily, hungry for the moment she could be alone and bang her head against a wall.

The Somerset Cat who had jumped Will was so different to her London incarnation that she seemed like some distant relative from Stupidland, who shared the same facial features but had been raised in a growbag.

Behind her own back Cat had nurtured feelings for Will, kidding herself they were a crush. *Crush.* Cat held the word between two fingers, declared it anaemic and tossed it away. She was a grown woman. And this was not a crush. It was desire. Subtle, and many layered, it was real, and warm, and she hadn't done it justice with that – there really was no other word for it – *snog.*

Except it's not a snog if the snoggee rejects the snogger. What Cat's desire deserved was a kiss. A good old-fashioned long and languorous kiss. She'd squandered so many might-have-beens with that one rough gesture. And all that gibberish about Hugh! Cat blushed as she recalled her daft, insulting soliloquy.

In the face of her self-loathing and regret, Cat clung to the memory of Will's 'I'm falling for you, Cat O'Connor'. 'He said it,' she reassured herself. 'He really did.'

The phone rang, its retro bell monstrously loud. Cat beat Germaine to it, snatching up the receiver, elation flooding through her. 'Dad?'

'May I speak to Mary please?' asked a high-pitched, nervous voice.

'For you.' Cat held out the receiver with as much grace as she could manage, then left the kitchen, and her untouched plate. 'I'll lock the chickens in.'

The fowl were amenable that night, sashaying up the drawbridge without complaint. As Cat shot the bolts, Lucy joined her.

'Thought you might need a hand. They can be tricky.'

This, Cat supposed, was as near to 'how are you feeling?' as Lucy could go and she was grateful for the reticence. She had never felt less like sharing. 'Do you ever want to run away from here?' she asked suddenly.

'Hmmm.' Lucy was masterful at this kind of noise. It could be construed as a yes, or a no, or neither or both. There was a short silence punctuated by the hens' imbecilic squawking. 'I don't need to ask if you know about Mary and me, do I?'

'Mary and you?' Cat attempted to look innocent, but gave up in the face of Lucy's patrician glare. 'She told me, yeah.'

'You two.' Lucy shook her head. 'You're like teenagers, telling each other every little thing.'

Riled, Cat said quietly, 'We're mates.' She paused. 'Besides, I saw you.'

That got a natural reaction, not one of Lucy's careful poses. 'How?' she asked, startled.

'I just did. You're not invisible, you know. If you stand around snogging somebody there is a possibility you'll be seen.'

'It wasn't snogging,' snapped Lucy. 'It wasn't snogging,' she said again, quieter and defeated.

In anybody else, somebody less Vulcan, this would be an obvious invitation to 'talk about it'. Cat couldn't be sure with Lucy, but she risked it. 'What was it then?'

'It was . . . beautiful.'

OK. So Lucy *did* want to talk about it. Cat sat on a tree stump, which happened to be the perfect shape for her capacious bottom. Listening to somebody else's travails would be a welcome holiday from her own: moreover, Lucy intrigued her, and touched her. She waited for Lucy to carry on.

'She's quite special, your friend.'

'I think so.'

'She's exactly what I didn't want to find down here.'

For Cat the commune was a ring-fence for her heart, but for Lucy, Cat realised, there was danger within. If fancying somebody can be considered dangerous. And, thought Cat, it bloody well can. 'Is she your type?'

'Don't have a type,' said Lucy. She was looking ahead, past the fanciful turrets of the hen house. 'Mary's so individual. And so transparent, especially when she's trying to be mysterious.'

'Thought you liked them lean?'

'That was mean of me.' Lucy looked contrite. 'True, though. But Mary's got something. She's full of life. Like a tap, bubbling water all the time.' She stopped abruptly. 'Listen to me. Going on.'

It was wonderful to hear Mary eulogised. Once in a while, Alun would grunt that she looked all right, and her shape prompted abrupt 'compliments' of the 'show us your boobs!' variety from men in the street. Lucy had *noticed* her. 'Mary's befuddled right now. You've been a bit off with her since . . .' Cat stopped, tongue tied.

'The kiss.' Lucy nodded. 'Yeah, I've kept my distance.' She chewed the inside of her cheek for a moment. 'Thing is, I came here to escape entanglements. Not make new ones. The last relationship I had . . .' She pouted. Her lips were very red. 'Not pretty.'

So, thought Cat, Lucy was on the run from her past too. The

commune was not the cool experiment she'd claimed in Group. 'In what way?'

'Classified,' said Lucy firmly.

'Oh. Sorry.' Cat felt castigated.

'She wasn't like Mary, this isn't some sappy rebound nonsense.'

'I didn't say it was,' said Cat gently.

'In fact, she was nothing like Mary. She was more like me. Reserved.' Lucy hesitated. 'Cruel.'

'Ah.' There was a broken heart in the mix.

Lucy spoke rapidly. 'I'm not, I'm simply not, going to be somebody's starter pack. *Just add water and grow your own lesbian.* I refuse to be her exotic holiday romance while she's off men.'

'Of course not.'

'I'm not in the market for anything casual. I'm after the real thing. Only I'm not ready for it.' Lucy paced in the dust. 'Do you see? What she's done to me?'

'Yes, yes, I do.' Cat was thrown by this change of demeanour. 'But listen, Lucy, she thinks she's done something wrong. Can't you talk to Mary like you're talking to me? So she doesn't feel so bad?'

'No. I don't want . . .' Lucy gulped, and winced as if there were burrs in her underwear. 'Look, I can't approach her about it, OK? It's not my job to sort out Mary's head.' She said, her lips barely parting, 'She has to come to me.' Lucy gave the hen house a restrained kick and turned for the back door.

'Goodnight, girls,' said Cat to the feathery tenants, set a-twitter by that kick. She trailed Lucy into the house, and saw her keep her distance from Mary as they both cleared the table.

'I'll help with—' began Cat, but found herself bundled into the pantry by Mary, who promptly locked the door behind them. 'What?' She sighed. 'Look, Mary, I'm not up to dissecting you and Lucy yet again, OK?'

'I'm going!' said Mary, her eyes glittering in the gloom.

'You can't!' Cat was panicked

'I can. I'm going over the wall. Tonight. And you're going to cover for me.'

Yanking Mary towards her by the neck of her faded blue tee, Cat whispered urgently, 'Don't drag me into this. If you want to go, go, but . . .' She relinquished her hold and whined '*Don't* go. What'll I do without you?'

'It's only for a night.'

Cat cursed Mary's talent for telling half the story. 'Where are you going?' She narrowed her eyes. 'Alun!' She recalled the strangely pitched voice on the phone.

'Yes. He's made me an offer I can't refuse.' Mary shrugged. 'Or one only a bitch would refuse, anyway.'

'Not . . .' Cat could barely shape the word. 'Not marriage?'

'Of course not feckin' marriage!' trilled Mary. 'This is Alun, remember? He goes into spasm walking past Moss Bros. No, he was calling from the Stag in Nether Fitzpaine, two miles away. He's booked us the four-poster suite. You know, the whole mini-break shebang. Log fires. Long walks.'

'It's too warm for log fires,' said Cat briskly. 'And Alun never walks further than the fridge.'

'Are you jealous?' Mary sounded amused.

'Yeah, I go crazy for men whose *Mastermind* subject would be Ball Scratching through the Ages. I'm *suspicious*, not jealous.'

'Not even a teensy bit?' Mary put a hand on her shoulder. 'After you know what?'

Too unspeakable to be referred to openly, Cat's *faux pas* had already become 'you know what.' 'Let's leave Will out of this.'

Mary defended Alun. 'Look, he's making an effort. I've been dropping hints about mini breaks for years and now he's actually booked one. It would be mean not to go.'

'Germaine'll go nuts. It's the central rule of the commune – no men.'

'But he's not coming to the commune. I'm going to him. I'll say I'm visiting a sick aunt.'

'That won't fool anybody.' Curmudgeonly Cat was being unco-operative for the sake of it and she could feel Mary's dismay.

'What'll I say then?' begged Mary. 'Dying gran? Nah. Germy knows all my mine are kaput. Jury service?'

'Audition,' said Cat with an air of finality.

'You are feckin' *brilliant*!' yelped Mary. 'Did you pick up this lying lark from Hugh?' She threw open the pantry door and called, 'Germaine! That was my agent on the phone – and guess what?'

48

It was cocoa hour by the time Germaine got back from dropping Mary to the station. Or cocoa and marshmallows and a flapjack-the-size-of-your-head hour in Cat's case. The women were hanging around the Aga, circling Beulah like sweet-toothed vultures, all eyes on the pot of chocolatey gloop she was slowly stirring.

Looping the minibus keys back on to their allotted hook by the pantry, Germaine looked around for Sarge.

'Still out. Still hiking.' Cat pulled a face to illustrate puzzlement at hiking when there was cocoa on offer.

'Really? In the dark?' Just as Germaine struck a note of puzzled concern, the front door slammed. 'Ah! There she is!' Germaine was relieved.

'Traitor!' barked Sarge from the kitchen doorway.

'I beg your pardon?' Germaine looked at her quizzically.

'Judas!' Sarge hadn't even taken her kagoul off.

Germaine studied Sarge's bristling little face for a long moment and a flicker of what seemed like comprehension crossed her features. 'Come on, Sarge,' she said decisively, approaching her with one arm out to guide her away, 'let's go somewhere and—'

'No. I'm calling a house meeting. Now!'

The others, eaten up with curiosity, gathered around the table. All eyes were on Sarge. Most were avid: Germaine's were unreadable.

'We've been betrayed. Double-crossed. Stabbed in the back.'

'Oh, for goodness' sake, if you've got some tale to tell on somebody, do get on with it,' sighed Lucy.

Her finger shaking, Sarge pointed at Germaine. 'Our leader, our so-called blooming leader . . .' Her voice shook too. 'She's been consorting with the enemy all this time.'

None the wiser, Cat looked from Germaine to Sarge. Then she looked at Antonia who was also looking from Germaine to Sarge, as was Beulah. As was Jozette. This looking at each other went on for some time until Lucy broke the cycle to ask testily, 'What do you mean, Sarge? I wasn't aware we had an enemy.'

'Men!' blurted Sarge, her eyes red. 'Germaine is having an affair under our noses.'

'Oh do shush,' tutted Antonia, folding her arms.

'There's nobody to bloody *have* an affair with,' said Cat peevishly. 'Unless it's the hay man.' She laughed and nudged Germaine. 'Is it the hay man, Germy?'

'No,' said Germaine. 'I'm having an affair with Jamie.'

It took a moment for Cat to recognise the name, then she was expostulating with the rest of them. 'As if!' she honked, as Antonia bent double, holding her sides and Beulah tittered into her handkerchief.

'Sarge, Germy isn't having an affair with anybody,' said Cat, feeling sorry for the deranged little woman. 'And if she was, she wouldn't pick on such an irritating little git.'

'He *is* rather dull,' agreed Antonia straightening up.

'Rather?' Lucy queried the understatement.

'And the laugh!' Antonia did a quick impression.

'Bang on!' squealed Cat. 'He sounds like a goose in labour!' She looked at Germaine and stopped laughing abruptly. 'You *are* having an affair with Jamie, aren't you?'

Germaine lifted the magisterial chin handed down to her by

generations of barking mad women with too much money. 'Yes. I've been seeing him in secret since the night we arrived.' The chin wavered. 'I'm very very sorry, sisters, but Sarge is telling the truth.'

Nobody responded. Lucy pulled out a chair, the scrape of wood against stone loud in the silence. 'Perhaps you should explain,' she said evenly.

'Explain?' Sarge was scornful as the others sat. 'What is there to explain? She's been betraying us, sneaking out to see that toyboy behind our backs, while lecturing us about her wonderful cause. She's a—'

'Yes, *all right.*' Cat held up one hand to halt the avalanche of bile. 'Germy,' she said, turning to her friend, a woman she'd thought she knew inside out until a moment ago. 'Talk to us.'

Germaine was as pale as the ghost that never was. The chocolate simmered forgotten on the Aga, as she looked around at the expectant, baffled faces and said, 'I'm at a loss to describe what's been happening except to say that when I met Jamie that first night, something happened.'

'Yeah, you bit his head off,' interrupted Antonia. She had only learned to interrupt recently and rather enjoyed it.

'*What* happened, dear?' Beulah's warm, weightless voice was encouraging.

'Something that had always been tight in me unfurled,' said Germaine, raising her voice as if soldiering through her guilt and embarrassment, determined to be unashamed. Her face softened: she looked twenty years younger and considerably less intelligent. 'It was as if a bell tolled my name. I couldn't ignore it.' She blinked, and came to. 'Perhaps it's more honest to say I *didn't* ignore it.'

'You didn't try very hard.' Tears were coursing down Sarge's face. She shrugged off the comforting touch offered by Cat.

'The shopping trips.' Antonia put two and two together. 'No wonder you never let us come with you.'

'The business to discuss with Jamie's father,' said Lucy.

'The minibus,' said Cat slowly, visualising a muddy field. 'It *was* in a different parking space after the county show.'

'Yes,' said Germaine in a dry voice. 'Jamie and I drove off. To be alone.'

'Urgh, please,' spat Sarge. 'No disgusting details.'

'It is not disgusting.' Stoppered-up tears mangled Germaine's diction. 'It is not,' she repeated dejectedly.

'It's a hell of an age difference,' mused Antonia.

'Twenty-two years,' said Germaine curtly.

'Nobody would bat an eyelid if Germaine was a man,' Lucy pointed out.

'That's very true,' murmured Cat.

Thumping the table, Sarge bared her teeth. 'Listen to you all! Don't you get it?' She wiped her eyes roughly with the back of a camouflage cuff. 'Never mind the bloody age difference. Germaine has lied to us and sabotaged her own experiment! We need to vote on what to do about it.' She stood back, hands on hips, her cheeks red. 'I vote to put an end to this hypocritical farce. I vote we all pack up and leave in the morning.'

Panic buzzed in Cat's ears. She sat silent, waiting for the others' reaction.

'I vote for hot chocolate.' Beulah put her hands on her knees and stood up heavily.

'We can't go home.' Antonia sounded scrambled. 'I can't.'

Germaine's head was down, her nose almost on the table.

'Don't say we have to go home!' Antonia's voice was growing shriller. She was travelling back in time, regressing to the personality she'd arrived with.

'I'm staying,' said Cat with conviction. She would have rather liked to fall apart à la Antonia but didn't feel able to.

'Me too.' Lucy blew out her cheeks. 'I see a thing through to the end.' She eyeballed Sarge. 'Don't you?'

'You people!' Exasperated, Sarge strode out.

Lifting her mass of curls, Germaine whispered 'Thank you'.

'I'm not doing it for you,' said Lucy. 'I believe in this experiment.'

'Aw Luce,' dared Cat. 'You are doing it just a bit for Germy, aren't you?'

'I don't like being called Luce.' Lucy shrugged. 'Just a bit. Maybe.'

Her fists rolled into balls, Antonia was breathing hard. 'I want a drink so bad,' she said, almost to herself. She seemed to be having a crisis of sorts, her lips trembling.

Germaine looked away as if Antonia had slapped her across the face. Cat guessed that she was feeling responsible.

'Stay calm, Antonia.' Lucy's voice was silky and authoritative. 'We're all with you. This will pass.'

'What if it doesn't?' whimpered Antonia, like a child scared of the dark and needing to hear a grown-up say it's all all right.

Beulah put a mug of cocoa in front of her. 'All things pass, dear. Trust me.'

'What about you, Beulah?' Cat twisted in her chair to follow her progress back to the pot. 'Do you want to leave?'

'No,' said Beulah. 'I have nowhere to go.'

Covering the kitchen floor in two paces, Germaine squeezed Beulah's soft, bowed shoulders. 'I'm sorry,' she murmured. 'I'm sorry, everyone.' She left the room.

The house was subtly changed, as if an enerating gas had leaked in through the ill-fitting casement windows. Germaine watched the others covertly at the subdued breakfast table, gauging their mood.

Demolishing dry bread with venomous bites, Sarge glared at Germaine. She had slept in her fatigues, and her puffy, unhappy face bore the marks of her pillow.

A fault line had opened up in the commune.

With synthetic high spirits, Germaine attempted to kick-start conversation. 'I do hope,' she said over her boiled egg courtesy of Hencat's nether regions, 'that Mary's audition is successful, she deserves a break.' She sighed philosophically. 'Something to go back to.' She looked from one face to the next. 'Only six weeks left, sisters.'

'Sisters!' scoffed Sarge.

Cat put down her spoon. 'Six weeks? Are you sure? It's only the sixth.'

'No, it's the tenth. Tenth of August.' Germaine looked taken aback at Cat's sudden exit.

'Antonia, another egg?' Cat heard Beulah ask as she leaned her forehead against the cool, thick walls of the narrow hallway.

The country house sale had been two days ago. Cat wondered if Harry had gone without her, if there had been a momentary '*hang on, didn't I promise to bring oh, what's her name, that daughter I abandoned more than twenty years ago?*'

She wouldn't cry. It was too late to cry over Harry. Even if she did feel like a six-year-old whose daddy hadn't picked her up from a party. Best to shove him into that attic space in her mind where Will now languished.

At least she'd managed to clear out some lumber. Cat retrieved the postcard – a view of Lyme Regis in lurid colours, taken decades ago – from her skirt pocket and placed it on the hall table to be posted. She checked the wording again, running her finger over the bold handwriting that Hugh so admired.

Hugh
Thank you.
Cat

The loose ends didn't matter any more.

'Yoohoo everyone!' An actress's voice utilising its diaphragm just like it had been taught, echoed around the house. 'I'm back from my audition!' Mary sought out Cat, just about to get physical with a muffin, and dragged her out to the yard.

Jozette was out there, weeding conscientiously around a dead runner bean. 'You're back early. How'd the audition go, hon?' she shouted.

'Very very badly.' Mary glared at Cat in a meaningful way. 'Disaster. Crap. Rubbish. Super-shit.'

'D'you think you got the part?' Barmy optimism was second nature to Jozette.

'I hope not,' said Mary, still eyeing Cat portentously.

Jozette got back to her task, and Mary led Cat to the far side of the hen house.

'So?' Cat cocked her head.

'It was like a horror film,' declared Mary. '*Invasion of the Body Snatchers.* Aliens took Alun and replaced him with a replica. It looked like him, it sounded like him, but it was doing all the wrong things.'

'Such as?'

'He held the door open for me. He didn't ask the waiter for the OAP special. He . . .' Her eyes widened in bewilderment. 'He asked me how I was.'

'That wasn't Alun.'

'He'd even had his hair cut. In a hairdresser's. And he's lost weight now I'm not around to cadge food from. His clothes were clean. He even smelled nice.'

'Like I said, that wasn't Alun.' Cat recalled Alun's aroma, a pungent bouquet of beer, Marmite, and his very old cat.

'The room was out of this world,' said Mary approvingly. 'Four-poster, plasma TV, tea and coffee making facilities, the works.'

'TV?' asked Cat excitedly, like a Third World child. 'What was on? Did you watch *Corrie*?'

'Didn't switch it on.' Mary shrugged. 'Didn't feel the urge, funnily enough. Besides, Alun had big plans for me. *Big*,' she stressed.

'And that is officially enough information.'

'Sorry, but I'm about to over-share. The sex was gentle, expressive, warm . . .' Mary groped for adjectives. 'Loving, generous, tender.' Her shoulders drooped. 'And shit.'

Cat yowled 'No!'

'Oh yes. It was like a Hallmark card. I've been more turned on leaning against the washing machine.'

'Did you,' asked Cat, fearing the reply, 'say all this to Alun?'

'Sort of. I left out the washing machine bit.'

'No man likes to lose his beloved to a spin cycle.'

'I told him to relax. He said I didn't like him when he relaxed.'

'Which is perfectly true.'

'So he asked what could he do to get things back the way they were. And I said I don't want them back the way they were. Cos they were rubbish.'

'Did you tell him about Lucy?'

A strange look contorted Mary's freckled face. 'Tell him what? What's to tell? Why would I mention Luce? What are you getting at?'

'Sorry! Sorry!' Cat put up her hands to defend herself.

'I've changed and Alun knows I have.' Mary leaned against the hen house and a chicken squawked within. 'I see him differently. It was cute to whisk me away, but it's also pointless. Typical bloody Alun.' She bent to tickle Chickensarge, who scarpered. 'He's such a contrast to Lucy.'

'Oh.' Cat cocked a sarcastic eyebrow. 'We're allowed to mention her now, are we?'

Ignoring her, Mary went on. 'She's so calm and precise. She says what she means. There's no waffle, you know. It's refreshing.'

Cat wanted to probe. She wanted to pry. She longed to know just how far Mary's relationship with Lucy had gone. But Mary would tell her when she was ready. And besides, she'd just heard Antonia shout 'Letter for you, Cat!'

Tearing at the envelope, Cat took the stairs two at a time. Full length on her bed she read '*Forgive me! Something came up. There's another sale on the eighth of October. Fancy going to that one? Your loving (and forgetful) Dad.*'

'I'll be gone by then, Harry,' Cat told the unheeding page.

Long gone.

49

Blacking the Aga was a two-woman job. Cat and Germaine were companionable but silent until Mary whirled into the room, her face ablaze with gratified horror.

'You sly old bat!' she shrieked. 'Germy, I never knew you had it in you.' Mary waggled her finger in mock consternation, giggling with disbelief. 'Pretending to be going out on oh-so-important commune business and all the time indulging in off-the-scale sauciness with a toyboy!'

'You've heard.' Germaine stood up, not mirroring Mary's effervescence. 'I'm sorry.'

'Sorry shorry,' scoffed Mary. She prodded the kneeling Cat with her foot and cocked her head at Germaine. 'She's a dark horse, isn't she?'

'Who told you?'

Cat's question threw Mary for a moment. 'Lucy,' she shrugged.

Feeling robbed of seeing Mary's face when she heard the news, Cat said heavily, 'We're all a bit shell shocked.'

'Why?' Mary goggled at her friend. 'Isn't Germy allowed some fun?'

'I had a duty to you all,' said Germaine dully. 'It was a betrayal, I know that.'

'Unbutton your hair shirt,' laughed Mary. 'You were caught out in an affair.' Her gaze slid over Cat. 'Not the first time in the history of the world that's happened.'

'No, but—'

'No but nothing.' Mary would brook no argument. 'You pulled a fast one, you were rumbled, you said sorry.' She clapped her hands. 'Case closed. You're not a martyr, Germaine. Nobody expects you to pack your libido in mothballs for our sake.'

Germaine winced at Mary's colourful imagery. 'But isn't that exactly what I demanded from the rest of you?'

'We're all human.' Mary took a step back to study Germaine. 'Tell me – do you love Jamie?' She looked sharply at Cat. 'Did the impromptu Spanish Inquisition think to ask that?'

'Very much,' said Germaine quietly, unable to stop the corners of her mouth rising a touch.

'All rules are off then!' Mary elbowed Cat. 'Oi, you. You're very quiet. Don't tell me you're in Sarge's camp, and you want to burn this poor cow at the stake?'

'No, of course not.' Cat basked in the warm blast of Mary's humanity. 'We all make mistakes.' The fault line rumbled and closed a little.

'And besides,' Mary said in a not-to-be-messed-with tone, 'love is where it falls. Germy happened to meet the one guy on earth who floats her boat and we have to accept it.' She patted Germaine on the back. 'Even if he is a dipstick.'

Her blackened hands at her side, Germaine said, in a tight voice packed with emotion, 'I'm not going to see Jamie again.'

'Yes you bloody are!' said Mary stridently.

'No, no, not until after the experiment is finished.'

'Oh. Well. OK.' The compromise seemed to satisfy Mary. 'I suppose you should follow the rules.' She winked. 'You made them up, after all.'

The news that Germaine had relinquished Jamie for the duration mollified bruised feelings. The women, in Cat's opinion, felt hurt, not angry: even Sarge who was slamming doors and kicking walls with a perma-scowl on her lean doggy face.

Yoked to Sarge on washing up duty, Cat stood shoulder to shoulder with her at the sink. 'Hey!' she warned, as Sarge banged a dried cup down on the dresser. 'You'll break something.' She hesitated. 'Your own heart, possibly.'

Making an un-spellable noise Sarge accosted another cup. 'Girly twaddle,' she muttered.

Taking the blameless little vessel out of Sarge's hand, Cat said, 'It's time to stop all this. You have to face facts. So your idol has feet of clay. They all have.' She thought of Hugh's clay feet which extended right up to his neck. 'Try and understand Germy or it will eat you up inside.'

'I understand her perfectly.'

'You make falling in love sound dirty,' chastised Cat. 'It's just a man and a woman doing what comes naturally.' Cat employed a new technique she'd christened WWBS: What Would Beulah Say. 'Forgive her, Sarge, for your sake as well as hers. Germy's given Jamie up. Meet her halfway.' She paused. 'What if I hugged you? Would that be good?' she asked gently.

'No,' said Sarge decisively. 'That would be bad.'

They finished their chore in silence, but Cat reckoned WWBS had worked.

Cat blinked and most of August was gone, leaving only a month or so of the experiment to go. Sarge had declared an uneasy truce and although she never looked directly at Germaine, she tossed the odd comment her way. The slavish adoration was history and Cat could tell that Germaine missed it.

Not half as much as Germaine missed Jamie, however. When Germaine would look up, heavy eyed, from a book, or drift off during a seminar on Eleven Ways To Kill A Man With The Contents Of Your Handbag, Cat would reach out a hand to her and it was never rejected. Forgiving her hadn't been easy, but it had worked: like applying a poultice to a boil, it got rid of all the bad stuff.

Whenever Sarge was otherwise engaged in bullying, instructing, or simply glaring, Cat understudied her as Antonia's AA chauffeur. Having delivered Antonia to her meeting one squally afternoon, Cat self-prescribed a cream tea. She was feeling introspective, a recurring problem since her relocation to the commune, and calories were the best distraction.

Contemplating her feast at the window table of Ye Olde Copper Kettle, Cat drew her initials in some spilled sugar before giving in and dragging out the postcard that had arrived that morning.

A view of the London Eye on the front, the other side read

No, thank you my darling girl.
For everything.
Goodbye

'Goodbye,' breathed Cat. She closed her eyes and let her head loll back. A door slammed shut somewhere, both in her mind and at the back of the café. She felt fresh, clean. Without the distractions of the past she had space for her new idea. It was radical. It would change everything. It scared her. And it was looking more attractive by the day.

Cat opened her eyes wide, and they met another pair of wide eyes. Will had stopped dead outside the window, an untranslatable look on his face.

Irresolute for a moment, Will's feet seemed uncertain which way to take him, until he pushed open the squeaky door of Ye Olde Copper Kettle. 'Hi,' he said, in a low impact, no pressure, what the hell am I doing here way.

'Hi yourself.' Cat managed a smile. 'I'm having a cream tea,' she said, stilted.

'So I see.' Will hesitated. 'Is it nice?' he asked, very much in the style of somebody with a broom up their bottom.

'Very nice indeed.'

Will shut his eyes. His furry lashes rested on his cheek for a moment before he opened his eyes again and suggested, with a smile, 'Let's start again. That was the dullest conversation I've ever had. And bear in mind that I talk about bovine rectal temperatures for much of the day.'

'You've put me off me cream tea.' Cat relaxed enough to risk a joke. She was sure she was red all over. Not the dainty coral blush of a Victorian maiden, but a ripe ketchup. 'Sit down?'

'I haven't really got . . .' Will checked the clunky watch on his wrist. Hairs straggled from the sleeve of his checked shirt, suggesting an arm much naughtier than his decorous, long-fingered hand. He raised his eyes to Cat. 'What the hell? The spaniel in Bridge Street can wait.'

'I'm flattered,' said Cat, hoping the puce tide was ebbing.

'Don't be. You haven't met the spaniel in question.' Will winced. 'I'm never going to get cast as James Bond if I carry on chatting to the ladies like that, am I?'

'No,' laughed Cat, grateful to Will for acting so normal in light of their recent history. She asked a passing waitress for an extra cup, noting surreptitiously that Will's late summer plumage suited him. Without the Barbour she could get a proper sense of his body. Broad and male-shaped, his chest was plump enough for the comfortable resting of a female head, toned enough to elicit a hearty phwoaar in the right circumstances. She approved. For a second, as she smiled into his blue gaze, she remembered his admission that he was falling for her.

That did it. Puce again.

'Have you caught the sun?' Will leaned over the tiny rickety table to examine her. She could smell his breath. It was sweet, as if he'd been chewing meadow grass along with his patients.

'No, I'm just a bit embarrassed, after, you know, last time we, when I . . .' Cat gabbled, taking a bite out of a scone.

'Forget it,' said Will. 'I have.'

'Oh. Right.' Uncertain whether this was good or bad (bad, probably, her pessimistic heart suggested) Cat regretted inviting Will to sit down. Frankly, he was a disconcerting presence. Near enough to touch across the gingham tablecloth, Will's masculine solidity in the midst of the doilies and teacakes set her thoughts racing.

Never a believer in skating from one relationship to another, Cat suffered emotional overload looking at Will. Will had become important to her, in the hundred subtle ways that a person can. They were on parallel rafts, drifting this way and that in choppy currents: sometimes close enough to brush fingers, but most of the time bobbing apart. It was, Cat consoled herself, watching Will fill his cup and drip tea on his spotless napkin, better that way. Post-commune, with a life and career to re-imagine, she would need to focus.

'How's the pig with the curliest tail?' asked Will.

'Happy as Larry. Whoever he might be.'

'No more trouble with her ears?' Will looked concerned. His frown made him look older. 'There may be a tendency to infection there.'

'Her ears are fine.'

No doubt there's a special circle of Hell where female souls spend eternity discussing pig health with the man whose underpants they long to remove with their teeth.

'And her trotters? You're checking them regularly?'

If this was a mission to render the conversation resolutely unsexy, Will was failing. 'Yes. Dave receives a level of service the royal family would envy.' Everything Cat did with Will was sexy. Going to the library would be sexy with Will; choosing a new sink plug would be triple X, if he undid his shirt a little more.

'I might be going to London in a few weeks.'

'London?' Cat reacted as if Will was off to Jupiter. London was *her* turf. 'Why?' she asked, as if there could be no guessable reason why a man in his late thirties might want to visit the capital city.

‘A wedding. My cousin’s getting married.’ His full lips thinned. ‘I’m not a wedding person. Not very good at dressing up.’

‘Just don’t upstage the bride.’

‘I’ll try not to.’ Will pushed back the determined comma of hair which insisted on working its way down his forehead. ‘I don’t suit suits, if you see what I mean. Or hotels. We’re staying in some fancy place, near Hyde Park Corner.’ He pulled a face. ‘I’d rather be at home. In jeans.’

‘With your forearm up a cow.’ Cat nodded in sympathy. ‘But think of all the fun you’ll have in London town,’ she said wryly. ‘Going up the apples and pears.’

‘Doing the Lambeth Walk.’

‘Cor blimey, guvnor, you’ll be ’avin’ it large.’

Will looked unconvinced. ‘I prefer small get-togethers. There are people coming from Australia for this do.’

‘Twenty hours in a plane for a ham salad and some speeches? Some folk will do anything for kicks.’

‘There’ll be second cousins once removed, great-aunts, relatives I haven’t seen since my own wedding.’

Speaking rather quickly, Cat said, ‘Yes, nice, second cousins once whatsit. Erm, did you say,’ she slowed right down, ‘*your* wedding?’

‘I was married. For three years.’

‘Oh.’ Cat’s mind raced. ‘Who to?’

Will cocked his head, amused. ‘I don’t think you know her.’ He chased a crumb across the tablecloth. ‘It didn’t last. Her mum and dad were still paying for the reception when we split up.’

In front of her, Will mutated from backwater boy with no emotional history (why, Cat wondered suddenly, had she assumed that?) to man of the world. Man of *his* world, not as wide as Hugh’s and certainly not as fancypants, but a fully rounded world all the same. ‘What happened?’ Cat qualified her question. ‘I mean, it’s none of my business.’

‘Rows. Niggles. No one thing in particular.’ Will turned his teacup round and round in his large hands, then said softly, 'unless you count us never really loving each other. That didn't help.'

'So why'd you get married? Don't tell me you're that desperate for a running buffet?'

'No,' laughed Will, his face creasing. 'Expectations. Our families took it for granted, and we sleepwalked up the aisle.' Will sat back, breaking the little circle they'd created amidst the rattle of cups and spoons. 'Look, am I boring you? Why should you be interested in my ancient history?'

'I'm not bored,' said Cat, with a plainness she didn't want to tarnish with a joke. Lust couldn't explain how right it felt sitting with Will, the pleasure she took watching him talk. Looking into his eyes while he spoke was something she could do indefinitely, whatever the topic. 'What else don't I know about you?' Her eyes flashed. 'Oh God, do you have kids?'

'Not yet, no.' Will lowered his eyes. 'Thought I'd have a couple by now, hanging off me, getting in the way. But it hasn't happened.' He shrugged.

'You'd make a good dad.' Banal *and* inappropriate: Cat bit her lip, literally and metaphorically.

'How did we get so heavy?' smiled Will, a fleeting look of discomfort banished by his habitual expression of puzzled good humour. 'I should make tracks. That dog will be looking at its watch and wondering where I am.' He rose awkwardly, bashing the chair of the octogenarian behind him.

As Will apologised and fussed over the old lady, Cat composed her features. She'd made a friend. Making a friend was good. Lovely, in fact. But it wasn't enough, as Cat's heart and loins were emphatically semaphoring. *Keep it simple,* she urged herself. *Relegate Will to the status of lovely/humiliating memory. Get on with your life!*

'What do I owe you for the tea?'

'Don't be silly.' Cat knew her smile was dilute. 'See you around.'

'Yeah.' Will half turned to go. 'Hang on. You've got a bit of cream just there . . .' He picked up Cat's napkin and gently wiped the corner of her mouth.

Her face felt scalded, as if all her blood had rushed to the spot.

Will stood very still for a long moment, before bending to place his lips gently on the spot he'd wiped. 'Cat,' he said, softly, and left.

How much later the banging on the window started, Cat didn't know.

'Cat!' Antonia was bellowing, hammering on the glass. 'Take me home!'

50

'Three weeks.' Germaine chewed the inside of her cheek and looked into the middle distance. 'That's all we've got left. I tried to extend the lease but it seems that Jamie's father has a buyer.' She looked around wonderingly at the ageing fabric of the commune. 'For *this,*' she said, as if surprised.

'I love this house,' said Lucy softly.

'Me too,' said Cat with feeling.

Jozette joined in. 'This house has a heart.'

An old table, found abandoned in an outhouse, was burning in the dusk. Flames cackled and hissed, feet from the women swathed in blankets dotted around the bonfire's edge.

'It's so wonderfully pagan,' enthused Germaine.

'She's perked up,' said Mary to Cat and Lucy, leaning either side of her like bookends. 'Do you think there's whisky in her hot chocolate? I wouldn't put it past her.'

Gazing into the flames that knitted the gathering together against the sooty night beyond, Cat put her forefinger to the corner of her mouth and stroked a spot she often petted. She hadn't clapped eyes on Will since he'd kissed the cream from her lip. She wouldn't admit to missing him – she was heartily tired of missing people – but she would like to see him one more time. A proper goodbye would be nice.

The swirling fog of her future had cleared. Cat had come to a decision. Mary wasn't going to like it, but there was no going back: she had made the pertinent call that afternoon.

Flopping down beside them, Jozette's eyes fizzed like the fire, full of energy. 'Guess what I did today?' she grinned, then burbled on before anybody could. 'Booked my ticket! I'm off, girlfriends. Home!' She bounced up and down, cross legged. 'Where they don't impersonate my accent!'

'What? Not Stoke Newington?' Cat sat up straighter, not reflecting Jozette's joy.

'Hmm.' Jozette pretended to think hard, that neon grin still in place. 'Miami versus Stoke Newington. It's a toughie. But *Miami wins*!' Her hot chocolate splashed into the fire, creating a tiny firework display.

'What about,' said Mary, 'Trev?'

'If Trev wants to follow me, he can.' Jozette's smile was a touch strained, but still in place. 'It's not so far.'

'Ten hours on a plane,' grumbled Cat.

'I'll be back.' Jozette shrugged. 'Maybe. Guys, who knows? I thought you'd be pleased for me. It took guts, facing up to facts about Trev and me.'

'No, no, we are, we are.' Cat rallied, ashamed of her selfishness.

Mary reached over to hug Jozette, letting Lucy thud to the ground. 'You're being very brave. And it's the right thing to do. Only . . .'

'We'll miss you.' Cat was determined not to cry.

'Come visit!' shrieked Jozette. 'I'm not dead, I'm in the States.'

'Trev will be devastated.' Cat put her hand to her mouth. 'Sorry Jo. You didn't need to hear that.'

'You're right, he will.' Jozette took Cat's hand in her own pleasantly dry one. 'But you know what, girl? Life is tough. It's him or me.' She tossed back her head, her Afro haloed in the firelight. 'And it sure as fuck ain't gonna be me!'

*

'It's not a funeral!' Jozette wailed, appalled at the red eyes and runny noses pressed against the window of her train carriage. 'Guys! Pack it in! You'll set me off.'

Automatic doors the length of the train hissed heartlessly shut, and Cat gulped. Never one to let the grass grow under her Jimmy Choos, Jozette migrated ten days after her announcement. The ragged little herd waved, woebegone, until the last carriage disappeared around the corner of the track. Cat felt the spirit of the commune gutter, like a candle flame in a draught.

The magic circle was ruptured, and the women were once again a ragbag of individuals. Time for Cat to dredge up her team-building skills. 'Right, you 'orrible lot!' she barked. 'Mandatory paddling. *Now!* Giddy up. Antonia, blow your nose. Mary, your eyeliner's running. Last one to the beach buys the 99s.'

The bluey grey waters of the Channel, expert at tempests and the sinking of ships, were in a gentle mood that day as they lapped around Beulah's chubby ankles. Her extra-broad sandals dangling from one hand, she peered at her feet as if they belonged to somebody else. 'It tickles,' she said wonderingly.

'We simply don't paddle enough,' said Cat, digging her toes into the soft gravel beneath the water.

'I've never done it before,' said Beulah.

'Never?' Cat was shocked. She pictured a much younger Beulah, one with ribbons in her brunette hair and a disappointed look on her little face. 'That's terrible.'

'Fun, you see,' said Beulah contemplatively, still watching her feet. 'He frowned on fun.'

'I won't be able to do this at the drop of a hat when I get back to London.'

'So you're definitely going back.' At last something wrenched Beulah's eyes away from her toes.

'Yes.' Cat shrugged. 'That place is a magnet.'

'And you're just a little iron filing,' said Beulah, almost to herself.

'This day next week, my dear, you'll be on the train.'

'I know.' Cat could contemplate her return to the big bad metropolis with something like equanimity. 'Don't let's talk about that now. We're all still together. Let's make the best of it.'

'I always do,' smiled Beulah, with that idiosyncratic way she had of giving each word equal and light meaning, yet making the whole sound profound.

Sarge was splashing like a mongrel through the shallows towards Cat. 'You can't drink seawater of course,' she proclaimed loudly, as if Cat was planning to. 'The kidneys would have to create twice as much urine as you drank, so you would die of dehydration. Quite literally wee yourself to death.'

It was no mystery why Sarge didn't get asked out much. 'Thanks for that,' murmured Cat, making for the shore.

Behind her, Sarge said suddenly, with much sniffing and shrugging and chin-jabbing, 'Have you seen Will? Since he kissed you in the courtyard?'

Taken aback, Cat protested, 'I kissed *him*, Sarge. He didn't kiss me back.' She peered at Sarge. 'I assumed you'd disapprove of such . . .' She searched for a Sarge-style word. 'Such twaddle.'

They'd reached the pebbly shore. Sarge bent down to pull her boots on. Cat couldn't see her face when she said, 'He seems nice, that's all. A nice man. Nice face.'

'If you thought that,' said Cat gently, 'why weren't you more friendly towards him?' She stuffed her feet into flip-flops with a rueful, 'I cocked it up. You might have got farther than me.'

'Hardly,' snorted Sarge, straightening up. 'I mean I'm . . .' She gestured at herself. 'And you're . . .' She waved a hand up and down Cat's figure. 'No contest.'

'Don't say that!' remonstrated Cat, hating the hinterland of insecurity it revealed.

'And don't bullshit me,' said Sarge.

A sharp rat-a-tat-tat at the front door interrupted the poignant chore of stripping Jozette's bed. 'Hello,' said Cat to the red-faced woman with hair made of Brillo pads standing on the doorstep.

'Where's the pig?' said the woman, whose ham hock arms needed more flattery than her sleeveless sundress afforded.

'Oh.' Cat took a step back. 'You're from the children's farm?'

'Yes. Margot. Hello. Pig?' A miser with words, she spent only a curt 'yes' in answer to each of Cat's catalogue of queries as they crossed the courtyard.

'Are you fond of pigs? Have you kept them before? Do you know about feeding? Mucking out?'

'I do run a farm,' said the woman eventually. 'I keep all sorts of animals.'

'But do you love them?' asked Cat desperately as they reached Dave's door.

'I tend them,' said the woman tartly as she entered Dave's inner sanctum. The scented candles were glowing, and Dave's fat neck sported a jauntily knotted Hermès scarf, Jozette's parting gift. 'This the pig?' she asked uncertainly.

'Yes. This is our beautiful Dave,' said Cat, her throat suddenly acquiring a boulder. 'She likes mashed boiled eggs for breakfast. She doesn't like anchovies, or kiwi fruit. I massage her back once a week.' Cat stopped short of listing Dave's beauty routine: Margot didn't look the sort to moisturise Dave's trotters. 'I understand you're interested in taking the hens too.'

'Always interested in good layers.' Margot paused, stroking the hairs on her chin thoughtfully. 'Do they have . . . special requirements too?' she asked warily.

'No, they're very independent. Although,' mused Cat, 'they are accustomed to living in a castle.'

Margot had brought her truck, but Cat, stalling brilliantly, had claimed that it was Dave's bath night and asked Margot to return the day before the commune closed down. Sitting with Dave after dinner, Cat rubbed the pig's snout and reminisced about the good times. 'I'll visit,' whispered Cat, vaguely aware that they looked like a spoof advert for a K-Tel Valentine's Day compilation.

'Listen to you.' Mary came in and the candles flickered. 'Sentimental old fool.'

'Very red eyes you've got there, missy. Been to see the hens?'

Rumbled, Mary sank to her knees on the other side of Dave. 'I kissed Maryhen all over. She didn't bat an eyelid, callous old chook.' Mary slapped Dave just the way she liked it, and the pig wriggled ecstatically. 'Wish we could take them home, don't you?'

'Hmm.' Cat's lips pursed. She looked away, busying herself with Dave's ear, hoping Mary wouldn't follow the obvious conversational route and start planning their flat search. She kept meaning to tell Mary about her plans, but her loins were still insufficiently girded.

Luckily, Mary's mind was elsewhere. 'How did Trev react to Jozette's decision?'

Cat made a scornful noise in the back of her throat. 'Ran home to Mummy as soon as he got the news. Apparently he's been under a duvet since he arrived. Just what Mum needs, *another* person to look after.'

'She's his mum,' said Mary. 'She won't mind. Sometimes we all have to run and hide away.'

'Yeah, fine, but where's Trev when Mum needs him?' Cat wasn't about to relinquish a comfortable prejudice just like that. 'He's useless.'

'He's just himself. Like Alun.'

'Pass me the brush, will you?' Cat titivated the hairs along Dave's long, rudely pink back. 'You love that, don't you, girl?' She returned her attention to Mary. 'At least with Alun you can chuck him. I can't chuck my own brother.'

Dashing the sentence off as if she'd been dreading it, Mary said, 'I'm going back to him.' She gulped. 'To live, I mean. I'm moving in with him.'

The brush faltered above Dave's bottom. 'Live with? Alun? Live with Alun?' recited Cat dumbly. 'But, Mary, that's not even going back to square one. That's going *further back* than square one.' She studied her friend closely for telltale signs of a prank. 'You're having me on.'

'I'm not. I really am going to live with Alun.' Mary's mouth twisted, fearfully. 'So you and I can't share a flat, Cat. I'm sorry. I know I'm letting you down. You have every right to hate me.'

'I couldn't do that.' Little did Mary know that she'd let Cat neatly off the hook. 'But why?' Cat was bemused. 'You said yourself he hasn't changed since you've been away, except to become more desperate. You're heading for a fall, Mary.'

With defensive hauteur, Mary asked so what if she was? 'It's my choice. I'm walking into it with open eyes.' She pouted. The cockiness wavered. 'I'm not brave, Cat. Better the devil you know.' She lowered her eyes, fidgeted with Dave's ear. 'Alun loves me. I know him inside out. We can't choose who we love, can we?'

'You haven't actually said you love Alun.' Cat dug tentatively. 'Is there somebody else in this picture? Somebody you're *not* brave enough to choose?'

Red eyed, Mary looked at Cat pleadingly, as if willing her to intuit something she daren't say. 'Mmm,' she nodded, lips tight together.

'Listen to your heart, Mary.' Cat put down the brush and reached across Dave to take up Mary's hand, noting with a pang its nibbled nails, like tiny ruined shells on the end of each finger. 'Don't go back to Alun just cos he's there. Go to the one you want to be with.'

'I can't. I'm not made like that. All the explaining. My mum . . .' she tailed off.

'Hmm, your mum.' Cat pulled an expressive face. The uber-Catholic Mrs Cavanagh could whip up a scene worthy of Wagnerian opera over who ate the last Jammie Dodger: presumably she'd burn the house down if introduced to her daughter's female lover. 'How far have things gone? Between you and . . .' Suddenly it felt inflammatory to say Lucy's name.

'Far enough,' was the curt reply. Mary ran her free hand over her face. 'I'm so fucking amazed at myself. I mean, wanting a girl. That's not me.'

'Well,' said Cat wryly, 'it is. Actually.'

Mary laughed, a snort unlike her usual hoots. 'I can't do it. Imagine how everybody would gossip.' She sighed. 'Alun would die.'

'You're more like your mother than you think, dramatising everything,' said Cat briskly. 'Alun would not die: fact. And so what if people gossip? What are they going to say?' Cat couldn't grasp the problem. 'There's somebody you like, and she's available, and I guess, willing.' She double-checked. 'Is she?'

'Yeah,' said Mary quietly.

'Love is where it falls. You said so yourself.'

'Don't go fecking quoting me back to me-feckin'-self,' snarled Mary.

Cat squeezed Mary's fingers. 'Please don't stumble back to Alun because you're too cowardy custard to be a lezzer.'

Finally, Mary laughed, a proper rich sound. 'I've always considered myself to be outrageous. Turns out I'm a bourgeois wimp.'

'You *are* outrageous. You're the one I rely on to flash your bra in Sainsbury's. The Mary I know can cope with a bit of gossip and her mother having a hernia over the breakfast bar.'

'The Mary *I* know,' said Mary, withdrawing her hand and rising to her feet, 'is small and scared and nothing like that wild woman flashing her bra.'

'Will you at least think about it?' All Cat's jealousy evaporated. Love was different. It had to be protected. And Mary was in love, anyone could see that. Nothing else could strip her down to her bare bones in this way. 'Promise?'

'I promise.' Mary lowered her voice. 'By the way, I discovered what she's writing. She finally told me.'

'Is it a novel? Or poetry?'

'It's product description for a website that sells outsize underwear.' Mary let that sink in. 'Pays well, apparently. All the time we thought she was creating poetic metaphors she was actually coming up with seventy different ways to say 'reinforced gusset'.

51

Mundane chores took on a profundity. 'Last time I sweep the grate,' thought Cat. 'Last time I wind the clock.'

The clatter of Dave's manicured trotters on the cobbles provoked a 'last time I walk Dave'. The pig heard all about Cat's audacious plan for her personal Brave New World in silence. Taking leave of Dave who always listened, never judged, occasionally stank, would be painful.

'We'll be all right,' said Cat bravely to Dave as they muddled through the bracken. 'Won't we?' She touched that corner of her mouth and it curved into a bittersweet crescent: Will would fade in time. He'd go sepia, then curl at the edges, and finally crumble into dust.

Picking up the pace, girl and pig ran back together to the solid old house.

A letter from Cat's mum prompted a sit down and a mug of chocolate. Smiling at the Jon chitchat (*our new occupational therapist looks like Cheryl Cole, I think he's in love with her!*), the news about her other brother propelled Cat off her cushion to seek out Mary, who was packing her case.

'Trev's gone to America!' burbled Cat. 'He's followed Jozette home. He's going to ask her to come back and make a go of it!'

'So a leopard can change its spots,' said Mary.

Cat read a few lines further on. 'Mum reckons he'd even take up a new career if that's what Jozette wants.'

'Greater love hath no man than that he lay down his traffic warden's hat,' said Mary gravely. 'What do you think Jozette should do?'

That was a toughie. 'Depends if I have my sister head on, or my friend head. As Trev's sister, obviously I want her to take him back. But as Jozette's friend . . .' Cat screwed up her nose. 'He's his father's son.' She imagined the phone echoing in an empty house this time next month. *If* Harry remembered. She pointed at a camisole in Mary's hands. 'That,' she said, glad of the distraction, 'is mine, by the way.'

The stone floors were swept. The door knocker was polished. The hen house stood empty. The door of Dave's vacated boudoir banged open and shut in a malevolent breeze. The commune was like a hushed stage set, ready for the final scene, the disciples' last supper. A place was laid at Jozette's empty chair.

'Shepherd's pie!' squealed Mary, brandishing her knife and fork in lusty readiness.

'Beulah, you're a saint,' said Cat.

Standing like a Dutch old master in the dying light, Germaine ladled out Desperate Dan size portions and asked Sarge to propose a toast.

'Me?' Sarge pulled her chin in. 'I don't do that sort of thing.'

'Oh please, Sarge!' cooed Antonia. Her volatile new personality had swung back to its super-feminine incarnation. For tonight, at least.

Mary was arch. 'Sarge, if you can talk for two hours about surviving up a mountain on a mini-Babybel and a hairpin, you can propose a bloody toast.'

Everybody laughed except Sarge. With great gravity she raised her chipped mug and said deliberately, 'To the commune.' She held the mug aloft for a moment longer. 'To Germaine,' she said.

The women looked at each other: *at last*, their expressions said. 'To Germaine!' they echoed, clinking their glasses and cups and mugs.

Germaine looked around the table, her face shining with gratitude, and found Sarge's eye. Sarge nodded curtly, and carried on, waving her mug. 'And to all of you,' she faltered. 'And to Jozette. This has been the best six months of my life.' She sat down abruptly, like a sack falling from a great height.

Taken aback, nobody spoke until Mary lifted her glass and yelled 'To Sarge!'

'To Sarge!' the others echoed.

'Not necessary,' snapped Sarge, looking as if she might burst with happiness.

Antonia coughed, a prelude to saying, all in a rush, 'I couldn't have gone to AA or kept it up without you, Sarge.'

Sarge harrumphed something that might have been 'thank you'.

'I mean it.' Antonia wanted to be heard. She raised her voice. 'All of you,' she said earnestly, eyebrows crumpled, 'gave me the kiss of life. And I don't know how to thank you.'

Cat didn't think she deserved gratitude and she said so, but Antonia was having none of it. 'This house saved my life.'

'If you really want to thank us,' said Lucy, handing round the big bowl of buttered cabbage, 'stay sober.'

'I will,' said Antonia 'At least, I think I can.' She took the bowl. 'Now.'

Looking at the cabbage, Cat couldn't resist saying, 'Dig in, sisters. After all, we grew it ourselves.'

Poker faced, Germaine simpered 'Mother Nature is so bountiful.'

A loud knocking at the front door echoed through the still, clean house.

'Whoever . . .' Germaine rose, but Sarge had trotted out already.

Cat had a wild thought. A wild thought involving a windswept vet and a declaration of undying love, but when Sarge returned she was carrying a huge unwieldy sack. 'Pig food,' she muttered. 'Forgot to cancel the delivery.' She coughed wetly and sat down.

'So,' said Lucy portentously. 'What are we most looking forward to about civilisation. Beulah?'

'Ah. Well.' Beulah looked stumped. 'I'm not over-fond of civilisation.' She winked at Cat as she reached for the gravy boat. 'Overrated, if you ask me.'

'My boys,' said Antonia, nodding furiously.

'Buses!' announced Mary. 'I'm looking forward to lovely big red shiny things that take you where you want to go.'

'Even if it's somewhere you've been before?' asked Lucy sourly without looking at Mary. 'Many times.'

Mary lowered her head and let her hair cover her newly pink face.

'What are you planning when you leave?' Cat asked Lucy sympathetically, guessing the subtext of her comment to Mary.

'I prefer to keep that private,' said Lucy smoothly, chopping at her cabbage.

'As you wish.' Cat withdrew, wounded.

Decimating the cabbage, Lucy looked at Mary's bowed head. 'Sometimes I wish I'd never clapped eyes on this place.'

'No, no!' Germaine sounded horrified.

'It's true.' Lucy gave the cabbage a respite. 'But mostly,' she said deliberately, 'I'm glad I came.' She swallowed. 'Really glad.'

'That's more like it,' beamed Germaine, who was not at home to Mrs Subtext.

Scraping back her chair, Mary muttered 'Loo' and fled.

Bottom hovering above her chair, Cat was irresolute. She knew that, coming from the taciturn, deeply private Lucy, that 'really glad' had been as public a declaration of love as Romeo's outburst beneath Juliet's balcony. She lowered her bottom: Mary wasn't a schoolgirl to be tailed to the bogs. 'What about you, Germy?' Cat attempted to lighten the tone. 'Are you looking forward to normal life?'

'What's normal?' Germaine was dim tonight, her electric outline not as vivid.

'Normal is television. Traffic. Earning money.' Cat rattled off a list she didn't much like. 'Job hunting. Relationship making and breaking. Crikey,' she said, 'I'd just hit my stride out here in the wilderness. Now I'm being tossed back to town.'

'I'm sorry,' said Germaine with such sincerity that Cat smiled.

'No, no, no, Germy. It's been wonderful. I've really . . .' Cat realised with a jolt that she'd been about to say *grown* but that would be a step too far into the realms of psycho-babble. 'I've changed. For the better,' she added hurriedly, as Germaine's face fell. 'But it's daunting going back to reality.'

'What a load of bollocks,' said Lucy civilly. 'So this isn't reality? This isn't *normal*? It doesn't count, because we're all women?'

'I didn't mean that,' said Cat, perturbed at being misunderstood.

'Are you blind?' asked Lucy, the mismatch between her harsh words and her bland tone unsettling Cat. 'We've handled as much stress as any CEO. There have been struggles, revelations, heartbreaks, the lot. We've had a soap opera's worth of problems to contend with together and you say it's not as difficult as your precious normal life?' She pushed her plate away.

'I only meant I—' Cat hurriedly stitched together a defence in her head, but was prevented from airing it.

'And *you*, Cat.' Lucy picked up her fork to jab it in Cat's direction. 'You've been one of the main struts in our shaky democracy. You've been a rock for all of us at one point or another.' Lucy threw her fork down in disgust. 'Give me strength! You don't even know how resilient you are, what a gift it is to engage so easily with other people. Why aren't you living in the moment? Relishing this as your precious normal life?'

Cat paused, aware that everybody expected her to reply. 'Erm,' she began, a smile teasing her face, 'Are you being horrid to me or,' the smile blossomed into a laugh. 'Or really really nice?'

After a second, Lucy laughed too, joined by all the women round the table. 'Sorry, sorry,' she waved her hands over her head. 'I forget how I come across sometimes. I'm being,' she gurned embarrassment at such a confession, '*nice*.'

'Then thank you,' laughed Cat. 'Even if I don't recognise myself from your description.'

'I do,' said Beulah.

'Cat, I'm just saying,' said Lucy, 'don't be afraid.'

'Funny you should say that.' Cat took a deep breath. Telling them would make it real: no going back. 'I've taken a leap in the dark.' She savoured the expectant faces. 'I'm retraining. I'm shaking the dust of advertising off my sandals. I'm going to college to take a diploma in social work.'

'What?' Mary was back, dabbing her eyes and squawking in surprise. 'You? A social worker at your age?'

'Yeah, me, a social worker,' said Cat, liking how that sounded. 'At my great age.'

'You'll be marvellous,' said Beulah with conviction.

'I would have liked to be a social worker,' said Antonia sadly.

'There's a course in Surrey. I can move home, stay with Mum and Jon while I get my qualifications. Then,' she said, excited, 'I can be of some use. I can contribute. Rather than just persuade people to buy stuff, I can be of real help to people who need it.'

'You're moving back home?' Mary was unconvinced. 'You get the heebie-jeebies when you visit, you can't *live* there, Cat.'

'I can,' said Cat, happily defiant. 'I've written to Mum, she's over the moon.' Cat hesitated, wondering if she wanted to share the private workings of her mind with these women. She did, she decided: of course she bloody did. 'I've been running from the situation at home for years and now . . .' She threw up her hands. 'I wonder why. It is what it is. They're my family. We get by. It's not perfect, but what is?'

'Indeed,' said Lucy.

'Good for you,' said Beulah.

Mary had been mulling, sucking her lips and tipping backwards on her chair. 'And what about Will?' she asked, slyly.

'He'll be here, being a vet and I'll be in London, being a penniless mature student.' Cat's voice shrank. 'Will's not interested. Not really.' Not beyond, she thought sadly, one creamy kiss. Despite his wild talk of falling for her. 'He's had plenty of opportunities to declare himself. So . . .' She waved her hands helplessly.

'And of course,' said Lucy, with a side order of sarcasm, 'you couldn't possibly do the declaring: that's a man's job.'

Cat stared at her plate. She was tired of 'understanding' Lucy's brusque ways and longed to lob a bread roll at her. How could she declare her feelings to Will when she hardly dared declare them to herself?

A glass was being tapped. Germaine was on her feet.

'Go Germy!' cheered Cat, grateful that the spotlight had moved.

'Sock it to us, Germaine!' roared Mary.

Wringing her hands as the women applauded, Germaine's mouth was pursed. 'I'll keep this low key,' she began, prompting a sceptical glance between Cat and Mary. 'You've had enough of my bombast by now.' Germaine looked them all in the eye, one by one, as she said 'I'm too afraid to ask what lessons you've learned here.' She sent a wary half-smile Sarge's way. 'But I'll share mine. I've learned, ladies, to love. To fall, and to like falling. Despite the repercussions, despite my guilt, I can't regret learning that lesson.'

'Hear hear!' smiled Cat, who'd never had occasion to say hear hear before.

'I imagined the commune would be paradisiacal, utopian. It wasn't, was it?' Germaine unbent a little, warmed by the wry 'no's and 'not really's. 'Sometimes it was hellish. We have weaknesses, peccadillos and bad habits, but put us together and watch out!' A little of Germaine's evangelical zeal crept back. 'Together, we are chain mail; we look delicate but we stop bullets.'

Cat leaned forward, her elbows on the table. She was caught up again, wanting to believe. She wanted to be one of Germaine's warrior women, striding out into the world to claim what was hers. She wilted: Cat daren't claim her prize without a gilt-edged invitation.

'That's not to say I didn't wonder about the point of it all at times,' Germaine continued. 'But I just leaned back on the chain-mail and found all the support I needed. This secret society around the table tonight is family to me. I hope you feel the same.'

Cat was surprised to see Lucy nod along with the others. She saw Mary's hand reach out to take Lucy's; after a momentary *froideur* it was grasped hungrily.

'I've never had children myself, not wishing to deliver innocents to a world of inequality, but if this family of ours has a baby, then it's Antonia's sobriety.' She laid a hand on Antonia's narrow shoulder and the woman jumped. 'It was born here and we all have a responsibility to nurture it and pick it up when it stumbles. Don't we?' she asked her audience.

Like a cornfield with the wind rippling through it, the women leaned towards Antonia, nodding, smiling, promising. She burst into untidy but happy sobs.

'What about men?' Mary was arch. 'Still hate them?'

'I never did hate them.' Germaine let the splutters die before saying, 'I hated their power and how women allowed them to wield it.' She lowered her lashes, flirtatiously: it looked wrong, like the Sphinx blowing its nose. 'I must admit, I'm starting to see the point of them'.

It was after midnight when the gathering shook itself, like a sleepy dog getting up from the hearth, and dispersed.

'The minibus leaves tomorrow at twelve sharp. Sharp!' warned Sarge as the table was cleared. 'Any latecomers will be left behind.'

'Charming to the last,' muttered Mary, dragging her feet to the sink to help Cat wash up.

Lucy stood up and stretched sinuously. 'Germaine,' she said, halting that woman's stacking of plates for a moment. 'Don't feel guilty about Jamie. You've given us all an adventure we'll never forget.' She looked boldly at Mary. 'Even though we might try to. If you and Jamie stick together for ten minutes or ten years, it will be worth it. Love,' she said, in a parched voice as she turned for the door, 'is where it falls.'

Cat watched Mary's eyes fill as they made a start on the smeared crockery. So much love goes to waste, thought Cat: there's probably an EU love mountain somewhere being sold off cheap.

Later, up in the dormitory, the air was different, thicker. It was a strange hiatus, this night before they said goodbye to the house. Climbing between sheets that smelled of the lavender growing under the washing line, Cat saw the narrow hillock of Lucy's body in the bed next to hers. She'd miss seeing that every night.

Dawn was creeping through the house, turning the shadows pink, when Cat gave up pretending that she could sleep. Down in the kitchen, quiet and unfamiliar at this hour, she found Sarge, blowing the steam off a large cup of coffee.

'You too?' said Sarge.

'Yeah. I feel nervy. Restless.'

'I just want to get away.'

Cat filled the battered old kettle and they sat in silence for a while, until it began to toot. 'In the beginning I didn't want to come here,' said Cat, in a wondering way, only partly directed at Sarge who surely wouldn't be interested. 'And now . . . I don't want to leave.' She shook her head at her own contrariness. 'What's the matter with me?'

'You're sentimental,' said Sarge.

'S'pose I am,' admitted Cat, her mouth downturned. She'd never thought of herself that way before. The yard outside, defiantly scruffy and unkempt despite the women's best efforts, was finding its colour under the early sun. The quiet was eerie, with no chicken to cackle 'good morning'. Cat opened the window, enjoying the weight of the heavy old latch, the scratch on her palm of the peeling paint.

'I'm disappointed in you,' said Sarge, joining her at the window.

'Gee thanks,' said Cat, rather enjoying how very Sarge-ish Sarge was being even in these last moments.

'I never had you pegged as a coward.'

Cat bristled. 'What's cowardly about retraining at my age? Taking a vast pay cut? Starting over?'

'Oh *that*,' said Sarge, as if swatting a fly. 'Yeah, yeah, very commendable,' she said glibly. 'I mean Will. You're letting him go without a fight.'

Cat goggled at her. 'You of all people . . .' she marvelled. 'He's a man, remember? On many an occasion you've advocated harvesting their sperm and sending them into outer space.'

'That's what *I'd* do,' said Sarge. 'But I'm not you. You need a man,' she said, with more sympathy than Cat had ever seen her display. 'You're made that way. You can't help it, it's like having sticky-out ears or a third nipple. Will and you are a good match. As men go, he's not the worst.'

'No,' agreed Cat, 'he's not.' Even Mary had just accepted that Cat would leave Will behind. She hadn't guessed at Cat's dark, blank panic at the thought of never seeing him again. Sarge, apparently, had. 'But I blew it.' She smiled at Sarge's quivering face: once again the little woman was a Jack Russell, one who'd seen a stick being thrown.

'See? Coward,' growled the Jack Russell, taut with annoyance. 'If I had your . . .' She tapered off, with an impatient grunt. 'So what if you make a fool of yourself? So what if he sends you away? You'd always know you tried.'

'This is silly, I'm all set to go. My ticket's bought. I have to say goodbye to the others. There's no time. I haven't even arranged when I'll see Beulah again. And Germaine is—'

'Come on.' Sarge banged her mug down on the draining board and snatched the minibus keys from the hook. She was out in the hall before she realised that Cat wasn't following her.

'I wanted to have a really nice last morning with everybody,' moaned Cat.

'Prioritise!' bellowed Sarge. 'This kind of dithering could get you killed in the wilderness. There's time to get back for a sentimental farewell if that's what you really want.' She stamped her foot when Cat didn't move. 'Get in the van,' she bellowed. 'THAT'S AN ORDER!'

Cat got in the van.

52

'Think positive.' Sarge was impatient with Cat's litany of can't do ('It's too early, I don't know what to say, he doesn't like me that much anyway, I haven't washed my hair for eight days') as she drove the familiar lanes rendered foreign by the hazy early light. 'Yes, you're right, it's very early but that means you'll probably catch him at home. And if you don't know what to say, maybe you'll be more honest than if you'd prepared a speech.' She ran a Mini Clubman into a ditch. 'I thought you had more spunk than this.'

'I used to.' The old Cat had spunk to spare; she'd faced down baying creative teams and bent them to her will; she'd charmed an extra twenty thousand on the budget from stingy clients; she'd eluded the howls of her conscience in hotel bedrooms, but this was different.

'If *I* wanted a man like Will, I'd tell him.' Sarge sounded very sure.

Cat looked at her, looked past the horrible khaki cap and the hair that was cut with a knife and fork, and found the plain, fine face underneath the attitude. 'You *do* want a man like Will,' said Cat. 'In fact, you want Will.'

'Do me a favour.' Sarge frowned, her nose in the air.

'You do.' Cat had learned to back her hunches at Percival Cant

Jablowski. 'That's why you've always been keen to call him, to have him around.' Her theory floundered a little. 'So why are you pushing me into his arms?'

'Because you have a chance,' said Sarge, in a clipped voice. 'Look, I'm not asking for flattery. Don't take me for a fool. I am what I am and I'm fine with it. I wouldn't know what to do with Will if I had him. You do know.'

Yes, Cat knew what she'd do with Will: seventy per cent of it was overwhelmingly rude. 'There. That's his place.' A sign was swinging in a breeze minted out at sea: 'Carlow and Son, Veterinary Surgeon'.

The minibus slowed to a stop.

'Out,' said Sarge, leaning over and opening the passenger door. 'I won't wait. You can get yourself back to the house.' She growled impatiently when Cat didn't move. 'Go on!'

'But . . .' Cat closed her mouth. Buts didn't go down well with Sarge. 'Thank you,' she said. 'Even if it all goes pear shaped, and it probably will, thank—'

'Oh get on with it.' Sarge shoved Cat out of the van so she landed awkwardly on the pavement. The minibus farted up the high street without a wave or a backward glance from its driver.

'Goodbye, Sarge,' said Cat quietly, to herself. Alone, she felt exposed. Her clothes were wrong: who wore a hooded sweatshirt to throw themselves at the feet of their true love? The sleeping street was quiet, like a wild west township before a gunfight. Cat's feet could feel every crack in the pavement, she could smell bread being baked, she could hear her own heart pogo-ing. Cat readied herself, trying not to think of the consequences for her self-esteem when Will guffawed in her unmade-up face. She stood at the door of the flat, breathed in deeply and lifted a shaking forefinger to the bell.

Get a grip. Cat.

Her finger was only halfway to the buzzer when the door flew open and Will was on the step, tugging on a jacket, a mobile phone clamped between his ear and a tweedy shoulder. 'I'm on my way,' he said loudly as he pulled the door shut with a bang. 'Which mare is it? The chestnut? See you in ten minutes.'

Will froze at the sight of Cat on the pavement. 'What are you doing here?' he asked, in what only the most optimistic onlooker could describe as a welcoming manner.

'Um,' said Cat.

'Move.' Will spun her by the shoulders and propelled her along the pavement. 'We'll talk on the way to my car. The Collet mare's in foal.'

Half trotting to keep up with Will's long-legged stride, Cat peeked up at him. He was flushed. His eyes were bright. He looked, she noted, preposterously sexy. And not at all approachable.

'So,' said Cat when it became apparent that he'd gone all caveman on her and wasn't going to observe social niceties, 'how have you been?'

'Busy.'

'Oh.'

Will turned abruptly down an alleyway. Cat sped past it, reversing clumsily to follow him.

'My car,' said Will, pointing his key at the familiar Land Rover, lurking down the alley like a mugger. A beep sounded and Will opened the door and threw his large leather bag on to the back seat. 'Cat, I can't hang about.'

'I know. The Collet mare. I know.'

Will's hectic body language slowed suddenly and he took her in properly. 'You're supposed to be gone by now,' he said in a muted voice.

'Not quite.'

'Is this a goodbye?' Will looked at his watch.

'Yes. No.' Oh God, she thought agitatedly, he's not making this easy. Cat stared at him tongue tied. She couldn't shoehorn all the stuff she wanted to say into a hasty interview down an alley. Mutely she stood, lemon-like, on the other side of the Land Rover.

'Get in,' said Will.

*

After a white-knuckle ride along back lanes, Cat was relieved when they pulled into a farmyard. Strewn with sharp-edged rural machinery, the Collet farm wasn't chocolate box. Eau de Poo hung heavily in the air, although neither Will nor the red-faced man in smut stained blue overalls who approached them, wiping his hands on a cloth, seemed to notice.

'All right,' said the farmer by way of greeting, turning as soon as he reached Will, and walking him towards a barn beyond the house. 'She's tired, Carlow. See what you make of her.'

Halfway to the barn, Will turned and flicked his head at Cat. 'Want to watch?' he called.

'Of course,' shouted Cat. She picked her way across the broken stone surface of the yard. She'd never seen anything being born. It was magical, so people said. She'd rather eat her own legs than witness a small animal emerging from the back end of a larger one, but Cat had unfinished business with the vet.

The barn, dark and damp after the sunshine outside, smelled tangy. In one of the stalls Cat could see the bulky shape of a handsome mare, standing erect and tense, her belly swollen. She emanated ferocious energy, her shiny auburn coat glowing as if lit from inside. Two young men stood by, one of them patting her ineffectually on her flank, the other frowning, his arms folded. Everybody's attention was on the horse: she was the centre of the universe. And she wasn't happy.

'Hello there, girl. Hello.'

Cat recognised the demeanour from Will's treatment of Dave. She watched him run his hand down the mare's rigid neck and along her body until he reached her rump, when he bent his knees and squatted. 'It's all going to be fine, girl,' he reassured the horse, whose eyes looked wild to Cat. She edged a little nearer, drawn by the elemental feel of the tableau.

'What's your verdict?' asked the farmer grimly.

Will was exploring the horse's stomach. When his hands veered towards her ruder parts, Cat looked away. Romance, she reckoned, can only survive so much.

'Foal's in the right position,' said Will in an undertone. 'If Mother will help me, we'll get it out safely.' He patted the horse fondly. 'You can do it, can't you, old girl?'

Yes I can, Cat almost answered. It was crazy that she should fancy Will all the more with his hand up a horse, but his movements were so sure and economical, his words so precise. He laid out surgical tools on a startlingly white cloth and marshalled the equipment he needed from the loafing onlookers – a bucket of warm water, a blanket – and suddenly the atmosphere in the barn changed.

'Here we go!' said Will, excitement frilling his voice.

Cat shivered. The air was charged. The mare strained, her front legs shifted and a tiny hoof appeared.

'Good, good.' Will's hand was on the hoof, but Cat could sense he wasn't pulling. She crept a little closer.

One bony leg, wet and slippery, was followed by another.

'That's my girl,' said Will encouragingly. 'Should be the head now.'

As he spoke a nose emerged. The mare moaned, a fluting sound that troubled Cat. She looked at Will and could tell he didn't like it either.

'She's exhausted,' he muttered.

The farmer tensed.

Will wiped the nose that was absurdly poking out of the back of the mother. 'Get a move on, little fella,' he advised. 'I've no intention of losing you, or your mum.'

An obliging little chap, the foal slithered out.

Cat blinked. It was like a conjuring trick. One moment two black nostrils were gaping at her, the next a newborn life was on the floor, its legs paddling drunkenly and its eyes rolling as it saw the banal wonders of its world for the first time. Cat held her breath as Will swiftly snipped the umbilical cord and gathered the awkward, raw-boned bundle in his arms. 'Welcome,' she heard him whisper as he placed the foal gently under its mother's nose.

The horse nuzzled the newcomer, puffing and grunting as she nosed him this way and that, checking out her creation. Cat felt a lump rise in her throat, and the scene blurred. She wiped away gate-crashing tears with the back of her hand: this was no sentimental made-for-TV movie, it was a farmyard. If the men saw her crying, they'd crucify her.

The farmer turned away from his horse, and passed Cat on his way out to the sunshine. His ruddy face was drenched with tears. He caught her eye. 'I never get used to it,' he said.

Standing back from his patients, Will wiped his hands. 'You know what to do, lads,' he said to the other two. 'I need this whole place swept and clean. Shout when the placenta appears.' He turned his gaze on Cat and smiled lazily. 'Right,' he said. 'I'm all yours.'

Cat preceded him out into the unkempt yard. She struggled to pull herself together, shaky and volatile after what she'd just witnessed. 'You were, I mean, that was incredible.' Cat bent to stroke a collie sunning itself beside an ornate old pump.

'Birth. Death.' Will grabbed the pump handle and worked it rapidly until a jet of freezing water splashed out on to the untidy grass forcing its way up between the cracks in the ground. 'You see it all as a vet.' He doused his face with water, then shook himself like a dog. 'Brrr,' he grinned. 'That's better.' He looked at her quizzically. 'Why are you here, Cat?'

'To ask you something,' said Cat, drawing herself up to her full height, a good foot less than Will. She looked around her: a lurking farmer would not help the situation.

Will had stopped smiling. Now that Cat was growing accustomed to his face she guessed that although he looked cross, he was actually concentrating. That's what she hoped anyway. She coughed. She swallowed. She picked a tiny piece of fluff off her shoulder.

'And are you going to ask me this something today?' checked Will.

'It's not easy.' Cat's gaze fluttered everywhere. Even the dog seemed to be waiting. Her eyes found Will's again. 'Oh, look, did that kiss in the café mean anything?' When Will didn't move or speak or run off or even blink, she motored on. 'What are you after, Will? I need to know. I'm off today, and I can't leave without knowing if you . . .' She faltered. It was too late, far far too late, to stop now. Absurdly, she thought of Sarge. 'I need to know if you want me as much as I want you.'

Will was chewing his lip. His eyes moved from Cat and narrowed, taking in the hills behind her. He sighed and rubbed a hand over his face. 'It was a done deal, Cat, the moment I clapped eyes on you walking your pig. Your hair was, well,' he gestured towards her ponytail. 'It was even worse than that. You were dressed like a bag lady. And I thought to myself, *there she is, there's my girl.*' He shrugged. 'But then I buggered it up. I thought it was too late.'

'Oh no,' gushed Cat. 'You haven't. It's not,' she reassured him, 'buggered up all.' She was gabbling: relief cornered her poise before lust saw it off altogether. She grinned at him. Will grinned back. She could already feel the kiss that was coming, and a tingle travelled the length of her spine, with a detour to her pants. She leaned towards him.

And he leaned away. 'This ex-boyfriend bloke,' said Will, holding up a finger. 'Where are you up to with him?'

'Gone. Finished. Over. Not happening. Done. Chucked. History.'

'In that case, come here.'

Will folded Cat into an embrace she'd imagined but failed to do justice to. His mouth, wide and masculine, was soft on hers. His breath was like a blessing and she swooned, just as he did, as they clung to each other at long last.

'Whahey!' whooped one of the blokes from the barn, suddenly between them like a very unwelcome genie. 'Get a room, you two!'

'Oh, we shall,' murmured Will, his blue gaze locked on Cat's.

'Will,' was all she could mutter.

'Placenta,' said the bloke.

Cat and Will pulled away from each other abruptly.

'I'd better . . .' Will jerked his head towards the barn.

'Yes, you go and, erm, whatever,' said Cat, smiling at him, complicit.

'You won't go anywhere?' Will backed away. He pointed at the ground beneath her feet. 'You'll stay right there?'

'I'm not going anywhere,' promised Cat.

Which wasn't entirely true.

53

'But do you *have* to leave today?' Will's voice was groggy with want as he held Cat's face between his hands.

Parked in the lane outside the commune gates, the Land Rover was the venue for their first sustained clinch. Hands were held, faces touched, lips locked, passionate words muttered, but now Cat had to draw a reluctant halt to such glorious lingerings. 'Yes, I do. *Will!*' Delighted, Cat scolded her new boyfriend – for that's what he was, they'd agreed on it, it was official – and slapped his hands away. 'I have an interview first thing tomorrow at college, and I'm staying at Mum's tonight. You know I don't want to go.'

'I don't know that.' Will's lower lip trembled playfully. 'You'll probably hit some classy discotheque in that there London and forget all about me.'

Despite her claims to be in a hurry, Cat breathed him in and nuzzled his neck. 'None of those disco boys could stick their hand up a horse the way you can.'

'True.'

'I don't even care if you leave wet towels on the bed,' said Cat dreamily.

Will put his arm around her, and leaned his head on the top of hers. 'We'll make it work, this long distance relationship stuff. Plenty of people do.'

'Soldiers,' said Cat.

'Actors.'

'Pirates.'

'We'll be fine.' Will sounded anxious when he said, 'Won't we?'

'Yes,' said Cat with certainty. 'Because I'm going to come down and see you. And you're going to come up and see me. And when all else fails, we'll meet in the middle.' Plans, big plans, involving motorways, trains, long weekends and snatched days had been laid. 'I won't let the distance get the better of us, Will.'

'You'd better not,' said Will, his eyes heavy lidded and smoky, a look Cat now recognised as the prelude to a kiss.

It was the last one. For the time being. 'Listen, I've got to get my stuff, see if anyone's left in the house.' Midday had come and gone: the minibus wasn't in the courtyard. Cat, after her shaky start, had found rather a lot to say to Will. He knew all about Hugh, all about her new vocation, and, vitally, all about Jon. The questions he'd asked about her brother, and the empathetic look on his face as he'd asked them, had tripled Cat's ardour for this sensitive, placid man but made her late for the commune's leave-taking. Deep down, Cat was relieved. She wasn't up to emotional goodbyes with the women who'd come to mean so much to her. Besides, reasoned Cat, she would always keep in touch with her oddball extended family.

Half out of the passenger seat, Cat froze and pulled a stricken face. 'Beulah!' she breathed.

'The old lady?' queried Will.

'She didn't give me a number or an address or anything,' whined Cat, jumping down to the verge. 'She's funny about things like that. I planned to do all that today but then . . .' Cat scuttled off, scattering anguished half-finished sentences in her wake.

'I'll be waiting!' called Will.

The gates were ajar. Jamie was manhandling a large suitcase into the back of a scuffed pickup. Noticing her, he laughed as heartily as if she'd done a ten minute stand-up routine. Cat ran past him, colliding with Germaine on the doorstep.

'There you are!' Germaine sounded both relieved and annoyed. 'We've all been fretting about you,' she said, waggling her curly fringe. 'Your cases are by the back door. Mary reckoned you'd scuttled back to Hugh.'

Cat groaned. 'Have I missed everybody?'

'Yes, you silly girl. All gone,' said Germaine briskly. 'It was rather draining. I do hate farewells. Everybody insisted that you call them when you're home. We're having a reunion in a month.' She lowered her voice. 'Mainly to keep an eye on Antonia. Alun picked up Mary. I think he'd combed his hair for the occasion, but it's so hard to tell. Lucy surprised me today,' she carried on contemplatively. 'Bawling, poor girl, eyes like golf balls. Sarge was, well . . .' Germaine paused in her pulling on of a tight red glove. 'Sarge was Sarge.' She waved over at Jamie. 'I'm taking my little toyboy back to town. My feminist book club will *die*.' At last she noticed Cat's expression. 'Cat, what is it?'

'I wanted to see Beulah before . . .' Cat tailed off.

Germaine smiled indulgently and hugged her. 'You're such a softie, Mrs Career Woman,' she said approvingly. 'Beulah left you something in the kitchen. Go and see.' She slapped Cat proprietorially on the bottom.

'Hang on.' Cat reached up and grabbed Germaine by the shoulders. 'Thank you, Germy.'

'For what? For fibbing my head off about courgettes and my sex life?'

'No.' Cat shook her head. 'For being brave and mad. I owe you a lot.'

'Mush, dreadful mush.' Germaine shoved her into the hallway.

'You're too good for him, you know!' laughed Cat as Germaine headed off across the cobbles.

'Obviously. All women are too good for their men.' Germaine picked up speed. 'Goodbye commune!' she yelled over her shoulder as she ran, arms open, towards where Jamie waited, lounging like an off duty Chippendale against the pickup.

The hall was gloomy. Cat savoured the familiar uneven floorboards and limewash walls as she made her way to the kitchen for the last time.

'Cake, dear?' asked Beulah, teapot poised.

'Eh?' Cat stood paralysed in the doorway. 'What?' she added.

'There's some fruit cake left. Or one little muffin that Mary missed.' Beulah padded comfortably back to the Aga and put down her teapot. 'Perhaps a sandwich?'

Cat looked about her at the kitchen. It was warm and humming with industry, as if she'd taken a step into the recent past and the commune was still a going concern. 'Beulah, everybody's gone home. Why are you making tea and baking cakes? Why isn't everything packed up?'

'You're still here, dear,' said Beulah calmly, stirring Cat's tea. 'There you are. Take it while it's hot.' She sat down and sliced a healthy V of cake.

Cat sat too. 'Can you give me an address?' she asked. 'So we can keep in touch.' Beulah's passivity worried her. By now the old lady should be on a train, or at the very least in her hat and coat.

'No,' Beulah shook her head.

'Beulah,' said Cat tenderly. 'You have to leave. It's over.' A horrible thought struck her. 'Beulah,' she said gravely, 'come home with me if you've got nowhere to go. We'll make room. You'd love my mum. We could set you up somewhere, it'd be—'

'I'm staying right here,' said Beulah. She flicked a crumb off the tablecloth. 'I bought the house, dear.'

Cat put her hands to her mouth. 'You!' She shook her head, delightedly. 'Beulah Beulah Beulah!' she laughed, leaning down to hug her friend.

Beulah didn't hug her back, but she accepted the grapple with grace and her smile widened a little. 'I should have told you earlier, but I wanted to surprise you. It's all mine,' she said, a little breathlessly, looking around the room. 'He left me well off, you see, once I'd sold that horrid place.' Beulah shuddered, but the cloud didn't settle and she carried on brightly, 'I bought this house for cash, which is unusual according to the nice estate agent lady.'

'Won't you be lonely?' was Cat's first thought, followed immediately by 'I'll visit! All the time. You'll be sick of me.' She envisaged Beulah all alone in the big unmodernised wreck of a house and didn't like the picture. 'I'll be in the area a lot.' She paused, before breaking the big news. 'I got it together with Will, Beulah. I'm his now, and he's mine.'

The anticipated wide eyes and congratulations didn't materialise.

'Thought as much,' said Beulah. 'Very nice, dear.'

'Yes,' said Cat, a little deflated. Evidently she didn't move in such mysterious ways as she liked to think. 'So I'll come and see you when I'm in Lyme. Every other weekend or so.'

'You'll always be welcome,' said Beulah, looking down at her cup. 'You're my very first real friend.'

'Beulah . . .' Cat couldn't, she reproached herself, cry *again*: it was becoming a habit.

'This house is my friend,' said Beulah, in her quavering voice. 'It rescued me. Well,' she smiled, 'along with the people in it. I've come to life between these walls, after being a corpse for so many years.'

'Really?' Cat reached out and took Beulah's hand. It was chubby and warm, but Cat could feel the lines scored into it.

'Oh yes.' Beulah nodded slowly. 'It got me thinking. There must be other lost souls out there, in need of a haven. I was lucky. I should share it. This will be a halfway house. For women who need refuge.'

'From men?'

'From the world. From bad situations. From men, from women,' said Beulah. 'This will be a place of acceptance, and peace. Women who have nobody to turn to, and nowhere else to go, women like me, can come here and heal.'

'You do have somebody to turn to now. Me. You know that?' said Cat urgently.

'I do know that, dear.' Beulah extricated her hand and patted Cat's gently.

'There's something else.' Cat swallowed. 'Your baby, Beulah. We're going to find her. We're going to find Matilda.'

Beulah looked scared. 'Could we really do that?'

'We could.'

Blinking rapidly, Beulah said simply, 'That would be very nice. Very nice indeed.'

A horn blared impatiently.

'Shush, Will!' laughed Cat.

'No, Cat, go to him.' Beulah leaned on the table and stood up. 'Go to your man, dear.'

Dizzy, wanting to stay, yearning to go, Cat kissed Beulah's cheek at the front door. 'I'll see you soon.' Beulah added a strong, shimmering strand to the web Will had woven, keeping her bound to Lyme Regis and this house. 'Very soon. Sooner than soon,' she gabbled.

'Be off with you.'

'You never know,' shouted Cat, as she lugged her bags across the courtyard, 'If things don't work out I might be one of your first lodgers!'

'Not you, Cat,' said Beulah as she shut the old front door with a soft clunk and leaned against it. 'Not you, dear.'

Also available from Sphere

HOW TO LOSE A HUSBAND AND GAIN A LIFE

Bernadette Strachan

'Warm, funny and witty, *How to Lose a Husband and Gain a Life* is everything you want from a good book – and in Ruby Gallagher presents you with the kind of lead character you'll wish you could make your new best friend!'
Mike Gayle

To the casual eye, Ruby Gallagher has the perfect life. Adoring husband, Manny: tick. Stunning home: tick. Fresh designer outfit every day of the week: tick.

If Ruby feels the odd twinge of doubt about whether she is actually happy, she learns to ignore it. After her turbulent past, there's a reassuring safety in predictability.

But when – suddenly and dramatically – it all falls apart . . . Ruby has to lean on somebody she's never relied on before: herself.

Is there life after Manny? Only one way to find out . . .

'an absolute treat. It's impossible not to love the characters'
Louise Candlish

Fiction
978-0-7515-4230-1

Other bestselling titles available by mail

	Title	Author	Price
☐	How to Lose a Husband and Gain a Life	Bernadette Strachan	£6.99

The prices shown above are correct at time of going to press. However, the publishers reserve the right to increase prices on covers from those previously advertised, without further notice.

sphere

Please allow for postage and packing: **Free UK delivery.**
Europe: add 25% of retail price; Rest of World: 45% of retail price.

To order any of the above or any other Sphere titles, please call our credit card orderline or fill in this coupon and send/fax it to:

Sphere, PO Box 121, Kettering, Northants NN14 4ZQ
Fax: 01832 733076 Tel: 01832 737526
Email: aspenhouse@FSBDial.co.uk

☐ I enclose a UK bank cheque made payable to Sphere for £ ....
☐ Please charge £ ...... to my Visa/Delta/Maestro

☐☐☐☐☐☐☐☐☐☐☐☐☐☐☐☐

Expiry Date ☐☐☐☐ Maestro Issue No. ☐☐

NAME (BLOCK LETTERS please) ....

ADDRESS ....

....

....

Postcode .... Telephone ....

Signature ....

Please allow 28 days for delivery within the UK. Offer subject to price and availability.